EXTREME MEDICAL SERVICES BOX SET VOL 4-6

Hunter Year

Extreme Medical Services Box Sets
Book 2

JAMIE DAVIS

MedicCast Productions

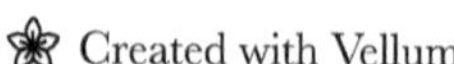 Created with Vellum

Get the prequel book "*The Vampire and the Paramedic*"
Free

Go to JamieDavisBooks.com/send-free-book

—

Eldara Sister Spinoff Series
The Nightingale's Angel
Blue and Gray Angel

—

The Huntress Clan Saga
(A 6-book Urban Fantasy series starting with)
Huntress Initiate

—

The Broken Throne Series
(A 5-Book Dystopian Urban Fantasy
starting with)
The Charm Runner

—

The Accidental Traveler LitRPG Series
(with C.J. Davis)
(A 6-book Epic Fantasy Series starting with)
The Accidental Thief

—

Lone Wolf Squadron Scifi Series
(A multi-book space opera series starting with)
Marshal the Stars

—

Follow on Facebook for updates, news, and upcoming book excerpts
Jamie's Fun Fantasy Readers Facebook Group

The Paramedic's Hunter

BOOK 4 IN THE EXTREME MEDICAL SERVICES SERIES

Chapter 1

The wounds were severe, at least that was the information coming in from the dispatchers over the ambulance's radio. Dean drove quickly through the nighttime streets of Elk City. He made good time but drove with due regard to safety and all traffic laws. It didn't do the patient any good if the ambulance wrecked on the way to the scene.

The call was for an animal bite. The dispatcher said that the caller was having difficulty stopping the bleeding. There were numerous bites to the patient. Dean worked hard to stay focused. He was distracted lately, ever since he found out his girlfriend, Ashley - an actual angel or, as she preferred, Eldara, had been abducted and was still missing. It was important for him to find her. It was also important for him to make sure he cared for his patients. He redoubled his focus on the dark nighttime residential streets in front of him.

Dean glanced over at his new partner. Barry Winston had been an experienced paramedic before he applied for the special Station U community paramedic program in Elk City. He had been unaware, just as Dean had been in the beginning, that their patients were not normal people. In fact, their patients were not human at all. The Station U paramedics responded to calls for emergency medical aid from what other people would call the creatures of myths and legends. Some might even say they were the monsters of nightmares.

Dean had come to know different. They were just people who were trying to live their lives alongside their human neighbors, without anyone knowing how different they were. Barry had been shocked at first, but was coming around. He was adjusting better than Dean had in the beginning. Barry was already a pretty good paramedic and that, plus a predisposition for reading fantasy and science-fiction books, had helped him overcome his cultural biases.

Barry operated the siren while Dean drove, changing the tone of it when they entered an intersection. Once they were through it and speeding down the road on the other side, he looked over at Dean. "What do you think caused the bite? It sounds serious. Could it be a shapeshifter like a werewolf or werebear?"

"Not sure, yet, Barry," Dean replied as he drove. "Whatever it is, it does not sound like a casual bite. Also, most shapeshifters are very careful about who they bite and infect with Lycanthropy. The disease is a blood borne illness and they take it seriously when someone is brought into their pack. It doesn't sound like that kind of bite. Whatever it is, we will see soon enough."

Dean turned the ambulance onto another residential street and started looking at the house numbers as the headlights illuminated the mailboxes lining the street. He was looking for number eleven-ninety-four. He knew he was getting close, and started looking on the right for the even-numbered houses. Most of the houses were modest ranch style single-family homes with large front yards. The street was lined with trees and didn't have any streetlights. Both of these things contributed to deep shadows and only a little moonlight filtering down to the ground.

He saw a flicker of movement ahead and turned the ambulance toward the shoulder of the road to shine the headlights onto one of the lawns in front of them. He saw a person crouched over a figure sprawled on the ground. The crouching individual, a middle-aged man, shielded his eyes from the glare of the headlights and then gave them a frantic wave. This had to be their patient, and the nine-one-one caller. Barry put them on location over the radio and was acknowledged by the dispatcher's voice in return.

"Careful on this one, Barry," Dean cautioned. "Whoever or whatever bit this person might still be in the neighborhood."

"Got it, Dean," his partner responded as he climbed down from the passenger side of the ambulance.

Dean grabbed the large flashlights from the compartment behind the driver's door on the ambulance, then he went around to the rear, climbed inside and got the heart monitor and oxygen bags out of the back. Walking around to the passenger side, he handed one of the lights to Barry. His partner had grabbed the trauma and medication bags from the compartment on his side of the ambulance. They hung off his shoulders by their straps. Switching on their lights, together the two paramedics walked across the lawn to the patient and caller. Dean shined his light around the yard to check for the creature that caused the bite. He had an itch between his shoulder blades and wished he could see better in the dark.

When they got to the side of the patient, the two paramedics saw she was an Asian woman in her fifties. Her entire shoulder on her left side was laid open so that Dean could see bone and tendon underneath. There were also deep slashing wounds to her abdomen. No wonder the caller couldn't stop the bleeding. It was a wonder she had lived long enough for the ambulance to arrive.

Because he was still on probationary status, Barry took the lead, with Dean observing and in support. The newer Station U paramedic held out the back of his right hand so the male caller could see it, and shined his light on it. That would reveal the hidden, ultra-violet ink stamp placed there. It showed the Station U paramedic emblem. It was invisible to humans, but it could be seen by their patients and other Unusual community members. The man nodded as he saw the fresh ink stamped there and he visibly relaxed. Dean showed his right hand as well. His mark was a more permanent UV tattoo of the Star of Life emblem. If Barry worked out in the long term, he would probably get one, too. All the Station U paramedics did eventually.

"Thank the Gods you are here," the man said. "My wife, she was attacked by some sort of demon-made-flesh."

"I'm Barry, and this is my partner Dean," Barry said as he set to work. "We are going to help your wife the best we can, okay?"

"Thank you," the slight Asian man said. "I'm called Yamo, and my wife is Akiko. Please help her. I did what I could but I'm not as powerful as she is."

Barry nodded as he started controlling the bleeding, slapping large, absorbent trauma pads over the wounds. Dean started collecting and assembling the IV supplies so they could get her some fluids. She had to have lost a great deal of blood.

"What sort of Unusual are you?" Dean asked. He had been unable to figure it out just from looking at them, or from anything that was said so far. That was normal. Sometimes you just had to ask.

"We are Hakutaku," the Asian man said. The woman groaned as Barry continued to work on her, packing her significant wounds with gauze and trauma pads. The groan distracted the man from Dean's inquiry. He knew a little of the Japanese and other Asian myths. The Hakutaku were healing spirits, and generally considered helpful and non-threatening. They were rumored to be related to the Chinese Bai-Ze spirits. It was times like this that his study of the extensive library of myths and legends back at Station U came in handy. It also explained why she was still alive. Her husband must have used some healing magic to sustain her.

Dean shined the light around in the darkness to check the area around them again. "Sir, did the attacker run off, or is it still out there nearby? Do you know what it was? Tell me what happened."

"I don't know," the man said. "We go for a walk every night. We love this neighborhood and enjoy the quiet after dark. It is a good time for contemplation and rejuvenation. Tonight, though, the natural world around us, was upset for some reason. We sought to understand why as we walked, but could come to no conclusion. We strive to bring healing and balance to both individuals and the world around us. This time we couldn't figure what was wrong. That was when the demon jumped out and slashed at Akiko. I was able to conjure a burst of light energy that drove it back. It screamed and ran off into the darkness. I turned my attention to my wife. I haven't seen it or heard it since. That was about fifteen minutes ago."

"You keep saying 'demon,'" Dean said. "What kind of Unusual being was it? A lycan? Another variety of animal shapeshifter?"

"No, no. You do not understand," Yamo said. "I think it was an Oni, a type of Japanese demon. I am sure of that much. I don't know how it got past the wards and entered this world. It must have sensed our true nature and set upon my wife right away. She's the stronger of the two of us."

The hairs on Dean's neck stood up. He had never encountered a demon before. He knew they were the evil opposites of the heavenly Unusuals like the Eldara. Those angels fulfilled the roles of messengers and agents of the gods of good and nature. The demons served another group, who sought to tear the world asunder, or so legend said. They were confined to the netherworld and kept there by a series of wards set in place millennia ago. An Oni was an Asian form of demon, though there were many varieties. Some were intelligent, but others were much more dangerous because of their unpredictable animal natures.

Shining the light around the yard, the paramedic saw nothing but the house and the trees and grass. He turned his attention back to the patient and her husband. If there was an Oni on the loose and attacking people, it would need to be dealt with, but that was a matter for someone else. He and Barry were here to care for this patient. They had to get her to the Elk City Medical Center trauma team.

THE ONI DEMON, called Tegu by its lord and master, watched from the roof of the house nearby. It had been easy to climb up there and watch for the arrival of its true target. Tegu had been told that it would know the one it was to kill by his aura, and the stink of an Eldara on him. The Eldara, the messengers of the gods, were the most hated of the adversaries faced by demon-kind. The master was right. As soon as the strange, loud vehicle arrived and the occupants climbed out, the Oni saw the white glow surrounding the driver. He was one of those touched by one of the hated Eldara. That was the demon's target. The man would not be without some sort of magical protections, so the demon watched and waited for the right opportunity to strike. He must kill this man. The master had ordered it.

———

DEAN FETCHED the stretcher from the ambulance and took it over to where Barry was finishing up his treatments to Akiko. She was semiconscious, only occasionally groaning in pain when Barry was forced to move her while binding her wounds. He had stretched out the clear plastic from a roll of plastic food wrap and had wrapped her chest to seal the wounds and help prevent what was commonly called a sucking chest wound. The lungs required a closed system to work effectively. When air was able to rush into the chest cavity without having to go through the mouth and nose, the lungs could not inflate properly. This was one of the causes of a collapsed lung. By wrapping her wounds in airtight plastic, Barry helped seal the wounds and prevent air from entering the chest cavity by another route.

Once the stretcher was rolled up next to her, the two paramedics carefully lifted her up onto it and then began loading their other gear up and around her so they could roll the whole package of patient and gear back to the ambulance in one run. Dean pointed to the ambulance and told Yamo to go get in the passenger seat of the ambulance's cab while they loaded his wife into the back. The two paramedics then rolled her over to the back of the vehicle. They took care on the uneven ground to avoid tipping the top-heavy load.

When they arrived at the back of the ambulance, Barry lifted the head end of the stretcher up and Dean helped him retract the wheels and roll it into the back of the ambulance. Considering his route to the hospital, he closed the doors and started to walk around to the driver's side of the ambulance.

TEGU SAW its opportunity as the two paramedics separated. Its target was alone at the rear and turning to walk to the front of the vehicle. The demon leapt down from its perch on the roof of the Hakutakus' home. This would be the chance to finish off the target for its master. It would be satisfying to kill one of the agents of good. Even if this human was just another minion, it would be satisfying to serve its master this way. As Tegu scrambled from the roof to the ground, the demon failed to notice another dark form detach from the other shadows at the corner of the house, following after it. The hunter was also the hunted.

Chapter 2

Jaz had been tracking this particular demon since her clan's oracle had detected its manifestation two days before. The small blonde hunter clanswoman shifted in her hiding place as she took in the scene in front of her. She was careful to make no sound. She crouched next to the bushes at the house's corner. Jaz had been too late to stop the attack on the Hakutaku woman and she didn't understand why the Oni had stopped short of killing the Japanese healing spirit, or her husband. Instead, the creature had moved to watch from a distance as the man wailed and cried over his injured wife.

This was very strange behavior for such a demon, and something that should be observed. She was close enough to see it on the roof above her. Maybe she could teach the other hunters in her clan something new about the Oni. Usually this type of demon was a blood-thirsty ravening animal and never stopped short of killing its target. They didn't stop unless they were killed first. That meant one of two things to Jaz - this demon had been driven back by some charm on the couple in the yard. The old man had manifested some sort of light magic in defense. She had seen that. The second option was that these two were not the creature's target.

The hunter thought back to her instructions, given to her by her father when he sent her out, alone. "Track this creature and when you have the opportunity, make the kill, fast and from hiding. The Oni are treacherous and not to be trifled with." She had already known that. Jaz had seen a lot in her twenty-two years.

She had asked why she was being sent out alone. She wondered if the creature was so dangerous, shouldn't a full strike team be used to kill it? All he would say was that the oracle had said it must be her, alone, to undertake this hunt. The whole situation was very strange. The strangeness continued as she started tracking it around Elk City two nights ago. The creature had made no kills on the previous nights' prowling. It was like it was searching for something or someone and hadn't found what it was looking for. The Oni, like many demons, was weakened by the daylight so it holed up somewhere in the city during the day. When it went to ground in the daytime, she lost the trail and had to wait until it surfaced again the next night. After it left its lair tonight, she had tracked it here and thought there was finally an opportunity to strike it down. They were away from the crowds of people that were always nearby in a congested city. Hunters must always try to hide their kills from the public they protected. The ignorant humans could not become aware of how close to death and damnation they were, each and every day, with monsters and demons all around them.

Jaz had tracked the creature here, and the strange behavior continued with the non-killing of the Hakutaku couple. What was this Oni demon up to? She double-checked her triple amulet, a three-sided pendant hanging on a chain around her neck to make sure it contacted skin. The amulet performed three simple magics to help her on her hunt. It masked her heat signature, since most of her prey could see into the infrared spectrum. It reduced her scent from those who might be able to sense her presence by smell. The amulet also allowed her to see nearly as well as any Unusual creature or demon in the night's near-total darkness. It was not perfect night vision, but it was better than any other human would be able to see on a moonless night like this.

Jaz checked her weapons to make sure all were at hand. The

Glock semi-automatic pistol holstered on her left hip was of little use with this particular demon. The bullets loaded in the magazine were infused with silver and arsenic. Those projectiles would slow it down a little bit, until it regenerated. They were more suited to taking down various shape-shifters and vampires. The small Bowie knife sheathed on her right hip was blessed by a priest, and had been tempered in both holy oil and holy water. That would do the job, but she was loath to get in that close. Those talons looked wicked sharp. She had seen the wounds caused by them on the woman on the lawn. That would leave the katana across her back. She preferred it anyway, truth to be told. It gave her a bit of reach beyond the arm's length of the demon's claws. It was also a holy blade, blessed like the Bowie, but more significant because of the additional power it held. It linked to her very soul and drew power from her life force. Every hunter in the Errington clan was gifted with one such blade upon their coming of age at thirteen years old. It gave the Errington hunters stamina and power few other humans could match. Her blade had been with her ever since and she would have felt naked without it.

The peal of an ambulance siren tore her from her consideration of her weapons and Jaz checked her quarry. The ambulance was likely one of those from Elk City's vaunted Station U. Those Unusual-loving paramedics were always out and about in the city, caring for anyone of the underworld's denizens who called for help. Jaz knew that not all Unusuals were evil. Most weren't, if she allowed herself the truth of it. What she hated was that so many of them tolerated those of their number who were evil, those who had done wrongs to humans. She snorted quietly. Those paramedics from Station U were relegated to a group that included the tree-huggers and rabid animal-rights types in her mind.

Jaz watched the demon vigilantly. She expected it to leave the area with all the attention and noise coming to the home with the ambulance. It didn't move back from the roof's peak but leaned forward, as if with anticipation. That was strange. Observing the Oni's behavior as it watched the ambulance arrive, she noticed it tense and heard a small snarl coming from its position on the roof.

Looking back at the ambulance, she saw that one of the paramedics, the driver, had come around the back of the vehicle just then. Could he be the real target of this creature? She settled back into her hiding spot and watched the scene as the paramedics set to work on trying to save the injured Hakutaku woman on the lawn. The demon watched as well.

The huntress was impressed with the efficiency and professionalism of the two paramedics. Even though they were caring for unusual creatures, they treated their patient no differently than she would have seen if the patient were human. Strange that they took so easily to helping the creatures living unseen beside their human neighbors. Jaz had been taught all her life that, while some Unusuals could be tolerated and even worked with, none of them were to be trusted. She watched while they stopped the woman's profuse bleeding and bandaged her wounds. Then the driver went back to the ambulance on the street and retrieved the wheeled stretcher, taking it back to the patient.

Jaz shifted her gaze to check on the Oni on the rooftop. It was definitely tracking the movements of the driver, ignoring the other three potential targets. She had never heard of an Oni demon leaving a kill unfinished, let alone using one attack to lure its actual target into range of a later attack. Whoever had conjured the demon and controlled it must be very strong. Controlling such a demon reliably from any distance was close to impossible by everything Jaz understood about the process. She didn't know of any human conjurer who would possess such power. The demon was clearly waiting for something. Jaz wanted to know what it was waiting for.

The team of paramedics packed up their patient and rolled her to the ambulance. Jaz watched as one of the paramedics directed the woman's husband to climb into the passenger seat while they loaded his wife into the back of the ambulance. When the paramedics loaded up the woman and the one paramedic climbed into the back with her, the driver shut the door. That was when the Oni moved.

Jaz heard the sound of the rushing attack before she saw

anything. The sound of the creature's claws, scrabbling down the roof's shingles, was her first warning. Damn, that thing was fast. Jaz reached over her shoulder, drawing her katana. She sprinted from cover to try to catch the demon as it bounded on all fours towards the back of the ambulance. The huntress caught up to the creature in the street, just as the paramedic driver turned the corner towards the front of the ambulance. It was springing forward to sweep at the paramedic's back with its extended claws. Jaz leapt forward in one last, desperate bound, her blade coming down and across beheading the demon in a single silent, slicing blow. The magical blade, which never needed sharpening, blessed by God, banished this demon back to hell with a single stroke.

The demon's head bounced once on the pavement before the head and body turned to a red mist, glowing in the brake lights of the ambulance, leaving Jaz standing in the street watching the emergency vehicle pull away. She wondered who that paramedic was that made him the target of such an attack. She would have to report back to her father on this development. He would want to investigate further. She stood in the street a bit longer as the lights of the ambulance faded, then she moved back into the shadows and headed home.

DEAN SLID the ambulance into gear, checked to make sure his patient's husband was belted in, then pulled away from the scene. He picked up the radio mic and notified headquarters they were on the way to the hospital. He was a little worried that the creature that had caused such a vicious attack was still out there. He made a mental note to notify James Lee, the vampire lord of Elk City about it, as well as the rest of the Station U paramedics. If one such attack happened, it was likely that more would happen soon.

As he drove away with his lights flashing, reflecting off the surrounding trees on this residential street, he shot a glance in the side view mirror. A small blonde woman with a sword stood there looking back at him. She wore all black, sported a pistol on her hip,

and held her sword in a two-handed, Asian-style grip. She was illuminated only briefly by the ambulance's taillights and rear emergency strobes while he pulled away from her, then she was hidden in
shadow and gone from view.

Dean blinked to clear his vision. Had he seen what he thought
he had seen? He had learned in the recent months with Station U to
trust his own eyes and instincts. There were many strange things in
the world out there. Lord knows, he had seen enough of them.
From diabetic werewolves, to watching his former partner turned
into a vampire in front of him, Dean Flynn had seen a lot of things
never experienced by other humans. This woman with a sword
should have been just another one of them, but something inside
him told him that she was important. Somehow, someday, he knew
he would see that woman again and he tried to remember her face,
framed in blonde hair pulled back in a ponytail.

All the way to the hospital, especially every time he stopped the
ambulance to check that an intersection was clear before proceeding
through, Dean found himself checking his mirrors. By the time he
got to the hospital trauma center, he wondered if he had imagined
the whole thing. Then he was distracted by the work at hand as they
unloaded their seriously injured patient and turned her over to the
ECMC trauma team. Dean told Barry to start on the paperwork on
the ambulance's tablet computer, while he took the old man inside
and showed him to the waiting area.

Yamo, the old Hakutaku man, took Dean's hand as he turned to
leave the waiting room after dropping the gentleman off there.
Dean stopped and turned. The paramedic was sure the man was
distraught about his wife's condition.

"She was real," Yamo said.

"What?" Dean asked. "Who was real?"

"The hunter girl," Yamo said. "I saw her, too - in the mirror as
we left. I think you two are tied together in some way. Beware, paramedic Dean Flynn. Hunters live by their own code, and they don't
easily associate with those who befriend Unusuals. You are tied, but
for good or ill, I do not know."

The Hakutaku man let go of his hand and returned his gaze to the door to the trauma rooms, waiting for word of his wife. Dean walked away, heading back to the ambulance bay at the hospital, thinking about what the man had said. If she was real, then what was she doing here in Elk City - and what was a hunter? Too many questions on top of his other worries. Dean sighed and walked back to meet up with his partner and put the ambulance back in service for the next call.

____

Chapter 3

____

Dean kept his thoughts to himself as he and Barry restocked the ambulance supplies at the hospital. They drove back to their station, tucked into the back of a run-down industrial park outside of the city. There was so much on his mind. Not the least of which was the woman with the sword he had seen in his mirrors at the scene of the earlier ambulance call. There was also the ongoing enigma of his missing girlfriend, Ashley. He felt guilty that he hadn't been thinking about her more often, but work had him busier than normal with the flood of patient calls coming in to the Station U paramedics.

Ashley was an Eldara Sister, an angelic healer. The Eldara were the messengers of the Gods serving many tasks for the divine beings on earth. She and Dean had been together for several months now. At least they had been until about five weeks earlier, when she had left town suddenly on what she would only call an important errand. Then, early last week, Ashley's twin sister, Ingrid, had shown up to announce to Dean that Ashley had been abducted. Ingrid said she needed his help to free her. Ashley's twin was a force to be reckoned with. She was an Eldara too, of course, but not one of the healing sisters. Ingrid was a warrior maiden, a Valkyrie, intent on collecting the heroes from the world's battlefields and escorting them to the afterlife where they would feast together and wait to return for the battle at the end of days.

Ingrid had left as quickly as she had arrived, giving her sister's boyfriend instructions to await her return. Great! Tell a guy he needed to rescue his girlfriend, then tell him to wait for an indeterminate time frame. That had been a little over a week ago. Since then, Dean had gone on autopilot, working extra shifts along with his regular rotations to keep himself busy while he waited. It was agony. He realized that tonight's call with the demon attack was the first time he had not been thinking about Ashley at all. He felt both guilty and relieved. He knew that he couldn't stay in that constant state of worry forever, which explained his relief. The fact that he had been able to forget her at all explained his guilt. Well that, and his distraction by the blonde girl's face in his rearview mirror.

All of this was on his mind as Dean returned to the station with his probationary partner. Barry was an experienced paramedic, but was new to the world of Unusual patients. Dean was his preceptor and was supposed to help break him in and oversee his adjustment to caring for their particular group of patients at Station U. Overall, the new guy was getting acclimated to their patients pretty well. He was doing his research in the station's extensive library of mythology and legend, and he was open-minded. Those were the keys to being a good Station U paramedic.

Paramedics normally had the mantra of Sempre Gumby - meaning always stay flexible. Every paramedic was forced to adapt and overcome challenges with every patient they encountered, even the humans. With Station U and their unique patients, that mantra became multiplied exponentially as they were forced to adapt to both the medical problems faced by their patients, and adapting to the individual mythical nature of each of them.

Dean pulled into the parking lot at Station U and waited while Barry got out to help him safely back up into their garage bay attached to the station. Once inside, he went about his normal post-call tasks of getting everything ready to go for the next 911 call. There was always a next call. Barry went into the station's squad room to complete his patient paperwork on the computer there, and prep it for sending off to the hospital and headquarters after Dean had a final look at it. Dean was heading over to the squad room door to check on Barry's progress when he got the text from Ingrid.

"Back in town. We need to meet up. Where are you?"

"I'm working," Dean replied back.

"Stay there. I'm on my way."

Ingrid was nothing like her sister, though they looked identical, except for a few extra piercings and tattoos. The differences didn't stop with the superficial items. The Valkyrie was much more direct in her approach to everything, Dean had learned. Ashley had once told Dean that she didn't want Ingrid coming to town to help them solve any problems because she usually left a certain amount of carnage in her wake on the way to getting the job done. He didn't want carnage, but action of any type would be preferable to just waiting as he had been doing.

Dean slid his smartphone back in his pants pocket and went into the squad room. Barry was still working on the computer, writing his patient care report for the injured Hakutaku woman. Since most Unusuals had pretty much normal human anatomy and physiology, the write-ups looked surprisingly mundane to the casual eye. The report system had a separate tab on the software's screen where the Station U medics could enter any additional care or details that pertained to their specific inhuman nature. A gravelly voice to Dean's left drew his attention away from his partner.

"I made a midnight snack for you guys when I heard over the radio you were on your way back. I have some cheeseburger sliders with sweet potato fries," Freddy said. Freddy was the station's resident chef. He was also a zombie. The paramedics had sort of adopted him after his run-down house trailer was firebombed by terrorists a few months before. He could never work in a restaurant again after his voodoo priestess girlfriend had turned him into a zombie for cheating on her. He was just about the best chef Dean had ever met, as long as you made sure all his parts were intact after he was done cooking.

"Thank you, Freddie," Dean said. "That will certainly hit the spot." Dean looked over at this partner. "Barry, how's that report coming?"

"I'm finishing up with it right now," the other paramedic replied. "I just need you to look it over and then we can send it in to the system."

Dean walked over to the other computer workstation and logged in to his own account. Because he was the preceptor, Barry's reports automatically came through his system for his approval before being sent in to headquarters and the hospital, to become part of the patient's records. Barry had been a paramedic for a while, longer than Dean, in fact. He was only getting the probationary treatment because of his lack of experience with the particular types of patients the Station U paramedics dealt with. Dean gave the report a quick review, found nothing that needed changing or adjustment, clicked the checkbox that added his electronic signature, and sent it off.

He was just getting up to go grab one of the mini-burgers Freddie had made when the locked parking lot door opened and a tall brown-haired woman dressed in a head-to-toe black leather ensemble stepped into the squad room. Dean didn't know how Ingrid was able to get past the lock. He knew she didn't have a key. Locked doors never seemed to bother her somehow. She just sort of ignored them. Maybe it was a hidden power of all of the Eldara, or maybe it was a Valkyrie thing. Either way, she always made her entrances unannounced.

"Hello, Ingrid," Dean said as he picked up a burger from the plate. "I'm glad you could make the time to come back. Now maybe you can help me find your missing sister. It's not like I was going crazy waiting for you or anything."

"Dean, you have no idea what I've been going through trying to get some assistance to find Ashley, so don't give me any sass. I'm not in the mood." While Ashley sounded as American as the typical girl next door, Ingrid's British accent gave her a certain aloofness that she used to her advantage. She crossed the room to the table where Freddy had laid out the food for them. She picked up a slider, took a bite and chewed with an eye-roll of pleasure, adding a nod and grunt of approval to Freddy before she sat down in one of the station's recliners.

"I'm simply famished," Ingrid said after she swallowed the first bite. She took another bite, finishing the first mini-sandwich off and leaning over from the chair to grab another off the plate. "I've been working hard to get my regular chores done and seek out information on where my sister is being held. It has been non-stop action since I've been away. Do you know how many small wars and battles there are around the world at any given time?"

Dean started to answer that he didn't know, but she waved him off and kept going.

"The problem is, Dean, I've been told, in no uncertain terms, that I can't go looking for my sister anymore. Partly because I haven't been keeping up with my quota of heroic souls for Valhalla." Ingrid paused to finish off another sandwich and looked up at Dean and Barry who just stood there watching. "You guys think you have a bureaucracy to deal with? You know nothing about bureaucracy compared to my superiors. They are the worst micromanagers of the Universe!" The last sentence was shouted at the ceiling.

Dean suspected that it might have more to do with wrangling an angel, who had what amounted to a divine case of ADHD, than pure micromanagement. He tried to get her back on track with what he wanted to know. What was she doing to find her sister?

"All I know is that she is somewhere in or around the Elk City region. That could mean anything within a few hour's drive," Ingrid said, grabbing a handful of sweet potato fries and dumping them on the paper plate she pulled over to her lap. She continued eating as she talked. "I also know that you are going to have to pretty much find her on your own. I've already done too much to meddle in what I've been told is none of my business."

"Is it Artur?" Dean asked. "Are there more members of The Cause that we didn't find when we broke up the group a few months ago?" Artur was an ancient vampire who tried to organize a hostile take-over of the rule of Elk City from the vampire James Lee. He attempted it by starting a terrorist organization of humans focused on getting rid of the Unusuals in their community. Dean and Ashley had helped shut down the conspiracy, and he thought they had rid the city of the problem. Artur fled the area as soon as his plans fell apart. Dean knew Ingrid and Ashley had a history with the meddling vampire. He also knew Ingrid still sought revenge against him.

"No, it's not him," Ingrid said with a snarl. "As much as I'd like to pin this on the little ferret, Artur is hiding out somewhere in East Asia and has nothing to do with this as far as I can tell. This is some sort of struggle between the powers that be. The divine and nefarious Gods are arguing about something, and Ashley got stuck in the middle. Frankly, it is just like her to get her nose into something with which she has no business getting involved. She was always the crusader for lost causes. Maybe that's why she was so attracted to you, Dean."

"Well, I don't know about that…" Dean started to object.

"Don't take it personally, lover boy," Ingrid continued, shoving another sweet potato fry into her mouth. "You're not the first stray pup she took under her wing. All things considered, you are one of the better ones and you might actually be useful since you are the one who is going to have to track her down and free her all on your own."

"What do you mean, 'on my own'? Aren't you going to help your sister escape from whoever has her?" Dean asked.

"Like I said. I've been told that it is not my job," Ingrid repeated. "I was not asked to stop. I was not requested to stop. I was told, in no uncertain terms, 'stay out of it'." She finished the last of her fries and got up to check the refrigerator. "What? No beer?" She grabbed a Mountain Dew, opened it and took a long swig from the bottle. "Look, Dean, I did some checking when no one was looking, and whatever Ashley is mixed up with falls into the realm of humans. That means some human or humans need to work to solve it. She found out that someone on the side of evil was making a direct assault on the area. That's a violation of the rules the Gods set up a long time ago. Still, the forces of good are going to play by the rules and rely on humans and other free-willed creatures here to solve the problem on earth. So that means it is up to you to figure out."

"Me?" Dean asked. "But I don't even know where to begin. How am I supposed to find Ashley if I don't know where to start looking?"

"Calm down. I was able to dig up a few items that might be of help to you." She glanced at the watch on her wrist and walked over to one of the windows overlooking the parking lot. She glanced outside and turned back to Dean. "I don't have a lot of time, so listen carefully to what I tell you. You can't find her on your own. You will need the help of two others." She rolled her eyes again. "This is so typical of how my bosses operate, by the way. They love to operate in threes. It has something to do with being a prime number or something. Anyway, back on track. You need three things to work in tandem to find Ashley and free her. You need a magical human, an anti-magical human, and a mundane to find her. You're obviously the mundane. I mean, look at you. You are the perfect average guy, just the kind of person the Gods use in all the stories."

Dean wasn't sure he liked the way she blew him off as average. He was, after all, the one who helped defeat the recent takeover attempt in Elk City. He was an accomplished paramedic, and had become something of a hero to his Unusual community of patients. He didn't think he was average or mundane at all.

Ingrid interpreted the look on his face correctly. "Don't take my words personally, Dean. Heroes don't look like some action guy in a film. They are ordinary men and women who choose to do extraordinary things. Don't forget that. What makes a hero is that they are mundane until they are called to act."

"So, if I'm the mundane in this equation," Dean asked, "How do I determine who I'm supposed to choose to fill the other roles? I mean, knowing I have to find the right person among both magical and anti-magical beings doesn't give me much to go with here."

"Hey, it would not be a quest if there weren't some work involved," Ingrid said with a shrug. She started towards the parking lot door. Grabbing the knob and pulling the door open, she turned and looked at Dean. "I may be able to come and help you, but only once. If you need me - really need me, you have the power to invoke me by saying 'Ingrid, I need you.' Don't use it frivolously. I'm counting on you to free my sister. If you don't, I'll be very cross with you." The Valkyrie turned and walked out the door, letting it slam shut behind her.

Dean just stood where he had been rooted to the floor the whole time she had been in the squad room. Ashley had once called her sister a force of nature. It was a good description of her. He looked at his partner. Barry had been eating a plate of food and watching the whole exchange as if he were watching a movie. He had a slight grin on his face when he caught Dean looking his way.

"Dean, you Station U paramedics certainly have interesting lives," Barry said with a laugh. "Where do I sign up for the supernatural girlfriend? I'm between ladies at the moment."

"I'm beginning to think they're more trouble than they're worth sometimes, Barry," Dean replied absently. His mind was distracted by the cryptic instructions from Ashley's sister. He had to find two others, two individuals who seemed to be polar opposites at first glance. He didn't even know where to begin. He told Barry as much.

"I have read a lot of the stories in our library since I got started with things here at Station U. Heck, I've read of stories like this my whole life. Maybe you're making it too hard," Barry suggested. "In all the stories, the party of heroes just sort of find each other. That is what makes it all so much fun."

"Well, Barry, this isn't a story. This is my real life and the life of my girlfriend." Dean sat down and started eating some food while he thought about Ashley.

Dean had the next two days off after his string of twelve-hour night shifts. He used that time for some in-depth research into what the instructions Ingrid forwarded to him could mean. He was supposed to assemble a team for a quest to get Ashley back, and that team was supposed to have three specific parts. Despite that information, as well as doing some targeted Google searches and reading, Dean felt no closer to getting Ashley's rescue underway.

He spent much of the two days in the Elk City Library's main branch, looking at every mythological and legendary reference on quests and searches for missing characters in the stories. He re-read and skimmed stories like the section from the Lord of the Rings trilogy where Aragorn, Gimli and Legolas hunted for the lost hobbits. Dean spent time searching online resources for tales of classic trios of heroes, all to try to narrow down what type of people he was looking for.

At the end of the two-day intensive search, Dean was only sure of one thing. In most quests, the heroes ended up together almost by chance. They ended up in a location to do one thing and soon found themselves tied together by a common bond that none of them really understood. He supposed it made for a good story, but from the viewpoint of living inside the unfolding tale, it just sucked. It was midnight on the last of his two days off when he finally threw up his hands and gave up. He hated to say it, but he had nothing to go on to lead him to Ashley. He was stumped.

The realization brought him to near tears when it hit him. Part of that was the exhaustion and the lack of sleep that hounded him. The other side of it was his intense connection to Ashley, and from his experiences alongside her during the previous months since he started at Station U. Ashley and Brynne, his former paramedic mentor and partner, had been important parts of his life over those stressful months. Now Brynne was a vampire and could no longer work as a paramedic. Ashley was kidnapped and held for some reason he didn't understand, and he was left alone to pick up the pieces. It was almost too much for him to bear. In light of that, he decided he might have to give up on all of them because he wasn't sure he was up to the task laid before him by Ingrid and the divine forces she and Ashley served.

Sleep eventually rescued him from his thoughts. It was the kind of sleep that took you when you had pushed yourself too long and too hard beyond your physical and mental limits. It was the kind of sleep Dean knew he needed and he surrendered to it, not caring about anything else anymore.

━━

HE WAS AWAKENED by the usual alarm for day shift on his smart phone. It was four-thirty in the morning. Time to get up, get some breakfast and get ready for his first day shift back in the rotation. He swiped to open his phone and saw that he had an urgent text message from work. Checking the message, and then looking at his emails for more detail, he saw that fire headquarters was pulling in all the paramedics by shift to undergo some sort of self-defense training.

An additional text message from Chief Ari, the fire department's deputy chief for emergency medical services, gave more detail on why the sudden need for this training. It was more informative than the department-wide email. Ari informed him that it was a response to the recent demon attack that he and Barry had responded to. There had been similar, but unconfirmed, demon attacks around the city. It was thought that a special set of scene awareness and defense trainings might help the EMS and Fire crews avoid dangerous situations until the culprit or culprits were found and stopped. The Station U crews would benefit from it especially.

He and Barry were to meet with all the city's C-shift paramedic crews for training at the academy that morning from eight-thirty until twelve noon. Then they would all head to work at their stations.

Dean looked at the email again and found some information on the outside contracting organization involved with the training. They were a security firm Dean had heard of, but only barely. Errington Security Outfitters were supposedly a high-end security and bodyguard service used by visiting celebrities and other important visitors to the region. They had offices in all the major cities up and down the east coast, but were based here in Elk City, according to their write up in the email. The training for the paramedics would be led by some guy called Jaswinder Errington. He possessed several black belts as well as certifications in martial arts and self-defense techniques.

Dean tried to approach all of their ongoing education classes with an open mind. He had to get over forty-eight hours of training every two years to maintain his Maryland paramedic license. Dean always looked forward to those unusual or different classes over the typical medical ones for which they all had to take refreshers. This self-defense and scene safety class might be one that would come in handy in his specific paramedic practice with the Unusual community. It certainly couldn't hurt.

He jumped in the shower and planned the rest of his morning. Since he didn't have to be at the station at six as usual and the class did not start until eight-thirty, Dean figured he had time to stop in and visit someone he had not had a lot of time to hang with in the last month or so. Plus this friend might have some ideas about where to find his quest partners. After he dried off and changed into his uniform, Dean pulled out his phone and dialed a number, waiting while it rang through to the other side.

"Well, hello Dean," the smooth southern drawl on the other end of the line said. "Long time, no talk. What can I do for you?"

"Hi, Celeste," Dean answered. "I wondered how Brynne was doing and if she was up to having visitors this morning?" Celeste was a vampire, and personal assistant to James Lee, the vampire lord of Elk City. James was the boyfriend of his ex-partner Brynne Garvey, the ex-partner he had decided would live on as a vampire after a fatal gunshot wound. She was still acclimating to the turning and was not always up to meeting with humans in the flesh. Their human heartbeats and freshly pulsing blood could be distracting to her, and that could be problematic for the object of her distraction.

"She has been doing much better, and I think with James and I present to watch over her, she would love to see you," Celeste replied. "When were you thinking of dropping by?"

"I have a training class downtown this morning at eight-thirty, and I thought I might come by there around seven to visit before class."

"That will be perfect," Celeste said. "I'll tell Brynne and James you are stopping by. They will be so excited you are coming over. See you later."

For a while, Dean and Ashley had lived in James' building downtown in an effort to protect him from attacks from The Cause. It had been fun living there like a stay at a posh hotel, but there was no place like home. Dean had moved back to his apartment in the suburbs, where he lived above a detached garage owned by a nice elderly couple. His landlords, Mr. And Mrs. Baxter, were very nice and he caught a break on his rent by doing odd chores around the house and yard for them. It was a good arrangement and he was glad to be back home.

Dean left his place, made sure he locked up, and headed down the exterior stairs to the driveway and the residential street where he had parked his white Ford pickup truck. It was still dark out, although the light of the coming dawn was starting to brighten the eastern sky. Dean unlocked the door and climbed in, starting the truck and heading towards the expressway that would take him downtown. He didn't see the red glowing eyes perched above the roof of his apartment, watching him leave. The eyes blinked twice, then the creature that owned them folded in on itself and disappeared in a red mist.

Chapter 5

Dean still had a keycard pass for the Nightwing building downtown, from when he lived in the building. He pulled up to the underground garage and slid the card in the reader, driving forward as the gate to the ramp rose. Driving down under the building, he parked in one of the open slots near the elevators and rode upstairs, again using the keycard to access the penthouse level. He walked up to the double doors in the entry hall and rang the doorbell there.

Celeste opened the door. Her smile was framed by shoulder length red hair. The vampire and self-described southern belle had been working for James Lee since sometime around the civil war. She wouldn't say how the two of them met but Dean was sure it was an interesting story. While she was his employee, she was also something of a comic foil, confidant, and companion to the vampire lord of Elk City.

"Dean," she said extending her hand in greeting. "It is so good to see you. We miss you since you moved back to the boring 'burbs."

"I like boring, Celeste," Dean replied taking her hand and shaking it. "I am starting to realize that excitement is overrated. And I miss you guys, too. Is Brynne doing alright?"

"She's still in transition," the vampire responded, her voice quieter. Dean knew that Brynne could overhear if they talked in normal tones and was nearby in the penthouse. "It took me almost a year to reach the point where James could trust me around potential meals unattended. Just be patient. She'll be her normal self again soon."

"I know, I'm just second-guessing myself and the choice I made on her behalf, that's all," Dean said.

"She is her normal self when it is just us vampires around. I think she misses all her human friends, but understands the reasons why she can't see everyone whenever she wants." Celeste turned and led him into the spacious penthouse. It had an open floor plan off the entry foyer. There were large plate glass windows around the perimeter that were carefully tinted to block most of the sun's harmful ultraviolet rays during the daytime. As he looked around, the blackout shutters were closed as the sun was already coming up. Brynne was too sensitive to sunlight to tolerate even a little bit of filtered UV light. It was another change her new existence had forced upon her.

Dean followed the red-haired assistant into the large open living room. All the furniture and carpets were white. Seated across the room were Brynne and James, together on the leather love seat. Celeste gestured for Dean to sit in a spot on the end of the sofa opposite them and she seated herself next to him. Dean was used to the precautions from his other visits to his old partner. With James and Celeste to intervene, Brynne could not get to Dean and feed without them stopping her.

Brynne was paler than she used to be, but otherwise looked the same. She was dressed in a pair of faded blue jeans and a vintage black Led Zeppelin concert t-shirt. Dean knew it was probably not a reproduction but one from a time when James had attended the concerts back in the 1970's. Her red-tinged eyes met his when he sat down.

"Hello, Dean," Brynne said. "I'm glad you came up to see me again so soon. I'm sorry for the need for the constant chaperones."

"Not me, Boss," Dean said with a chuckle. "You'd eat me without them. Right?"

She sighed and smiled a bit. "Yes, that is true. Sorry, but you do look delicious." She licked her lips, exposing the elongated canines in her mouth. James laid his hand on hers from where he sat next to her. He was in his characteristic all black outfit, this time black jeans and a black long-sleeve button-down shirt to match his dark eyes and hair.

"Uh, I'll leave that one where it is, Brynne," Dean said.

"It is unusual for you to call and come by on such short notice, Dean," James said. "Is there something you needed? Have you gotten any more word on Ashley's whereabouts? You know if there is anything I can do to help you, you just have to ask. It concerns me that an Eldara Sister has gone missing from my domain."

"I thank you for that, James," Dean replied, "and there is something I need advice about." Dean proceeded to tell them all about his encounter with Ingrid two nights before. He tried to include every detail of the conversation he'd had with the Valkyrie, every item of information he had gleaned from her. If there was something important he was missing, James, with his millennia of experience, or even Brynne or Celeste, might have some inkling of what he was supposed to do next. He talked about his research and all the dead ends he had reached. When he was done dumping everything he knew, he stopped and looked at them each in turn.

James pursed his lips and thought for a moment. Dean heard Celeste utter a quiet "Oh, my," from where she sat next to him. Brynne was the one who broke the silence.

"Dean, just to be clear, she said you need both a magical being and an 'anti-magical' being?" Brynne asked. Dean nodded and she continued. "I agree with Ingrid that you are the mundane in the equation. She sure has you tagged correctly. What do you think, James?"

"I agree with you and Ingrid about Dean, but I'm not sure I can offer much to help you with the other two parts of the team you must assemble to find Ashley. A magical being could be any number of Unusuals or magical humans from a Djinn, like our friend

Kristof Algar, to that crazy half leprechaun who owns The Irish Shop downtown. It's the anti-magical part that is interesting. Usually that is reserved for those opposed to us, the humans who would have us gone from their communities."

"What about one of the Hunter Clans?" Celeste offered. They all looked at the red-headed vampire. "I mean they are human, right? But, they are diametrically opposed to the use of magic to influence and lord power over their fellow humans."

"The problem is that they are unpredictable," James said. "A few of them have some sense of honor and can be dealt with on a limited basis. Others are little better than terrorists like The Cause group we just defeated here in Elk City."

"Hunter Clans?" Dean asked. He had never heard of them and wondered why. Brynne had been very thorough in educating him when she was his supervisor and mentor at Station U.

James sighed and answered. "It dates back to the very beginning of human-kind's dealings with the Unusuals in the world. There were some who took it upon themselves to protect their communities from the more predatory of us. In the beginning they just served as defenders of human-kind, but eventually most of them turned into clans of human predators against any Unusuals. Modern society and social norms have mellowed some of those predatory practices, at least here in the United States, Canada, and Western Europe."

"So they don't hunt you all anymore?"

"Not unless they perceive someone as acting outside of the law and can't get our leadership to act first. Now they mostly focus on the beings of the netherworld who break out into this world," James clarified. "Don't misunderstand me. Even the best of them would just as soon stake me, Brynne, and Celeste as talk to us. They see us as preying on humans, even if we do it in a consensual way."

"How do they feel about the Eldara?" Dean was concerned about the reaction to Ashley if he took one of these hunters on a quest to find her.

"It varies from clan to clan, Dean," Celeste said. "Some see themselves as squarely on the side of good and tolerate the Eldara as connections to the Gods. Others seek to rid humanity of Unusual influence of any kind."

"It's a long shot, though," Brynne said. "My understanding was always that the Hunters avoided places like Elk City, where the two communities, human and Unusual, were more integrated and tolerant."

"That is true, my dear," James said, smiling at Brynne. "But there are Hunters around from time to time including one family that is based here. They travel a lot but I try to keep tabs on them when one of the clansmen comes to my city. There are a few in town right now, but they appear to be just passing through on business. Most of the clans have set up broad networks of business fronts to support their efforts over the years. They are involved with almost everything in some way, from banking, to import/export businesses."

"So, maybe one of these hunters or maybe not one of them. Which is it?" Dean said, shaking his head. "I'm no closer to finding Ashley than I was two days ago."

Brynne laughed aloud and Dean looked up at her, feeling hurt by her callous outburst. She held up a hand as she got control over herself.

"Dean, you always go down the path of feeling defeated before you've even gotten started," his former partner said. "You said you did your research. You've received word from on high, as it were, that you are to go on this quest. If that is the case, then the members of the quest will assemble around you. You may have already met or encountered one or both of the other two you are to join up with. Trust yourself and your instincts. They will carry you through this mystery and help you find Ashley."

James laughed then, too. "She's right, you know, Dean. It is something right out of a storybook. You're the hero, and just like Robin the Hood stumbled on his greatest companion, Little John, in a seemingly random encounter, you are going to stumble upon your sidekicks in this endeavor. Just keep your eyes open, and be ready to ask for help when you think you need it. The right people will come along to help you soon enough, probably when you least expect it."

"I wish I had your confidence, James," Dean said.

"How's the new probie working out for you?" Brynne asked. "Is he driving you nuts?"

Dean was relieved for the moment with the change in subject matter. "Barry is a pretty good paramedic. He had a lot of experience before he came to Station U, so his learning curve is not as steep as mine was, fresh out of the academy. Plus he already had a lot of the lore and legends under his belt from his penchant for reading fantasy and sci-fi novels. Chief Ari says that they are going to focus on getting more experienced team members like him to fill vacancies in the future. He thinks they will adapt better once they are screened for their open-mindedness."

The discussion changed to talks about the Unusual community and their use of the medical resources from the Station U paramedics and the ECMC emergency department. Dean listened and participated a little, but his heart was not in it. He was still thinking about Ashley as he did almost all the time. He wondered who had her, how she was being treated and whether she would survive the captivity. He knew she could not be killed in the human sense. Eldara were eternals. Their corporeal form on earth could be destroyed for a time, but there was very little out there that could destroy the core of her being. All that would happen to the Eldara if they killed her human form was that she would return to her higher plane for a time while her corporeal form regenerated. Dean didn't want that to happen to Ashley. The process could take up to a hundred years. He couldn't wait one hundred years for her to come back to earth. He would be long gone by the time she returned.

Dean checked his watch. It was time to head over to headquarters and go to this defensive scene awareness class. He told Brynne he would come back and see her again soon, and said goodbye to James and Celeste. The assistant walked him back to the elevators.

"Dean, if you do seek out one of the Hunter Clans for your team, be careful," Celeste said. "They have their own agenda, and they are indoctrinated from birth to follow their leadership's orders. If you, or anyone else you care about gets in the way of what they think is their duty, they will not hesitate to sacrifice you to achieve their goals."

Dean nodded and told her that he would be careful as the doors to the elevator closed in front of him. He would be careful but only as far as he had to be in order to rescue Ashley. That was all that mattered to him. All that mattered in the world.

Chapter 6

Dean parked his truck in the municipal parking garage next to the headquarters complex and headed into the training academy building. He nodded to a few of the other paramedics from the C-shift crews around the city as he entered the designated training classroom. There was some idle chatter around him regarding what this particular class would be about. There was a tap on his shoulder and he looked behind him to see Ray Burkhardt from station 7 across town.

"Hey Dean," Ray said. "Have you heard anything more about this Jaswinder guy? He's supposed to be some big security expert and bodyguard to the stars. I heard Errington Security is made up of former Special Forces and other military types who served overseas, but I couldn't find anything about this particular person on their website. I wonder if it's he's related to the Errington that owns the business?

"I don't know anything about them other than what was on the flyer attached to the email I got," Dean replied. "Still, if he has some Special Forces training, it might be an interesting class to take. Not the usual boring same-old, same-old medical topics again and again. Am I right?"

"You got that right." Ray said. "Hey, have you heard from your old partner Brynne? I heard she took a sudden leave of absence. You guys at Station U have some serious turnover, don't you? I suppose it's because it's so boring out there in the sticks."

"I hear from her from time to time. She's alright," Dean responded. "And, yeah, it's nothing like you'd expect a paramedic assignment to be, believe me."

Ray snorted a chuckle and started to respond when a clear soprano voice caused them both to turn their attention to the front of the classroom. A woman in her early to mid-twenties stood at the front of the room with two very large men, one white and one black. She was dressed the same as the two men - all in black, from black cargo pants with baggy pockets and a black belt, to a black t-shirt with some sort of family crest on the left breast pocket. She was also wearing a black baseball cap bearing an embroidered "E," and her blonde hair was pulled back into a ponytail through the hole in the back of the cap. Her piercing blue eyes took in the assembled paramedic crews with a glance as she greeted the assembled students.

"Hello," she began. "I'm Jaswinder Errington, Vice President of Personal Protection at Errington Security, Limited. My companions and I were asked by your Chief to come here and relate to you some concepts and techniques in personal safety and awareness. In the class today, we will…."

She trailed off as the door opened and Dean's new probationary partner Barry walked into the room. He had a cup of coffee and a big grin on his face.

"I didn't miss too much, I hope?" he asked.

"You're late, sir," Jaswinder said. "Do you arrive late for all your important meetings, or just your patients and others you intend to show disrespect to?"

"I was just running late today, that's all," Barry replied, some confusion showing on his face. "The line at the Starbucks was pretty long and I got tied up." He raised his cup of coffee to show verification.

"My colleagues and I were asked here to teach you all as a favor to your Chief, an old family friend, sir," she said. "Who should I tell him thought coffee was more important than what we intend to learn here?"

Barry looked around the room for some support and Dean took pity on him. "That's my probie, Ma'am. If anyone is going to humiliate him, it will be me. I'll take care of his tardiness issue."

The woman spun around and fixed Dean with a glare. Apparently she didn't like to be interrupted. He also got the impression that she enjoyed busting balls in her everyday work.

"And you are?"

"I'm paramedic Dean Flynn, Ma'am," he replied. "That's my probationary paramedic and I'll be the one that handles him and any discipline that needs to be handed out. It's my responsibility."

"Flynn, huh?" she said, fishing in one of her large cargo pockets and pulling out a small tablet computer. She tapped it and scrolled through something there, then looked back up at him. "You and your partner are at the City's U Station?"

Dean nodded in response.

"I would think that the two of you would be much more attuned to what we are trying to teach you here. Attacks and violence against EMTs and paramedics is on the rise, and if I understand my briefing for this class, your station has seen more than your share of these types of negative events. Is that true?"

Dean felt uncomfortable as all the eyes in the room focused on him. This woman, who didn't look old enough to have the experience necessary to teach a class like this in the first place, was a very unpleasant person. He didn't want to end up on her bad side, but it appeared it was too late for that. He didn't know how to get out from under her stare or answer her in a way that would get her off his back, so he lashed out.

"I don't think you, a bodyguard to pampered rock stars, would know much about what I, or my partner, do on the streets," he said. Dean regretted the outburst as soon as he said it, but he was tired, emotionally drained, and distracted with worry about Ashley. He didn't have time for some girl to tell him what he needed to know to survive on the streets.

"I see," was all she said in response. She turned her attention to Barry again. "Take a seat. It's time we got started with a little introduction on the work my team and I do." She gestured to one of her assistants and he walked over to dim the lights. The other one lowered the large projector screen on the main wall of the classroom. She picked up a remote and keyed on the projector. As it warmed up, Dean looked at the image on the screen. It was Jaswinder, standing next to a Humvee in what looked like a village in the Middle East. She was dressed in desert camo, had a black and white checkered scarf around her neck, and sported a military assault rifle. There was a pistol strapped on one hip and a knife on the other. She also had what looked like a sword hilt, of all things, jutting up over one shoulder. It looked like her two classroom companions were in the photo with her, dressed and armed in a similar fashion, minus the sword.

"My team and I just got back from guarding a team of journalists traveling behind the lines in Syria. We filmed civilians who'd been bombed by one side or another in that civil war, watched as emergency crews responded through the carnage and destruction, and fended off three separate attempts to kidnap or kill our clients." Jaswinder paused and looked around the darkened room at her assembled students. "I have been trained as a combat and tactical responder, and unfortunately, have had to use those skills in the field on more than one occasion. The point I make is, we were chosen for this assignment in particular because it was thought our experiences gave us some understanding of what you all have faced here in the civilian emergency medical services sector. I know it's not the same as everything you've all seen, but I believe it gives me the right to be able to share my experiences with you about situational awareness, and to help you be prepared to defend yourselves if you get in a tough spot on the streets." She fixed Dean with a blue-eyed stare. "It also gives me the right to command a certain amount of respect."

Dean felt very petty all of the sudden. He had let his temper get the better of him, and instead of showing some respect for an invited guest speaker at the academy. He knew it was not his best moment.

"Mr. Flynn," Jaswinder said. "Will my qualifications, and the qualifications of my team be suitable to continue teaching this class?"

"Yes, Ma'am," Dean said.

"Excellent," she said. "Then in that case, let us all move forward. We have a lot to cover in the …" she glanced at her watch, "… two and a half hours remaining, so let's get to it." She clicked to the next slide and proceeded on with her lecture. She covered surveys on violence on healthcare professionals, EMS, and fire professionals, talked about specific cases and situations from the news, and then broke the class up into three groups to discuss and talk about individual's own experiences.

After a brief break, they proceeded to talk about scene safety and situational awareness. She spent a good amount of time on this topic, urging them to not operate as if they had blinders on that kept them from noticing what was going on around them. The final hour of class was spent on specific personal self-defense techniques, including how to use their gear - like their medication or trauma bags, or even their heart monitors to fend off an attacker and keep them at bay. She wrapped up the morning by handing out business cards with her contact information and a request to please send her any information or ideas that she could use to improve the class.

By the time Jaswinder and her team were finished, Dean was feeling like a complete idiot for his outburst at the beginning of the training session. He lingered after class as the room emptied out and waited until the Errington team had packed up their computer and other gear. She looked over at him standing by the door and motioned for her team to carry the stuff from the room, then came over to him.

"Did you have something you wanted to say, Mr. Flynn?" she asked as she walked over to him.

Dean felt his insides squirm, but he clamped down on his discomfort and nodded. "Ms. Errington, I would like to say that I made some hasty conclusions and voiced them aloud at the beginning of this class. I was wrong and should have kept my mouth shut. Your class was both relevant and informative, and I think we all learned a lot." He ended with smile and extended his hand. "I hope that you will accept my apology."

"I appreciate that, Mr. Flynn," she said taking his hand. She did not return his smile. The two of them walked out into the hallway and back towards the academy's large entry hall. Grim-faced, she said, "I meant what I said in class. You and your partners at Station U would be the ones who I would expect to want this class the most. Your, shall we say, unique patients, require you to be prepared for extra dangers and risks all the time."

Dean was surprised that she was aware of the nature of his patients, but if he had learned nothing else over the course of the past three hours, it was to not underestimate this woman. "My patients do present some challenges, but for the most part, I believe they are no more dangerous than most of the human patients out there."

She stopped him where they were walking in the hallway with a hand on his arm. "You really believe that?"

He nodded, "Of course I do. I've seen nothing that leads me to think that my patients are any different when you come right down to it. If you know anything about recent events here in the city, you know that it has been humans who have been the most dangerous by far."

"I fear you are a fool, then," Jaswinder said. "There are many more dangers out there lurking in your patients' community than you know. You would do well to watch your back. For all you know, something could be hunting you right now."

Dean laughed aloud. "I doubt that. I'm not that important. No one has any reason to hunt for me." He said it and kept up a brave front, but inside he was wondering if what she said had some flavor of truth. He had already made an enemy of Artur, one of the oldest vampires in the world. Would that qualify as dangerous? He certainly thought so.

"I have to go relieve my previous shift," Dean said, checking his watch. "I'll remember what you taught us about maintaining aware-ness on our scenes. Thank you again for the excellent class." Dean left her standing there in the hallway, where she turned to talk to her team members who were waiting nearby. He did have to head off to the station. Brook and Tammy would be waiting for him and Barry to get there. He pulled his key fob from his pocket as he headed outside and across the street to the garage where his pickup truck was parked. It was time to go to work.

JAZ WATCHED as the naive paramedic walked away from her. She had been expecting some sort of pushback when she was tasked to lead this class for the city. She dealt with it head-on, just like she always handled the doubters and haters out there. She knew she was young, and a woman, and she knew what that meant to some of the people she encountered in her line of work. She was used to being underestimated by men meeting her for the first time. She was also used to putting such men in their place when they got out of line, and to be honest with herself, she looked forward to it.

She told Chad and Grant to head down with the gear to their black SUV where it was parked in the underground garage. She needed to head upstairs and meet with the Chief and her father to give her evaluation on the paramedic crews' preparedness level based on her assessment during the class. The two Station U paramedics in particular weren't ready for what was out there right now. Not ready at all.

Barry had gotten there a few minutes earlier. As usual, Dean and his probie partner went through the shift checks on the gear and the ambulance.

"Hey, Dean, thanks for drawing fire from me in that class earlier," Barry said.

"No problem. She didn't need to do that to you in front of the whole class," Dean replied. "On the other hand, I don't think you'll be late to class again. Am I right?"

"You got that right," Barry laughed. "Still, she didn't have to be such a colossal bitch about it."

"No, probably not," Dean agreed. "Still, you have to admit that she knew her stuff, and she had the qualifications to teach that class, after all. I can't imagine how tough she must be with all she's had to have seen. She's got to be my age, after all."

"The same could be said about us, Dean," Barry reminded him. "There are things we've seen that we just can't un-see."

"True," Dean said as he zipped up the bag he was checking and placed it back in its compartment in the ambulance. "True indeed."

They were interrupted by the alert tones from the overhead speakers in the ambulance bay, followed by the sound of the dispatcher's voice over the radio: "Ambulance U-191, respond for an injured subject, at 4782 Seventh Avenue."

"Time to load up and do our jobs," Barry said. Dean nodded and headed around to the driver's side so that Barry could take the lead. He was doing a great job, and Dean knew that while his probie was an experienced paramedic in the normal sense, he was still learning how to manage their particular patients. But, he was a fast learner and he was getting to the point where he knew as much about Unusuals as Dean did. He was doing his research and making sure that he learned something from every call. Barry was a good example of the quintessential EMS professional.

Dean navigated across town to the area of the 911 call while Barry operated the lights and sirens to help clear the traffic in front of the speeding ambulance. The follow-up information was not very helpful. The dispatcher had very little detailed information on the call, only saying that another responder was reportedly on the scene ahead of them. Dean hoped whoever it was who was on the scene would be able to fill them in on what was going on.

The ambulance turned onto Seventh Avenue, where some rather large homes were situated on broad lawns set back from the road. This was an old and affluent section of town and Dean had never been on a call here before. Most Unusuals either lived in poorer neighborhoods or tended to blend into the urban counter-culture of the downtown scene. Dean started checking the GPS instructions because the house numbers were not well marked and homes were too far back from the street to easily read the numbers on the front. Then he saw something he knew marked the house in question. There, parked under the overhanging porch roof on the side of one house, was a beat-up white van Dean knew very well. The responder reporting from the scene was Gibbie.

Dean pulled the ambulance up into the driveway behind Gibbie's van. Together he and Barry gathered their gear and went up to the front door, which was ajar. The two paramedics heard voices coming from inside the house, shouting or arguing, Dean couldn't tell which.

"Hello. Paramedics here," Barry called as they entered the

home. As Barry pushed open the door with Dean behind him, something large whizzed by in the air at head-height and crashed onto the wall just inside the entry foyer. No, not just onto the wall. Whatever it was went through the wall, leaving a soccer-ball sized hole in the dry wall on both sides of the foyer. Dean saw that there was even a chunk taken out of the wooden two by four stud inside the wall.

He and Barry started to back out towards the door when the door was slammed shut behind them. Something large impacted the interior side of the front door pushing it closed. Dean looked behind him at the now closed door and saw a large frozen bird carcass, maybe a large chicken or a turkey, lying on the floor. It still had its label and packaging on, and Dean could even see the supermarket bar code. As he looked at it, the frozen bird started quivering and then, without warning, launched into the air, flying past his head in a whoosh, bouncing off the walls down the entry hall before turning the corner, and flying into a room on the left. There were screams of alarm and more crashing sounds.

"Dean, is that you?" A familiar high-pitched voice sounded from down the hallway.

"Yeah, Gibbie. It's me and Barry. What's going on?" Dean replied. Gibbie was a middle-aged, somewhat flamboyant vampire who had been trained as a civilian first responder. He and Dean had run black market EMS calls together when Dean had been suspended from the fire department a few months back. Life was never dull when Gibbie was around.

"Dean, Barry, watch out. There's a frozen turkey flying around," Gibbie called.

"We already figured that out. Thanks for the heads'-up before we got here, by the way," Dean quipped. "Where's the patient? Is he or she with you?"

"Yeah, he is in here with me and Kristof," the vampire responded. "If you keep low, you can usually avoid getting hit by the bird."

"Kristof is in there, too?" Dean wondered just what was going on. Kristof was the owner of a very successful restaurant downtown called Sabatani's. He was also a Djinn, more commonly known as a genie. "Is Kristof alright?"

"I'm fine, Dean," Kristof called over the crashing and Gibbie's swearing coming from the other room. "Sorry about this whole mess. I didn't think it would be a problem."

Dean didn't know what he was talking about, but that was not the problem at hand. There was a patient here, and there was a definite scene safety issue, too. Dean looked back at Barry.

"Let's stay on the floor and commando crawl down the hallway until we can see around the corner into the room they are in."

"Sounds like a plan," Barry said. "I'm certainly not standing up while there's a frozen turkey flying around." The statement was punctuated by the whizzing again at standing head height. The bird crashed into the wall and through into the next room where both paramedics could hear it crashing around, breaking everything in its path.

Dean snorted out a chuckle as he heard the words come from his partner's mouth. The things he had seen and heard while on the job at Station U were the types of things that he never would have expected, even from an exciting job as a paramedic. He turned and pushed the heart monitor in front of him on the ornate tile floor, while he started to crawl down the hallway. Barry came up behind him, pushing the medication and trauma bags in front of him.

When Dean got to the open doorway, he saw a high-end residential kitchen with a built-in double refrigerator against one wall. One of the freezer doors was open. There were custom wood-paneled appliances of other sorts around and two granite-topped islands in the center of the room. Crouched next to one of the islands were the two Citizen Emergency Response Team members, Gibbie and Kristof, and they were bent over another man Dean did not know, who lay supine on the floor. Gibbie held a wad of gauze to the man's head. That must be their patient and he seemed to be unconscious.

"Thank God you're here, Dean," Gibbie cried in his high-pitched voice. In other circumstances Dean might find the situation and his friend's flamboyant nature humorous. Now was not the time to laugh, though. There was a patient to attend to.

"What happened, Gibbie?" Dean asked as he crawled over to the patient.

"It is my fault, Dean, not Gibbie's," Kristof said. "I was paid to offer this man a wish. As one of the Djinn, I cannot refuse a wish once payment is made. I always warn my client of the risks of accessing my wild magic. It's unpredictable at the best of times and I warn them, but that almost never changes their minds."

"So what happened to this guy?" Barry asked. He had crawled up next to Dean and was starting a hands-on assessment of the patient. "Hey, he looks familiar. I've seen him on the TV before, haven't I?"

"Yes, Mr. Jones here is Cam Jones from Cam Jones Automotive Mile over on Route 40. He does those ads where he tells everyone how crazy he is to make deals, and smokes those big cigars." Gibbie said.

Kristof ignored the distraction of the man's celebrity and answered Barry's first question. "His new wife hates his cigar smoking, but he was having trouble giving them up. He said he tried everything from e-cigs to hypnosis, but was unable to quit. He knows me and understands my true nature after selling me several cars over the years. He came to me to ask for help. When he called me over here to his house I thought he was calling to book my restaurant to cater an event. When I realized what he was doing, I tried to stop him, telling him that it was a bad idea. He had discovered the formal words to request the granting of a wish from me, however, and I had no choice.

The frozen bird carcass flew by overhead, careening around the kitchen and bouncing off the cabinet doors before zooming out of the room through an open doorway. Everyone ducked and stopped talking while it bashed from wall to wall above them.

Once it left the room again, Dean looked over at Gibbie. "How did you get mixed up with this?"

"I came along because Kristof's car was in the shop and he needed a ride," the frumpy vampire said. "I was just going to stay in the van since it was daytime, and I needed to stay behind the window tinting. But when we got here and I saw that the carport overhang by the front entrance blocked the sun, I just had to come inside. I love Cam's ads on the TV and I wanted to see if I could get a selfie with him for my social feed."

The frozen turkey flew by again and Dean looked up as it went by overhead. Then he looked at the unconscious patient and smelled the acrid odor of cigar smoke still in the air. He shook his head as it hit him what had happened.

"Don't tell me," Dean started. "He handed you your fee for the wish and then actually said it didn't he? He went and wished he could quit 'cold-turkey'?"

Kristof nodded and looked a little ashamed. "I told him, just like I told you the first time you asked me about it. I can't control how my magic acts. I'm just a conduit for the wild magic. It interprets the words and acts upon them. Sometimes it gets it right, but most of the time, not."

Dean looked at his partner. Barry had completed his assessment. "How's Mr. Jones, Barry?"

"He's unconscious and unresponsive. He has one pupil in his eyes that is slower to react than the other to light, and the whole right side of his head is swollen," Barry said. "He's definitely got a closed head injury and needs to get to the trauma center. He probably has a brain bleed. That means his brain is starting to swell inside his skull. If we don't get him out of here, his brain is going to turn to mush."

"Agreed," Dean said. "My guess is that the turkey is going to follow him unless we can find a way to deactivate the magic." He blinked and rubbed at his eyes. That cigar smoke was really irritating him. He was allergic to smoke. "Kristof, there has got to be a way for you to turn this off. Think. There has got to be something we can do."

"I told you, Dean," Kristof said, chastised. "I have no control over the magic. Once it is activated, it has to play out on its own."

Dean sniffed, and wiped his nose. His allergy was really kicking in right now, probably because they were in an enclosed space of the kitchen with the smoke. Dean stopped and looked around, ducking as soon as the bird flew by once again. He sniffed the air, trying to zero in on the source of the smell. He saw it, as soon as he started looking for it. There was a smoldering cigar against the far wall by the kitchen sink. It had rolled under the lip of the cabinets there. He darted over to it, dodging the frozen bird once again, and grabbed the still-lit cigar. He reached up from his crouched position, flipped up the faucet lever to turn on the water, and held the cigar under the faucet.

Gibbie shrieked, "Look out, Dean."

Dean turned and saw the frozen bird turn and zip right towards his head, but just before it got to him, it fell to the floor and skidded into the cabinet by his knees and lay still. Dean let out a sigh of relief, realizing he had been holding his breath.

"Huh," Gibbie said, letting out a long breath. "That was really easy." He looked at his partner. "Why didn't we think of that, Kristof?"

Dean and Barry shared a glance and then the two of them went to work on their patient. Gibbie had done a good job of stopping the external bleeding, so that was already taken care of. They hooked up the heart monitor and blood pressure cuff to start getting vital signs and then Dean looked at the Djinn.

"Come with me, Kristof, and help me get the stretcher."

The genie nodded and followed Dean outside and to the ambulance. On the way, the Unusual CERT team member tried to apologize the whole way to the ambulance.

"I hate using my wish magic, Dean," Kristof said. "I avoid it at all costs, but sometimes there is nothing I can do."

"Nobody is blaming you, Kristof," Dean said as he pulled the stretcher from the back of the ambulance. "I know you can't control it. You told the guy the truth. It's on him. Besides, maybe this will really get him to quit smoking, right?"

The two of them brought the stretcher back into the mansion and then the four of them lifted the portly used car magnate up onto it. He had to weigh over three hundred pounds. As the paramedics took over rolling the stretcher outside with all their gear,

Dean looked at the two **CERT** responders. They looked a little shell-shocked by the whole incident.

"Come by the hospital while we drop Mr. Jones off," Dean suggested. "I'll get you some supplies to refill the gauze and stuff you used up back there to treat him before we arrived, okay?"

They nodded from the shadows of the Mansion's front door, Gibbie was careful to stay back away from the sunlight. Dean waved after he shut the ambulance's rear doors and then he climbed in, flipped on the lights and siren, and drove their patient to the trauma center.

Chapter 8

When Dean and Barry came out of the ER's ambulance entrance to get back to their unit, Gibbie's van was pulled up next to it. Dean had a bag of supplies he had retrieved from the restock room at the hospital. Walking over the to the passenger side sliding door of the van, he slid it open and handed the bag to Kristof.

Barry walked up next to him and laughed aloud. Dean looked at him with a raised eyebrow.

"Oh, I was just thinking of what Ms. Jaswinder Errington would say about staying safe and sound with a flying frozen turkey as your enemy," Barry said, continuing to chuckle.

Dean laughed and turned to explain the joke to Kristof and Gibbie. He stopped when he saw their faces. They had both assumed a shocked and maybe even frightened expression.

"What?" Dean asked. "You act as if we just invoked the devil himself."

Gibbie was the first to speak. "Did you say that Jaz Errington is in town? Is her father, old man Earnest Errington here, too?"

"I don't know her by that name, or if her father is here, but I guess that's the same person," Dean said. "She was in headquarters earlier today teaching us a class on scene safety and self-defense. She was a bit of a hard-ass, but seemed to know what she was talking about. Why do you ask, Gibbie?"

"Because the Erringtons are one of the great Hunter Clans," Gibbie replied. "They are known primarily as demon hunters, but they are just as happy to kill off any Unusuals they encounter who are not playing nice with humans."

"Yeah, Dean," Kristof said. "In the home back there, someone like Jaz Errington would have found another, more permanent solution to the problem of uncontrolled Djinn magic. She would have killed me to cut off the magical flow."

"You're kidding," Dean said. "It wasn't your fault. You warned the guy against invoking it and he did it anyway."

"I'm afraid the Erringtons do not see things that way," Kristof replied. "They are not as bad some of the other Hunter Clans out there. I mean, they don't kill indiscriminately, but they have their own code and they live by it in everything they do. If one of the Erringtons think you are an Unusual who is a risk to humans, they'll take action."

Barry asked, "But what are they doing here? She told us all in the class that they had just got back from a bodyguard mission in Syria."

Kristof nodded, "It would make sense that the Erringtons would want to be involved there. The various terrorists are destroying ancient ruins there because they represent Gods that are not their own. A lot of those ancient holy places were built in their locations because of a nexus with the netherworld. If they break the seals on the gateways during the destruction of the temples, they could cause an opening that demons would use to infiltrate the world. It could cause havoc if left unchecked."

"That's true," Gibbie said aloud. "We Unusuals are all scared of the Erringtons, but demons are terrified of them. They have become very proficient demon hunters over the centuries. Rumor has it that Jaz Errington is the best to come along in the last one hundred years. I'd bet that if she is here, she is following a demon of some sort.

Dean took in all they were saying, listening and filing all of it away for future reference. The thing that had him thinking the most was that nagging feeling of deja vu he had since he had first seen Jaswinder Errington in class that morning. It was the feeling he had seen her somewhere before. Until now, it hadn't occurred to him that the two recent events could be related, but in light of what Gibbie and Kristof were saying, he could not ignore it. There had been a series of demon attacks in town recently. He and Barry had responded to one a few days earlier. Dean could still see the image of the woman with the sword standing behind the ambulance as he drove away. Now he was sure he knew who it was. Jaz Errington had been there that night.

Barry clapped him on the shoulder to get his attention and it brought him back to the present discussion. He looked around and saw the three others just staring at him.

"You alright, Dean?" Barry asked.

"Yeah, you look like you've seen a ghost," Gibbie said.

"I don't think it was a ghost, but I might have seen our Ms. Errington before," Dean replied. "Barry, remember the animal or demon attack our last night shift rotation?"

Barry nodded. "Yeah. That Hakutaku couple claimed that they were attacked by some sort of Japanese demon called an … Oni, wasn't it?"

"Well, I didn't tell anyone, but as we were driving away, I thought I saw a woman, dressed all in black, holding a sword," Dean said. "I saw her when I looked in the rearview mirror as I pulled away from in front of the house. I looked away for a second, and when I looked back, she was gone. I chalked it up to seeing things after a few long night shifts. Now I have to wonder if she is the reason the Oni demon didn't come back and kill the couple. It would make sense if she was there and killed it before it could return."

"If she was there, Dean, then she has been in town for a little while," Kristof said. "There have been rumors of netherworlders, or what you would call demons, floating around the Unusual community for almost a month. Folks have claimed sightings all over the region. That might be what drew the Erringtons here. If they heard rumors of demons roaming around Elk City, they'd come running to find the source and stop it."

"Whatever the reason she and her family are here in Elk City, it spells trouble for those of us who they might like to hunt," Gibbie said. "I'm going to spread the word of their arrival, and then I'm going to ground for a while. I am not getting staked or beheaded by one of those maniacs." The middle-aged vampire started up the van to punctuate his statement. "Kristof, I'll drop you off at your place downtown, then I'm disappearing for a while."

"It's not fair that you feel like you have to run and hide, Gibbie," Dean said. "Let me talk to James. There has to be some way to reach out to them and see what is going on locally that has brought them to town."

"You can try, Dean," Kristof said. "The Erringtons don't always play well with the Unusual leadership in a town. I doubt that James is going to be able to do anything. Remember, they'd just as soon stake him as talk to him. The only type of beings they will not kill, according to their code, are humans and the Eldara. At least that is what the legends about them say."

"Well, if that is the case I guess I'll have to deal with them myself," Dean said. He was getting angry about these groups of interlopers coming into his town and threatening his friends. First it was The Cause, now it was these hunters. "I will have to set up a little meeting with her. I need to have a few words with Ms. Jaz Errington about what she is doing here."

"Yeah," Barry said with a snort of laughter. "Because you made such a good impression on her at the training class this morning. She is definitely primed to listen to you now."

"I don't care, Barry," Dean replied. "Let's load up and get back to the station. I need to figure out how to contact her and set up a meeting. We need to find out what she is doing here before we she goes and kills one of our patients in her zeal to follow her family's calling."

Dean and Barry climbed into the ambulance's cab and waved to Gibbie and Kristof as they pulled the ambulance away from the van at the hospital. Dean was thinking about the connection between the hunter woman and his own situation. James and Brynne had both suggested that there might be a hunter clan connection to him in his quest to free Ashley from her abductors. Was Jaz Errington's presence here in Elk City a coincidence? He doubted it. If Ashley had taught him nothing else, she had impressed upon him how the Gods liked to use little connections and coincidences to influence events on earth indirectly. They were forbidden to act directly by some agreement with the forces of darkness long ago, instead relying on the free will decisions of the people and Unusuals populating the earth. They could put situations in front of people to influence a decision, or even force a decision to be made, even if they weren't sure of the outcome of the decision to be made. Dean wondered if that was what was happening here.

He didn't like feeling manipulated, especially if it was going to force him to work with this Hunter. She stood for everything he was against. She was a killer. He was a healer. She believed in one group of the city's occupants being inherently better than the other, while he believed in equal opportunity and treatment for everyone, human and Unusual alike. Dean didn't know how he was supposed to find the common ground to work with her. He was going to meet her and find a way, though. Ashley was depending on him and he owed it to her to try.

Jaz wanted to stomp her foot but she forced herself to stand still and tried her best to appear calm. Her father had told her after their meeting with the Fire Chief that she was to come back and meet him here at their corporate offices downtown. Now she was here in front of him, feeling like a little girl all over again, caught sneaking out to the gun range after lights-out.

"… I said, 'are you paying attention to me', young lady?" Earnest Errington asked his daughter.

Her eyes darted up to meet his too late and she knew he had gotten his answer. His lips pressed together, forming a thin line under his salt-and-pepper mustache.

"Father, I have met the man in question. I tell you honestly, I don't believe he will be much help to us in solving our particular dilemma," Jaz said, keeping her voice level and professional. The fact that did not feel professional was hidden under the surface of her demeanor, barely. Ugh! Why did her father always make her feel this way?

"Jaswinder, I do not recall asking your opinion of the man," her father stated. "In fact, I don't believe I asked for your opinion about any of this. This is your assignment and I'll ask you to fulfill it as you would any other task I assign to you. Is that understood?"

"But Daddy, he is so infuriating, and I've only met him one time," she pleaded with her father. "Imagine what a colossal douchebag he'll be after spending a few days or weeks with him." She snapped her mouth shut, knowing she had gone too far.

"Don't 'but Daddy' me," her father said. "I heard about the way you dressed him down for his unprofessional demeanor during the class. You told both me and the Fire Chief in our meeting after the class. You also heard the way he responded. Dean Flynn is what he called 'one of the most valuable members of our Station U paramedic team.' He went on to call him a natural and intuitive medical professional who knows his job and responsibilities. Perhaps your single meeting was more a matter of your impression on him, and not the other way around?"

"I don't see how that could be the case," Jaz said in defense of herself. "I was putting a late arrival in his place for tardiness when Mr. Flynn stepped in and interrupted me, defending him."

"Who was the man in question in relation to Mr. Flynn?"

"It was his probationary medic, apparently," Jaz replied. "He took issue with me berating his guy."

"So he came to the defense of his direct subordinate?" Earnest asked. "And this makes him a 'douchebag' because?"

She hated when he turned things around with logic. She knew where he was headed with this, and it was making her even more angry. "Look, Father. I know you are going to tell me that I would have done the same thing if someone had laid into one of my subordinates. In fact, you've seen me do it. That makes no difference here. I'm sorry, he just rubs me the wrong way."

"Well get over it," Earnest said, standing up from behind the desk to walk around it in the well-appointed office. "This is not just me saying it. This is not just another assignment. This is for the honor of the whole clan. The clan oracle herself decreed that it must be you to fulfill this responsibility."

"I still don't understand why this is our problem anyway," Jaz complained. "Some angel gets herself abducted and we are honor bound to help because …?"

Jaz's father sighed. "Jaz, you know the legends. A long time ago, this particular Eldara assisted the Clan by keeping us from being duped by one of our adversaries into doing their bidding. Your great-great-great-grandfather made an arrangement with her that we would watch over her when she required our assistance. This happened just before our clan followed that adversary to the United States in the late 1850s. It is a centuries-old obligation and we will not be the generation to sully the honor of the clan because you don't like one of those who must be enlisted to help. Not under my watch."

"Father, the Oracle said that a hunter, a healer, and a hexen must take up the quest for the missing Eldara," Jaz said. "What makes the Oracle so sure this one is the healer we must use?"

Her father's answer was a burst of laughter that continued until he nearly had tears in his eyes. She was not amused by her father's jocularity. Finally, he composed himself. "Daughter, you have always had a stubborn streak, but I never thought even you would question the veracity of something proclaimed by the clan's Oracle herself."

Jaz started to say something but her father held up his hand to stop her.

"She has spoken and names the one called Flynn as the healer, just as she named you as the hunter," he continued as she listened.

The younger Errington hunter felt herself deflate a little. She knew better than to fight this, but she kept pushing anyway. It stemmed from her need to be the one in charge, and years of having to put men in their place. It was something she was unable to do with her father. Must it always come down to some sort of Daddy issue?

"Okay, so the hunter is me and the healer is this Flynn guy," Jaz asked. "Who is the hexen? How do we discover the identity of this witch we need to join up with? Has the Oracle been of any help with that?"

"The only variable left is the witch. The Oracle was unable to pierce the veil of the hexen's identity, only that she, the witch, was involved or connected to this matter in some way. It is as if she does not exist in this world. The Oracle suggested that you and Mr. Flynn would have to work together to figure out who this unknown witch is."

"So I have to work with him, I get it," Jaz said. "I dressed him down in front of his peers while he openly challenged my authority, and now we have to find a way to make nice and get along for the honor of the clan." Jaz sighed. Her temper and need to outdo everything the guys around her could do had gotten her into trouble before. This was one of those things she had learned to deal with. For some reason, though, this time it seemed to bother her more than the others.

"See, I knew you would figure it out," her father said, a broad grin on his face. His phone chirped on the desk and he picked it up to see the message. His grin widened. "It seems that you will have the opportunity to set forth on your task sooner than you think. Mr. Flynn used our company website to request your contact information. He wants to meet up with you."

"Oh, joy," Jaz said, rolling her eyes.

"I will forward you the contact request and you can respond directly to his request. May I suggest you take a different tone with him this time?"

Jaz turned and left the office to the sound of her father's laughter ringing in her ears.

▭

FOUR HOURS LATER, she rolled into the parking lot at the nondescript diner. The neon sign on the top of the classic diner-car restaurant was supposed to read "Hank's Place" but instead read "ank' lace." Jaz was early. She always liked to arrive at meetings early. It gave her a chance to get the lay of the land and establish an advantage over her opponents.

Jaz did a visual sweep of the parking lot and then sat back in the driver's seat as she parked the black Ford Expedition SUV. Old habits died hard and she never let her guard down, at least not all the way. The fact that she had just been in Syria hunting a particularly nasty group of demons freed by terrorist radicals there, caused her to be a bit more on edge. That, and the fact that she didn't look forward to this meeting with the paramedic.

Her father drove her nuts, not just because he was the clan's leader and she had to obey him. It was also a matter of his being right every time he ordered her to do something she didn't want to. She knew that this paramedic, Dean Flynn, should not be able to get under her skin so easily. That she had allowed him to do so was a problem. She knew that. The fact she had allowed it to surface in an argument with her father was infuriating.

She settled back and did some deep breathing exercises to calm herself. It would do no good to go into this meeting with her dander up. Her temper was legendary in her family. She chalked it up to being the only girl, besides her mother, in a family of men. Her brothers had all teased her as the youngest of the brood. They told her she could never be the top hunter in the clan. They told her it was a man's job. She had eventually proved them all wrong, but not without cost. She was the best hunter in the Errington clan, a fact she had proven with both individual kills and the successful team raids she had led. But the victory was bittersweet. To be honest, Jaz had never wanted it, never wanted to be a hunter in the field, but fate had a way of twisting everyone's desires to its own pattern. Each of her four brothers had died on missions before she had reached the pinnacle of her abilities. Now, as badly as she wanted to show them what she could do, what she had done, that could never be. It was too late.

Her last remaining brother, Anton, had died in a raid on a demon lair in Siberia six years ago. He had been the eldest, the heir apparent; the golden boy. Now he was gone, gutted by a hidden Scara demon before he even knew what hit him. She had become the Errington clan's heir at that moment, and with it came the powers that went with the title. That was the moment she entered into her own realization of her abilities. She had always been looking forward to going to college and having a somewhat normal life, at least as normal as could be for the member of a hunter clan. Once she became the heir; that had all changed.

Her father changed the direction of her education as soon as word came back of her brother's death. Jaz didn't even have time to grieve. Everything she did became more urgent and everyone told her she needed to work harder. She had always trained with weapons and learned the lore, but it all became more intensive and more real then. She started going on trips with other hunters, shadowing them and learning from them. She went to college, but it was through an online program that focused on criminal justice and military history, not the art history major to which she had previously aspired.

None of that changed the here and now, she knew. Jaz had worked hard to embrace her new role and live up to what she saw as the expectations of her father, mother, and her lost brothers. Now she was here, in this small, boring city in Maryland, fulfilling a quest started by some ancestor in exchange for a debt with which she was not involved. To top it off, she was forced to do it without her usual team, the team of hunters with whom she had defeated some of the worst demons to break through the wards and walk the earth. No, Jaz was forced to do it essentially alone, with an obstinate paramedic who was dedicated to saving the monsters living among the human population. Then, the two unlikely allies were supposed to team up with a witch of all people. The combination was an affront to everything she stood for as a member of those sworn to protect the human race from the things that no one even believed in anymore.

Jaz stopped her rumination on the situation as a beat up white pickup truck passed in front of her SUV and pulled into a parking spot down the line. She checked her watch. It was six-fifteen. It was about the time she expected the paramedic to show up, based on travel time from his station. She was correct, as she saw Dean Flynn climb out of his vehicle and walk up to the diner's doors. She watched through the diner's front windows as he greeted one of the waitresses and pointed to a booth at the back. The waitress nodded and Dean walked back to the booth and sat down.

She did another sweep of the lot then looked at her passenger seat. Attached to the back of the seat, facing the front, was a pocket organizer that held her selection of weapons and other assorted odds and ends. She considered her choices. She never went anywhere unarmed, and as a private security agent and bodyguard, she had a license to carry a firearm. She was also considered a licensed deputy with the U.S. Marshal's office. That was a special arrangement the Marshals had with the Erringtons dating back to the 1860s.

Jaz looked over the weapons before her. Her katana was too unwieldy and long to be hidden, so that must be left behind. She settled first for a brace of throwing knives, which she attached to a Velcro panel inside the left side of her leather jacket. Once those were in place, she took the Glock from the holster mounted on the cargo carrier and leaned forward to slide it into the hidden holster clipped to her belt at the small of her back.

Finally, she took the small Bowie, in its sheath, and clipped it to the slot in her shoulder holster. It held the blade under her right armpit, with the hilt hanging downward towards her belt. She snapped the keeper flap from the knife sheath to her belt to keep the hunting knife in place and settled her black leather jacket back over it. Feeling less naked now that she was suitably armed, Jaz exited her SUV, clicking the key fob to lock the doors. The heavily tinted windows hid the contents of the front seat weapons caddy from passersby. Making another scan of the area, Jaz looked to see that her target was still in his location inside the restaurant, and then headed for the front door. Time to get this mess started. The sooner she found this missing Eldara, the sooner she could return to the work she really wanted to do.

Chapter 10

Dean looked up from his phone's email app to see Jaswinder Errington crossing the diner to his booth. He pushed down his discomfort with this whole situation and decided to stick to his guns. He had to find out what she was doing here and what danger she represented to his patients and his friends.

She walked up to him and extended a hand. "Mr. Flynn," she said. "Thank you for getting in touch with me. I am glad we have the chance to follow up on our unfortunate encounter in class this morning."

"Please, call me Dean," he replied, rising to take her hand and shaking it. "May I call you Jaswinder? It really is a very interesting name." He sat back down as she slid into the booth across from him.

"I prefer Jaz, actually," the woman said. "Jaswinder is a family name that dates back to antiquity. Only my father and mother call me by it, usually only when they are annoyed with me."

Dean felt himself smile, despite the reason for the meeting. Even Hunters had families that functioned much like most families out there.

"Well, Jaz," Dean began. "I was surprised you responded to my email so quickly. I had expected it to take several days to hear back from you, if I heard back from you at all."

"Errington Security is a respected business with fully integrated technology resources," Jaz said. "Your contact request was forwarded to me as soon as it was received. It seems that we have a lot to talk about, starting with the words we exchanged this morning. I want to assure you that nothing personal was intended. I teach a lot of military teams and I have found that establishing alpha status as quickly as possible is a useful tool, especially for a female. I'm sure you understand."

Dean did understand, and it surprised him to find himself agreeing with this woman. He had expected to disagree with her about nearly everything. It caused him to rethink his approach to this conversation and he took a leap of faith that his instincts on how to deal with this situation were right.

"I can accept that. Until very recently my paramedic mentor was a woman," Dean said. "What I really wanted to ask you, if I may, was what you were doing behind my ambulance three nights ago out in the suburbs?" Dean watched her face as he asked the question to see if he could discern any clues, should she decide to deny she was there.

"I wondered if you saw me," she chuckled. "I got a little sloppy charging after that Oni demon. It was determined to have your heart for dinner. I decided that I couldn't allow that to happen." She met his eyes with an even stare. "You're welcome, by the way."

Dean stared back at her. He knew he had been right about seeing her, even though it had just been a glimpse. There was a glint in those blue eyes, challenging him in a way. It was disconcerting to think about what she had done if that demon was really there and had almost killed him. He met her eyes, the eyes that held his as if challenging him to deny that he owed her something. He declined to offer to fight, instead opting to defuse the situation.

"Thank you, I guess," Dean said. "We knew the Oni must still be around. I'm glad you were around to help stop it. I doubt I would have been able to avoid being attacked otherwise."

He saw what he thought was surprise in her expression when he didn't take the bait to argue with her. He was pleased with himself. Score one victory for him. He picked up the menu and slid hers over to her.

"I can recommend just about everything they serve here, Jaz," Dean said. "I haven't had a bad meal yet. They serve breakfast all day, too, if that is up your alley."

She nodded, took the offered menu and started to look it over. Dean didn't need to look at his. He knew what he was getting. He looked up and caught Daisy's eye. She was the waitress who seemed to always take care of him when he was in. She came right over.

"Hi, Dean," Daisy said. "What can I get you two to drink?"

He deferred to Jaz and she placed her order for ice water. Dean ordered a Sprite. They were both ready to order so they put in their orders for dinner. Jaz ordered steak and eggs, while Dean ordered a burger and fries. They both watched Daisy leave and then their attention turned back to the matter at hand.

"I guess we should get down to why I wanted to make sure we met up," Dean offered as a start to the conversation he suspected they both were waiting for. "It's because I know what you do and who you are, just as I know that you are aware of what I do for a living and the people I treat."

Jaz opened her mouth to speak but Dean held up a hand. "Please. Wait until I am finished with what I have to say."

She nodded and he continued. "I want you to know that I'm very protective of my patients and I won't put them in a position to be injured or killed by someone on some vendetta based on an old, outdated code of honor. I also want to know why you are here, and what can be done to expedite your mission so that those of us living here in Elk City can all live together in peace again."

He finished his prepared challenge and watched her for any sign of a response. The only thing he decided was that he never wanted to play poker against her. She sat there, stone faced and quiet for a full minute before she answered him.

"You know nothing of what it means to be a Hunter, or what my clan sees as our duty to mankind," Jaz began. "Errington's do not kill any being indiscriminately, unless it is a netherworlder here on earth, bent on destruction, as they all are."

"And who do you consider netherworlders, if I may ask?" Dean leaned forward, ready to argue against her reply.

"Demons, daemons, and all their ilk, of course," Jaz answered. "Creatures escaped to earth and spreading evil intent everywhere they go like the Oni demon I killed while it stalked you."

"So you don't see all Unusuals as creatures to be slain in your quest for a pure human world?" Dean asked.

"I will not lie to you, Dean," Jaz said leaning forward in a whisper. "There was a time when the Hunter clans were charged with killing any that weren't human living among us. But we have, uh, evolved I guess you would say. My family and I are more lenient towards Unusuals now. As long as they bear no ill will to the people they live among, we will ignore them. If they are found to be causing harm and local authorities do not or cannot take action on their own, then we may act in the cause of justice. There are also those, human and Unusual, who collaborate with netherworlders in their plans to do evil on this earth. Those who do so forfeit their lives just as they have already forfeited their souls."

She finished the last statement with what Dean would only call a bloodthirsty grin. She seemed to enjoy this stuff. Was she some sort of psychopath to look forward to killing that way? Dean wasn't sure. He had gotten his answer, though, and it was different than what he had learned from Gibbie and the others about hunters. How could he be sure she was telling the truth? Dean decided that he couldn't know in the near term without seeing what she was doing in Elk City.

"So you aren't here to enact some slaughter of my friends and patients? That is good to know," Dean said.

"I know some of what you all recently dealt with here in the city. That kind of carnage is harmful to all and is not what we are about," Jaz said. "In the end, you were fighting against the vampire lord, Artur Torrence. He is an ancient adversary of ours as well. Had I been in town when these events were occurring, I and any other Errington would have been firmly on your side. In fact we are still attempting to track that particular creature. We owe him a very old debt that we would like to collect. Perhaps someday we will end his cruel machinations on earth."

Dean thought on what she said. Could he have been more wrong in his estimation of her and her motives here? Was she even telling the truth?

"So if you are not here on some sort of a hunt, what is your reason for coming to town?" Dean asked. "I can't believe it was just to teach a class to the paramedics in the city about staying safe on the street."

"You are correct, at least in part," Jaz said. "We do consulting and training work like I did with your class this morning. It is not usually me who does it, but we do that at Errington Security."

She paused as Daisy came back with their drinks and set them down along with two sets of silverware, each wrapped up in a paper napkin. When the waitress walked away, Jaz continued.

"Dean, I am here because of an old debt, a debt we owe to someone as a clan. I understand you are a friend of the Eldara Sister Ashley Moore?"

"Yes, you could say that," Dean said. He didn't want to give away too much about his relationship with Ashley. Where was this going?

"We owe the Eldara a debt earned more than one hundred fifty years ago," Jaz continued. "I am here to seek her out where she is held captive and bring her abductors to justice."

Dean started to ask how she knew about Ashley's abduction but the hunter woman kept going.

"There is more, Dean. I am charged to enlist you in that search, along with one other." Jaz finished and sat back, as if to wait for Dean's reaction.

"You're one of the three, just like me," Dean said. He could see his answer caught her by surprise.

"What do you mean, the three?" Jaz asked.

"Ashley's sister, Ingrid, told me that I was charged to find two others to assist me in looking for Ashley. One was to be a person who was magical in nature; the other was to be one who shunned magical things. I'm guessing the latter is you."

"I, too, have a directive from my clan to gather two others to seek out the Eldara and free her," Jaz revealed. "Our oracle prophesied that we must have a hunter, a healer, and a hexen to make the rescue have a chance at success."

"I get the first two," Dean said. "But what's a hexen? Is it some sort of magical creature?"

"A hexen is our word for a witch," Jaz explained. "What you would call a witch, I believe. As for the other two, you have guessed correctly. You are the healer, and I am the hunter mentioned by our Oracle. There was no guidance on who to choose for the third role. I do not associate with witches so perhaps it was to fall to you to choose one you knew. What do you think?"

"I don't have any close witch friends," Dean replied, making sure to use the correct term for the women who channeled magical powers. "I am acquainted with a local coven, but I already owe them a significant debt. I'm not sure they will let me undertake another debt to them." Dean referred to his agreement during the recent troubles with the terrorists of The Cause, to offer his firstborn girl child someday to the coven, so she can be trained in the witch ways. He didn't think he should tell Jaz about that. He was sure her response would be less than positive.

"I think that is wise," Jaz said. "I would not want to owe a debt to them either. I sympathize with your plight. Still, I was charged to find a witch, and find one I will so that the clan may discharge its debt to the Eldara."

She stopped. The lights had gone out in the diner. The sudden darkness caught them both by surprise. Dean looked around, trying to peer through the darkness when screams started at the far end of the diner by the entrance. He couldn't see anything, but heard rumbling snarls amid the screams, snarls that were coming closer.

"Shit," he heard Jaz say from across the table. "That's another Oni demon and someone has sent it here for the two of us, unless I miss my guess. We need to get out of here. I need my sword and I left it in the SUV outside." He saw her reach behind her in the darkness, and then he saw the unmistakable silhouette of a semi-automatic in her left hand.

"Is that a gun?" Dean exclaimed.

"Yes, but it's not going to do much good against an Oni," the huntress said. "The best I can do is slow it down a little. We need to get out to the parking lot. Is that the only door at the far end of the restaurant?"

"I'm afraid so," Dean said. He was still looking at the gun he hadn't known she was carrying. It was a bit of a shock.

"Okay, get behind me, Dean," Jaz said as she stood up and faced the sound of the snarls and screams coming from the other end of the restaurant. "Grab one of those chairs and bust out the window behind us next to the booth. We'll have to go out that way. Hurry up! It is going to figure out where we are any minute."

Dean picked up one of the diner chairs. It was heavy, made of tubular chrome steel with a red vinyl cushion. He looked at Jaz but she had taken a shooter's stance with her pistol aimed downrange towards the far end of the diner. How was she going to use that thing without killing some innocent person? He could not see more than a few feet past his nose.

"Dean, what are you doing?" Jaz said, turning to look back at him. "Break that window out. Now!"

Dean turned and hefted the chair, holding it by its back and swinging it hard at the window, striking the glass with the chair legs. He was surprised when it bounced off. Then Dean heard two gunshots behind him and he picked up the chair and swung harder. The glass broke under the blow this time, shattering and falling around him on the floor and outside. He turned and saw Jaz squeeze off four more shots in rapid succession, the muzzle flashes illuminating her face in the darkness with each shot. He heard a howling roar of pain from the darkness beyond her.

"You go first," Dean said.

"Don't be an idiot, I have the gun," Jaz shouted. "Get out the window. I'll be right behind you."

Dean used the chair to sweep some of the remaining glass from the window frame and swung his legs over to the outside, then jumped the four or five feet to the ground. The streetlights in the parking lot gave him better visibility than he'd had inside. He turned back to look in the open window to see four more muzzle flashes and then Jaz dove out the window, executing a perfect midair flip and landing on her feet next to him. There was a snarl of rage from inside the diner and then Dean saw the Oni demon for the first time as it reached the open window.

The demon was roughly man-shaped but was covered in scales and patches of coarse fur. The head was elongated like a wolf's and the teeth were the largest the paramedic had ever seen. He stood rooted to the spot while the creature looked in his direction and roared as if it recognized him. Jaz jumped in front of him as he saw her slap another magazine into her pistol and then emptied the fresh clip into the demon's face. Dean saw the bullets impact it, and the force of the impacts drove it backward as it screamed in rage and pain.

Jaz grabbed his hand and yelled, "Come on!" as she pulled him away from the diner and across the parking lot. He turned and ran beside her. She held something up in front of her and he saw the lights of a black SUV blink about fifty yards away. It was an awfully long way off with that thing chasing them. He tried to run even faster and make it to the relative safety of Jaz's car. When they reached the side of the SUV, Dean heard the roar of the demon behind them and turned to see it leap out the window, fall to all fours and run across the parking lot towards them. Jaz threw open the driver's door, leaning inside to grab something. Dean couldn't see what it was. He was focused on the demon chasing after them. No, it was looking straight into his eyes. It was chasing after him. Then his view was blocked as Jaz dashed in front of him. In her hands, held in a two-handed grip, was the sword he had seen her holding in the mirror at the Hakutakus' house days before.

She swept the sword down at something and Dean ducked to avoid the impact from the demon as it charged into Jaz to get to him. He opened his eyes to a reddish mist surrounding both of them. The snarling and roars had stopped. He stood from where he was crouched behind the hunter and looked around.

"Where did it go?" Dean asked. Jaz was just standing there, her sword held out to her side, one-handed. Her heavy breathing was the only sign that she had exerted herself at all. She was still as a statue otherwise.

"Where did it go?" Dean asked again.

"Shhh. I'm trying to listen to see if there are any others around."

Dean looked around, startled at the thought. Could there be more of them?

He watched in silence as she scanned the parking lot, looking and listening. Then she turned and shoved him over to the passenger side of the SUV.

"Get in," she said. "We've got to get you out of here until we figure out why they are targeting you."

Dean started to say something but thought better of it when another snarling roar sounded in the distance. He went around to the passenger side while she climbed into the driver's side. He couldn't get in because of the weapons caddy attached to the seat. Jaz reached over and detached the strap holding it in place to the headrest.

"Just throw that in the back. Get in."

Dean got in and was still buckling his seatbelt as the hunter gunned the engine to life and, with a squeal of tires, drove off into the night, leaving the carnage of the attack behind them at the diner.

Chapter 11

Dean's heart was pounding in his chest as he thought about what just happened at Hank's Place. The diner had always been a safe haven and in the past had served as a neutral meeting ground with his enemies, real or imagined. He had met with Mike Farver there several times. His former mentor had turned out to be one of the lead terrorists in the attacks on the Unusual community a few months before. Dean had first learned of his betrayal at the very diner booth where he and Jaz sat this evening. Now there were possibly injured people back there who needed his help and he was speeding away, running from demons who seemed to be seeking his blood.

Another thought occurred to him about the carnage at the restaurant. He turned in his seat and looked at Jaz. She had been part of that carnage, firing her pistol blindly into the darkness during the blackout.

She noticed his attention and shot a glance his way while she was driving. "What?" she asked.

"I'm just wondering how many of your bullets missed the Oni and maybe hit other patrons or staff. Was it a good idea to fire off your weapon blind like that?"

"I was not firing blind, and I don't miss what I aim at," she hissed in reply. She kept the SUV's speed up even as she took a sharp left turn at the next intersection.

"Oh sorry," Dean said, rolling his eyes. "I didn't know you could see in the dark. Why didn't I think of that?"

"I can see in the dark," she replied. "I'm a hunter. It would not do much good if I wasn't on some sort of even footing with my adversaries." Jaz shot Dean another glance as she sped down the road away from the attacker.

"Wait, you're not kidding," Dean said, a bit amazed. "But how? I know you are human like me, and it couldn't be magic. You all hate magic."

"We don't hate magic," she clarified. "We hate when it is used against humans for gain by our adversaries. My hunter amulet gives me the ability to see in the dark, as well as in the UV and infrared spectrums, among other things." She touched the ornate three-sided pendant on a chain at her neckline.

Dean was chastened but not any less curious. He always wanted to know more about the hidden world he had known nothing about only a year before. He was hungry for knowledge about his patients and their lives. That included the hunters, he supposed.

"Can you sense the demons? How did you know there would be more coming?" Dean asked.

Jaz glanced his way again as she continued driving. She looked up into the rearview mirror and then pulled the SUV over to the curb, stopping there.

"I can't sense them any better than you, other than the seeing in the dark thing," she said after they stopped. Dean noticed that she kept looking around as she talked. He guessed it was the bodyguard training she must have had; that or paranoia. "Like I said, I can see in the UV and IF spectrums, too, so I can sense when someone is possessed. In those situations the demon sort of leaks out around the edges and shows up in the person's aura. Other than that, I have to use my normal human senses and sensibilities."

"So possession is real?" Dean asked. "Like as real as in movies like Exorcist?"

"I'm surprised you're so naive, Dean," Jaz replied. "You've seen so much and you are smart and well-read. Why wouldn't all of it be real?"

"I don't know," Dean replied. "I guess I'm just still surprised that so many of the legends and myths are actually true. I didn't grow up in this world the way you did."

"All of the legends and myths are true, at least in part," Jaz responded. "And you grew up with the same stories I did, you just never had anyone tell you they were true."

Dean watched as she checked her mirrors and then scanned the area around them. He got a sense that very little missed her attention.

"Someone is sending the Oni demons after you," Jaz said. "Someone or something. We need to get you somewhere safe, but I'm not sure we can trust any of the normal places. Is there somewhere you can think of that no one would think you would go? Somewhere isolated, where we can think and plan?"

Dean pondered the question. He, like most people, was a creature of habit. He had his apartment, his work, and his favorite places to hang out, like Hank's Place. He liked to go places where people knew him and he could feel at home and relax. There was nowhere he could think of that would give him a place to hole up like Jaz described. There was James Lee's Nightwing building downtown. There was plenty of security there, but that wasn't hiding and it would put more of his friends in danger. Dean looked at the huntress and shook his head.

Jaz took out her smartphone and tapped it a few times. He figured she was sending a text message when she started tapping away with her thumbs in rapid succession. Dean waited while she sent her message. He started looking around. It made him itch to think that there was at least one more of those Oni demons around out there, hunting for him. She finished whatever she was doing and slid her phone back into the pocket of her leather jacket.

"I just sent my father a message that we were tracked to the diner. He'll send a team there to make sure any Oni hanging about will be dealt with," Jaz said. "I also told him that we were going operationally dark. That means no messages, in or out, from now on. Turn off your phone so no one can track you. My phone is scrambled so we'll have to rely on that for now."

"I can't just disappear," Dean said. "I've got work in the morning. I'll lose my job."

"Daddy is smart," Jaz said. "He knows you're with me and he will let your Chief know that you are on an assignment with us as a tactical medic or something. That should cover you. He and your fire chief go way back. Now we need to keep moving until we can figure out where we can safely hide."

She continued to look at him as she slid the gear lever out of park and into drive. She gripped the wheel and started to move. Dean looked forward and saw a girl, palms of both hands outstretched, her eyes squeezed shut. She was standing directly in front of the vehicle.

"Look out," Dean shouted.

Jaz looked forward, jamming on the brakes. They had nearly run the girl over. Her outstretched hands were now resting on the hood of the SUV. Jaz drew her pistol. "Dean, get down. If she can't see you, she might not be able to connect the spell she's casting. She's a hexen; a witch. I can see her drawing in magic."

Dean didn't duck. He was looking in the girl's face. She was only about fifteen or sixteen he would guess, dressed in a flowing long print skirt, with a white peasant-style blouse and a brown vest. She looked like someone from a renaissance faire or something. She also looked sort of familiar, like he had seen her somewhere before, like he should know her.

"Don't shoot her," Dean said on impulse. "I think she's with us."

"What do you mean, 'she's with us?'"

"Look," Dean said. "I know you're a shoot first and ask questions later type of person, but we have to work together here. You said that, not me. I'm telling you that for some reason I know her, even though I've never seen her before. Just look at her, she's not threatening us. She is just standing there."

The girl in front of them had opened her eyes and was staring forward at them through the tinted windshield as if she could see into the darkened interior. She had a wild sort of grin on her face, standing there under the streetlights in front of them.

"I am looking at her," Jaz said. "I can see the UV waves of her spell. She's casting something right now. How do you know she isn't calling the Oni on us?"

"How do you know she is?" Dean countered. He watched as the girl lowered her hands and walked around to the driver's side of the Expedition.

Jaz put the window down but kept the gun in her left hand, just below the edge of the window, ready to use. Dean spoke up before the huntress had a chance to speak.

"Hey, good thing I saw you before my companion here ran you over," Dean said with a smile. "What were you doing standing in front of us like that, if you don't mind my asking? It's kind of nuts, you know."

"I was masking your vehicle from scrying spells," the girl said. "The revenants are already trying to track you both after the attack at the diner." She looked at Jaz, a broad smile on her young face. "You can put the gun away, Jaswinder. I mean you no harm. You both were just about to go looking for me anyway, so I decided to come to you."

"Jaz," Dean said looking at the driver. Jaz turned to meet his gaze and nodded. "I think we found our hexen."

"Yeah, I think so, too," the hunter replied. She leaned forward and reached back, sliding the semi-automatic pistol into its holster. Then she reached up and pressed the button to unlock the doors. "Climb in back," Jaz said to the young witch girl. "We need to keep moving. Even if your masking spell worked, there are still mundane ways to track us."

The girl kind of bounced at the invitation to get in the vehicle with them. She jumped into the back seat and slid to the middle, looking around at the gray and black interior. She extended her hand to Dean when he twisted back to look at her as she got situated. Jaz pulled away from the curb and started driving again.

"I'm Jo. That's short for Joanna," the girl said, shaking his hand. "But I prefer just Jo."

"Nice to meet you, Jo," Dean said. "I'm Dean and this is Jaz. But I guess you must know that already." He noticed she was still bouncing slightly as she sat forward on the edge of the bench seat behind them. "Hey, Jo, sit back and buckle up. We can still talk but you need to be belted in. Okay?"

"Okay, Dad," she said rolling her eyes. Then she giggled and sat back to buckle in.

Typical teenager, Dean thought, viewing any adult telling her what to do as a parental figure.

"What were you doing out here in the first place, and how did you find us?" Jaz asked.

"My coven knew that I needed to come here and help you so they sent me directly to this place and time to make sure I was here when you arrived," Jo said. "They spent a great deal of energy to make sure I was here to help you find the missing Eldara."

"So you know about our mission?" Dean asked.

"You are seeking to free Ashley Moore, an Eldara Sister abducted by revenants who seek to use her divine energy to create a large breach in the warding that separates the netherworld from ours." Jo stopped her recitation and looked from Dean to Jaz and back again. "How'd I do?"

"Pretty well," Dean said. She seemed to know more about this than either of them. There was so much he wanted to know more about. Who were these revenants? Where were they holding Ashley and how could they free her?

"Revenants," Jaz said. "That's not good." Dean saw her make eye contact with their back seat passenger in the rearview mirror. "Are you sure they're revenants?"

"Yep," the teen replied. "They are determined to kill one of us. If they do, it will stop us from rescuing the Eldara. They have their own seers and they know of our quest, too. They know it has to be the three of us."

"Well revenants are high order netherworld demons of a sort," Jaz told Dean. "They are the damned souls of the most evil of men, reformed into magical creatures of the netherworld. They can be very powerful."

"How do we beat them?" Dean asked. In the stories the bad guys always have some sort of weakness.

"I don't know," Jaz said. "I've never faced one of them before."

"You can kill them, or at least banish them with a holy blade, like the one you have Jaz," Jo said. "Beheading will do the trick if you catch them unawares. It just destroys their corporeal form and sends them back to the netherworld but it would be enough for our purposes."

"How do you know all of this?" Dean asked.

"Oh, I feel like I've been preparing for this all my life," Jo said.

"How old are you?" Jaz asked.

"I'm fifteen," she responded. She sounded defensive all of a sudden. "I just passed my acceptance ritual into the coven. I'm an adult now, so don't tell me I'm not old enough to be here doing this."

There's that teenager thing again, Dean thought. Naturally pushing back against authority figures.

Jaz laughed. "You're not going to get an argument from me, girly-girl. I killed my first demon on a hunt at fourteen. It wasn't my first hunt, just my first kill."

"Cool," Jo said. "You'll have to tell me about it. I haven't heard that story about you before."

"Time enough for stories later," Jaz said. "Right now we need to get out of here to someplace safe."

"So, where are we headed?" Jo asked.

"We need a place where no one will expect to find us," Jaz said. "Someplace we can regroup and reorganize while we figure out our next steps."

"How about the mountain cabin?" Jo asked.

"What mountain cabin?" Jaz said.

Dean looked back over his shoulder at the witch teen and saw her looking back and forth between the two of them. She seemed puzzled that they didn't understand.

"There's a cabin in the woods on a lake to the west of here near the mountains," Jo explained. "It belongs to the Eldara."

"That might work, but I don't know what you're talking about."
Jaz said.

"No, no I guess you wouldn't. Okay, Ashley Moore owns a mountain cabin she bought from a nurse friend of hers," Jo said. "It's remote and it should be safe enough for now, especially with my spell in place over us."

"Wait, I think I know that cabin," Dean said. "I didn't know that Ashley had bought it, but I know the one you're thinking of." It was weird how Joanna knew so much about them, and Ashley, for that matter. She must be from the local coven and had been briefed on them by Asha and the other women there.

Dean turned to Jaz. "Head south to I-95, then we'll swing over and get on I-70 westbound. The cabin is in the mountains of Western Maryland about two hours from here. I think Jo is right. It will be a perfect place to hole up until we get our bearings again."

Jaz nodded and turned the car onto a nearby on-ramp to get up on the interstate. Dean sat back in silence. He had started that day without a clue about how to get started finding Ashley. Now he had his trio to get to work finding her. Despite the recent events with the demon attack, he felt pleased for the first time in a long time. He finally had the jumpstart he needed to find her and get her back.

Chapter 12

The trip to the cabin was several hours long and after some time trying to plan out what they were going to do, everyone was quiet for a while. Dean looked back at Jo in the back seat. She was settled back, with her earbuds in, watching something on her phone. Jaz had cautioned her about connecting her phone to anything online and the girl had told her that she would access only stored media on the device. Dean thought about who she might be. He was uncomfortable with running around on this mission with a fifteen year-old child. She had said the coven saw her as an adult, but he noticed that she never said anything about what her parents thought. The more he thought about it, the more he started to think she was some sort of runaway. If that was the case, it could make things worse for them. He would have to talk to Jaz about it the first chance they were alone. There had to be a way to verify her story.

He knew that he needed to have three people in their team in order to find Ashley. He was willing to risk just about anything to get her back. It seemed like Jaz was the right person for one of those slots. She had her own prophecy of some sort that matched up with what Ingrid had told him he must do. The wild card was Joanna. She fit the slot in their team they had open, and there was also the fact that she had found them and identified herself as the one they were looking for. Still, with his concerns about her legal status and age, was he willing to endanger her life to get Ashley back?

He knew what Ashley would say. She would never condone putting anyone in danger just to rescue her. She would say she was the one who did the rescuing. He didn't feel the same way about Jaz. She had demonstrated that she could take care of herself. Heck, she could take care of him, too. With demons chasing after him now, he felt safer with the blonde huntress around. He looked over at her as she drove. He wanted to know more about her and her training. It was a new side of the mythical world in which he found himself at Station U. Dean was always curious to learn new things. Maybe he could learn more about caring for his patients by learning more about the hunters and their backgrounds.

When they stopped for gas about an hour outside of Elk City, Dean learned just how paranoid Jaz was about keeping them off the grid. Dean was going to head in and get a soda to help him stay awake and offered to buy something for the others.

"How much cash do you have?" Jaz asked when he turned to leave the pumps to go inside the WaWa convenience store.

"Not much, but I have my debit card," Dean replied.

"No credit or debit cards. It is just like keeping our phones off or in airplane mode," Jaz said shaking her head. "We can't afford to leave a trail behind us. Come around back of the Expedition."

Dean and Joanna got out and followed her to the back where she opened the lift gate. There were three black Pelican cases lying in the cargo area, two large cases and one smaller case. Jaz looked around to make sure that no one else was around and then dialed in a combination on the embedded lock before opening the small case. Jo laughed as she saw the open case and turned away as if she wasn't that surprised. Dean couldn't take his eyes off the contents. The case was full of cash, stacks of it. The bills were all bundled up in bank wrappers and neatly arranged in rows.

"How much money is that?" Dean asked.

"It's one hundred thousand dollars in various sized bills," Jaz said, taking one of the stacks of fifty-dollar bills out of the case before she closed it and rolled the combination dials to lock it again. She peeled off a few of the fifties, handing them to him, before putting the rest into an inside pocket of her black leather jacket. "Use that to buy anything you want, I'll take a coffee, one sugar and some half and half. Put the other fifty down on the gas here at pump number 2."

"Ooo, I want a smoothie," Jo chimed in. "I love WaWa smoothies."

"Do you always drive around with that much cash in the back of your car? What if someone tries to rob you?" Dean asked.

Jo laughed aloud. "Rob her? That would be like committing suicide. Come on, I'm thirsty." The teen headed towards the convenience store entrance.

Jaz shot a look at the teenager and then said, "It's about being discreet and careful. I'm never as concerned about the cash as I am about the weapons. And, yes, all our Errington vehicles are prepped to go dark at any time. Since we have to be prepared to provide the best security for our clients, we have to be prepared for anything. That includes doing what we are doing right now, heading to a safe house to regroup. Go get my coffee. I'll pump the gas."

Dean shook his head as he wondered what was in the other cases in the back. She had mentioned weapons and he was sure there were other surprises as well. She certainly liked her mysteries. He walked into the convenience store just behind Jo. The teen witch seemed to take everything in stride as if she was used to traveling around a lot. It made him wonder about her legal status again and he wished he could turn his phone on and make at least one call to ask Asha about her. If the coven really sent her to them, she would tell him.

Dean got Jaz her coffee while Jo used one of the touch screens to order herself a smoothie. He strolled up and down the aisles, looking for something to snack on while he waited for the smoothie to be finished. After all, his dinner had been rudely interrupted. He selected a bag of pretzels large enough for all of them and headed to the counter to pay. He handed the clerk one of the fifties and told him to put it on the SUV getting gas at pump 2. He used the other fifty to pay for their food and drinks. He noticed that the clerk was staring at the back of his right hand. It was where his UV ink tattoo was located that identified him as a Station U paramedic. Only Unusuals could see the mark. He let his eyes come up and met the clerk's eyes. They had a slight yellow tint around the corners of the irises. He was some sort of lycan, an animal shapeshifter. The clerk just smiled at him and made an adjustment on the screen.

"Police and public safety don't pay for coffee, sir," the clerk said.

"I'm not on duty," Dean said. "I don't mind paying." He knew that some places gave discounts and freebies to policemen, fire and EMS crews. He took advantage of them all the time while he was on duty. This was the first time someone had noticed who he was off duty.

"Not a problem, sir. Thank you for your service, I'll just ring up the other items," the clerk said.

Dean nodded in thanks and picked up the coffee cup and the bag with the pretzels and bottle of soda. Jo strolled over with the stamped receipt to pick up her smoothie at the deli counter. Once she had the fruity concoction the two of them went back to the SUV. Jaz was just finishing up filling the gas tank. He was surprised it had taken so long to fill up, even with an SUV the size of the Expedition. He mentioned as much to Jaz.

"It's got dual custom gas tanks so we can go twice as far on a tankful," the hunter explained. She took the coffee from Dean and took out her keys while she climbed in.

"I can drive," Dean offered.

"No, I've got it," Jaz said. "I don't like it when other people drive my vehicle."

Jo laughed from the back seat. "Some things never change."

Dean shot her a glance at the strange comment, but didn't argue with Jaz. If she wanted to drive, that was fine by him. He could get some rest. He was tired after working all day and getting up early.

"How's the free coffee?" Jo asked. "Dean got comped a free cup when the clerk spotted his invisible ink."

"He what?" Jaz said, concerned.

"It's no big deal," Dean said. "A lot of convenience stores offer free coffee and fountain soda to public safety officers. He spotted my Station U tattoo and said the coffee was free. He was some sort of lycan, if I were to guess."

"He was kind of hot, too," Jo said. "But most shifters have that vibe going for them."

"Dean," Jaz said. "I told you we have to stay under the radar and you go and expose us to the first convenience store clerk we run into. Are you crazy?"

"I told you that it is no big deal. I forget about this tattoo when I'm not working," Dean explained.

"Yeah, but you are one of, what, ten or twelve people in the world with that tattoo?" the hunter asked. "So if word gets around that one of you was here on the way out of town, how long do you think it will take our adversaries to put two and two together and figure out it was you?"

"Wow, paranoid much?" Dean asked. "What makes you think that anyone is going to go to those lengths to track me down? It was a chance encounter, that's all."

"I stay alive by being paranoid. If you let me, I'll keep you alive, too," Jaz cautioned him as she started up the SUV and drove back towards the highway ramp. "We know they are tracking you somehow. Until I figure out how they got to us at the diner, I will assume that any compromise is potentially fatal."

"So if we weren't in a hurry, you'd go back and kill that kid to cover our tracks?" Dean asked, only partially joking.

Jaz shot him a glance and then went back to paying attention to the road ahead. The glance turned his blood to ice. If she thought it would work, that is exactly what she would do. Dean had to remember that at the heart of it she was a killer. Maybe she did it for the right reasons, maybe not, but she was his opposite. If the situation called for it, she'd kill without a moment's thought and without remorse. He shivered and wondered again about who he was teamed up with on this mission.

"How about some music?" Jo offered from the back seat. "It's like riding in a hearse in here. Put the radio on and get us some tunes."

Dean reached up to the dashboard and turned on the radio. When he switched it on, he caught a Baltimore news broadcast in progress.

"… Identified as Jaswinder Errington, a private security specialist. Ms. Errington is being sought in relation to a savage animal attack where shots were fired in Elk City earlier this evening. Her companion, Elk City paramedic Dean Flynn is also sought for questioning in the incident. They were last seen leaving the scene of the incident in a black SUV and should be considered armed and dangerous. Do not approach them yourself. Call 911, Elk City Police, or the Maryland State Police if you have information of their whereabouts. We'll be back in a minute with tomorrow's weather forecast after these messages from our sponsors."

"I thought you called your father and told him what we were doing? He was going to square things away," Dean said.

"I thought so, too," Jaz replied. "It appears our adversaries have more resources than we thought."

Jo chimed in, "At least they didn't mention me."

"Yeah, but you two are on the security cameras at the convenience store and if that lycan back there puts two and two together, he's going to report us to the police. They are going to have descriptions of all three of us on the radio as soon as he does."

"Well we're only another hour from the cabin," Dean said. "It is isolated and no one will look for us there. There is no connection to us."

"I hope so, Dean, I hope so," Jaz said. "Because isolated cabins make great places for a concerted attack, too, where no one can hear the noise and raise an alarm."

The SUV's occupants fell silent as they drove onward, thinking about that final statement. It did not bode well for them.

Chapter 13

Dean paced the floor in the cabin's open great room while he thought about the situation he was in. "I can't believe I'm being chased by the police again," he complained. "I just got murder charges against me dropped. I promised myself I would never be in that situation again."

"You're not charged with anything," Jo said. "You're a person of interest in an ongoing investigation. The police search is just our opponent's way of getting help tracking us down."

"She's right," Jaz said. She was seated on the sofa against the wall. She had her handgun broken down to its component parts, all laid out on the coffee table in front of her. She was wiping the barrel with a cloth coated with some sort of oil. "This is just a ploy to get the police to track us down for them. It keeps us on the run and not getting on with our task of tracking down the missing Eldara."

"That's easy for you to say," Dean quipped. "You're used to living on the run and being tracked by demons."

"This is a kill or be killed game you're mixed up with, Dean," she said. "And, no, I'm not used to being in trouble with the police. We usually try to work with them and not against them. It makes me wonder what my father is doing to get all of this worked out.

Something must be keeping him from getting us off the police's radar."

"Maybe he's got other things on his mind," Jo said. She pointed to the TV she was watching. There was a video of a large building fire. The caption read, "Gas Explosion Destroys Elk City Building."

"Turn that up," Jaz and Dean said together.

"… Fire department investigators are making no statements as to the cause of the explosion, but bystanders claim they smelled gas just before the blast that leveled the Errington Security Building and damaged surrounding structures as well. There are no reports of the number of casualties in the blast and subsequent fires, though there are several reports of firefighter injuries while fighting the blaze."

Dean looked at Jaz. She looked pale and lost all of a sudden. It was the first time he'd seen her with her guard down. He heard a sob from his left and looked over to see that Jo was crying. He didn't know what she was crying about. It was Jaz's father that might be missing after all. Maybe she was just shocked by the carnage.

"Jaz," he said. "We don't know that your father was in the building when the explosion happened. We have to hope for the best until we know for sure."

"He was there, Dean," she said. "He was staying in the clan apartments upstairs. We keep them there for when we are in town. My mom was there, too, along with most of my cousins. This mission was important. All hands were on deck to help out. Now we're on our own." Her shoulders sagged and she turned her head away, probably so he couldn't see her crying.

Jo walked over, wiping tears from her eyes and sat down on the sofa next to Jaz. She put one arm around Jaz's shoulders to comfort her. The hunter started to pull away and then she gave in and the two of them shared a tearful embrace. Dean wasn't sure why Jo was so upset, too, but he supposed it was good she was able to give Jaz a shoulder to cry on, given the circumstances. He had never known his own father and had only the vaguest memories of him. His mother had never talked about him, no matter how many times Dean had asked. He moved over and picked up the remote from on top of the TV and turned the TV off. He looked around for something to do. With all that had happened to Jaz this evening, his troubles didn't seem so important.

He looked at the cabin. Ashley had made a few upgrades to the place since they'd been here. He had come here once when she had borrowed the key from an ER nurse friend of hers. Since she had bought the place, he found that she had put in a small satellite dish and added a generator to power the place if the main power went out. The pantry shelves were stocked with canned goods and it looked like someone came in periodically and cleaned and dusted the place.

He wondered if the caretakers were members of the nearby Unusual community. He and Ashley had helped a family of Dryads living in the forest nearby when they had been here before. They had saved the oldest daughter from a life-threatening infection and he was sure that family would have felt obligated to help the Eldara again if they knew she bought the cabin. He might want to try and contact them. He thought he could find their place through the woods again if he tried. He looked at his watch. It was nearing midnight. Would that be too late, or should he wait for morning?

"I'm going to go for a walk. I've got to connect with someone who might be able to help us out," Dean said.

"No, we can't afford to let anyone know where we are," Jaz cautioned.

"These are friends of Ashley's and they owe her a debt," Dean explained. "You understand how that works. We need some help, at least in the short term. They could be of service to help us stay supplied and informed about what is going on in the outside world. Trust me. These people can help us."

The huntress just looked at him for a moment with her red-rimmed eyes, the pain showing in her expression, even though she tried to appear in control. She nodded, almost imperceptibly, and he grabbed a flashlight from where he had left it on the counter and left to go and find some Dryads in the dark.

▭

DEAN STEPPED outside the cabin and shined the flashlight's beam into the woods. It had been a while since he had been here, but he thought he could find the path that led to the Dryads' house in the woods. If he could connect with Enric, the head of the family and one of the leaders of the Unusuals in the mountain valley, they could hide here in the cabin for a while before anyone found them. Playing the flashlight's illumination on the ground in front of him, Dean started to look along the edge of the trees for where the path began.

It didn't take him too long, no more than fifteen minutes to find where he thought the path began and he walked into the dark woods, following the trail. It was probably a bad idea, he thought. Dean was a child of the city. He had grown up in and around Elk City all his life and had not spent any appreciable time in anything approaching a wilderness setting. The forest here was alien to him in many ways. In daylight, the paramedic might have been able to keep his bearings while walking, but with the darkness, even with the help of a flashlight, he soon became lost.

The first clue was when he stumbled through an opening in the trees and found himself on the edge of the mountain lake that filled the center of the valley. He had started on a path that led away from the lake. The fact that he had gotten turned around and ended up next to the water meant that he had no idea where he was. He checked his watch and realized he had been gone for almost an hour. The walk to the dryad's cabin, when he had taken the trip before with Ashley, had only taken about twenty minutes.

Dean looked around in the darkness. It was cloudy, so there was no help from the moon or stars to lend light to the landscape. He played the light from his flashlight on the dark waters of the lake and then turned in a circle, shining the light into the woods behind him. Dean supposed he could just walk along the lake's bank until he got back to the cabin, but the cabin was not right on the lake and he was not sure he would see it in the dark. He was still contemplating his options when there was a sound behind him. It was a ripping snarl, like that of a large cat. Spinning around, the light's beam showed the tawny form of a mountain lion, eyes glowing in the light's illumination.

Dean started to panic. His chances of fending off a mountain lion on his own without even as much as a knife were slim. He held out the flashlight in his left hand, keeping the beam on the lion, which stood watching him from the edge of the tree line. He extended his right hand in a calming gesture, palm extended, fingers wide. Dean didn't know what he was doing, or why, but he knew that if he tried to turn and run, the big cat would catch him without any trouble at all.

Then the lion did something he didn't expect. It sat down and extended its right fore paw. If Dean didn't know better, he would think it was copying his movements. The cat's head tilted as if puzzled by something and it let out a low rumble from its throat. It wasn't a growl exactly, but it did send chills up Dean's spine. He had a sudden thought and turned his right hand from palm out to show the mountain lion the back of his hand. He wasn't sure if the hidden tattoo there glowed in the UV spectrum in the dark so he shined the edge of the flashlight's beam on it briefly, just to illuminate it.

The lion looked from meeting his eyes, to his outstretched hand and then nodded. At least that was the way he would describe it. It looked like a nod. He decided to try something else.

"I'm Dean Flynn, I'm a paramedic and a companion of the Eldara, Ashley Moore. Do you understand me?" His voice sounded loud in the darkness amid the chirps and buzzing of the nighttime insects.

The mountain lion nodded again, and Dean felt his shoulders relax a bit. This wasn't a mountain lion. It was a lycan of some sort who had shifted to lion form. He decided to keep talking since that seemed to be working.

"I was looking for Enric's home, the Dryad chieftain in this valley. Do you know him?"

Again, a nod from the large cat.

"Can you take me to him or his family? I need their help." Dean asked.

This time the head tilted again and then swung from side to side. So it was a no. He wondered why the shifter didn't just turn back into a human form and talk to him normally. All but a very young shape-shifter could change back at will. The ability to shift forms came with adolescence and the swings in mood and emotion that came with puberty also made changing back and forth difficult for the younger shifters. The change could also be brought on by anything that altered mental status, but that wasn't the case here.

"Why aren't you shifting back to talk to me as a human?" Dean asked. "Are you too young to shift back until morning?"

Another nod confirmed his suspicions. Okay, so now he had a connection to the Unusual community, but he'd have to wait until the morning to talk to them. For now he was stuck communicating with the shape-changer with yes and no questions only.

Dean settled down on a large fallen tree trunk at the water's edge and started thinking of ways to keep the conversation going. He wasn't afraid of the big cat anymore, but he was afraid the kid would lose interest in this conversation with the lost human and go about his business, leaving Dean alone in the woods again. He was still contemplating questions to ask when he heard voices from behind him. The mountain lion stood back up and looked past him into the woods, then, with a quiet snarl, turned and bounded off into the darkness.

Dean turned the flashlight the other direction, towards where the voices were coming from. He thought he recognized them. He watched as Jaz and Joanna exited the tree line at the edge of the lake about a hundred feet away.

"See, I told you I could find him," Jo said. "You shouldn't doubt me. I have skills you don't appreciate."

"I didn't doubt you, I just didn't think it was a good idea to have another one of us wander off into the woods alone to get lost," Jaz countered. "Anyway, yes, you did find him." In the illumination of his flashlight, he could see she carried a large tactical shotgun with a folding stock, and he could see the hilt of her katana jutting up over her left shoulder. "You alright?"

"I'm fine," Dean lied. "I was just taking a break. I found a lycan and we were talking when you showed up."

Jaz cursed under her breath and swung the shotgun back and forth along the trees at the edge of the forest, searching for a target. Dean thought this was going to be an ongoing problem for them if Jaz just assumed that every Unusual was a potential target for her hunter skills.

"Jaz, it was a peaceful encounter," Dean said. "Anyway, the kid ran off as soon as you two arrived. What are you doing out here? I was fine," Dean lied again.

"Jo here said you had gotten lost, that she could sense it," the hunter replied. "She was going to come out looking for you on her own and I couldn't let her do that, so here we all are."

"I wasn't lost, exactly," Dean explained. He was curious how the witch girl had figured out that he was lost. He was pretty sure that sort of spell that required a certain level of intimacy or connection unless she was very powerful for her age. "I got turned around in the woods, but when I found the lake, I real-ized I could follow it back to the cabin. Then I met the lycan youth."

"How do you know it was a young one?" Jaz asked. She was still watching the surrounding woods, scanning the area with her night vision charm for any movement.

"He or she couldn't change back on their own until morning," Dean said. "The ability to shift at will comes with age and practice. The kid was probably out for a normal night of hunting when he came upon me. I showed my tattoo and we started talking. Well I talked and asked simple questions. The lycan's answers were just head bobs or shakes."

"So what did you learn?" Jo asked. "Can we get help from the Unusuals here?"

"I think so. I was about to get to that part when you all showed up and scared the kid away."

"So, are you ready to head back to the cabin, or did you want to stumble around in the dark a little bit more?" Jaz asked.

"Yeah, Dean," Jo added. "At least let me cast a glamor on your eyes so you can see in the dark."

"Uh, no spells, thank you," Dean said. "I'm happy with my normal human abilities."

He joined them as they walked back along the bank of the Lake. They only walked about five hundred feet before Jaz turned and led the group back to the cabin. Dean felt a little silly that they were so close to the cabin the whole time he was thinking he was lost. He decided to keep that thought to himself.

Chapter 14

Dean woke up the next morning and stretched in the early morning light coming in the cabin's first floor windows. He had taken the couch for the night, while the ladies shared the queen-sized bed upstairs in the single loft bedroom. He was a little stiff since the couch cushions weren't all that soft or comfortable when it came to sleeping on them. He thought he was the only one up, but then the front door opened and Joanna came in from outside. She was carrying her sandals in one hand and a small bouquet of wildflowers in the other. She smiled at Dean when she saw him sitting up on the sofa.

"I didn't want to wake you up. You looked like you could use the extra sleep," the witch girl said.

"You didn't wake me," Dean said. "I needed to get up anyway. I expect we'll have visitors this morning after last night's encounter with the lycan youth. What were you up to outside?"

"It's a little morning ritual I like to do," Jo said. "It helps me to stay grounded and remember who I am within the world."

Dean did not know what to make of that. He hadn't found much for himself in the spiritual realm. He didn't begrudge it to those who believed in something larger than himself, but Dean had never been that guy. It was surprising considering his relationship with an angel and all.

"You should have let someone know you were going out, that's all," Dean said. "We have to stick together and know what each of us are doing if we are going to stay safe.

"I told Jaz when I got up," the girl said. "I thought she might want to join me, considering what happened to her parents last night. It's a great way to center yourself and lose the worries and cares of the world around you."

"I don't need to forget what happened," Jaz said from the stairs as she descended to the first floor. "I need to keep focused to take the revenge called for by my parent's death."

"It was a fire, a gas explosion, Jaz," Dean said. "The fire department told reporters that. It's tragic, but it happens from time to time. I'm sorry for your loss, but not everything is an attack. It could have been an accident."

"It wasn't an accident," Jaz said with firm belief in her words. "I don't believe in coincidences, and this is too closely related to the time we were attacked at the diner and went on the run. There have been many attacks over the years that have reduced our numbers. This was a final step to remove the Errington clan, once and for all."

"She's not wrong, Dean," Jo added. "The revenants want to bring on the end of the world ahead of schedule. They need certain players out of the way in order to do that. It's why they took Ashley."

Jaz looked over at Joanna. "You mentioned the revenants before. How do you know they are behind this?"

"Very powerful revenants control several levels of the netherworld and would love to be able to freely cross the wards that keep the worlds separate," Jo answered. "I was told by my coven leader that revenants sought a breach in the wards between our worlds."

"I still can't believe I didn't know anything about these revenants until now," Dean said.

"You had all those books on Unusuals, myths, and legends at the

Station, Dean," Jo said. "Why didn't you learn more about what you could run in to?"

"I paid attention to the living and corporeal creatures I was likely to see on my calls," Dean replied. "I didn't pay much attention to the part about ghosts and creatures from beyond the grave. And how do you know about the library at Station U, anyway?"

"Uh, I mean, doesn't everyone?" the teen replied. "Anyway, we need to find out where the revenants are holding Ashley. The coven's scrying told us they plan to leach her power away and use it to open a permanent hole in the wards between our worlds."

Dean thought for a moment. "So these revenants are the ones sending the Oni demons after me. Why?"

"We have to figure that out," Jaz said, "among other things. The attack on my family, the attacks on you, and Ashley's disappearance are all tied together. Once we find the common threads we'll...."

A knock at the cabin door interrupted her thoughts. Dean turned to answer the door, but Jaz drew her pistol and jumped in front of him, picking up her katana where it was propped by the door. When she was set with sword and pistol in hand, she nodded to Dean to answer.

A glance through the peephole in the door showed two men. Well, actually a man and a teen boy of about fourteen or so. Dean looked at Jaz, shrugged and opened the door.

"Uh, can I help you?" Dean asked.

"My son said you were here and maybe in some kind of trouble," the man said. When Dean looked at the boy and then back to the father, the man continued. "He said you met last night by the lake?"

"Oh, the lion," Dean said. "Please come in." He stepped back and gestured to the pair. The father led the way and the boy followed. The man stopped and Dean heard a growl deep in the man's throat. He shot a glance back at Dean, showing his teeth.

"You invite us in, but have an armed hunter waiting to kill us?" the man said. He crouched and turned to snarl at Jaz. She shifted to a defensive stance and raised her sword up over her head.

Dean jumped between the two of them. He pressed his hands

outwards to stop both of them from advancing on each other. "Stop. Stop right now. I mean it," Dean shouted.

He looked back and forth between the two. Jaz looked ready to kill Dean on the way to the pair of shifters. Her eyes were blazing in fury at him. The man was no less angry but they had halted their advance on each other.

"Jaz, put the sword down," Dean said. "These people have done nothing to harm us. The boy was the lion I met last night during his shifted travels." Dean turned his head towards the man, "Sir, we mean you no harm. We have traveled a long way, and have had troubles with those who follow us. That is why she answers the door armed."

Jaz started to lower her blade, but didn't really relax. The man took a step backwards, though Dean noticed that the fingernails on his hands were slightly elongated and ended in points. He had partially shifted. Still, he had not attacked, and they were ready to talk, not fight, and that was a step in the right direction.

"I'm Dean, Dean Flynn. I'm a paramedic from Elk City." He held up his right hand to show the tattoo to the father.

"I'm Albion Nutt and this is my son Arlo," the man said. "Arlo says you talked to him and he said you needed assistance. He said you mentioned the Eldara who visits this place?"

"Yes, Ashley Moore. She is a good friend of mine." Dean said. "She is missing and in our quest to find her, her abductors attacked us. We were forced to flee here to plan our next actions."

"Way to go, telling everyone our whole plan, Dean," he heard Jaz mutter.

Jo came over and introduced herself.

The man looked at the three of them and gave Dean a crooked grin. "You three are an odd group of companions to quest for a missing Eldara."

Jaz said, "Don't get me started. It wasn't my idea."

That comment made Albion laugh out loud. He kept laughing until he noticed the others staring at him. "I'm sorry. I know this is no laughing matter to the three of you. The whole valley is honored by the visits of the Eldara to this region. It makes us proud that she would choose our quiet lake and forest to make a place of rest and solitude in-between her travels. Of course we will help you."

Albion looked to Dean, "Have you tried to reach out to the Dryads? Their patriarch is the leader of the vale, Enric. He would know best how to help you."

Dean smiled. "That was where I was headed last night when I got turned around in the woods and ended up by the lake with your son."

"Well, we can take you there now, if you'd like?" Albion offered.

"I would like that," Dean replied.

"We would like that," Jaz said after clearing her throat. She looked at Dean. "I'm not letting you get lost traipsing around the woods again. We'll all go together."

"If that is your wish," Albion said. Dean thought he seemed uncertain about taking the hunter along on the trip to Enric's house but decided not to argue about it.

"Albion, my interests in this quest are no less important than Dean's. My family owes the Eldara a debt of honor and I would repay that for my family." She stopped for a moment and stared off past Dean for a moment, gathering herself before continuing on. He knew she must still be reeling from the apparent loss of her parents last night. The fact that she refused to break their radio silence to check on them was a surprise to Dean, but she said that it would only serve to pinpoint them to the enemy.

"A debt of honor I understand," Albion said with a nod. "May I have your assurances that you mean no one in the valley harm?"

"I mean harm to none who don't wish to harm us," she replied. She met the werelion's eyes. The two considered each other for a time and then the elder shapeshifter nodded, as did Jaz. That was settled.

"So, when can we get started?" Dean asked. "I'd like to see Enric, Asha and their family again."

"You know them?" Albion asked, then he snapped his fingers on one hand. "Of course. You are the paramedic who was here and helped heal Enric's daughter, Zora."

"That's me."

"I'm sure they will want to see you as well, then," Albion said. "They talk about how you helped the Eldara and were her chosen companion. A great honor. Let us go, then."

Dean agreed and he, Jaz, and Jo gathered their limited things for a walk in the woods. For Dean, that meant his duty jacket. He was still wearing his uniform from the previous night. He had no additional clothes. Jo had a few things in her shoulder bag, but not much. Jaz was the most prepared for their sudden departure from Elk City. She had a full evacuation kit in the back of her SUV that didn't just include bundles of cash. She had several changes of clothes and the two large cases that Dean had helped her carry into the cabin the night before. She would not tell him what the contents of the cases were and he was not sure he wanted to know.

Jaz slipped her sword belt over her shoulders so that it settled across her back with the hilt jutting up diagonally over her left shoulder. She already had her pistol holstered on her left side and what she called her small Bowie knife on her belt on the right side. Albion waited while she gathered her leather jacket, which showed a brace of throwing knives still attached by Velcro to the interior of it.

"Are you expecting trouble, huntress?" the shifter asked. "I assure you that none in this valley mean you harm if you come in peace."

"If those who seek us come for us, you will be glad I have come prepared," Jaz said. "Let's go."

Albion and Arlo led the way out of the cabin and Dean brought up the rear, locking the door behind him and pocketing the key instead of replacing it under the fake plastic rock by the front porch where he had retrieved it the night before. He had wondered when they arrived how they would break in to the cabin but Jo got out and went right to the rock even in the darkness and giggled with glee when she came up with the key. He figured she had used some spell to find it.

The five of them headed off into the woods, this time in daylight, seeking the Dryad cabin.

Chapter 15

The journey to the Dryad community did not take that long. The tree fairies lived deep inside the forest and occupied a cabin built into a wooded hillside. Dean knew the rooms extended deeper into the hill than most would expect. Albion, Dean and Jaz were silent on the twenty-minute walk through the trees. Jo and Arlo, however, chattered the whole way there. She asked him about where he went to school and when he said he was taught at home by his mother, she laughed and said that she was home schooled, too, after a fashion.

Dean listened to the conversation with some amusement at how easily teens connected with each other. It was also the most he had heard about Joanna's family life or where she came from since they had met the night before. When Dean and Jaz had questioned her about it, she was evasive and did not give any direct answers to their queries. He wished they were walking longer because of what he might learn from the teens' conversation.

As they entered the clearing where the front of the cabin showed from the hillside, Dean recognized it right away. There was no one outside so Albion went up and knocked on the door. "Enric, Asha, come out. It is Albion and some guests."

There was no answer, and Dean and the others looked around the clearing for some sign of the Dryads. Albion knocked again. As he stood waiting, the door burst outward, knocking Albion backwards from the covered wooden porch. Then the Oni demon was on top of him. Dean watched as the shifter transitioned immediately to his mountain lion form and then the scaled demon and the enormous lion were rolling on the ground, in a snarling and roaring battle for their lives.

Dean didn't have much time to watch. Two more demons burst from the cabin's doorway and ran out at them. He saw Arlo shift form and join his father against the demon he was fighting. The sudden violence caused the shift to happen spontaneously. He heard shots to his left and saw Jaz, pistol in a two-handed grip, drop one of the charging demons with a full magazine worth of bullets into its head. He knew it wouldn't stay down for long from the experience at the diner the night before.

The final demon made it past Jaz and was headed straight for him when he saw it intercepted by a bolt of white light from his right. The demon seemed to stop in midair as it was leaping towards him. Then it fell to the ground as the light turned to white-hot fire that consumed it and left the netherworld creature a charred carcass on the ground in front of him. He looked to his right and saw Jo standing there, her right hand outstretched, palm forward, fingers spread wide as if she were trying to signal someone to stop. There was a glowing ball of white the size of a baseball rotating in front of her palm.

Dean turned back to the scene in front of him. Jaz had drawn her sword and held it in one hand as she ran over to the Oni she had shot. It was struggling to rise after taking a flurry of bullets to its head. With a sweeping motion, she hacked through its neck from above and removed its head. As soon as she did so, the demon's body turned into a red mist that dissipated into the air. He turned to see that Arlo, in his lion form, smaller than his father but no less powerful looking, had now latched his jaws on the neck of the Oni demon atop his father. He twisted his head from side to side as his jaws clamped down tighter. That must have done the trick because, with a snap of the younger lion's head on the demon's neck the Oni stopped struggling and went limp. Then, it too turned to mist and the two lions were left there on the ground, glancing around with puzzled looks.

Jaz walked over the still smoking corpse of the third demon and poked at it with her sword. She looked over at Jo. The young witch still stood wide-eyed with the ball of energy or magic or whatever it was swirling in front of her outstretched palm. She looked around at her companions and then back at the demon, a look of disgust and horror on her face, then she raised her hand upward and the ball of white light burst upward into the sky out of sight. The girl then collapsed in a heap, crying, after releasing the pent-up energy. Jaz ran to her side.

Dean looked around and tried to decide what he could do to help. He had been of little value during the attack itself, but perhaps he could do something now. Looking towards the shifters, he saw that Albion had returned to human form. He had a few scratches and scrapes on him from the demon's claws but Dean knew he would heal. Shifters regenerated after a time. Arlo was still in lion form and his father was talking to him in a soothing voice while the lion paced back and forth, letting out occasional growls and snarls. The younger shifter had less control over his transformation and would shift back once he had calmed down.

Dean decided that Jo needed help the most right now and went over to her. She was holding her right wrist in her left hand as she sat on the ground and sobbed. Jaz had an arm about her shoulders but was scanning the tree line and shooting glances towards the cabin door. He knew she was expecting another attack. Looking at Joanna's right hand, Dean saw what looked like a nasty, circular second-degree burn on her right palm. It was already blistering and the area around it looked red and painful. He didn't have a first aid kit with him but he did have a pack of four by four gauze in his uniform pants pocket. He wanted to keep that burn wound clean until he could dress it properly. The gauze would have to do until he had more supplies.

"Jo, I don't know what it was you did back there," Dean said, "but I want to thank you." He opened the pack of gauze and laid it gently on the wound in the girl's palm.

She looked up at him, blinking tears from her eyes. "I couldn't let the demon kill you, Dean."

"What was that?" Jaz asked. "I have never seen a demon outright killed like that. That one will never return. It is dead, dead, dead."

"I've seen you kill a demon before, Jaz, like back at the diner," Dean said. "They just kind of go 'poof' don't they?"

"That is what happens when you destroy their corporeal forms here on earth," Jaz explained. "Their spirit forms return to the netherworld, from whence they came. There they must regenerate for a hundred years before they can manifest again. But what Jo did was something different. She killed it, spirit and all. That demon will never return to kill again."

Jo looked up at Jaz. "It is called sun-fire. I have never done it before and it takes a great deal of power to do it just once. I basically open a small portal to the center of the sun and release a ball of fusion plasma from there in the direction of my choosing. It will consume, body and soul, anything it strikes."

"Plasma from the sun, huh," Dean said. "No wonder you burned your hand. I'm surprised the wound is not worse."

"I was stupid. I summoned another ball before I checked to see if I needed it," Joanna said. "I shouldn't have held it so long. The spell comes with wards against fire and heat, but it's the sun, you know, so it's not normal heat or fire. I also used up my power. I have a splitting headache and there's two of everything I look at right now."

"I have never heard of this magic before, but it seems dangerous," Jaz said. "If it strikes an innocent or one of us, we'll be consumed as completely. You must be careful."

"Of course I'll be careful," Jo said, rolling her eyes at the hunter. She sighed and held a hand to her head. "To be honest, I didn't know I could do it. I'd read about it and learned the theory of it, but no one has been able to cast it for centuries. Then again, no one has needed to try since the demon wars in the dark ages I think."

"That's probably why you didn't know what it was, Jaz," Dean said. "I'm sure she'll be careful using it in the future. If she hadn't used it here and now, though, I would be demon chow." He turned and looked around the clearing again. The last time he was here, there were children playing in this clearing and several families lived here. Where were the dryads? A horrible thought occurred to him.

He stood up and ran to the cabin set back in the hill and went inside. He looked around the outer room and then started to head back the hallway, into the hill's tunnels to the other rooms there. A hand on his shoulder startled him and he turned to see Jaz and Albion standing there.

"Let us go first. We can see better in the dark back here," Jaz said, handing him a penlight. "Here take this flashlight for yourself while we go in."

Dean stepped back as he turned on the flashlight to let the others take the lead. Albion went first and Dean could see he was partially shifted again, his talons extending past his fingertips. Jaz followed with her sword in hand. They hadn't gone far when Dean detected the characteristic scent of death and heard the moans and cries of the wounded. Albion must have been able to smell the stench and hear the cries from the first room. It was why he looked so grim. He kept up with them as they went down the long hallway, checking each room to the right and left. These were the bedrooms belonging to the extended dryad family that lived here. They had shown Dean and Ashley such hospitality in the past when they had traveled to the valley on a weekend holiday.

They got to a room at the end of the hall. There were bodies piled in front of the door. The men in the family must have defended the door to the last against the demons. Albion looked back at them. "This is not going to be good," he said. "Prepare yourselves."

Dean had seen death and dying before but this carnage was beyond his experience. The men and parts of men were strewn about the floor. The smell was overpowering in the enclosed space. Dean heard retching behind him and he turned to see the werelion teen behind him turn and vomit on the floor. Jo had tears streaming down her face and she looked a bit pale, but when she caught him looking at her with concern she stood up straighter and nodded that she was all right. Arlo wiped his mouth with the back of his hand and tried to give Dean a weak grin.

"Arlo," Dean said. "Why don't you go back out and watch our backs. We don't want to be caught from behind by more demons. We've got this covered here."

The shifter boy nodded and looked grateful for the excuse. He turned and headed out to the front of the cabin. Dean turned back to face the door, standing amidst the bodies.

"Thanks for that, Dean," Albion said. Dean nodded in reply.

Dean looked around at the bodies and then saw movement. My God he thought. Some of them were still alive. He kicked himself for not doing his job right away and started gently pulling the grisly pile apart, checking each of the ten or so men and boys for a pulse. Four of them were still alive. When he found the first live survivor, he had to clear a gobbet of clotted blood from the teen's mouth and tilted the head back to open the airway. He wished he had a portable suction machine, but he didn't. Once he had succeeded in doing this much the boy's breathing eased some.

He felt a presence next to him and saw Jo at his side. He looked over at her and, despite the pale and startled look on her face, she nodded and took over holding the boy's airway open while he went on to find the next survivor.

"I need medical supplies, or these four survivors are not going to survive," Dean said.

"I have some things from the SUV back at the cabin," Jaz said. "I'll go with Arlo and bring back one of our medical kits."

"What's in it?" Dean asked.

"It's a standard combat medic's kit. There are two of them, plus a few personal kits," Jaz replied.

"Bring both of the larger kits. Hurry." Dean urged.

While Jaz ran off toward the front of the cabin, Dean took a SOF-T tourniquet out of the cargo pocket of his duty pants. He always carried one and this was another instance he was glad he did. The next survivor was bleeding from a gash in his upper arm and had already lost a lot of blood. The arm below the elbow had been ripped or bitten away. Applying the device and tightening the strap by twisting on the attached windlass he was able to stem the blood flow from the mangled limb.

Two down, two to go. Dean heard Jo ask Albion to hold the tilt on the first victim's head so his airway would stay open. He glanced over at her as he continued his work. She had started tearing strips from her long skirt and pressed the improvised cloth bandages into the worst of the first victim's wounds. There were several areas that appeared to be bite marks on the torso and she was trying to manage that patient's bleeding with her application of direct pressure and wound packing.

"You're doing a good job, Jo," Dean said. "Someone taught you well."

"My father was training me to be an EMT before I left to join the coven. He hadn't finished but we had gotten to the module on traumatic injuries. I can help," the witch teen said.

Dean nodded and went back to sorting the living from the dead. He had pulled the final two survivors out and was continuing to manage their serious wounds with what little he had when Jaz and Arlo returned with two black tactical backpacks. Jaz unzipped the first one so that it opened up with all its medical supplies exposed and laid out for him. Dean started grabbing supplies, including a needle decompression kit that he was going to need for victim number four to manage what he suspected was a tension pneumothorax or collapsed lung.

"Jo, do you know how to set up an IV bag for infusion?" Dean asked.

"Sure," Jo replied. "Doesn't everyone?"

Dean smiled. "I saw two IV bags in the first pack. There are probably two in the other as well. Get two set ups to run fluids for these patients when I get the IV's started on the worst two. Be ready to spike the other two and get them ready if I need them. Okay?"

"Got it," the teen replied and she set to work.

He thought he could get these four survivors stabilized for the time being now that he had the supplies he needed but they were going to have to get to a trauma center in order to survive. He looked around and saw Jaz and Albion pulling the dead from in front of a single door that ended the hallway.

Jaz reached out and tried the door handle but it did not open. Albion stepped forward and set his shoulder against it to shove. It did not move.

"It's barred or blocked from the other side," the shapeshifter whispered.

Dean looked at the men on the floor and then looked at the barred door. "What if there are more survivors on the other side? There are only males here. No women or children," Dean observed.

Albion nodded. "That makes sense. Let me try something." He stepped up close to the door again and called out. "Hello, is there anyone on the other side of the door? It is Albion and some other friends here. The demons are gone. It is safe to come out."

There was nothing so Albion knocked on the door and repeated his message. Finally a muted voice came from the other side. It was a woman's voice.

"Albion, it is Asha," the voice said. "How do we know you are not some trick of the demons? They tried to get past the door with force. Perhaps you are trying to trick us?"

Dean called out from where he was working on getting another IV started, "Asha. It's paramedic Dean Flynn. Do you remember me? I helped to heal your daughter Zora last year. I am Ashley Moore's companion."

"Paramedic Dean," Asha's voice called. "I remember you. Tell me, what were my daughter's injuries?"

"She had two broken legs and a serious infection, Asha," Dean said. "A tree had fallen on her when she tried to stop human loggers from cutting in the forest."

There were murmurs and scraping sounds from the room on the other side of the door and then the door opened a crack with some light from the other side spilling out into the hallway. Albion stepped into the opening. Dean thought he was trying to block the view of the carnage in the hall from those in the room. A face appeared in the partially opened doorway. It was Asha. She looked both worried and relieved at the same time.

"What of Enric and the other men?" she asked. "We heard the fighting and screams and feared the worst."

"There are some survivors, but I'm sorry Asha," Albion said, "most of them gave their lives protecting you. Dean is working to save the few survivors now. We want to get you others out of there, but let us clean up the hallway a bit first. Don't come out until we call you."

The dryad woman choked back a sob, but she nodded at him and stepped back from the door, closing it. Again, Dean heard frantic voices from the other side and then cries and sobbing. He could only imagine what it must have been like to be on the other side of that door, listening to what was happening out here in the hallway.

Jaz said, "I'll get some sheets from the other bedrooms. We can cover the bodies out here and clear a pathway to get them outside. It will shield them from the worst of it."

Albion and Jaz set to work shifting the dead bodies, and parts of bodies, from in front of the door so they lay against the sides of the hallway. Jaz used a pile of sheets to cover the remains. There was now a path through the hallway to the outside.

Dean was finishing up his work on the final survivor when Jaz rapped on the door again. "Asha, it is all right to come out now. Carry the children, and stay to the middle of the hallway."

The door opened again, this time wider, and revealed a small bedroom packed with the women and children of the dryad clan. Asha and Zora were the first Dean saw and the older dryad woman rushed over and pulled Dean close in a hug. He felt Zora join in. He held them while they expressed their relief.

"Come on," he said, breaking the hugs. "Let's get everyone out. I've got more work to do on the survivors, then we can talk and share what happened here together."

Asha nodded and started gathering the women and children. Albion led the way while Dean and Jo continued their life-saving work. Jaz stood by in another doorway. As they passed the women saw the shrouded shapes on the floor and blood on the walls and the crying began. Dean knew he would hear that keening sound in his nightmares for a long time to come. He redoubled his efforts to save the living and went back to work packing wounds and assessing his remaining patients.

Chapter 16

It took Dean and Jo another ten minutes to finish stabilizing the four patients as best they could. Then he used some more sheets to fashion litters to move them all outside. He'd have more light there and could do a better re-assessment than in the darkened hallway with his single flashlight. He didn't know how Jo managed as well as she did and chalked it up to better eyesight.

Asha, Jaz and Albion came back in and helped him move his patients out into the clearing in front of the cabin while Jo stayed inside until the last had been brought out. When they got into the sunlight, he noticed that all the injured appeared somewhat improved. Then Asha and some of the other women began to bring small pots of something over to injured dryad men. The women pushed Dean aside and started peeling off the clothing that Dean and Jo hadn't already removed from the patients. When the men were nearly naked, the women started smearing a green paste on the exposed skin. He watched as the paste was instantly absorbed adding a greenish tinge to the skin of his patients.

"What is that, Asha?" Dean asked.

"It is tree paste," she said. "You would call it chlorophyll. It

111

comes from the trees that sustain us and we use it whenever one of us is injured. It helps the body sustain itself while it heals."

Dean looked down at his four patients. Their bleeding had slowed or stopped soaking through his bandages and their faces had more color. Far be it for him to doubt the healing abilities of his patients. They would still need some sort of advanced medical attention but he could see that it was much more likely now that they would survive.

"Asha, that is a good thing, but they all still need to go to a hospital. They have internal injuries and need stitches," Dean explained.

"Some of the women will take them by car to the city. It will be faster than waiting for an ambulance to get all the way out here," Asha said. "Zora and I will remain here with the others and tend to the children."

Dean nodded. It wasn't a perfect solution but she was right in that it was probably thirty minutes before an ambulance could get here in the remote valley. They could be halfway to the nearby county hospital by then.

"I know you don't like to use human facilities, Asha. Do you want me to come along?" Dean asked.

"No," she replied. "There is a doctor there who knows us and knows of our differences. He trained in Elk City with one of your doctors. He will watch out for us."

She motioned to one of the other dryad women who went and started a beat up old Chevy Suburban parked under the trees nearby. Dean and Jo helped the women package their patients and arrange them in the back of the SUV as best they could. Two other women climbed in with the driver and then the vehicle left.

"At least the demons didn't get all of them," Dean said as the makeshift ambulance pulled away down the long dirt lane. "That has to be one small blessing in all of this."

"But what were those creatures doing here in the first place," Albion said. "I haven't heard any reports of other attacks nearby and our valley is sheltered and off the normal travel routes around the state."

Jaz, Dean, and Jo all shared a look and the elder werelion picked up on it.

"That is what has been chasing you?" he asked, pointing to the burnt carcass nearby. "Why didn't you warn us?" He sounded angry.

Dean spluttered in an attempt to come up with an answer. The fact was he was blaming himself a bit for this, too. Jaz stepped in and spoke.

"I'm not sure they came here for us," the hunter said. "If that were the case, why come here and attack the dryads when we were just a few minutes away? It doesn't make sense. No one knew we were coming here. It couldn't have been us that brought them."

"Well, if you didn't bring them here, what did?" Albion asked. He was frustrated and it showed in the way he flicked his still-manifested talons against each other, making a clicking sound.

"I think it may be this," another voice said, entering the conversation. It was Asha. She approached them carrying a bundle she had retrieved from the cabin. Dean wondered what it was. What could have drawn the demons to attack the dryads here?

"About two months past, the Eldara Ashley Moore came and visited us. She told Enric and me that she had bought the cabin in the woods and would be staying there for a time. She also gave us this bundle and asked us to keep it safe and hidden, telling no one we had received it. We were honored to receive the gift of trust from an Eldara and we owed her a life-debt anyway." Asha glanced down at the long, thin bundle she carried. It was about three feet long and a few inches across. It was wrapped in white cloth and tied up with rough twine.

"Eldara Ashley told us that if she disappeared and did not return to claim it in one moon's passage, that we were to take precautions to protect the cabin. Also, we were only to give this to one known to us as Ashley's friend, relative or companion." Asha held the bundle out to Dean and bowed her head slightly. "Paramedic Dean Flynn, we know that you are companion of the Eldara Sister. I believe she meant this for you if she did not return in the allotted time."

Dean took the bundle. It felt lighter than he expected based on how Asha was carrying it. As his hands touched the cloth, and he ran his fingers along the length of the bundle he thought he knew what it was. At least, he knew what if felt like. He pulled at the knots holding the fabric wrapping on the object and pulled the covering away, revealing a shining silver sword blade. It felt unusually light-weight, considering how big it was and that it was made of metal.

There was a gasp from everyone around him when he held it up so all could see it. Even Jaz seemed surprised by what she was seeing. Albion looked like he was about to bow down before it and Dean both. Only Jo seemed unsurprised by the arrival of the shining sword in their midst. Why had Ashley left some sword behind in the care of the dryads and told them to give it to him when the time came? He filed that away in the list of questions he had for his girlfriend when they reunited.

Dean didn't believe it was a real sword. While it was shiny, it had very little heft to it. He thought it might be plastic painted to look like metal with some sort of glossy covering. He went to wave it and take a few practice strokes in the air, but Jaz came forward and laid a hand on his arm.

"Don't do that, Dean. You act like you have no idea what you're holding," she cautioned.

"It feels like a really well made plastic replica of a sword," Dean responded. "You hold it, but it has no weight at all." Jaz stepped back from him and she had a look of, something, fear or horror in her eyes. "What? I thought you liked swords."

"That is a heavenly blade, Dean," Jaz said. "Every Eldara has one, even the Eldara Sisters. It is the manifestation of their divine power and mission here on earth. No mortal should even be able to touch it. Yet here you are swinging it around like a fool." She tilted her head to one side, giving him a quizzical look. "What are you?"

"I'm human, just like you, Jaz," Dean said. He looked at the blade again, trying to decide what to do with it. He touched the blade end with his thumb and, before he knew it, had cut himself rather badly across three of the fingers on his left hand. The blade was so sharp that it didn't hurt immediately, which was why he had managed to cut himself so deeply before he noticed. Drawing the hand away as if touching a hot pan on the stovetop, he clenched his fingers into a fist to stop the bleeding. As he watched, the little bit of blood on the blade, smoked to ash and fell away, leaving no evidence of it behind.

"See, I'm bleeding. I told you, I'm human," Dean snapped, a bit of anger at his stupidity coloring his voice. "Anyway, you're also partly right. It's a real sword of some sort. That blade is razor sharp." His hand was starting to throb and he held his clenched fist close to his chest while holding the sword away at arms-length. Someone needed to wrap that blade up again before someone else got hurt messing with it.

Asha came in and picked up the cloth in which the sword had been wrapped. Without touching any part of it directly, the dryad took the sword from him and wrapped it back up again. Her daughter Zora came over and helped tie the bundle of cloth-covered sword closed.

Dean watched the blade get put away and when his fingers separated from it, he felt like he was losing part of himself. It was strange, but it was like the blade had connected to something deep inside of him and now that it was taken away, he noticed a hole inside that he had never noticed before. This was not a new void, but one that had always been there, unknown, until his contact with the sword had filled it. It was strange and it made him feel a little queasy.

"Dean?" Jaz asked. She was looking at him with growing concern. "Are you all right? You just turned pale as a ghost."

"I think it's just the pain in my hand," Dean lied. "It will be better soon. I just need to dress the wound and wrap it up." He looked down at his hand where he clutched it to his chest. There was no longer any blood dripping from his clenched fist so he had gotten the bleeding to stop. It would probably start up again as soon as he opened up his hand. He still had a few of the gauze dressings in his pockets. He pulled them out and opened his hand. They'd do the job for now. He was probably going to need stitches. The cuts had been deep.

He looked down at his hand and searched for the wounds amidst the crusted and dried blood on the inside of his hand. He remembered cutting his fingers and still felt the pain, sort of. Come to think of it, he realized he was feeling the memory of the pain. As soon as he thought about it, he realized that the pain was gone. His hand ached from clenching it so tightly for so long to stop the bleeding, but that was it.

He examined the inside of his fingers between the two joints, looking for the cuts from the blade. They weren't there. Instead there were lines of thin, white scar tissue there where the cuts had been. It was like he had cut himself weeks ago and the wound had healed perfectly. The dried blood was there to prove he had done it, but not just minutes before. He didn't want the others to see, so after wiggling his fingers a little, he pressed the small stack of gauze squares against his fingers and closed his hand again.

"It'll be all right," Dean announced to the others watching him. "I got the bleeding to stop and I'll finish bandaging it up when we get back to the cabin." He held out his free hand and took the sword bundle back from Asha, taking care to grip the package by the hilt end of the sword and not the blade.

He looked around and his gaze stopped on Joanna. She was looking at him with a grin on her face. She held a finger to her lips and pursed them in a shushing gesture. She knew he had healed, he was sure of it, but how did she know? He wanted to go over and ask the teen witch, but could not right that moment, here in front of everyone.

"Dean we need to get these women and children situated somewhere," Jaz said. "They can't stay in there and we cannot bring them back to the cabin, either. There's not a lot of room and that is where the next attack will likely take place if there is one."

Dean looked at her, not knowing what to do. She was right about them not staying there until the interior of the dryad's cabin had been cleaned up. He looked to Albion with an arched eyebrow, forwarding the question to him. The elder shapeshifter glanced about the clearing and nodded to his son.

"Arlo, go home and tell your mother what has happened here,

then go to the rest of the valley council and tell them the same," he said. "Tell them we need to provide shelter for the dryads and also need the strongest of the area to begin patrolling the valley. If there are more of these demons around, we must find them and stop them before they attack anyone else."

The boy nodded and ran off at a trot for the forest's edge. He was gone from sight in seconds. Dean wondered aloud about what the other Unusuals of the valley could do if the demons returned again.

"Between Arlo, his mother, and I, we can handle a large portion of this side of the valley," Albion began. "There is a small pack of werewolves that live at the far end of the valley. They don't mix with us often but this is an emergency. They'll do what needs to be done. Then there's Old Barney. He's a werebear. He's more than a match for one, or even two of these things. We'll keep this valley safe. It's our home, after all."

"We need to go back to our cabin and regroup, too," Jaz announced. "Dean and Jo, come on. We've got some planning to do. That sword's presence here gives me an idea of how we can find our missing Eldara, or at least find out what happened while she was here."

Dean didn't want to leave the dryads alone in the woods after their ordeal, but when he looked around, Asha had already organized them into small groups and they were salvaging things from their cabin. They had assembled a few sacks of clothing and were spreading a cloth on the ground to prepare some food. It appeared they didn't need his help right now after all.

Jo and Jaz were already waiting for him at the edge of the clearing. He nodded to Albion. "Come get us if you need anything from us, or if you learn anything new."

The other man nodded and Dean joined the two women at the other side of the clearing. Together they headed back down the trail. He had questions for his two companions about this heavenly blade and what they knew about it. Then they had to plan. It was time to do more than just react to everything that was happening. It was time for them to intervene on their own behalf.

Chapter 17

The walk back to the cabin was a quiet one. Jaz led them with Jo following her. Dean brought up the rear. He held the bundled up sword in one hand while he clutched the unneeded gauze in his left hand. He was looking forward to getting back to the cabin. He knew he needed to clean up that hand and look at it carefully, but still did not know how it healed so quickly. The amount of blood was proof of the severity of the wound. So what had happened back there?

Everyone seemed shocked he could touch the sword. It was a bit like King Arthur removing the sword from the stone. Was he the chosen one in some fashion? Dean was still marveling at the sword, too. He could still picture the silvery, reflective surface, the light weight, and the razor's edge. He also could picture the blood burning off the blade, turning to ash and flaking away, leaving the blade unblemished. If nothing else, seeing that with his own eyes had assured him that the sword was magical in some way.

Jaz had said she had a plan to find Ashley by utilizing the sword. He wondered what it could be. He was still pretty new to the world of Unusuals and knew there were many things that he didn't know. Jaz had been raised in and around the lore of that world, even if it was as an adversary to those he considered friends. She must know a lot more about what can be done with an artifact like the heavenly blade.

He was still contemplating the true nature of the sword when they arrived back at their cabin. There seemed to be no signs of intrusion but Jaz didn't take any chances. She stopped them at the edge of the woods and observed the cabin for a few minutes from a hidden location. Then she had them stay behind her while they approached the front door. The hunter had her sword out in one hand and a pistol in the other. They stepped up on the porch and checked the door. Still locked. Dean retrieved the key, unlocked it, and they went inside. Jaz did a quick sweep of the small building and when she was finished with the upstairs loft bedroom, she nodded.

"It's clear," she announced. She holstered her pistol and sheathed her sword, and then removed the sheathed blade from across her back, propping it against a chair before she sat down.

"I've been meaning to ask you, Jaz," Dean said. "Why do you use a pistol when your sword is needed to kill the demons?"

"Two reasons, really," she said. "The pistol can't stop the demons permanently but it still injures them for a time. A series of well-placed headshots on any demon will scramble their brains. Sure, they'll regenerate enough to keep coming in a minute or so, but that gives you options to do other things like run away, or run in close and finish the job with an enchanted or blessed blade like mine. The other side of it is if you are close enough to a demon to use your sword, they are close enough to reach you, too. All things being even, I'd rather slow them down with a few, well-placed bullets, then banish them back to hell with a sweep of my blade. That's the better option every time."

She got up and crossed to the two large pelican cases they had carried in from the SUV the night before. Dialing in the combination lock on one, she opened it and pulled out a small zippered pouch. She closed the lid before Dean could see the other contents. Walking back to her seat, she unzipped the pouch and pulled out a rag, a can of some sort and some assorted tools, laying them on the side table next to her. He realized she was cleaning her pistol after firing it that morning.

Dean walked over to the kitchen area and turned on the water in the sink, letting it run while he unclenched his left hand. He half expected to see the wound had returned, that he had imagined it healing. When he opened his hand though, aside from the dried blood and a thin silvery scar, there was no evidence it had ever happened. He started washing the blood off in the sink and wondered what he should do.

"Here, Dean, let me help with that," Jaz said. "You can't bandage that hand on your own."

"It's okay," Jo said from across the room. "It's already healed."

"What?" Jaz hurried over to Dean and looked into the sink where he was washing his bloody hand. "That's impossible. I saw you cut it. I saw the blood. It was a deep wound." She looked at him again as she took a step backwards. "Dean, you have not been honest with me. With either of us," she said gesturing to Jo. "Are you some sort of shifter? That would explain the regeneration, though not the fact that you can touch a heavenly blade."

"I'm as human as you, Jaz. I assure you," Dean said. He was pretty sure he was telling the truth, though he was beginning to think he didn't know the truth.

"Well, no human heals that fast, Dean. So come clean. What are you? If you aren't going to tell us your powers and abilities, how can we be a team on this quest? I need to know so we can maximize our chances for success."

"I'm not lying to you," Dean said. He was starting to get angry with her. Why wouldn't she believe him? "Look Jaz, not everyone in the world is out to get you or is your enemy. I'm the same guy I was when you met up with me yesterday. I eat regular food. I sleep in a bed. I walk in the sunshine. I'm as human as you are. Why won't you believe me?"

"Because you are hiding something. You are jeopardizing this mission, and this mission is all I've got left," she said. Dean could tell that she was getting angry with him, which just angered him more.

"Oh, you think you've got a monopoly on this mission's importance? You, the big hunter girl." Dean was shouting at this point. "I've got every bit as much tied up in this mission as you do. Don't try and take this whole thing over for your own agenda."

The hunter stepped towards him poking him in the chest. "If you insist on lying to me, I can't trust you. If I can't trust you then this partnership is over, period. Tell me the truth about what you are so we can get on with things."

He brushed her hand away. "Don't touch me. I didn't give you permission to touch me. And I'm not sure you're the right person for this mission in the first place. You are all 'kill first, ask questions later' and that is not the way I run things."

"Run things?" Jaz shouted at him. "You are not running things here. This is a mission of honor to the whole clan, or what's left of it. I'll not have some half-breed monster of some sort messing that up."

"Half-breed monster!" Dean shouted. He stepped up until he was inches from her face, staring down into her blazing blue eyes. "You trigger-happy whack-job, I told you I'm human. You don't get to label me like that…."

"Mom. Dad. Stop it. You can't fight right now. Not when Aunt Ashley is still in danger. Stop it, stop it, stop it!"

They stopped as Jo's voice reached them. She was standing up, fists clenched, tears rolling down her cheeks. Dean wasn't sure why she was crying and why did she call them that. Was she mocking them?

"What did you say," Jaz asked the witch girl. "Why would you call us that?"

"Because you two fight all the time. I want you to be the parents I remember, not these people, ready to kill each other. I miss you both so much. Please stop fighting." Jo pleaded.

"Wait, we remind you of your parents?" Jaz said. "I mean that's nice and all, but honestly, I'm a bit young to be your mother."

Dean looked from Jaz to Jo and back again. The blonde hair was the same, as was their build. Could it be true? But how? Jaz would never let her daughter become a witch, he was sure of that. Then he froze. She wouldn't do it unless the child was already spoken for - unless someone had already traded the life of her first-born daughter for a spell. Dean's heart sank. This was not going to be good. If the last fight was a bad one, this one was going to be a doozy.

"She doesn't mean we remind her of her parents," Dean said. He looked to Jo. "Isn't that right?"

"You know me?" Jo said taking a step towards him.

"I do, I just don't know how it could be, not yet at least," Dean responded.

"Oh, Daddy, I've missed you so much." The teen ran up to him, throwing her arms around him. He felt awkward as he patted her on the back.

"Will someone tell me what is going on here?" Jaz asked. "I feel like I'm missing something important."

Jo turned to her as Dean let go of the embrace. The girl wiped away her tears as she laughed. "You always hated this part of having me. You never accepted that I had to become a witch, Mom."

"Look, stop calling me that," Jaz said. "It is impossible for me to be your mother. I'm only twenty-two. I can't have a fifteen year-old."

"Asha warned me that you'd resist the truth if I revealed it to you," Jo said, laughing through her tears. "She said I'd have to show you something to convince you."

"Who is Asha? What are you talking about?" Jaz asked. "This is crazy. No Errington would become a witch. It would not be allowed."

"Asha is my coven leader," Jo explained. "Take off your jacket and show me your birthmark."

"What are you talking about? How do you know about my birthmark?" Jaz looked a little frightened. It was the first time Dean had seen something resembling fear in her eyes.

"Your family birthmark," Jo said. "The same one I have. Show it to me."

Jaz slipped out of her leather jacket. She was wearing a black tank top underneath. He saw what Jo was referring to right away.

There was a light brown birthmark in the shape of a shield on her left shoulder. She reached a hand up to cover it absent-mindedly.

Jo took off her brown vest and then pulled her white blouse over her head. Dean started to turn away then saw that she was wearing a camisole underneath. There, on her left shoulder was a matching birthmark.

Jaz looked at it, amazement in her eyes. She reached out a hand to touch Jo's exposed shoulder. She touched it, tracing the borders of the birthmark. She shook her head.

"There has to be another explanation," Jaz said, stepping back. "Maybe you're a long lost cousin none of us knew about. I told you, you are just too old to possibly be my daughter."

"Well I'm not from now, Mom," Jo said, laughing. "You don't have me until you're, like, twenty-eight or something like that. I came back from your future to help you find Aunt Ashley. Asha told me I was needed. That's the purpose for which I was born and training had begun. The coven cast the spell to send me back in time to you both. The spell worked better than I thought it would, though I had to run out in the street to stop you before you sped away."

Jaz looked at Dean. "Why aren't you arguing with her? This story is crazy. It's ridiculous." She stared into his eyes. "Isn't it? No Errington would become a witch. It would never happen."

Dean just shook his head. He had no idea how to explain this to her. He thought he had years to go before he would have to address the price he paid a few months ago for a particularly dangerous spell from the Elk City coven. They had demanded his firstborn girl as a price, saying they would take her in as she reached school age and train her as one of their own.

"I didn't have a choice, Jaz," Dean floundered for a way to say this. "The coven demanded a price and when they asked for a child I didn't even have as payment, I just went with it. It didn't seem to matter at the time."

"Wait, you're not kidding," Jaz said, staring at him, the fire returning to her eyes. "You gave away your daughter, my daughter,

OUR daughter, to become a witch and you say it didn't matter at the time."

"Look at her," Dean said, pointing to Joanna. "She turned out fine."

"She's a witch!" Jaz shouted. "How is that fine?"

"Here we go again," Jo muttered under her breath nearby.

Dean flinched as he saw Jaz's reaction start to build after their daughter's offhand comment. He steeled himself to take the brunt of it and to take his time explaining himself. This was going to be an epic argument. One for the ages.

Chapter 18

Dean puttered around the cabin straightening up and trying to stay busy. To say the level of stress was high in the small enclosed space was an understatement. It had been nearly eight hours since the heated argument between he and Jaz had died down. The sun was getting low in the western sky. It had been a long day. Since the argument, she had not said a word to either him or Joanna. Joanna had drifted off to a corner of the room and had put her earbuds in to listen to music. She was not talking to either of them either. Dean wondered what he was supposed to do.

When he had agreed to the coven's terms for casting their scrying spell a few months back, he had thought he would have years to face the consequences of the decision. Now he had been literally slapped in the face by them. That had been the point where Jaz had walked away from the argument and ceased talking, when she slapped him. Dean's hand drifted up to his face to touch the place where she had hit him. He wondered if this was considered domestic abuse.

He went over and sat down where the heavenly sword bundle still lay on the dining table. Having run out of things to do to keep busy, Dean decided to look more closely at the blade. He would be more careful this time, though he apparently healed from the blade's wounds quickly.

The argument about his 'powers' was still unsettled. It had been deflected by the fight about who Jo was, but it would have to come up again. Jaz insisted that the fact he could even handle the blade made him an Unusual of some sort, and that he had been hiding his true nature from her. How could he get her to understand that if he were different in some way, it was hidden from him too?

Dean reached over and untied the twine that held the bundled sword's cloth wrapping closed. He carefully pulled the cloth aside and looked down at the blade as it was exposed. The sword's brightness and gleam was not diminished in any way by the darkness that had filled the room as night started to fall. It didn't glow exactly, but the reflective surface of the blade seemed to capture any available light nearby and reflect and magnify it. The sword was beautiful, with delicate etching on the blade that seemed to be both decoration and words or runes of some sort. Dean didn't recognize the language or even the letters that made up its alphabet, but he was sure the blade's decoration meant something to the right person. Ashley, Ingrid, or another Eldara might be able to decipher it for him.

Moving his gaze up the blade to the hilt, he saw more intricate work there. The cross guard was of the same silvery metal of the blade and seemed to meet the blade without a seam of any kind, as if it were forged in one piece. The grip of the hilt was covered with a glossy white leather of some sort. When Dean leaned forward to examine it more closely he noticed the leather didn't have grain but tiny scales that made up its surface. Continuing his examination, he looked at the pommel where gripping silver talons, those one might see on an eagle or other raptor, clutched a multi-faceted white crystal.

He reached out to touch the sword and gripped the hilt in his right hand. And then he wasn't in the cabin any longer. It was disorienting and it took the paramedic a moment to realize he was seeing the new location through another person's eyes. They were walking through a cave or a cavern of some sort. No, it wasn't a cave. The walls appeared to be finished in some way. There were squared-off timbers supporting the walls and roof periodically along the passage. Here and there, he saw an old-fashioned oil lantern hanging from one of the supports, providing pools of yellow light along the way.

Dean tried to turn his head and look backwards but was unable to do so. He was locked inside the viewpoint of whoever this individual was. Dean and whoever's head he was in continued on their shared journey down the passage until they reached a junction in the corridor. Turning left down a different, narrower passage, they walked a bit further to a stout wooden door set in the rock wall ahead of them. There was a hinged panel in the door and a white, cadaverous hand reached up and opened the panel, leaning forward to peer through it into the room on the other side.

There was a figure, dressed in a dirty white gown, seated in a chair in the center of the room. No, the figure was tied in the chair, her hands bound to the chair's arms, and her ankles tied to the chair's legs. He couldn't see who it was. The long, dark and filthy, matted hair hung over the face as the person's head sagged down with her chin resting on her chest. He peered closer to see who it was, and as he did, the individual lifted her head and her familiar green eyes looked back into his.

"Dean, you must leave me," Ashley rasped, her voice rough as if she had been yelling or maybe screaming for an extended time. "It is too dangerous."

He tried to answer back as the cadaverous white hand slammed the panel in the door shut. As the latch clicked something rocked his body to the side and jarred his vision. He blinked and then he was back in the cabin. Someone was shaking him by the shoulder.

"Dean, can you hear me? Wake up, snap out of it. Are you all right?" He heard Jaz's voice, but it sounded far away, as if he were in both places at once even though he could see the cabin and the table and sword in front of him. He pulled his hand back from where he had been gripping the hilt and the rest of the vision vanished leaving him firmly in the cabin with Jaz and Jo.

"I said, are you all right?" Jaz repeated. Her annoyance was evident in her tone.

"I saw her," Dean said. "I saw Ashley."

Jo rushed over then. "You saw her? How? Where was she? Is she alright?"

"She's bound and looks like she's been mistreated. She sensed me looking in at her somehow," Dean said, relaying what he had just seen. "She told me to stay away."

"Are you sure it was her?" Jaz asked. "It could have been a delusion of some sort, or a spell cast on you."

"I wasn't a spell, Mom. I would know," Joanna said.

"Don't call me that," Jaz snapped.

Jo spun around and walked back to where she had been sitting. Dean could see she was hurt by Jaz's response.

"You don't have to take it out on her. She's not responsible for this. I am," Dean whispered.

"I know who is responsible and it is not, I assure you, Dean Flynn," Jaz replied. She shot him an angry glare. "You will not get off that hook anytime soon. We will have more than one long discussion on this issue, but now is not the time. I am honor-bound to help find the Eldara, and I plan on reuniting you with your true girlfriend as soon as possible. Then I will put as much distance as possible between us. Now go over what you saw again. Take it step by step."

Dean went over the vision from the first moment he found himself inside the other's head to the moment when he was wrenched back to the cabin and his own body. Jaz asked him several times to describe the hand he saw opening the panel in the Eldara's door. She seemed intrigued by it and Dean asked her why.

"I think you were occupying or sharing the vision of a revenant," Jaz said. "We know they are involved with this, and the dead-looking skin on the hand would match up with what I know about them and how they look."

"I could grab the hilt again and try to reconnect," Dean offered, reaching out to the sword on the table in front of him.

"No," Jaz said. "The revenant might have noticed your presence from either your own bumbling around in its head or from Ashley's direct communication with you. We have to be careful using that link moving forward. Do you know how you activated that ability?"

"I was thinking of her while looking over the sword up close," Dean said. "I jumped into the vision when I gripped the hilt."

"Okay, let's try not to do that until you learn to control what you can do better," Jaz said.

"How come you think it's me and not something the sword is doing?" Dean asked. "I want to understand more of what this blade can do. If it can help us find Ashley sooner, we should be using it."

"There's plenty that blade can do, Dean," Jaz said. "In the hands of a being from one of the higher planes, it is said to be able to heal that which cannot be healed. It also has a negative effect on those from the netherworld, the lower planes. If you strike a fatal blow to a netheworlder, you kill it, not just banish it back to regenerate in a hundred years, as my sword does. That blade severs not just skin and bone and sinew, it severs the soul's connection to the body of the creature it strikes. It's why I, and other normal mortal types cannot touch it. The divine power vested in it would consume us. The fact that you can handle it is proof that you are more than you say you are."

Dean started to object and Jaz raised a hand to stop him.

"I know you don't understand it any more than I do. I accept that. But, just the same, we need to understand it. It could be important to how we act later on in this quest. It could change what we do."

"So what do we do?" Dean asked.

"I could attempt a scrying spell," Jo offered from across the room. "We know that Dad-uh-I-mean-Dean connected with Aunt Ashley somewhere. Perhaps if I center the spell on him it will tell us where she is."

"No, it's too dangerous, Joanna," Jaz said. "That kind of spell puts you at risk if there are any sort of defensive wards in place. You would be opened up to the backlash."

"Aw, Momma, you do care," Jo said.

Dean saw Jaz tense up. He spoke up and tried to defuse the situation before another argument started.

"You can't have it both ways, Jaz," Dean said. "You can't treat her like your daughter one moment and turn around and tell her not to call you Mom the next. I say we treat her as a full member of the team, just as we have since the beginning. It's a calculated risk but one that would get us on the path to completing this quest."

Jaz looked at him and back to Joanna before she nodded. "All right, you can do the spell, but I want you to take precautions. If you detect any sort of wards in place, back off."

"I'm not stupid," Jo said. "Anyway, Asha says I'm more powerful than any of the other sisters in the coven. I can do this, especially now that we have the new connection between Dad and Aunt Ashley."

Dean looked at Jaz. She nodded and he nodded in return. "Okay, kiddo, let's do this. What do you need me to do?" Dean asked.

"I'm going to need to spend a few minutes meditating," Jo replied. She was bouncing a little in her seat in her excitement. "I need to settle myself down a little. This is going to be awesome. Okay, in the meantime, you can try to clear your mind. I don't want you to think about anything. When the time comes, I'll ask you to reach out and touch the sword hilt again but don't try to reconnect with Aunt Ashley. Just think about the blade. I'll make the connection through you."

"All right," Dean said. "You will be careful with this, right?"

"Absolutely," Jo responded. "You get set. I'll be ready in a sec."

Dean and Jaz watched their newly revealed witch daughter settle onto the floor, sitting on a throw rug in front of the cabin's rustic couch. She crossed her legs as she sat down and rested her hands on her knees, then she closed her eyes and was still for a minute or so. The other two in the room sat at the table and waited until she was ready.

Jo opened her eyes and Dean almost thought he could see a white glow surrounding her. It was as if her image was shimmering, like she was a video of a person superimposed on the image of the room. He reached out and laid his hand on the hilt of the blade, working to keep his mind clear as he did it by thinking about random EMS drug protocols. As his hand contacted the sword, the room again vanished from in front of him, swirling away into darkness. It had begun.

Chapter 19

Jaz sat at the table, watching Dean and Jo as the spell took effect. Dean sat up straight and started staring straight ahead, but his eyes glazed over and were unfocused. Jo sat on the floor nearby, like a statue, immobile and almost humming with magical energy. Jaz' amulet's night vision function let her see into the non-visible light spectrum that humans could not ordinarily see. That let the hunter catch a hint of, well, some sort of waves emanating from the witch girl.

She still couldn't quite wrap her head around the upheaval in her life that had struck her in the last two days. Her mother, father and the rest of her clan had likely been wiped out in the explosion and fire at their offices in Elk City two days ago. She couldn't even come forward to ask for information about them because of the nature of their quest, and the authorities probably counted her among the dead anyway. Then she had discovered, against everything she had been raised to believe, she had a daughter, who had come back from the future in some manner. A daughter who was a witch. Hunter children didn't grow up to be witches and use witchcraft, they grew up to guard against them. But, then, that particular wrinkle was Dean's fault.

Jaz thought about Dean. She knew they had not started off on the right foot with their clash in the self-defense and safety class she taught at the fire academy. To his credit, he sought her out to try and make things right. That didn't make him any less infuriating, however. He was good at what he did, and he knew it. He also had learned to accept the Unusuals in a way she thought she never could. She knew that her upbringing carried a certain prejudice with it. That was necessary to maintain the skepticism and vigilance to catch the creatures that were out to harm mankind. Now it appeared he had some sort of supernatural background himself, not that he was likely to admit it to himself. Jaz accepted that it was something he honestly didn't know and she did not have a clue as to who or what he could be. Touching that heavenly blade uninvited should kill any human or normal Unusual on contact. At the very least, Dean should have received some sort of shock or burn from it.

But he was sitting here in front of her, his hand laid across the hilt of that divinely wrought sword as if it were made of plain steel. It was as if he did not understand the rules, so he just chose not to follow them. There was that sort of obstinacy to admire in the man. He didn't give up easily on a concept or on people he knew. That type of loyalty was hard to come by. Once he joined a team, he was with that team one hundred percent. She had seen it happen with their small team. Or should she call it a family? It was a dysfunctional one, if it was a family at all. She shook her head in disbelief. Somehow, someway, the two of them were supposed to get together and then stay together long enough to raise a daughter who knew them as her mother and father.

As she watched his face, she wondered what he was seeing in that intense stare. She was not aware of any way to join their magical conference call with whatever connection Dean had with the Eldara to whom her family owed a life debt. Jaz chuckled to herself. The man who was to be the father of her future daughter, was the very committed boyfriend of that same Eldara. How was that going to work out for any of them? Jo called her Aunt Ashley, so she knew the woman. It was just that Jaz could not see how she would let any man she was with associate with a former lover after they started seeing each other. Not that there was a whole lot of men in her life. She had dabbled with some random encounters when the mood struck her, but none of them had meant anything to her, and they were certainly not the type who she would count as a long-term love interest.

She had always envisioned that her mate would be someone who would remain behind while she went out on hunter missions and encounters. He would be someone who would understand her non-traditional background and lifestyle. It would almost have to be someone from outside the hunter clans. Men in the hunter clans would never take a backseat to a female hunter. In their patriarchal world, she would be expected to hang up her sword and turn out hunter babies to replenish the clan's ranks. That would be their version of an honorable role for her. The very thought of it disgusted her. No, she would find new blood to bring into the clan. It was not unheard of, and she would have set her own expectations for the newcomer about what a woman in the clan was expected to do.

Her eyes were drawn back to Dean again. He might have been a perfect person to fit that role in her life if she didn't already despise him so much. As she watched him, his back stiffened and his eyes widened as if he were seeing something startling. Again she wondered what might be there wherever his mind was, and what he was seeing. She shifted her gaze to Joanna, but nothing had changed there. The witch girl still held her position on the floor and looked to be silently meditating if it weren't for the barely visible waves of energy coursing from her.

Jaz settled back, taking a whetstone from her baggy utility pants pocket. She drew her Bowie knife. She had been taught an idle hunter was a dead hunter, so she began the long careful strokes of the blade on the stone that honed it to a razor's edge. She was a hunter. She knew how to wait for things, be it her quarry or the answers she sought.

AS SOON AS his hand made contact with the sword's hilt again, Dean found his point of view changed. He was staring out of another' eyes at a forested hillside. His angle of view was from above and looking down the side of a large hill, or small mountain. The dark green of the treetops below blanketed a broad valley with a lake in the center. The sun was just setting beyond the ridge to the west casting the mountain's shadow across the valley floor. The image shifted as whomever it was turned and walked back into a cave set in a mountainside. From the finished look of the cave corridor, Dean was confident this was the same cave system that he had seen before. He was close to Ashley again and he tried to remember and note every detail that might help him and his friends pinpoint its exact location.

He walked back down the long, rough-hewn rock corridor leading back into the mountain, proceeding straight until a side passage to the right opened up. Turning down that branch of the cave system, Dean watched as the individual whose point of view he shared took him down a sloping path until it opened into a cavernous chamber deep in the mountain. There was the sound of running water nearby in the darkness, and though he could see well in the dark given his host's abilities, he could not penetrate to the depths of the large room's far walls.

There was a strange purple glow to one side and that was their destination. On one wall of the cavern there was a large oval of glowing purple energy swirling on the wall. It was easily ten feet tall and six feet wide and looked like a sickly purple and yellow bruise projected on the wall. Whoever his host was, they stopped together in front of the shimmering surface of the energized oval. It filled his field of vision. He heard a raspy voice and it took him a moment to realize that it was his host's voice.

"The hunting party sent to secure the blade has not returned," the voice said. "I fear it has been intercepted."

A second voice answered from the other side of the magical field. "This is both fortunate and not," the second voice said.

It would have sent chills down his spine, if he was in his own body right now, Dean thought. It had the same quality as the scratching of a thousand cockroaches all at once in his head. It continued.

"We have lost more of our Oni brethren and they are a finite resource in this endeavor. That is unfortunate. But our seers warned us that the Hunter, the Healer, and the Hexen were on their way to us. Who else but they would have the power to stop a hunting party of three Oni?" Dean watched as the swirling purple oval pulsed with each of the other voice's words.

"So they are here?" Dean's host said. "How is that fortunate?"

"Because they have not realized their full power yet as questers," the voice from beyond the purple portal said. "They must accept their shared bond in order to become as powerful as they could become. Before they will be able to accomplish that, we will reach our goal and drain the soul of the Eldara in order to hold open this portal indefinitely. Then there will be nothing they can do to stop us from taking this entire area for our own."

"We must still pay our benefactor for helping to secure the Eldara for us in the beginning," Dean's host said.

"He demanded the healer be taken alive and the hunter clan eliminated," the portal's voice pulsed. "We will fulfill our end of the bargain. The clan has been removed from the picture, yes?"

"All indications are that the rest of the clan was consumed in the fire," the host's body said with sickening glee. "There will be no descendants other than the one who has come to us. There will be no one to continue to hound our benefactor's long-term plans, I assure you."

"He will be pleased with that news. Now we must finish the task assigned to us so we will gain the knowledge from him to use the Eldara's soul to maintain this portal indefinitely." The portal's colors shifted and began to coalesce into distinct shapes. "I will send through a larger party of Oni to complete the final part of our bargain. Use them wisely. They are among the last available to us."

"As you wish, Master." Dean's host stepped back from the portal as the shapes continued to solidify. He knew what to expect based on the conversation, so he was not surprised when the first Oni demon stepped from the purple borders of the magical oval on the rock wall. What did surprise him was that the procession of demons continued for some time. Dean lost count at fifteen and was pulled out, back to his seat at the table in the cabin. It took a moment to refocus his eyes and he blinked while his vision returned to normal.

The paramedic looked around the room and saw Jo leaning forward where she sat on the floor, her fingertips rubbing at her temples. A glance to his left showed Jaz sitting in the chair next to his at the table. She had that frighteningly large knife out and appeared to be testing the blade's edge with her thumb. She looked up at him and quirked up an eyebrow in question while returning his gaze.

"Jaz," Dean said. "We've got trouble. They know we are here."

Chapter 20

"But how much do they know about where we are?" Jaz asked again. She was pacing from window to window, looking out at the cabin's surroundings for trouble.

"All I know is that they know we are in the valley here," Dean said. "They figured it out when the three demons we killed at the cabin didn't return. Oh, and they have some sort of prophecy or something like it of their own. The voice on the other side of the portal mentioned seers and the three of us."

"Okay, tell me the whole thing again from the beginning," Jaz said. "Don't leave anything out. Every detail could be important."

Dean closed his eyes and, for the third time, recounted what he could see and hear from inside his host's head in the vision. When he was done, Jo jumped up and pointed outside.

"That's it," she said. "I missed it before, but it's obvious now. They are somewhere in the mountains around this valley. That is why the demons came through the portal all at once like that. They are close enough to travel here on their own power. There must be old caves or something in these hills they are using."

"It makes sense, but that is bad news for us," Jaz said.

"Why?" Jo asked.

"Because that means the demons are closer than we think," the hunter said as she resumed her pacing to check the windows as the late afternoon sun streamed in from the southwest.

The knock on the cabin's door made them all jump. They relaxed when they heard Albion's voice from outside.

Dean opened the door as Jaz and Jo walked over to join him in the cabin's entryway. They saw Albion and three others standing outside on the porch. There were two men and a woman who Dean did not know.

"Hi, uh I thought I'd bring the other shifters from the area down to meet you guys while we were on patrol," Albion said. "Dean, Jaz, Joanna, this is Mark, Dawson, and Hannah from the pack at the north end of the valley."

Dean nodded and the three of them nodded in return. He looked at Jaz who stood still just staring at the three newcomers with a suspicious gaze. He nudged her with an elbow and she shot him a glance and then nodded to them herself. Jo stepped out onto the porch and shook all their hands, greeting them enthusiastically.

"Man, we can sure use you guys right now," Jo said. "After what we just found out, we can use all the muscle we can get."

Albion looked from the teen to Dean and Jaz with an alarmed look. "What is she talking about?"

"We just cast a little spell using the Eldara's blade to try and locate her," Dean said. "We think she is being held inside this valley somewhere. I was able to see caves or passages in the mountain rock shored up with wooden crossbeams. It all looked very old and broken down in parts. Does any of that ring a bell?"

Mark scratched his beard for a minute in thought, but it was Dawson who spoke up first. "It might be the old silver mines at the south end of the valley. They have been boarded up and closed for over 150 years now. It would be a good place to hide out."

"It's not just a hideout," Jaz added. "They have opened a netherworld portal there and are bringing demons through to attack the valley. The last count was fifteen demons before we lost our connection."

Albion looked worried and Mark let out a low growl. Hannah

was silent, but Dean noticed her fingernails had suddenly elongated into claws. The four shifters shot each other glances and then looked back at Dean and the others in the cabin's doorway.

"Do we know where they are going or what their intentions are?" Hannah asked.

"It seems that they kidnapped the Eldara in order to drain her life force to create a long-term portal to the netherworld. I think they need her sword to complete the process," Joanna said. "The newly transferred demons are here looking for us, since we have the ability to throw a monkey wrench into their plans and rescue her."

Jaz jumped in, "I do not think they knew specifically where we are in the valley, though they will surely check here, and at the dryad's cabin, too."

"We cannot allow them to open a permanent portal here in our valley," Dawson said. "We would all become subservient to them and that is unacceptable."

"I don't know what we can do, Dawson," Mark said. "If they are already in the valley and heading this way, we won't have time to contact other packs to help, and we aren't strong enough to take them on by ourselves. There are only six adults in the pack, plus Albion and Arlo, and there's Old Barney the werebear, if we can find him. Even with the hunter, the witch and this human, it will never be enough to stop more than fifteen demons."

Jaz shook her head. "We need to take advantage of the demons being out in the valley looking for us and not in their hideout. Now is the perfect time to go there and try to get Ashley out." She looked at Dean and Jo.

Dean nodded and when he looked at Jo, the witch teen nodded, too. It made sense, even though it abandoned the rest of the valley's inhabitants to fend for themselves. He wished he could come up with a solution for them. Then he got an idea.

"I might have a way to get you all some help while the three of us head off on our rescue mission," Dean said. "We have to try and shut this portal down and get Ashley out of there before they get too strong. Jaz is right. This is the perfect opportunity to do that. But, there is another person who has a vested interest in this, someone who might be the best solution of all, if what I've heard about her is true."

Jaz looked at him with a curious glance, but Joanna seemed to see where he was going and nodded enthusiastically.

"Ashley, the Eldara, has a twin sister," Dean explained. "For reasons she can't tell me, she is unable to participate directly in the rescue of her sister, but she is a Valkyrie. I suspect she might enjoy coming to the valley to help you all deal with the demons. Does that sound like a good idea? I don't know her very well, and I've heard she makes a bit of a mess wherever she goes, but I think she's a ferocious fighter."

Albion smiled for the first time since he had heard about the demons on the loose in the valley. "A Valkyrie or two would be a welcome addition to our little militia," the werelion said. "I agree. They are strong warriors, and I think they would be interested in ridding the world of a few demons, seeing as how they are destined to face them in the final battle at the end of the world."

"Good, I'll contact her." Dean said. He looked up at the sky outside the cabin. "I don't know exactly how long this takes, but here goes." He took in a deep breath and shouted, "Ingrid, I need you."

"There's no need to raise your voice, you know," the smooth tones of Ingrid's British accent sounded behind him in the cabin.

Dean and Jaz both spun around in surprise. There stood Ingrid, dressed in her black leather pants and jacket outfit, just as Dean had last seen her. Joanna ran forward and wrapped the new arrival in a hug.

"Aunt Ingrid, I'm so glad to see you," Jo said. "Things are a little tense here and I could use a friend right now."

"Hey, Kiddo," Ingrid said with surprise. "What are you doing here and now? Aren't you a little out of place?" Ingrid looked at Dean and Jaz and then back at Jo. "Do they…?"

"Yes, they know who I am," Jo said. "That's why it's been a little tense."

Ingrid let out a long laugh at that statement. "Oh, I'll bet it has been, and more than just a little tense." She looked back at Dean and Jaz, "Don't worry you two. I know it's a bit of a shock, but you will both get over it eventually."

She walked forward and took in the four shifters standing outside. Turning to Dean, she said, "I assume you are using your one chance to call for help? Remember I cannot participate directly in Ashley's rescue. That option has been forbidden to me."

"I told them," Dean said. "But I think we have found a way you can help without directly fighting to rescue Ashley. How would you feel about helping this valley's residents fend off a few dozen Oni demons?"

"Ooo, you've got my attention," Ingrid cooed. "Go on, I'm interested."

Dean and Jaz explained the situation in the valley. Albion and Mark jumped in occasionally to lend their input about what the valley's residents could do. Dean pointed out that if they could tie up the demons in the valley, it would allow him, Jaz and Jo to slip around them and get to the abandoned mines at the caves.

Ingrid listened, asking questions when she didn't understand something about what Dean had learned through the sword's strange connected visions. When they were done explaining what they had in mind, Ingrid gave them a large, feral smile, showing her white teeth.

"This is going to be great fun," the Valkyrie said. "Plus, I think I can persuade one or two of my Valkyrie sisters to join the party, too. We haven't had a good demon hunt in years. I've got to go and make a few inquiries. I'll be back just after dark. We'll stage here at the cabin and lure them in. That should give you, Dean, along with your lady friends, a chance to move around them in the dark and make your way to where they are holding Ashley."

Dean nodded, cringing inwardly at the way Ingrid called his companions his lady friends. Albion nodded too, and he along with the three werewolf pack members trotted off into the woods north of the cabin. They had to gather their forces and get back here before dark.

Ingrid watched them leave and turned back to Dean. "This is going to be our one chance to get Ashley, Dean. You understand that, right?" He just looked at her. "If they can't have her for their portal, they will likely destroy her corporeal form, and her soul will be banished to the heavens until she can regenerate. She will be gone for the next one hundred years. We can't have that. There's a lot she has to do here on earth, so don't screw this up." She held his gaze for a moment longer and then looked up. "I've got to get going if I'm going to bring anyone back with me to help. See you in a bit."

Dean watched in amazement as a set of white-feathered wings spread from behind Ingrid. She launched herself off the porch and into the air, shimmering a little and then she winked out of sight as she flew away through the trees. He watched for a minute then came back to the present when he heard someone clear their throat behind him.

"Are you done ogling your girlfriend's sister, Dean?" Jaz said. "Because we've got some work to do here. If we are going to move quietly and without being seen in the dark by the Oni demons when they approach this house, we need to put some things in place. I have my amulet, but that just works for me. Joanna, can you create a spell of some sort to mask yourself and Dean from demon senses?"

"I have my hunter's amulet, too, I just didn't wear it because I didn't want to give away who I was. You gave me the amulet on my thirteenth birthday, just before I left to join the coven," Jo replied. The teen thought for a bit and said. "I could try something else for Dad, but I have to think about how I can pull it off."

"Good," Jaz said. She looked at her watch and then the surrounding skyline. "You've got two hours to figure it out and get it in place. Get started. Dean and I will pull together the gear we are going to need from the cases we brought in from the SUV."

Dean watched the hunter take charge as they finally had a plan of sorts to act on. This was her element and he was impressed as she opened up the larger pelican cases and set to work. He knew she was right. They didn't have much time.

Chapter 21

The three of them set to work. Jo sat down on the couch and began going through her large satchel purse. She had components of her spells and other items in there, including a few items of spare clothing. Jaz called Dean over to where she was opening up the two large cases. He had suspected at the time that the cases carried weapons a hunter might need on their operations. He was half right.

When Jaz unlocked the rolling tumbler locks and lifted the lids, Dean did see a startling variety of weapons. But there were also the two medical bags with two tactical medical kits. She pulled the medical bags out and handed them to him. He took them over to the table and slid Ashley's sword to the side so he could open them up and inventory their contents.

These medical kits weren't the same. He had the two tactical kits they had used with the dryad attack. There was also a standard individual first aid kit also called an IFAK. It was meant to be carried by an individual and had basic trauma supplies to treat and manage immediate life-threatening emergencies. It held a pair of black medical exam gloves, a SOF-T tourniquet, a few various combat gauze dressings, plus trauma shears, a needle decompression kit and basic airway management tools. It was all packed in a black bag with elastic loops to hold everything in place when it was unzipped and fully opened. The bag could be clipped to a belt or pack and was small and compact.

The other small kit was a little bit larger and was contained in a small black backpack carrier. It had everything included in the first kit, plus additional supplies he was glad to see. There was a 500 milliliter bag of lactated ringers IV fluid and a full IV kit. He also found several quick clotting solution impregnated gauze dressings and various bandages. There was a surgical airway kit and some basic field surgery supplies including a small suture kit to do stitches. He was also happy to see a medication pack attached to the inside by Velcro. It carried small containers of ibuprofen and acetaminophen for aches and pains in the field, plus there were also small vials of morphine, and naloxone to counteract an overdose and syringes to administer them. There was even an epinephrine auto-injector for severe allergic reactions.

Dean wasn't sure what he would need and opted to carry both since he wasn't going to be armed. At least he'd be prepared to provide care for Jaz, Jo, and eventually Ashley when he got to her. He attached the IFAK bag to straps on the bottom backpack so that it would sit below the small tactical backpack when it was worn. He was adjusting the straps and making sure it fit comfortably when Jaz came over and dropped something on top of the pile of medical gear on the table. It took him a moment to realize what it was. It was an empty sword scabbard and belt. He looked up at her where she stood next to the table.

"What's that for?"

"It's for your blade, stupid," Jaz said. "I took out the sword that was in there. It should fit your blade pretty well. You can't just carry it in your hand the whole time."

"I wasn't going to carry it at all," Dean told her.

"You can't go on this thing unarmed, Dean," the hunter said. "I need to know you can take care of yourself if everything goes to crap. Try it out and see if it fits, otherwise I'll come up with something else."

Dean thought about arguing further, but opted out. She was

probably right. He needed to be ready to defend himself and if he took the sword along, he could return it to Ashley. She might have some magical use for its powers. He picked up the blade and the scabbard. The blade slide home and seemed to fit pretty well for being a replacement. Jaz nodded in approval and walked back to her cases where she was organizing her kit.

Dean took a moment arranging the sword and scabbard on the belt. He was trying to figure out if he should carry the blade like Jaz did across his back or wear it on his hip. He decided that he could attach the scabbard to loops on the side of the medical backpack. He removed the sword belt from it and set to work using some spare Velcro straps to secure the scabbard to the medical bag so the hilt would stand just over his right shoulder. It was a bit thrilling to envision himself in the rig and he put the assembled medical pack on and stood to check out the look in the mirror on the wall.

"Looking good, Dad," Jo said.

"I really don't think you should be calling me that, Jo," Dean said. "I know it is true for you, but it just doesn't make sense in my brain. You are from twenty years or so in my future, right?"

Jo nodded and looked disappointed. It must have been hard for her to hide her true feelings for the two of them when she first arrived. He started wondering what he would do in her situation and started feeling sorry for the teen. He remembered how much he had needed his mom at that age. His dad had never been in the picture and he had only vague memories of him.

"Okay, look," Dean said. "You can call me Dean, or Dad, or whatever you want if that makes you feel better, but understand that I'm not there yet. I'm still wrapping my head around all of this. I know that it's possible you are my daughter come back from the future to help with saving a kidnapped angel. It is going to take me some time to adjust to this, okay?"

He suddenly found himself wrapped in a hug, and then the teen bounced away with a big grin on her face. He smiled back at her and went back to admiring his getup in the mirror. He reached up and tried drawing the heavenly blade free. It slid out of the scabbard easily with a soft rasping sound of metal on metal. He couldn't get the angle right to return it to the scabbard, though and figured that it took practice to do so. He shrugged out of the pack and then replaced the blade in the scabbard. He looked at his assembled pack on the table when he was finished. He was pretty much set to go. He turned when he heard the two women arguing behind him.

"No, absolutely not," Jaz said. She shook her head for emphasis, her ponytail whipping behind her head.

"But why not?" Jo pleaded.

"I'm not giving you a gun, Jo, and that is that."

"Look Mom, you need to get over this," Jo said. "You raised me. Do you think you, the last Errington hunter, didn't teach me how to handle weapons?" The witch teen pointed to something in the case in front of Jaz. "Unload that Glock and I'll show you I know what I'm doing."

Jaz hesitated for a moment, then reached into the case and extracted a pistol that looked like the twin of the one she now wore on her hip. She removed the magazine and racked the slide to check and make sure the chamber was empty. When she was sure the gun was not loaded, Jaz handed it to Joanna.

Jo sat down with the weapon and, in a series of fluid motions that only came from long-practiced muscle memory, proceeded to take the pistol apart. When she was finished she had the component parts laid out on the cushion next to her. She looked up at her mother with a grin. Then she reversed the process in another series of well-practiced moves, handing back the reassembled weapon. Dean had never had weapons around his home growing up, so he wondered again about whether Jo really grew up in a house with him as the father. He did not think he would allow guns in his house.

Jaz took the reassembled gun from Jo without a sound, inspected it. She slid in the magazine and racked a round in the chamber, then removed the magazine. She pulled back the slide to eject the shell in the chamber and expertly caught the bullet as it was ejected into the air. She thumbed it back into the magazine before replacing the magazine into the pistol's grip. The hunter stood staring at the girl on the couch before her for a moment, then reached into the case and pulled out the pistol belt with holster and three pouches full of spare magazines. She handed the pistol and rig to Joanna, who squealed with delight as she took them from her outstretched hands.

"So much for my mother-of-the-year award," Dean heard Jaz mutter and then she went back to work organizing her own kit.

He saw she had pulled out a small backpack as well and was stuffing it full of blocks of something he couldn't make out. The paramedic walked over and watched as she filled the pack.

"I don't suppose I get a gun, too?" he asked.

"Have you ever even fired a gun before, outside of a video game?" Jaz asked him without looking up from her work.

"No," Dean said.

"Then, no, you don't get a sidearm," Jaz said.

"What are those blocks you put into your bag?" Dean asked.

"C-4, detonators, and some preconfigured door breaching charges in case we need them," Jaz said. "And don't tell me it's overkill. We have no idea what we are going to encounter when we get to the mines."

"I wasn't arguing, just curious," Dean said.

Jaz glanced at him and snorted at his pack and sword arrangement.

"What?" Dean asked.

"It's fine, but we need to get you out of that light blue uniform shirt," Jaz replied. She dug in the second case and turned to toss him a black, long sleeve turtleneck. "Put that on. Your navy blue duty pants are fine, but you need a different shirt so you draw less attention, especially at night."

"Thanks," Dean said. He took off the pack, then swapped out the light blue uniform shirt for the new black turtleneck. He caught Jaz watching him change and wondered if she liked what she saw. She wasn't hard on the eyes either, he admitted. If he wasn't so committed to Ashley, he could see himself with a woman like her. Dean looked around, trying to find Jo. He asked Jaz.

"Where did our future daughter go?"

Jaz shot him a glance that wasn't quite angry. "She went upstairs after I gave her the Glock. She's your daughter, why don't you see what she's up to."

"Jaz, I didn't come to that decision lightly, you know. When I was asked to give up my firstborn daughter to the coven, I was thinking of all the people who were hurt or killed by The Cause in their terrorist vendetta."

"Dean, I know that you think you meant well," Jaz said. "But hunter children do not become witches. They are raised to be hunters." She looked to the stairs and then back to Dean. "If she is my daughter, she's the last heir to the Errington Clan after me. There is a lot that goes along with that responsibility. I can't see a way I would give her up to be trained as a witch."

"She's good at what she does, Jaz," Dean said. "And you must have trained her in some hunter stuff, too. I saw her field strip that pistol. It looked like she knew what she was doing. You thought so yourself, or you wouldn't have given her the gun."

They were interrupted by the sound of the teen coming back down the stairs. Dean glanced in her direction and was surprised at what he saw. She had changed out of her long skirt and baggy blouse and vest outfit. She was wearing a skintight black body suit. She had her long hair pulled up in a ponytail like Jaz's and had a holstered pistol on her left hip and a Bowie knife just like Jaz's on her right. Both the pistol holster and the knife scabbard had straps that secured them to her thighs on either side. She looked like something out of a spy movie.

"I don't think you need to worry about her forgetting her hunter roots, Jaz," Dean said. "Damn, in that getup she looks just like you. You could be sisters."

"Where's your sword?" Jaz asked Jo. "If you were raised by me, I'd have made sure you were given your blade when you turned thirteen."

"I couldn't bring it back with me," Jo said, disappointed. "The coven said its magic wouldn't penetrate the time travel spell's field with me when I went through. Besides, you would have recognized it. It was Grandmother's sword."

"I suppose that would make sense," Jaz said. "I would have

given you my mother's blade if I had been able to recover it from the explosion."

"I don't need it really," Jo said. "I'm supposed to focus on my magic, Asha says. She says my attachment to weapons of war keeps me from reaching my potential."

Another voice behind them from the cabin's doorway interrupted them. They all turned to see who it was.

"Well, well, well. Don't you all look like one big happy family," Ingrid said, walking through the cabin's doorway.

Dean just stood and looked at her. Two companions followed her into the room. The three Valkyries stood there, looking like they just stepped out of a Wagnerian Opera. They all wore gleaming armor, polished to a mirror finish. Each was holding a winged helmet under one arm.

"These are my battle-sisters, Elsa and Antonia," Ingrid said. Elsa had a large two-handed sword she had propped point-down on the floor. Antonia carried a spear with an eighteen inch long gleaming double-edged blade at the business end. They both nodded in response to the hellos from Dean and his companions.

Antonia looked around and thumped the butt of her spear on the floorboards, giving a wicked smile. "So, when does the fun start?"

It was just after sunset when the shifters returned to the cabin. Mark, Dawson and Hannah came first with three other members of their pack. Albion and Arlo showed up next and were accompanied by a gray-haired, bearded man who was wearing furs and buckskins like something out of a mountain man movie. Dean guessed that was Old Barney, the werebear. Trailing behind Albion and Arlo were the dryads Asha and Zora. When Dean asked what they were doing there, they told him they were there to defend their valley. They said they could help with any wounded injured during the coming battle.

Dean, Jaz, and Joanna stood on the front porch facing the assembled shape-shifters and the dryads as night fell. The Valkyries stood off to one side, inspecting their weapons, as if they didn't have a care in the world. He supposed they didn't. This was the kind of thing they lived for. Jaz cleared her throat and went over the plan one more time.

"Okay, Albion, you and the rest of the shifters will wait inside the cabin with the lights on to draw the attention of the Oni demons to you." She waited as the group of shifters nodded.

"Asha and Zora," Jaz continued, "You will be upstairs and stay out of the way until you are needed or called for." The dryads both said yes, they understood. The hunter turned to look at the battle maidens.

"Yes, yes. We understand," Ingrid said. "We stay unseen above the forest canopy until the demons are engaged at the cabin's doors and windows. Then we swoop in and pin them against the cabin between us and the shifters inside."

"Zis is going to be zo much fun," Elsa said in her thick French accent.

"Right," Jaz said. She continued, looking right and left at Dean and Joanna. "Dean, Jo, and I will be out to the side, in the woods, watching. Once the Demons are engaged by the Valkyries, that will be our signal to move from our hiding place and start heading south to the old mines."

"Have you figured out how you are going to mask Dean from the demons' senses?" Albion asked. "I can see and smell him clearly. The two of you are nearly invisible to me according to my Unusual senses."

"Jo says she has a solution to that," Jaz said. She hoped it worked. The witch girl had not been very forthcoming about what the solution was, just that she had worked something out. Jo had her own amulet, similar to Jaz's, that masked her scent and cooled the heat pattern to hide it from Unusual senses beyond the normal visible light spectrum.

"Well, you three better get to your hiding places then," Old Barney rumbled. "The forest is telling me that there's trouble coming fast. The demons must almost be here."

"See you on the other side," Ingrid said. She and the other Valkyries spread their wings and launched themselves skyward, winking out of sight as soon as they left the ground. Dean knew that they could mask their presence from anyone if they chose to do so. The shifters started into the cabin with the two dryads, leaving the three of them on the porch. Jaz stepped down to the ground and headed to the northwest side of the cabin followed by Dean and Joanna.

They walked about a hundred feet from the house into and

among the trees until they arrived at a large fallen tree lying on the ground amidst the brush and undergrowth. They climbed over it to the other side and found a sheltered area where the three of them could spread out and lay down on the ground. There was enough open space under parts of the tree so that they could still see the cabin through the brush. They were mostly hidden from view, especially in the dark.

Dean looked around. Now it was time to see if Joanna had been able to come up with a solution to mask his presence from the Demons as they approached the cabin. Once they were engaged, it would not matter as much and they could slip away to the south.

"Okay," Joanna said to Jaz. "I came up with something that will extend your amulet's effects to cover a larger area than just an individual. That should mask Dean as well. The challenge is that the area of expanded coverage is dependent on contact."

"What do you mean by contact?" Jaz asked. She shot Dean a look.

Jo sighed and gave them a sheepish grin. "You two have to be touching, as close as possible, in order for it to work."

"Wait a minute, how close?" Dean asked.

"Really close," Jo replied. "Look, the amulets are our best protection. I can expand their area of effect but it has to be through contact. I decided that if it was with me it would just be weird, so it has to be you and mom."

"When this is all done," Jaz hissed between her teeth, "you and I are going to have a long talk, young lady."

"Oh joy," Jo said, rolling her eyes. "Look, we don't have much time and I have still have to cast the expansion spell, so lie down."

Dean watched as Jaz lay on her stomach behind the log, then he lay down beside her so that their adjacent arms and legs touched. He craned his neck around to look at Jo. She was shaking her head.

"No, you two have to be really close, closer than that," the witch teen said.

Dean looked over to his left and looked at Jaz where she had turned her head to look at him. This was going to get very uncomfortable.

"Fine," Jaz said. She rolled onto her side. "Spoon up behind me, but don't you dare enjoy this."

"I wouldn't dream of it," Dean said. He waited until she was still and then he moved up behind her, pressing his body against hers. He could smell the shampoo in her hair as he got closer.

"And don't breathe on me," Jaz said. "I hate that."

"Don't breathe, got it," he replied.

He heard Jo giggle a little and then she said, "Perfect." He heard her mutter a few words under her breath from behind and above them.

"Okay, the spell's in place," Jo said. "Don't move and it should be fine. I'm going to go over here a little ways and get settled."

As she moved away, Dean whispered in Jaz's ear. "You know this is straight from the child of divorce's handbook. You know, come up with a way to force your parents back together, or in our case, to get together."

"Well, if I detect any evidence that it's working on your part, you're going to be sorry," Jaz hissed in reply.

"Noted," Dean said. He still had to admit it would be funny if the whole situation weren't so deadly serious. He settled in to wait and distracted himself by peering into the darkness towards the cabin. He found he could see much better than usual. It must be part of the amulet's effects. He could make out details in the dark that he would never be able to see under normal circumstances. He looked at the woods to the south of the cabin and tried to see if he could detect movement there that would signal the coming of the demons sent to kill them.

Dean didn't have to wait very long. They were hidden only about ten minutes when he saw something coming through the woods, then another form moved up with the first. He thought they could be deer or something at first. That changed when two changed to five and more of the forms moved up, then more of the creatures were present. The demons were bunched in a group and he couldn't get a good count. They spread out in a line and moved towards the cabin. As they moved into a line, he was able to refine his count. There were eighteen of the demons here. He wondered if there were more kept back at the mine, waiting for them to arrive. That was important to keep in mind.

The closest demon in the line was going to pass within about twenty-five feet of their hidden location. Dean held his breath as the creature passed by. He could make out the scaled hide of the beast as it reached its closest point to them. It paused to sniff the air and Dean wondered if it had picked up on something. Whatever it was, the demon soon continued forward, finding nothing worth investigating.

The approaching line of demons curved around the southern edge of the clearing in which the cabin stood and stopped just inside the tree line. Dean watched them as they took up positions behind trees as if they expected an attack from the house. He wondered what they were waiting for, but then with a unified snarl, the demons all rushed forward towards the cabin. They split into groups. The bulk of them went for the front porch with its front door and single window for access. The others split into groups of two or three and headed for the other ground floor windows visible on the south side of the building.

As the demons reached the cabin, there erupted a chorus of wolf howls, lion roars, and a loud growling snarl that must have been from Old Barney in bear form. Then the melee began. The demons struggled to get in their chosen entry points and the defenders inside, slashing and biting with claws and teeth to keep them out.

"Almost time," Jaz whispered. "Be ready to move."

"Got it," Dean replied.

As if on cue, three shining forms materialized just above the ground. The light they emitted in the UV spectrum, as Dean could now see, aided by the amulet, was blinding. The Valkyries shouted battle cries together and charged into the rear of the mass of demons clustered on the porch. The surprise attack was successful and the cries of the demons were cut short as the battle maidens' blades slashed through their tough hides without effort. As each of the Eldara warrior's holy blades swept home, the demons cried out and then fell to the side in a burning heap of smoldering flesh.

Their blades, like Dean's, would actually kill the demons, not just banish their corporeal earthly forms back to hell.

"Okay, now," Jaz said shifting her position behind the log to rise. It was awkward because of how Dean was pressed up behind her. He rolled backward away from her to give her room to rise. He got to his feet and turned to see that Jo had joined them as well.

"Dean," Jaz said. "I know you are not going to be able to see as well where we are going in the woods. We will keep you between us and try to warn you of any obstacles. Try to keep up with our pace. We won't have much time to reach the southern end of the valley before the cabin attack's results are known to the Revenant at the mines."

Dean nodded, checked his gear to make sure was all set and attached where it would not get in his way as he followed the women through the woods in the darkness. Jaz took the lead, with Dean following and Joanna taking up the rear. She set a pretty rapid pace, jogging off between the trees. He already missed his enhanced vision as he stumbled over a root, but he wouldn't let that be the reason they failed this mission. He steeled himself to keep up and watch as best he could for hindrances in the darkness. He would keep up.

The three would-be rescuers set off together into the deep woods of the southern end of the valley. Hopefully they would reach their destination before anything happened to their objective. Dean thought of Ashley. He thought about her and how she counted on him with each step and that kept him going. Soon they were out of sight of the cabin and the sounds that came from the battle there. They could focus on the task that waited ahead.

Chapter 23

It took the trio nearly an hour to make it to the foothills that made up the southern base of the valley. Dean considered it a good pace, given that he could barely see the whole time. Jaz didn't seem to agree with the paramedic based on the way she kept pushing him to go faster. As the upward slope announced their arrival at the south-ern-most point of the valley, the hunter finally called for a halt to rest and start the second part of the journey: finding the location of the mine's entrance.

Old Barney had told them the entrance was likely hidden by a lot of undergrowth that would make it difficult to locate even in daylight. Jo said she had a plan to help with that and both Dean and Jaz looked to her.

"The demons are netherworlders who do not belong here," Joanna explained. "That means they should leave a trace of their passing in a forest this thick. The plants themselves will react to their touch, which will start to destroy the leaves and branches as they pass. I think I can recognize it. Once we find the point where they came down the mountain, we can follow it back to their lair, in theory."

"Are you sure?" Dean asked. "When you first mentioned this to us, you acted like you had cast this spell and seen it work before."

"I mean, it should work," the teen said. "It's just a simple contrasting nature spell."

Dean shared a look with Jaz, but they both chose to keep their thoughts to themselves. Dean figured they had already committed to this plan. They would just have to stick with it until something proved them wrong and they had to adjust.

"What do you need to do the spell?" Jaz asked.

"I need you two to stay behind me while I cast it," Jo replied. "I have to keep it up until we cross their path down the mountain. Once we have that, it should be little trouble for either of us, Mom, to backtrack their trail to where they exited the mines."

Dean stood up, adjusting his pack where it dug into his shoulders, and got in line behind Jo. Jaz got behind him.

"I'll stay back here and watch our backs," Jaz said. "Dean, you keep your ears open. Listen for anything that changes in the sounds around you. Things like the insects quieting down or other changes to the usual forest sounds. They could signal the return of the Oni demons from the cabin."

He nodded and started listening, wondering if he, the city boy, would notice anything at all since he didn't know what normal forest sounds were like at night. He paid attention to the sounds anyway as Jo started on a track perpendicular to their first path of travel. She was paralleling the base of the mountain, trying to find the track used by the demons.

They walked for about a half hour before Jo stopped them. She had taken them on a very slow walk. It was so slow, in fact, that Dean had little trouble picking his way along in the darkness. Now he peered ahead as Jo and Jaz conversed in low tones. The witch teen was pointing out something on the side of a bush Dean could barely see ten feet ahead of them. Jaz nodded and the two of them came back to where he waited.

"We found it," Jaz announced. "I'm going to take the lead now. Jo will follow me to help pick up anything I might miss. Dean, you'll come last. Try to keep up. We are going to pick up the pace again as long as the trail is easy to follow. All those demons coming down the hill in one group has torn up the ground pretty well so I think we can easily follow this trail back to the mine's entrance."

"Got it," Dean said with a nod. "Keep up."

Jaz and Jo turned up the hillside and started moving through the brush. Dean stumbled along behind them, doing his best to move silently the way they did and failing at the attempt. He did, however, manage to keep up with the two women. He had thought of Joanna as a witch, a peaceful spell caster. Seeing her in this element alongside Jaz showed him that she was a hunter as well. He wondered how she managed the two sides of her nature and what the rest of the Elk City coven thought of her hunter skills when she arrived at their doorstep, in the future.

The move up the side of the mountain was steep and grueling, and Dean was panting and soaked with sweat despite the cold night air by the time the women called another halt. Jo came back to him where he crouched, gasping for breath. She seemed unfazed by the uphill climb.

"We think we spotted the entrance. Mom is going to check it out and make sure it's clear, then we'll go in," the teen said. She noted his heavy breathing. "Boy, you are really out of shape, Dad. Catch your breath. The exciting stuff happens now."

"Running up a mountain in the dark wasn't in my exercise plan," Dean replied. "And remember, exciting is not always a good thing."

He could make out the broad grin she gave him in reply and realized that she didn't agree with him. Though their ages were not that far apart right now in this time and place, the things Dean had seen over the last year had aged him prematurely. He knew better than to take things for granted or assume that everything would work out the way they planned. The paramedic thought that his hunter counterpart, the teen's eventual mother, would agree with him.

Jaz came back down the hill to where they waited. She looked around and then described what she saw.

"There's an old rusted metal door set in the hillside up there," the hunter said. "I listened at it for a while but didn't detect anything on the other side. The demons definitely came that way and since I don't see them shutting a door after they leave, I have to assume there are other, more intelligent inhabitants inside who closed it after they left. I can see light leaking around the door, so there is light on the other side." Dean liked the sound of having some light for a change.

"What's the plan?" Dean asked.

"We'll go up and you will open the door while Jo and I stand ready to deal with any guards on the other side," Jaz said. "Then we go in, shut and hopefully lock the door behind us to keep anyone from sneaking up on us from behind. If all goes well, we will be able to begin our search. I'm hoping your memory of what you saw in your visions will help us navigate inside.

Dean wasn't sure if he'd be able to do that, but maybe he would remember some landmarks in the passages along the way. He just nodded in response, not wanting to give voice to his concerns.

Jaz must have figured out his lack of confidence, even in the darkness. He remembered she could see his expression clearly because of her amulet.

"Look Dean, you just pay attention to what is going on and tell us when you think something is important. You will remember more than you think you will. I'm going to take the lead and Jo will bring up the rear. We will take care of security, but if things get hairy in there, don't be afraid to use that sword. Its mere presence will keep some of them away from you. Any netherworlder will be able to sense the finality it represents for their otherwise eternal existence."

Dean adjusted his shoulder straps and reached up to touch the hilt of Ashley's sword over his right shoulder. He was as ready as he was going to be. He gave a firm nod in response and Jaz turned to go back up the hill with Dean right behind her.

With Dean's eyes adjusted to the darkness and wide open to any light source, he noticed the outline of the doorway right away. He could see the light leaking around the edges of the door. It had the yellow tinge of fire or lantern light, but he was relieved that he would have some normal light for a change, and any light source would do as far as he was concerned. He reached a flat area in front of the door and Jaz pointed to the door's handle without saying a word. She had drawn her sword and he noticed that Jo was standing just behind him with one hand outstretched and the other resting on the grip of her pistol in its holster.

He gripped the cold metal of the old iron door and looked to his companions. They both nodded to him and he turned the handle and pulled outward. The door swung open with a groan of metal on metal from the rusted hinges. Light spilled out from the entrance and Jaz and Jo both rushed past him in silence. He looked around the door and saw a small room on the other side with a passage leading off from it into the mountain. The two women stood looking down the passage. Jo turned and looked his way with a grin and single thumbs up to tell him it was okay.

Stepping into the room, he pulled the door closed behind him. He looked around the inside for some sort of latching mechanism but didn't see anything. Then he noticed a large iron bar leaning against the wall and the bracket on the door meant to hold it in place. He lifted it up and slotted it into the brackets with one end extending past the door to wedge against the inside of the stone wall. It would hold that door securely for the time being. He was not sure how strong an Oni demon was, but he knew he would not be able to pull that door open from the outside now.

Dean turned to look at his companions. "What now?" he whispered.

Jaz returned a feral grin that was mirrored in their daughter's face. "Now we hunt," the hunter clanswoman said. "It's time for some payback."

The passage back into the mountain sloped downward a bit, with a dirt and stone floor and the same rough-hewn stone walls with occasional timber supports for the ceiling of the passage. Every twenty or thirty feet or so, the support beams held a kerosene lantern against the wall of the passage from a hook. They created pools of light with long shadowy sections of darkened passage in-between.

Jaz lead the way again, walking in a slight crouch, her sword out in her left hand. Dean figured the gun would make too much noise, alerting others of their presence, plus it might not be effective against their netherworld foes. Dean wondered if he should draw Ashley's sword. He decided that it would just get in the way for now. His hand drifted up again to check it was still there over his right shoulder.

Joanna was behind him, a few steps to the rear. He saw when he checked on her that she turned to look behind them periodically. She was making sure no one caught them by surprise. When she noticed him looking back at her, she gave him a broad grin as if to say she was having the time of her life. He smiled in return and then turned back to pay attention to the passage ahead of him. He tried to remember the view from his visions and tie any detail from there to what he was seeing now. Nothing had clicked for him yet but he hoped that when he saw a defining feature of the passage that he'd recognize it.

There were no side passages for some time and so no decisions about direction needed to be made. They continued on their gentle downward slope for about ten minutes without any changes. While the passage wasn't completely straight, they could see some distance ahead of them with a slight bend in the distance blocking their view. That was why the attack came as a complete surprise.

They had only occasionally looked upwards to check the uneven ceiling. There were the supports that held up the lower sections of the passage but the rest of the ceiling arched upward in dark pockets of shadows that Dean couldn't pierce. There was an upward shaft leading to another level that Jaz missed as she passed under it. A shape dropped down directly in front of Dean between he and Jaz and with the powerful sweep of one arm, knocked him to the ground. He had barely shouted his pain and alarm at the sudden blow before the attack happened.

Jaz didn't have much notice, but Dean saw that it was enough. She twisted in place and grabbed the outstretched clawed hand that reached for her neck, pulling it and using its own momentum to propel the assailant past her into the passage ahead. She was knocked to the ground but had avoided the brunt of the attack. Dean still couldn't make out what it was that attacked. They were between lanterns in the passage so he couldn't make out details, just that it crouched to the ground and was snarling and growling. It landed on the ground just past Jaz and turned to leap back at her where she had been knocked against the wall. Dean was sure that she was going to be unable to defend against it as she struggled to rise.

Jo rocketed past him in a bound. She had her hands outstretched and he could make out her saying something under her breath as she went by. A cobalt blue light glowed from her hands and then he could see a similar glow appear around Jaz. The creature reached the glowing boundary around Jaz and shrieked in pain, drawing backward for a moment. That was all the time the hunter needed to recover. She turned, sweeping her sword through the air and the creature's head was rolling off its shoulders, a brief fountain of blood, colored black in the darkness of the passage, appearing in its place. Then the body collapsed to lie next to the head, still rocking in place on the ground. A moment later, the body and detached head disappeared in a red mist.

"What the hell was that?" Dean asked in a whisper. He tried hard to keep his voice under control but he wanted to scream. He hated getting startled like that. It was why he avoided haunted houses.

"Another Oni demon," Jaz replied. "It must have been set there to guard the passage. Well, where there is one, there are likely others. It just adds to the things we have to watch out for. This one was on me. I should have checked the ceilings for hiding places."

Dean was glad she could so easily adjust to the advent of a new threat. His heart was still pounding out of his chest. He needed a minute to collect himself and the women paused to wait for him to get squared away. He could see them exchanging glances, but he didn't care. He was a paramedic. He was not trained to go into dark places and fend off attacks from monsters and demons. Dean took a few deep breaths to calm his nerves and then nodded that he was ready to go on.

A short time later the passage opened up into a small chamber with two other passages branching off from it. The three of them used the small room to take a brief break while deciding to move onward. Jaz checked the passages leading deeper inside the mountain. One sloped upward from the chamber, the other continued down, deeper into the mines. Keeping their voices low, they talked over their options.

"I can see where both branches show signs of recent usage, so I'm not sure which one to take," the hunter said. "Dean, does anything look familiar yet?"

He shook his head. "The general look and feel is right so I think this is where they are holding Ashley, but I haven't picked up on any specific landmarks yet. If anything draws me one way or another, it is to take the downward passage. It feels right."

"I'd go with his feelings on this, Mom," Jo added, ignoring the look Jaz shot her. "He's the one who's come closest to walking this path before."

"Well it's as good a choice as the other," Jaz said rising to her feet. "Let's get going."

Dean got up and joined them as they continued on the descending path. He was frustrated. Every wall, lantern and support looked the same to him. He tried to watch and pay attention to the little differences, but he could detect nothing. Then, when the path had leveled out for a bit, he saw a passage branch off ahead. He whispered for Jaz to stop. Jo came up to join the other two.

"This looks familiar," Dean said. "I think that side passage leads to the cell where Ashley is being held."

Jaz nodded and turned back to look up the length of the passageway. Dean looked around and followed her gaze. Still no sign of anyone else, which was good news. They were on an even tighter guard since the demon had attacked them. Jaz had figured it had been an isolated sentry set there to guard the entrance passage. They moved up to where the passage branched and Dean looked left and recognized the passage he had seen in his first vision. There was a stout door about ten feet down the passage. It stood open, not closed as he had seen it before.

Before she could stop him, Dean rushed past Jaz and ran into the small room where Ashley was held. Correction. Where she had been held. He saw the armchair there where she had been tied up. The ropes that had secured her were coiled and looped over the back of the chair spindles. Jaz and Jo joined him looking at the chair.

"This was where they were holding her," Dean said. The room was tiny and probably served as a secure storeroom when the mine was in operation. It only had the one exit. "Where is she?"

"She didn't escape or get rescued," Jo said.

"Why do you say that?" Dean asked. He wanted to think she had gotten away.

"The ropes," she said, pointing to the chair. "They're coiled. Whoever took her, took the time to leave the ropes in a way that they can be used again. My guess is that she was taken somewhere else in here and they expect to bring her back here later."

"Good thinking, Joanna," Jaz said. "So do we keep looking for her or wait here for them to bring her back?"

"We have to keep looking," Dean said. "Who knows what they are doing to her right now. She's an immortal, but that doesn't mean she can't feel pain."

"I'm not saying you're wrong, Dean," Jaz said. "We can go on searching and return here if we don't find anything or anyone else down here. We know she's been here and will likely be returned here."

"I say we keep going," Jo said, adding her opinion to the mix. "We only suspect they'll come back with her, and every minute we spend waiting is that much sooner that any of the demons might return from the attack on the cabin."

Jaz thought for a moment and nodded. "I'm inclined to agree, Jo. Let's keep going and find her. Dean, can you find the path from here to the room with the portal? My guess is they are trying to use her in some way to hold the breach in the wards between our world and the netherworld open."

"I think I will recognize it," Dean said. "It has to be close to this location. Let's keep going down the main passage and see where it leads."

"Be ready for anything," Jaz said. "If I were the leader of this group of revenants from the netherworld, I'd be at the nexus of the connection."

Dean found his hand drifting upward to the sword again and then pulled his hand back. The sword was still there, and checking on it would only make him look scared. He couldn't let that happen in front of either of his companions. Sure, it was a stupid macho thing, but it also helped him stay focused on them and not his own quivering fear. He never liked enclosed spaces and thinking of how deep they were in the mountain with tons of rock overhead just made his knees weak.

Jaz took the lead again and Jo had moved up closer to Dean rather than hanging further back and checking behind them. All eyes were focused forward. It didn't take too long for the sound of the rhythmic chanting to resonate up the passage to them. The grunting and snarling nature of the voices grated on his eardrums and made Dean's skin crawl. They sounded as inhuman as the beings to whom they must belong.

The three companions stopped at a bend in the passage. There was flickering purple light pulsing from beyond the turn ahead. The chanting was clearer now. It was not a language Dean recognized, if it was a language at all. For all he knew it could be a random collection of phonetic sounds. Dean looked at his colleagues as they paused in the passage and Jo answered the question.

"It's Aramaic, an ancient language used by many netherworlders, as well as their divine counterparts," she whispered. "I don't speak it, but I know enough words to recognize it. I can feel the power emanating from down the passage. They are casting some sort of spell. Whatever they are trying to do down there, it takes a lot of magical energy. The air is crackling with it."

"I think we have found the portal room," Jaz said. She looked at each of them. "When we round that corner we need to have a plan of what we are going to do. Dean, if Ashley is in there, our goal will be to get to her first. Once we get there, while Jo and I keep them busy, you try and free her. Get her out and away if you can. That is our priority. If we have to beat a hasty retreat, we want her to be able to join us."

She turned her attention to the witch teen. "Jo, can you draw on that sun-fire spell again?"

"Yes," Jo nodded. "But only once, or maybe twice. I have some other tricks, though, and the Glock. I can cover my area of responsibility." She patted the gun holstered at her side.

"Okay, then. Based on how you described the portal chamber you saw, Dean, it's a big room." Jaz looked to him for confirmation and Dean nodded. "We will get as close as we can without being seen, and try to see how many we are dealing with in the way of guards and revenants." She paused for a moment and looked at the passage around them. "Okay, I have an idea. Give me a second to rig something here in the passage."

Dean watched as the hunter took off her pack and started pulling a few items from it. He recognized several blocks of C-4 plastic explosive. She took some sort of metal stick and shoved one into each of the blocks. The huntress walked over to the nearest ceiling support where it met the vertical wall support beam and slid the block into a narrow crevice between the rock wall and the wooden crossbar that supported it. When she was finished placing the charges, she came back over to them and handed Dean a small hand-held device.

"That is a detonator, Dean," Jaz said. "If you get Ashley free and you are the last one out, or the only one of us left, you run past here as fast as you can with her and once you are around the bend, flip up the safety and hit the button hard, twice. Two times, close together or it won't work. Got it?"

He nodded, and started to argue the specifics of what she wanted him to do. She shut him down with a hand raised in the air.

"Jo and I are going to be busy in there, at least in the beginning," Jaz said. "In all likelihood, we will be running along with you when you blow the passage. But one way or another, someone needs to seal up this portal for the time being until the magic dissipates and it closes up on its own. You've seen what these demons will do if they get loose. We can't let them run wild in the valley, or get into more populated areas."

Dean thought about all he had seen the demons do and then thought about how the average uninformed human would respond if one showed up where they lived or worked. They couldn't be allowed to get out of this mountain. Dean nodded and slid the detonator into a cargo pocket in his duty pants.

"Alright, that's done then," Jaz said. "Now let's scoot forward, carefully, and see what we can see before we go running in there."

Chapter 25

The trio crouched and advanced along the corridor until they could start to see into the chamber beyond. Just as Dean had seen in his vision, the room opened up into a huge cavern with the far reaches lost in darkness. Again Dean could hear the sound of running water in the distance. The strange, sickly purple glow filled the room with an eerie light source, casting long shadows on the floor and into the passage where they hid.

Jaz motioned them down and then forward. They all belly-crawled up to the entrance and looked into the room. There was a group of figures clustered in a semi-circle in front of the pulsing portal in the cavern wall. Dean stifled a gasp as he spotted Ashley, held between two humanoid figures in front of another robed figure who wielded a strange curved dagger. The blade was of some sort of black metal or stone and had a serpentine shape. The figure was waving it before the captive Eldara while he and the others surrounding her continued their chanting.

There were seven individuals participating in the ceremony as Dean and the others watched. The one carrying the dagger wore a brown hooded robe and only his forearms and hands showed. The skin showing was pasty and white, like the skin of a dead body drained of blood. He guessed that was the one whose head Dean had seen from when he had his visions assisted by the heavenly blade. The others were dressed in lighter tan robes. The whole group swayed in tandem with the tempo of their chants.

Jaz tapped Dean on the arm and motioned them backward into the passage. The three edged back until they were out of sight of the room's occupants. Then they all leaned close while Jaz outlined their plan.

"Those are all revenants, unless I miss my guess. It is hard to tell for sure from behind." Jaz said.

"So what do we do?" Dean asked. "Can we handle seven of them by ourselves? I'm not so sure we can take on that many on our own."

"Speak for yourself, Dad," Jo said. "Hunters have their own methods to deal with them, and I have my magical resources, too. We can beat them."

"The bullets in our pistols are going to hurt them but not put them down permanently," Jaz told him. "The bullets in our magazines are blessed and infused with silver and arsenic. Those will put them down if we strike clean to the head or the heart. If we miss those vital areas, the slugs will still slow them enough to do what we need to do."

Dean shrugged. He'd have to take their word for it. "So what do I do?"

"You make a beeline for Ashley, Dean," Jaz said. "I'm going to take on the three nearest us, then I'll charge the lead revenant. He'll have to pay attention to my sword. It can certainly send him back to hell, whatever protections he might have." Jaz gave him a grim smile. "When he lets go of Ashley, pull her to the side and get her ready to run."

She looked to Joanna and paused a moment. "You are going to have to take on the demons on the other side and then finish off any I miss from the shots I fire at the first three. Are you up to this? I hadn't tackled anything this advanced at your age and you don't have all my training."

"I've got this," Jo said. "You worry about the leader. I'll make sure nothing gets you from behind."

"Okay then." Jaz said. "We can do this. I'll go first, followed by Jo. Dean, you'll follow at the rear. Stay right behind me and grab Ashley as soon as you can."

Dean nodded, checked the sword hilt again to make sure it was there. He didn't know much about how to use it, but it was his only weapon for defending him and Ashley once they got in there. He got in line behind Jo and watched the teen ahead of him bouncing on the balls of her feet in her black boots. She had drawn her pistol, and he saw her rack a bullet into the chamber, flicking the safety to off with her thumb. She shot him a broad grin and turned to look forward again.

Jaz gave one last check behind her to make sure they were all ready and then, with surprising speed, sprinted forward into the room. There was no battle cry or sound at all beyond the scrape of her boots on the rock of the passage floor. Jo was right behind her and Dean was left there, scrambling to catch up. Then the chaos of the battle took over.

Dean entered the chamber to see the closest of the demons in the tan robes go down as its head exploded in a shower of gore. The robe then flattened to the ground, empty as the dispatched demon disappeared in a puff of red mist. One down. The other spun around with multiple bullet impacts and fell to the ground. Dean saw no red mist so he knew that one was still alive. The third took several shots to the torso and then misted as the robe fluttered to the ground. He followed the women in as he ran past the single creature writhing on the ground. He saw the three demons on the far side spin away under a flurry of bullets from Jo's pistol and then a ball of white light erupted from her extended palm, consuming two that were close together. They burst into white-hot flames and soon their charred forms fell to the cavern floor.

He turned his attention to the central figure in the darker brown robes. Jaz was still several yards away, charging in. The hooded face turned and the cadaverous face with sunken red glowing eyes bored into him as it took in the attackers. The lips peeled back in a fierce grin showing dual rows of needle-like teeth in the mouth. As Dean watched in horror from where he charged up behind Jaz, the revenant took his curved dagger and plunged it into Ashley's side, then flung her to the ground in the charging hunter's path. Jaz had to leap to the side and that gave the revenant time to reach into its robes and draw a matching serpentine-bladed scimitar from beneath them. Dean only had a moment to take all of this in, then the hunter and the demon were battling each other with a mad, flashing flurry of blades.

Dean had no time for that, though. He had to get to Ashley. He rushed over to where she lay on the floor and gently rolled her onto her back. Blood was pouring from the wound in her side and the paramedic flung off his pack, opening the attached IFAK pouch and pulling out a trauma pressure bandage and a pack of quick-clot impregnated gauze to stop the bleeding. He ripped the package open with his teeth and pressed it deep into the gaping wound in the Eldara's side. He followed the gauze with the trauma pressure bandage that had an absorbent pad and the dressing that could be wrapped around her torso and secured by tying on the opposite side. She was an angel on earth, but she could bleed and die. Depending on the nature of that curved blade, her fate might even be worse. He had to keep her alive.

"Dean," Ashley whispered. "I told you not to come."

"Yeah, because you knew I'd listen to you," Dean answered her with a wry laugh. "We'll get you out of here as soon as we finish off the revenant and his goons."

"You found Jaswinder Errington and the witch girl, I take it?" Ashley asked.

"You know about them?" Dean asked. "How?"

"I have been tied to the Erringtons for a long time," she replied. "After some time spent with you, I knew that you would be tied to them, too."

Dean had too many questions to be answered here and now. He needed to do something to stabilize his patient and get her ready to move out of here. Looking up from where he was crouched in front of the portal he saw Jaz still battling with the revenant, their blades moving more quickly than he could see. Jo was circling a pair of wounded demons in the tan robes. He could see scaled skin on their arms and clawed hands that ended in wicked-looking talons. The teen had drawn her Bowie knife in her left hand and held out her hand in a palm out gesture that showed a glowing white light beginning there.

A rustling sound behind him caused him to turn and then scramble backwards as the demon that Jaz had shot, but not killed, crawled toward him. He kicked out at its scaled, flat face with its mouth full of fangs. The creature snapped at him and he kept going backward until he remembered his sword. Reaching back with one hand, he drew the blade and jabbed it forward in the direction of the advancing demon. It shrieked and drew backward, eyeing the blade warily.

He knew they were in a standoff right now. Jaz and the revenant were still battling around the room. One of them was going to make a mistake and lose this battle and Dean was not sure what to do if it was Jaz. Jo had drawn her remaining adversary away from where he was located, but he couldn't get to Ashley and carry her to safety until he took care of the demon nearest him. He got to his feet, and keeping the sword in front of him, walked toward the demon where it crawled on the floor. Its legs must be paralyzed by the bullet wounds but who knew how long that would last. He suspected the creatures would regenerate quickly from anything but a fatal wound. He did not have much time.

It swiped at his ankles with a clawed arm and he skipped backward out of the way. He was not a fighter and was not sure he could do this. The alternative, however, was to let Ashley and the others die here in the cavern with more demons coming out of that portal in the future. He moved forward again, and when the demon took a swing at him with its other arm, the paramedic stomped down with his booted foot to crush the clawed hand beneath it. Moving quickly, Dean lunged forward and plunged the heavenly blade into the exposed face of the demon. Black blood fountained out of the wound where it cleaved through the nose and roof of the mouth, then the creature began to shake as if in a seizure and the area around the sword blade began to sizzle. The skin nearest the blade turned black, the charred color spreading outward until the whole head was a blackened, cracked mess.

Dean pulled the blade free and saw the charring of the flesh spread to the exposed arms and clawed hands. Then the beast was still and he was left standing without an adversary. He heard a hissing sound close by and saw the black blood coating the end of the blade smoke, char and flake away, leaving the pristine silvery metal in its place once more.

A flash of white light from behind him caused him to spin around. Jo must have fired off another blast of her sun-fire spell. The demon dodged the ball of solar plasma and took that opportunity to charge at her from the side. He shouted a warning. It plowed into her, grabbing her outstretched arm in a clawed hand and biting down across her forearm. The teen screamed in agony and brought her other hand around clutching the broad bladed knife, and jammed it into the creature's neck.

The two of them fell to the ground and rolled over and over several times. Dean watched in horror, holding his sword out but unable to lend a hand, knowing he'd just as likely stab the girl as the demon while they fought on the floor like that. The struggling stopped with the brown-robed figure atop the girl. There was a screeching sound and then the brown robes were empty, as the body disappeared in a puff of red mist. Jo levered herself up on one elbow, still clutching the Bowie knife in her left hand. There were rips in her black body suit where the demon's claws had scraped her and she was clutching her other arm to her side. She got up and came over to him.

"How's Ashley?" Jo asked, her shoulders heaving as she struggled to catch her breath.

Dean looked her over and then moved back to where he had left Ashley on the floor while he battled the demon. "I think she'll be all right if we can get her out of here. I've got her patched up as best as I can for now." He reached out to look at the ragged wound on Jo's forearm where she had been bitten. It was bleeding and the skin was torn in multiple places. He needed to get a dressing on that wound, too. "Come over here and talk with Ashley to keep her awake while I wrap up that arm."

The clash of metal on metal across the cavern drew their attention as Jaz continued to battle the revenant. They were off in the darkness somewhere at this point and Dean couldn't even see them. "Jo, can you make out what is going on?"

"Mom and that revenant are still battling," Jo said. "That thing is good. I need to get over there and help her."

"Stay here and let me bandage that arm," Dean said. "There's got to be a way to distract it or weaken it."

"The sword," Ashley croaked from nearby.

"What?" Dean asked.

"My blade, Dean. It can close the portal," the Eldara said. "That will weaken the revenant. He's too strong for the hunter to beat right now."

"Aunt Ashley, the blade is tied to you, won't that pull you from the earthly plane?" Joanna said.

"It must be done," Ashley said. "We can close this portal forever but we have to do it now, while the revenant is distracted. He doesn't know you have it here. Do it. Now."

Dean looked into the darkness, hearing the clash of swords there. He had to help, but he also had to save Ashley. He looked back at the Eldara lying on the cavern floor. He could still get her some help. A medevac helicopter could get her to the trauma center in time to save her.

"Dean, you saved me," Ashley said. "You already did it by coming here, and by keeping them from using my life force to open the portal permanently. I'm only going to go away for a while. It will only be a few years, ten or twenty at the most, I promise. I'll find a way to come back. I have too much to accomplish here with young Joanna." She looked him in the eyes and reached out to squeeze his hand. "Do it, before it is too late."

Dean felt lost. He had come all this way to rescue her and now he had to let her go again. Everyone who was important in his life was being torn away from him. He looked down at the blade in his hand. The silvery metal gleamed with a light all its own. It was a pure light, unlike the sickly purple light coming from the pulsing portal.

He stood up, letting Ashley's hand slip from his grasp. Walking over to stand directly in front of the portal, he looked back at the Eldara where she lay on the floor nearby. Her eyes met his and she smiled at him. His heart melted under that smile. She nodded to him in encouragement. Dean held up the blade and wondered how he should do this? Did he just throw it into the portal to the nether-world? No, that wouldn't be right. Instead he shifted his grip on the blade, and with two hands gripping it over his head, he stabbed it forward into the center of the swirling mass. He half expected to fall into the pulsing maw of the opening between worlds but the blade struck home and wedged up to the hilt inside the inter-dimensional doorway.

There was a roar of agony in the darkness behind him that was choked off with a shriek. Then the blade disappeared from his hands. One minute it was there and the next it was gone. Gone as well was the purple light illuminating this end of the cavern. It plunged him into total darkness for a moment. He turned and strug-gled through the inky blackness to get back to where Ashley lay on the cavern floor. As he was making his way back, the golden glow of a pool of light was lit nearby. It was Jo. She pulled her hand down from above her head, but the small ball of soft yellow-golden light remained in the air above her and Ashley. He rushed over, surprised that she was still there.

"Ashley, you're all right, you're here." Dean said as he knelt next to her.

"I wouldn't leave without saying goodbye," she said with a smile. "Besides we don't have much time and you need to tell the hunter something important."

"Okay," Dean said. "I'll tell her whatever you want, just don't go."

"I have to go and I can't hold on too much longer. Listen to me. Tell her that Artur Torrence is behind this. Tell her that the Errington Adversary lured me here. It was all part of an attempt to destroy her family once and for all." Ashley squeezed his hand. "Do you have that? Jo, you too. Remember it. It is important."

Both Dean and Joanna nodded. They had heard her.

"Dean, I have to go now," Ashley said. She looked into his eyes and gave him a smile. "We will see each other again. I promise. In the meantime, you must live your life and fulfill your destiny. You are so much more than the person I thought you were in the beginning. You will figure in many changes coming to this world. Enjoy the time you have and the people around you. Trust in that, and continue to show the good that is within you to the others around you. Promise?"

He nodded, his eyes welling with tears that clouded his vision. He couldn't see her clearly anymore.

"Goodbye, Dean."

He blinked his eyes to clear away his tears, eventually using his hands to wipe them away. When he did so, she was gone.

Jaz watched as the revenant's form burst into the familiar red mist in front of her as she pulled her blade from its heart. She had never taken on a greater demon before on her own and she had barely survived this one. She had always had a full attack team backing her up and they had worked together to terminate the target. If this was under other circumstances, she would have swelled with pride and dialed up her father to tell him what she had done. But she could not do that, ever again. She paused, sheathed her sword, and scrubbed at her damned leaking eyes with the heel of her left hand. Her right hand was hanging limp at her side, blood dripping from her fingertips to the floor from a long gash high on her shoulder.

The hunter craned her neck to try to get a look at the wound. The revenant had almost finished her with that attack. She had been forced back under a flurry of cuts and slashes that had ended with that slashing blow to her arm. Only by luck did she duck under the follow-up to the attack that would have sliced her head from her shoulders. She had used it to her advantage, though. She started favoring her right side. It wasn't hard to do. It hurt like hell. It created a pattern the revenant started trying to take advantage of, and when the demon went to complete an attack where that pattern said she should be, Jaz launched her own final, desperate attack. Then just as she was spent, her energy waning, the creature shrieked aloud. It stood up straight and turned to look back across the cavern to the portal. Using the sudden opening in the revenant's guard, she was able to finish it with a single, almost anticlimactic thrust to the heart.

She looked back to the other end of the cavern, hoping against hope that Dean and Jo survived, or at least fought there so that she could lend aid to them in time. She saw that the ugly purple glow of the portal was gone from the far end of the room. There was also the soft yellow glow of witch light hovering over two figures seated on the ground. She saw no others so she hoped that they had been successful in defeating all their foes. Stumbling along, the loss of blood and fatigue starting to take over control of her body, Jaz worked her way back across the broad cavern to the welcoming pool of light at the other end.

As Jaz got closer, she realized that she could not see the Eldara with Dean and Joanna and fear welled up in her. She had undertaken this journey in order to fulfill the clan's duty, and honor their debt to the Eldara Ashley Moore. She had never even met the angelic messenger, but had heard the stories of how she had helped the Errington's on many occasions over the previous two centuries. Had she, Jaswinder Errington, the last of her clan, failed in the quest to save her? She struggled to speed up her pace to get back to where she saw her companions clustered together in the pool of light.

Dean looked up at her as she approached, his eyes red-rimmed with tears. The sword was gone from the scabbard at his back and was nowhere to be seen. Neither was the Eldara. Had she been consumed in the portal? She looked to Joanna. Jaz still couldn't bring herself to think of the witch girl as her daughter.

"Jo, where is Ashley?" the hunter asked.

"She's gone. Her injuries were severe, and Dean and I were not able to save her," Jo answered through her tears. "Her sword might have been used to help her draw on healing energy to save herself, but she had Dean use the blade to seal the portal so that you could defeat the revenant. She said it would kill you otherwise."

"So we failed?" Jaz asked. She looked up and stared at the cavern's jagged ceiling far above them.

"No," Dean's voice cracked as he answered. "We did not fail. Ashley was saved and then she chose to have me save you."

Jaz thought she sensed a hint of anger in his tone. Of course that made sense. She was his girlfriend, even though that relationship was destined to end someday.

"We need to get out of here, then," Jaz said. "I know you are upset about having to leave without Ashley, but we need to go before any surviving Oni demons from the cabin attack return. They will sense the closing of the portal, as well as their master's demise. My guess is they will return here."

"You're hurt," Dean said, looking up at her arm. "Sit down here and let me get a dressing on that wound. While I do that we have a message to give you from Ashley."

Dean had her sit down next to him as he set to work on bandaging her arm. The initial gauze he put on turned warm as soon as it soaked with her blood. She knew the quick-clot formula impregnated in the gauze he used was responsible for the heat she was feeling. When her paramedic companion had finished securing a pressure bandage on her shoulder, he set to creating a sling for her arm to support it while they got moving. His hands were gentle, and she watched him working. He was careful and watched her for signs of pain and avoided moving her arm unnecessarily. When he was done, he pulled out a pre-filled morphine syringe and looked at her with a question in his eyes.

"How's your pain level?" Dean asked. "Do you think you need this?"

She thought about it. They had a long way to walk to get back to the cabin and she was going to need to be clear-headed. On the other hand, her arm throbbed. The pain was a little better now that he had bandaged it, but it hurt like hell.

"Can you just give me enough to take the edge off?" she asked.

"I'll give you half now and if you need more, make sure you tell me, all right?" Dean said.

She nodded in reply and watched as he checked the dose. Then he gave her an injection in her opposite shoulder. He asked Jo to massage the injection site gently for her since she couldn't do it for herself with her arm in a sling. The teen leaned forward to rub her shoulder muscle with her fingertips. Jaz noticed her hands were trembling.

"You did well, Jo," Jaz said. "Is this your first time in a battle like this, other than the fight at the dryad cabin?"

"Is it that obvious?" Jo asked, looking away. The hunter realized she was ashamed.

"Don't look away, Joanna," Jaz said. "I was a complete wreck after my first firefight. I understand what you are feeling, I really do."

"It's different than at the cabin," the teen choked through the tears. "I didn't have a chance to do much thinking before that happened. It was so sudden. Here, I thought I was better prepared, but Ashley's loss and your injury has me realizing how close of a call this was. We almost lost."

"Yes, but we didn't lose," Jaz responded. "Hold on to that. That will help for now. Later, we will have a talk about how to deal with the stress of an event like this. It's the same chat my father had with me, once upon a time. It will help you, I promise."

The hunter looked around the room, seeing little of the aftermath you would ordinarily see in such a desperate battle. That was the way it was with fighting demons and other netherworlders. You destroyed them, sure, but you often had no bodies on the battlefield to mark your success. In those situations there was nothing to show but your own wounds and exhaustion.

"You had a message for me from the Eldara?"

"She told me to tell you that Artur Torrence is behind this attack on you and your family," Dean said, spitting out the words like venom. "I assume that means something to you? It means something to me. Now I have an additional score to settle with Mr. Torrence."

Jaz stiffened at the mention of the hunter clan's hereditary adversary's name. Artur Torrence was the reason behind why the Erringtons had long ago become a clan of hunters. Legend had it that they had been nothing more than peaceful farmers, coming from somewhere in what was now the Middle East. Artur Torrence had come upon their farm and almost succeeded in wiping out their simple farming family before he tired of his sport and moved on. Her surviving ancestors followed, seeking vengeance. Over the intervening years, the family legends say they came close to catching up with him many times. Often they were able to foil his sinister plans, but always missed out on finishing him off.

"Mom," The teen's voice interrupted her thoughts. "Artur has never come after the family before like this, has he?"

"No," Jaz replied. "I don't know if it was because he never had the opportunity, or if it was because we had him on the run so often that he could not spare the time and energy to do it."

"We need to find him and finish him," Jo said.

Jaz turned her head and looked in the girl's eyes. She saw a familiar face as she looked at the witch girl. Her blue eyes reminded Jaz of her own eyes, and her mother's. She still didn't want to accept the revelation that Jo was her daughter, back from the future, but the concept was growing on her. There had never been a witch-trained hunter to her knowledge. It was why she resisted her instincts that the girl's claims were valid. Dean didn't deny it. He had accepted it far easier than she did. Jaz knew that she needed to get over her doubts. They were all that was left of the clan, after all.

"Yes Jo, we do," Jaz said. "We need to finish him, together."

"You aren't alone in this, ladies," Dean said. "I want in on this vendetta, too. Artur's machinations have hurt those I care about twice now. I've met the vampire lord, and I've seen the way he views and treats humans and others he considers lesser beings. I want to be there when he gets brought down."

"It might take a while, Dean," Jaz told him. "We Erringtons have been tracking and chasing him for centuries. If the legends are true, our vendetta dates back to the beginning of recorded history, before the Christian era. We've learned a certain amount of patience in that time frame."

"I can be patient, as long as we are successful," Dean said.

"Then welcome to the family, Dad," Joanna said. "You're an honorary Errington now."

He sort of smiled at that, Jaz saw, as she watched him packing up his EMS supplies and donning his black backpack. Dean Flynn wasn't a bad sort of fellow. She had never had time to get involved with anyone before, and she certainly didn't have the time now, but she admitted he was the kind of guy she had always imagined for herself. Strong and confident, but willing to let her be the hunter she was trained to be.

"Come, on, let's get out of here," Jaz said. "I want to get back to the outside, and I want to make sure we seal up this room before we leave."

"But we closed the portal," Dean said. He pointed to the section of wall where the pulsing purple doorway to the netherworld had been just minutes before.

"That portal is closed, but the tear in the wards between worlds will not heal completely," Jaz said. "Another could come here and try to force the doorway open again if they were able to harness enough power. By sealing off this chamber, we can go a step further and limit easy access to this location. It's not as much as I would like to do, but it will have to be enough."

She watched as they all stood up, each looking more than a little beat up. Time to get this team back to base. The three of them walked out of the cavern, returning up the passage they had used to enter. When they passed the place where she had placed the C-4 plastic explosive charge, she double-checked with her good hand to make sure it was still there above the support beam. She took them further down the passage, turning a bend in the mineshaft before stopping them about two hundred feet away.

"Dean, you can do the honors," Jaz said.

The paramedic took the wireless detonator from his pocket and flipped up the safety cover, revealing the button underneath. He looked at her again and she nodded. She watched as he thumbed the button twice, clicking it quickly in succession. The rumbling blast sent a rolling wave of rock dust down the passageway at them and she heard the continuing fall of rocks tumbling down from the heart of the mountain above them. The portal's location was sealed away for now. It would have to do. Turning to look at her companions, Jaz nodded and led them out of the mines, beginning the long trek back to the cabin in the woods.

Chapter 27

Dean was exhausted by the time they returned. It was near dawn as the trio trudged into the clearing surrounding the lakeside cabin. They approached with caution. There were some broken windows visible to show that something had happened here, but no other signs of the battle. As Dean, Jaz, and Joanna walked up to the front porch the door opened and Asha the dryad stood there with Ingrid and Albion on either side of her. She smiled as she saw them.

"Paramedic Dean, it is good to see you and your companions return to us safe and sound," the dryad woman said.

"We are safe, but some of us are not so sound," Dean said. "What happened here, is everyone safe?"

Ingrid gave a broad smile, "My battle sisters and I have not had such fun in years. It was a great way to prepare for the final battle. It will be a story that will make the other battle maidens jealous." She looked at Dean. "I felt Ashley leave for the home planes. Thank you for freeing her."

"But I didn't save her, Ingrid," Dean said. The guilt that told him he had failed wracked him. "I couldn't bring her back with me."

"You succeeded in keeping the revenant from using her to create a breach between the worlds," the Valkyrie said. "She is not destroyed, and she will return to this plane to help people again. It will not be long. You saved her very existence, Dean, take heart in that."

"How did the battle here go?" Joanna asked.

"It was glorious," Ingrid said. "My sisters and I pinned the demons against the cabin when we attacked them from behind. We destroyed five of the eighteen before they even realized we were here. When they turned to face us, the shifters exploded from the cabin's entrance and pushed them into our blades. We destroyed twelve of them with our heavenly blades, and the shifters sent the others back to their masters in hell. None escaped."

"That's good," Dean said. "It was better than I hoped would happen. Were there any major injuries on our side?"

Albion shook his head. "A few of the shifters suffered some bites, cuts and bruises, but they have all regenerated. Ingrid told us that she sensed your success in rescuing her sister, so the others all returned to their homes. Asha and I waited for your return to see if there was any further assistance we could provide. We owe you a debt for ridding our valley of this threat."

"We banished the revenant for now and sealed the portal. We also blocked off the mine shaft with explosives," Jaz said. "There should be no further trouble here."

"There is one thing, Ingrid," Dean said. "Artur was behind all of this again. I don't know how, but he rebounded from the last failed attempt to disrupt lives in Elk City and instituted this whole series of attacks to provide the revenants a foothold in this world."

Ingrid's eyes burned with a feral gleam. She looked at Jaz and said, "Your adversary returns, Ms. Errington. I, too, have long had a score to settle with this one. I have looked for him over many years, in between my other travels. I know that your clan has been hunting him as well."

Dean watched Jaz for a response, but it was limited to a hardening of her eyes and pressing her lips together until they disappeared. She had found out back at the cave that the vampire lord

Artur Torrence had destroyed the rest of her family. Now he discovered that Ingrid and Artur had history, too. It was something else that connected the two of them.

Ingrid continued, "Jaswinder Errington, I pledge my services to you and yours now and in the future in the hunt for this creature. We have been working separately, but now let us work together to track and defeat this evil."

Jaz looked the Valkyrie in the eyes and nodded, extending her good arm to clasp hands in agreement.

"Good, that is settled," Ingrid said. "I will watch for signs on my travels and send word of anything I find. Dean knows how to invoke me if you need my assistance, since the two of you are tied together in this, as well. Until then, I must return to my work gathering souls of warriors in preparation for the last battle." She turned to Jo and pulled her in for a quick hug. "Hang in there, kiddo. Your parents are good people. Give them the time they need to get used to having you in their lives."

"I will, Aunt Ingrid," Jo said.

Ingrid took a step back away from the cabin in the clearing, manifested her great white wings again, and launched herself skyward with a few broad strokes. Then the Valkyrie was gone, blinking out of sight as she sped away skyward.

Asha took the opportunity the break in the conversation offered and came forward to Jaz, pointing to her injured arm. "And your injuries? We must do something for you. Come inside and let Zora and I make you something to eat and treat your wounds. Come." The dryad woman gestured to the open cabin door and Jaz led the way inside to enter and rest.

Dean watched her go inside and turned to Albion. The werelion had been a strong ally in this fight for the valley's residents and against the demon incursion into this world. Dean hoped he could keep that friendship alive. He stepped forward and extended his hand to shake the other man's hand. Albion took it and merely nodded, then he turned and started off into the forest. Dean watched him leave and then turned to go inside. Jo had already gone in following Asha and Jaz.

Once inside, they sat while Dean looked at Jaz's injured left arm again. She needed stitches to properly close that gash in her shoulder, as well as an antibiotic and a tetanus shot. They could stay here for a few hours, but he needed to get her to a hospital for the needed treatment. Asha and her daughter set to work providing a breakfast for all of them. It was good to sit and relax in relative safety for a change. Dean looked around the room at the assembled group. Asha walked around with a smile serving the breakfast meal and doting over Jaz, worrying over her injuries. Jo and Zora were in the corner chatting together, bonding as only teens in the presences of adults, or in this case, parents, could. They were close in age and he was glad that Jo had relaxed enough to find a friend here.

He felt like someone was watching him and when he looked around the room again, he caught Jaz staring at him. She smiled a little when their eyes met. A lot had happened to them in the last few days. He was concerned about her. She had yet to deal with the loss of her family in the explosion back in Elk City. Dean knew that it was probable that she was the last of her hunter clan. A series of giggles from the two teens on the other side of the room distracted him and he remembered that, no, she wasn't the last of them. Somehow Joanna was the continuation of the Errington line, and while he had trouble believing in the beginning when it was revealed to them, he could see what might attract him to Jaz. It was not impossible at all that, in some way, the two of them would end up together.

Dean shook his head. Ashley was only a few hours gone. What was he thinking? He felt guilty that he was considering another relationship so soon. But, this was different, wasn't it? The two of them had not hit it off in the beginning, but the last few days of events had brought all three of them closer together than he would have thought in the beginning of this quest.

The paramedic's thoughts drifted back over the previous year. He thought about his time in the fire academy to become a paramedic, his initiation into the Unusual world at Station U, his realization that, despite the true nature of his patients, they were people in need of care just like anyone else. Now he had fought his way through a series of battles that had truly been about good versus evil. It was so different than what he had become used to. Getting back to Station U and the ambulance calls serving his Unusual patients would be a welcome return to normal. It would be good to get back home.

Epilogue

Ingrid had only flown a short distance away, using her innate ability to mask her presence in the mortal world to disappear from view of those on the ground. The Valkyrie stopped and hovered in the air over the cabin. The other shining form before her exuded a blinding light that dazzled even her divinely created eyes. Vaguely humanoid in shape, it hovered before her in the air where she flapped her great wings to maintain position.

"Does he know his true nature yet?" the light pulsed as the form spoke to her, more like words echoing directly in her mind than spoken in the air.

"No, my lord," Ingrid said, inclining her head in respect. "He did not question how he could handle the heavenly blade without harm, nor his position in this conflict. I followed your instructions to keep it from him if I could, though you know I cannot lie in response to a direct question."

"It is well that he remains in the dark for the time being," the form pulsed. "It is not yet time to reveal his relationship to all of this."

"My lord, Dean Flynn is not an ignorant or foolish man," Ingrid said. "He will begin to question what happened here in this valley and the things he was able to do."

"When the time comes I will reveal myself to him and explain his place in the world," said the voice in her mind. "For the time being, I must attend to your sister. She was sorely injured by the revenant scum. I will assist her recovery so that she may regenerate faster and return to earth to continue her work there."

"Thank you, my lord," Ingrid said, bowing slightly again. "I know my sister will appreciate that."

"In the intervening time, Ingrid, you must undertake the task of watching over him, assisting him to fulfill his destiny. My son must come of age in his own time but time is short and he must be ready for the battle when it comes. Everything depends on it."

"I will do as you say, my lord," Ingrid said, bowing in the air again as the form faded from sight. She glanced back down at the cabin below before soaring higher into the blue morning sky, setting off to Valhalla, awaiting the time when she was needed again on the earthly plane. Needed again to help Dean Flynn realize his destiny.

▭

Read on for Book 5 - The Paramedic's Witch

The Paramedic's Witch

BOOK 5 IN THE EXTREME MEDICAL SERVICES SERIES

Chapter 1

The baby werewolf tried to bite him while he worked on his assessment. "How long has she been like this?" Paramedic Dean Flynn asked the concerned parents standing in the doorway of the baby's bedroom.

"We heard the growls coming from her room about 15 minutes ago," the mother said. "When we saw her we called 911 right away."

Dean was glad to be back on the job at Station U after the events of the past few weeks. He had rescued his kidnapped girl-friend Ashley, an actual angel from heaven, only to have her slip away as a result of her injuries during the ordeal. She wasn't dead, but it would be years before she could manifest again in person on earth. Along the way to rescuing Ashley, he had teamed up with a female demon hunter named Jaz Errington and a witch named Joanna. The surprises and complications continued when he and Jaz found out that Jo was their daughter, returned from the future to assist in their quest to rescue the angel.

So managing the snarling werewolf baby in the crib in front of him was a welcome change of pace back to his normal life of treating his special type of emergency patients. Those patients were the creatures of myth and legend, called Unusuals, who lived alongside their unknowing human neighbors. Dean, his partner Barry, and the other paramedics of Elk City's Station U were tasked with helping these underserved members of the city's community.

"I thought that Lycans didn't start changing until they reached adolescence?" Barry asked, trying to hold the baby without getting bitten by the were-child. "What do you think is going on, Dean?"

"My guess is that the baby is having a seizure of some kind that is causing it to shift and change sooner than expected," Dean surmised. He turned to look at the concerned parents standing nearby. "Has she been sick lately, had a cold or flu bug, or anything?"

The mother answered. "She has not been sleeping well and had a fever last night when I put her to bed. I didn't think anything of it. Did I let this happen? Is it my fault? I've never heard of one of us shifting form so young before. Is she going to be alright?"

"I think she is going to be fine," Dean reassured her. He wasn't sure, but he thought the baby was having a febrile seizure. It was a common enough occurrence in some infants when they spiked a high fever suddenly. It kind of caused the brain to reset. That might be what happened here. The seizure must have triggered the change to werewolf.

"You're thinking febrile seizure?" Barry asked.

Dean nodded. "So what do we do?" The paramedic asked his probationary partner, testing him.

"Actively seizing infant, we give Midazolam IM or IN," Barry replied. He meant give the drug commonly known as Versed by injection or aerosolized spray up the nose. It was a sedative that would break the seizure and hopefully, the baby would return to human form. Hopefully.

Dean nodded in the affirmative and took over securing the snarling infant, avoiding the snapping teeth. Barry crouched down to draw up the medication in a syringe while his partner secured the patient. The new guy was coming along alright, Dean thought. He wasn't a new paramedic, which helped. He was just new to the knowledge that some of his patients were creatures like werewolves, even werewolf babies.

Barry stood back up with his syringe and supplies and Dean turned the baby on her side so Barry could give the injection. Barry used an alcohol prep to swab the little hairy butt and then gave the intramuscular injection. It would take a few moments to begin to work so Barry took over holding the struggling and snarling infant from his partner after putting the needle and syringe in the sharps box in the side of their med bag.

"Now we just need to wait and see if the drug we just gave her does the trick," Dean told the concerned parents. "In the meantime, while a febrile seizure is usually an isolated incident, given the startling change that occurred, we should probably take her in to the hospital to get checked out. Okay?"

"Are you sure she'll be alright?" the mother asked.

"Look," Barry said. He had let go of the child. The snarling had stopped and as Dean and parents leaned over the crib to look at the baby, they saw the tiny werewolf shift back into a normal baby girl. Her clothes were a little shredded from the previous struggles, but she was sleeping comfortably and looked none-the-worse for the experience.

"See," Dean said. "She seems to be just fine. Like I said, it's probably an isolated incident but I'd like to have you come with us while we take her into the hospital and get checked out. It may never happen again. Still, it's better to be safe."

"We can go to the hospital if that's what you recommend," the father said. "Thank you so much for helping us. I come from a long line of Lycans and I have never heard of that happening before."

"It's new to me, too," Dean said. "Still, this job is all about new and exciting experiences." He chuckled and started helping Barry pack up the gear. He would head out to the ambulance and get the car seat for the baby set up in the back of the ambulance while Barry got the baby ready to transport and brought her and the parents out to the ambulance behind him.

When they got there, mom climbed in the back with Barry and the baby while Dean pointed to the front passenger seat for the father. Dean got in behind the wheel and waited while the dad buckled his seat belt. He checked the rearview mirror to see the thumbs-up from Barry in the back that signaled him it was time to go and he pulled the ambulance out from the residential driveway, onto the street. Then they were on the way to Elk City Medical Center.

———

BY THE TIME they got back to their station after dropping the baby off at the ECMC ER with the nurses and doctors there, Dean was ready for the end of a long night's work. It was nearly dawn, and he and Barry worked together back at the station to get the ambulance restocked and make sure everything was done for the end-of-shift checks. The next crew of paramedics came in at six in the morning to relieve them, and another emergency call could come in at any time so the ambulance and gear needed to be ready.

The restocking didn't take long and the two paramedic partners walked into the squad room to the smell of a delicious breakfast in the air. A gravelly voice across the room in the small kitchenette area of the station called to them.

"I've got steak and eggs with home fries for you guys to round out your shift," the shambling chef said. That was Freddy, their live-in chef. He was a zombie who had been a premier chef on the national restaurant scene until his voodoo priestess girlfriend had caught him cheating with one of his waitresses. One spell later and he was one of the undead, forcing him to leave the profession he loved. Dean and the other paramedics had adopted him after his house trailer was burned out in a hate crime. Now he lived in the station and made the paramedic teams five-star, restaurant quality meals in gratitude. The food was great as long as Freddy checked to make sure he hadn't lost any body parts during the cooking process.

"Man, I'm starved," Barry said. "Keep it warm for me, Freddy. I have to finish up my paperwork from the last call. It'll only take a few minutes."

"Will do," Freddy croaked.

"Well, I'm not waiting," Dean said. He took the plate offered by the zombie chef and grabbed himself a bottle of water from the fridge before sitting down to eat in the Station U squad room. The room served as an office between ambulance calls, as well as a lounge during their downtime. There were two recliner lounge chairs and a sofa, as well as a large flat screen TV mounted on one wall.

The best part of the station, in Dean's estimation, was the extensive library on myths and legends in a bookshelf on the wall. The volumes were annotated with notes from various Station U paramedics over the years to help teach later crews the lessons learned about their special patients. Dean made a note in his smartphone to remind himself to make an annotation on one of the werewolf stories about his encounter with the werewolf baby, the first he had ever heard of.

Once he set up the reminder for later, he dug into the plate of delicious food. Savoring every bite, Dean took his time with his breakfast. That was unusual in itself. He knew that most paramedics ate their meals as fast as possible to make sure they finished before another ambulance call came in. Dean used to be that way, too. He had changed in the last few months, though. There had been a lot going on. Racist hate crime attacks on his Unusual patients, a takeover attempt of the whole city by a rogue vampire lord, and the kidnapping of his girlfriend by demons had all left him with a new perspective on life. He was determined to enjoy and savor these quiet, peaceful moments whenever he could. He knew all too well how quickly they could shift into chaos and loss.

His phone buzzed on the table next to his plate and he checked to see that a text message had come in. It was from Joanna, his recently revealed fifteen-year-old daughter. He was still getting used to that fact himself. He was too young at twenty-three to have a daughter that age under normal circumstances, but she had traveled back in time via a powerful spell to come here and help rescue

Ashley. She was from twenty years in his future and only knew him as her dad. He was still struggling with thinking of her as his daughter, let alone that he was somehow responsible for her while she was here in this time and place.

He checked the text message and saw that she was up early and wanted a ride over to her mother's apartment. Jo was staying with him because he had a spare room in his place, though he knew nothing of raising a teenaged girl. Now she wanted to go over to her mother's place. She probably wanted to help her mother continue the job of sorting through the few remaining items left after her own parents and much of the rest of the extended family had been killed in a suspicious gas explosion and fire just a few weeks before. Dean sighed. He supposed he could take her across town to Jaz's apartment after he got off work. This was his final night shift in the rotation and he had a few days off, so he had plenty of time to give her a ride over before he got some sleep after working all night. He could use his tiredness as an excuse not to stick around too long.

Dean didn't relish running into his parenting counterpart. She had been as surprised as he was by the revelation they had a child together at some time in the future. It was doubly awkward because the two of them had not hit it off well when they first encountered each other. Jaz was a strong-willed individual and took umbrage whenever anyone tried to tell her what to do, or worse - didn't immediately listen to her commands when she was in charge. Dean was willing to stand up for himself when he or someone he knew was being wronged. This dichotomy led to the two of them arguing over who had the right to reprimand Dean's probationary paramedic Barry when he was late to a class Jaz had been teaching.

It had not gotten much better when Dean and Jaz had evaded a demon attack aimed at him and had to leave town, picking up a stray witch on the roadside who turned out to be their future daughter. The daughter who wasn't to become a hunter like her mother, but was already committed by her father to becoming a member of a witch coven. Dean saw nothing wrong with joining the coven at its most basic level. He had made a difficult decision that affected not only him, but two other people as well. He had been the one who made the deal with the coven for his firstborn daughter to someday join them in exchange for a spell they cast on his behalf. 'Someday' had seemed so far away at the time.

This was the root of the awkwardness that lay between he and Jaz Errington. Then there was the problem that existed because of their opposing careers. She was a member of a hunter clan, committed to hunting down demons as well as those Unusuals she perceived as evil. She drew that line at anyone taking advantage of humans or perpetrating crimes against humans with evil intentions. He, on the other hand, was a healer and a paramedic committed to saving many of those same individuals when they needed medical care. They said opposites attracted, but he thought this was not what the proverbial "they" meant when it was said.

Dean picked up his phone and texted his daughter. He told Jo that he was fine running her over to her mother's place. He told her to be ready when he showed up after work. She texted back a thumbs-up emoji. He finished his excellent breakfast and prepared to welcome the next shift. Bill and Lynne, the next shift's paramedics, both showed up soon after he was finished eating. Grabbing his gear as six o'clock rolled around, Dean said goodbye to Bill, Lynne, and Barry, and headed out to his pickup truck to drive home and pick up Joanna.

Chapter 2

Dean drove the few miles back to his apartment, located over a detached garage in a residential neighborhood on the outskirts of Elk City. When he pulled up out front, Joanna was there waiting for him in the driveway. She was dressed in shorts and a tank top, carrying her purse on one shoulder. They had gone shopping for some new clothes when they returned from their rescue mission in the mountains to the west. Jo had been transported back in time pretty much with just the clothes on her back. Her outfit at the time was not what a normal teen in this day and age would wear. Apparently, twenty years from now, the fashions revisited what he would have called nineteen-sixties' "hippie" style. Now, at least, she looked like any other teen he saw walking down the street.

"Hi, Dad," she said as he climbed in the pickup with Dean. "I appreciate this. Mom will, too, I think. She's having a problem adjusting to being the last living member of the Errington clan. She's overwhelmed with all the responsibilities to run the security company, plus having to manage getting her parents' estates in order."

"Did she invite you or are you inviting yourself to go help?"

"She would never ask for help. You know that, Dad."

Dean was still getting used to this whole family man thing. A week ago, he had been a normal single guy. Okay, maybe not normal, but certainly not the father of anyone - especially not a fifteen-year-old girl. Now he not only had a teenaged daughter, he also had a future - what would you call her? Wife? Girlfriend? Baby-momma? He still had trouble seeing him and Jaz Errington getting together, even with the apparent proof that they did sitting in the truck next to him.

"Have you given any more thought to how and when you're going back to when you came from?" Dean asked.

"I can't do it on my own. I have an idea of how it's done, but the spell has to be cast on me by another witch. It took a group casting to send me back here. It might take more than one of us to send me back."

"We should contact the local coven then. They sent you back here in the first place, at least their future selves did." Dean was getting a headache trying to wrap his brain around the whole time-travel thing.

"I want to stay a little longer and help Mom out. She is all alone now. She doesn't even have you to lean on yet. She needs someone else to help her through this."

That comment brought them to an awkward silence. They were mostly quiet the rest of the ride downtown. Jaz had taken an apartment about a block away from the location of her family's bombed-out building. The fire marshal and the feds at the ATF had determined that it was not a mere gas explosion as had originally been reported in the news. Since they were federal security contractors, it was being treated as a potential terrorist incident, given the company's federal security ties, especially since Jaz and her team had just returned from an unnamed mission in Syria. Dean knew from the news how dangerous that middle-eastern country was. It was a testament to how tough Jaz was, and to her skills as a demon hunter that she had been sent there and survived to come home again.

Dean found a spot on the street, thumbed a few quarters into the parking meter, and followed Joanna into the building. They caught the elevator up to the sixth floor where Jaz was staying and knocked on the apartment door.

Jaswinder Errington opened the door. She could have been Jo's older sister, they looked so much alike. Dean saw right away she had been crying. He knew that she would be embarrassed by his noticing it, so he shot her a big grin when she looked his way and pointed to Jo.

"Look, I brought you a teenager to lend you her snarky comments while you work."

"Oh, joy," Jaz said stepping back and gesturing to them. "Come on in. I told you I didn't need your help, Joanna. It's busy work for the most part. It's stuff that I just have to slog through and get it done."

"No one should have to do this stuff alone, Mom. Besides, Dad is off for the next two days so he can stay and help, too. Together we can get it done faster than you could do it alone."

"I told you, Joanna. Stop trying to force Dean and me together. I don't doubt that we are your parents anymore. That is something I accept now. I do doubt that we are going to become more than friends just because you keep coming up with ways for us to stay in close proximity to each other."

"Jaz is right, Jo." Dean jumped in to help Jaz out. "If we end up as more than friends in the future, it will have to happen in its own time and can't be forced. I mean, you didn't want us to just start jumping on each other as soon as you snapped your fingers, did you?"

"Ew, Dad, don't be gross. That is not an image any daughter wants to think about."

"Well, then, leave us alone," Jaz said. "Let things happen naturally. You aren't even born for almost five years, right? Dean and I have plenty of time yet to get to know each other."

Dean saw the teen's shoulders sag a little. If he thought about it from her point of view, he could understand how she felt. She wanted to see the parents she had left behind in the future. They were a happily married couple, not the barely-friends she saw when they were together here in her past. He had very little memory of his own parents together before his father left him and his mother on their own. He had been three when his father left them. After that, his mother had avoided talking about him, at least in front of Dean. He knew almost nothing about the man who had fathered him.

Dean changed the subject. "On the bright side, we are here together now. Let's see what we can do to get some work done. What do you think, Jaz? Do you have any work for the kid and me to help you with?"

"The fire marshal dropped off some boxes of personal items recovered from the fire. I have not wanted to, but maybe since you both are here with me, we can sort through them. I've got nothing else to do until a conference call coming up at noon with some of our satellite office managers. I need to make sure that all the Errington private and federal security contracts are being served."

Jaz's family had been one of the world's great hunter clans, serving as the guardians of humans against demons and those Unusuals who saw fit to take advantage of them. Once they moved to the United States before the Civil War, the family set up a security and private detective firm to serve as a basis for them to investigate demon and Unusual attacks on humans. Since then, the Errington Security Firm had become one of the preeminent private security and personal bodyguard companies in the nation. They provided protection to people like movie stars and corporate leaders around the country. They also took special jobs from a clandestine federal agency related to their core mission, hunting demons who broke through to the human world from the netherworld. It had been one such group of demons the three of them had battled to rescue the angel, Ashley Moore, just a few weeks before.

"So where are these boxes?" Dean asked looking around the room. He saw a stack of six large cardboard boxes on the far side of the room along with some charred, hard plastic Pelican cases in various sizes.

Jaz pointed to the boxes and Dean and Jo walked over to them.

"Where do you want us to start, Mom? Do you want us to just pick a box or case and dig in?"

"Yeah, sure. Pick one. I don't care."

Jo picked up one of the cardboard boxes and moved over to the dinner table with it. She unfolded the flaps and looked inside. Dean noticed the smoky odor coming from the contents of the box. Jaz came over and the three of them started to pull some picture frames and other odds and ends from the box.

IT TOOK them about two hours to go through all the boxes, and it wasn't until they got to the last box that Dean found something strange.

"Jaz, what's this?" Dean asked. He pulled a small jade figurine from the bottom of the box. It had been hidden under a piece of charred linen.

Jo hissed in alarm and Jaz drew in a sharp breath.

"Dean, where did you get that?"

"What? It was in the box. Here," he said trying to hand it to her.

"Don't hand it to me. Just set it down on the table, quickly. You shouldn't touch it at all." Jaz looked at Jo. "Do you have any protection magic that will counter that?"

"Just a normal ward against evil. It might work."

"Cast it. Now."

Dean was confused but set the figurine down. Jo closed her eyes and started chanting under her breath. He looked at the jade figurine. It was about the size of his fist and portrayed a short, squat man-shaped figure holding a sword. It appeared to be smiling, but as he looked closer he saw there were double rows of sharp teeth in the figure's mouth that made the smile more of a grimace.

The hair stood up on the back of Dean's neck as Jo's chanting got louder. He didn't understand the language, but knew that many spells were spoken in Latin, Greek, or even other, more ancient languages. She finished and opened her eyes. Looking at Dean and the figurine, she nodded.

"That should do it, Mom."

Jaz stood up and looked in the box Dean had been unpacking. He looked inside, too. It was empty except for a few scraps of paper.

"Crap, where are the other two?"

Jo looked alarmed. Dean looked from one to the other, still not understanding.

"There were three?" He asked.

"Yes, a matched set of three that were kept in a specially warded box. The wooden box must have burned in the fire, but the jade would have survived, as we've seen."

"Will someone please explain to me what is going on?" Dean asked, careful to stand very still. He had been afraid to move and touch anything.

"It's a summoner, Dean, and Jo's spell should serve to contain it for now. They are meant to be used to summon the presence of a demon lord to earth. They work when all three are set at three of five points of a pentagram scribed in a warding circle."

"They can also cause really bad luck to those who hold them, Dad. Like evil sorts of bad luck! I think I cleansed the effects from you with my spell. You only held it for an instant."

"Why would your family have a way to summon demons, Jaz? You're demon hunters after all."

"Dean, we didn't use them, we kept them safe from others using them. My clan captured them centuries ago when we wiped out a ring of demon worshipers back in the old country, if I remember the family lore correctly."

"Wow, Mom. I know you can't see it but the aura radiating off that thing is disgusting and really powerful. If I look at it for too long it makes me queasy. I can't imagine what it would be like with all three of them in one place. We need to see if we can find the other two. If someone else picked them up in the rubble of the fire and ran off with them, we could have a big problem on our hands."

"So it causes bad luck. So what?" Dean asked.

"So what, you say? The problem, Dean, is that this is evil associated directly with bad luck," Jaz said. "Like Jo said, it won't just be stubbing-your-toe, or tripping-over-a-fallen-branch-on-the-sidewalk kind of bad luck. This will be run-out-of-gas-in-the-middle-of-a-rail-road-crossing-while-a-train-is-coming bad luck. This is the kind of bad luck that brings down a fully loaded passenger airliner while you're on board."

"And it will get worse unless it can be contained. There could be other effects on an unprotected person, as well," Jo said.

"Well, let's head over to what's left of the building," Dean suggested. "There's a construction crew there. Maybe they have seen something or someone. If not, we'll see if we can find the other figurines in the rubble. Jo, you can see the glow of the figurine's aura, so if we get there and the other figurines are there, you should be able to find them, right?"

"In theory, Dad, yes."

"Good. Then let's go before some homeless guy decorates his cardboard box with a new knickknack and brings down an asteroid on the city."

"LOOK HONEY," Sam said. "Today was my lucky day. I found these cool bookends on my demolition job. I thought we could use them on our bookshelf."

The matching figurines he held were set on the shelf and turned so they looked out over the construction worker's small apartment. Sam didn't see the eyes flare with an internal light for an instant, glowing and pulsing a sickly green before they faded.

Chapter 3

Dean, Jaz and Jo left the apartment building and started the short, two-block walk to the burned out remains of the former Errington Security headquarters. They had just gotten to the intersection across the street from the site when a delivery truck swerved out of passing traffic. It hopped the curb heading straight for Dean. He wasn't paying attention. He was going through some emails on his phone and looked up, startled by the noise and shouts, to see the truck barreling towards him. He couldn't move. He just froze in place.

He tried to move out of the way, but felt like he was mired in glue. Then he felt an iron grip clamp onto the collar of his uniform jacket and yank him backwards out of the path of the out of control vehicle. He fell backward as he lost his balance, and landed on top of whoever had rescued him. He realized after a moment of struggle that it was Jaz.

"You can get off me now," she said.

"Oh, sorry." Dean rolled off of her onto the sidewalk and got back to his feet. He extended his hand to help her up, and after looking up from the ground for a moment, she took it and he helped her back to her feet. "Thanks for that. I couldn't move. It was all going in slow motion, kind of like one of those dreams where you can't get away, no matter how hard you try."

"Dean you need to be more careful. I mean seriously, Jo and I told you that you've touched a demonic idol that will bring you bad luck. You would think that you'd be more aware of your surroundings when you know your luck is compromised."

"I thought Jo's spell solved that problem." Dean looked at his daughter. "What was all that mumbo jumbo back in the apartment about if it wasn't to protect me?"

"It was a protection spell, Dad, and it worked. Mom grabbed you and saved your life. You were lucky. That truck could have splattered you all over the sidewalk."

Dean turned to look at where the truck had come to a stop just before crashing into one of the shops that lined the street. The store owner had come out and was shouting at the driver. Dean looked around to make sure no one else was injured. There didn't appear to be any other casualties, just his own pride.

"Come on, Dean, we need to get over there and find the other two figurines before it's too late," Jaz said.

Dean joined the two women and together, after carefully checking that all oncoming traffic was stopped by the light, crossed the street to the newly erected construction fence that surrounded the remains of the Errington Security building. The three of them had to walk halfway down the block to get to the construction entrance where trucks and workers were coming and going from the site.

"Let me talk to the construction foreman when we get inside. They are pretty careful about anyone but their demolition workers coming on the site," Jaz said once they got inside. She walked up to an office trailer nearby and went inside.

While she was inside, Dean and Joanna looked around as the workers went about their work knocking down the remaining brick walls. A front end loader was scooping up rubble and filling a dump truck nearby.

"Do you see anything, Jo? Any sign of the other figurines?"

"No. They could be covered by the rubble and wouldn't show as easily, but I think I would still see the aura emanating from where they were."

Jaz came out of the trailer, followed by a tall man in work khakis and a blue button-down shirt. He was wearing a white hard hat and carried two others. Jaz was putting a similar hard hat on, adjusting it for her ponytail.

"Guys, this is Joe Anderson, the construction foreman."

Dean shook his hand and took the offered helmet, putting it on. Jo did the same.

"Yeah, we need to be careful," the foreman said. "I've had three guys injured in the last three days by fluke accidents and the insurance inspectors are due here any minute. Everyone on the site has to wear their helmets and I have to ask you three to stay back from the work. I know you are looking for some personal effects and I've had my guys keeping an eye out. We've been putting whatever we find over in that storage trailer over there. If you'll follow me."

The three of them filled in behind him as he walked over to storage container trailer nearby. Dean brought up the rear and leaned forward so that his companions could hear him over the machinery. "Fluke accidents sounds like we have a confirmation that the other idols were here, right?"

"I was thinking the same thing, Dean. Jo, keep your eyes open."

"I am, Mom. Nothing pops out to me so far."

Joe unlocked a padlock and opened the other trailer. There were a few boxes and dusty items set on tables inside. There was no light in the trailer, just what streamed in the door.

"I'll be outside if you need anything. I've got to keep an eye out for that inspector," Joe said. He stepped outside the trailer and left the three of them to look through the piles of stuff.

Jaz went in first. To Dean, it seemed as if her steps were tentative, as if she didn't want to be there. He knew this must be tough for her. Jo followed her and stayed close to her mom.

Dean kept back a few steps to give the two of them some space. This was all that was left of her family. To Jaz and Jo this was something like visiting a grave site. Jo had grown up hearing about this in the future.

After a bit of searching, Jo let out a squeal of delight and rushed forward past her mother to one of the tables. Dean thought they had found what they were looking for. He craned his neck to look past Jaz in the dim light streaming through the open trailer door. He saw Jo pick up something and turn around holding it out in triumph.

"Look, Mom. It's Grandma's sword. My sword. You gave this to me when I turned thirteen."

Jaz stepped forward and took the katana in its scabbard from her daughter. She held it in front of her, brushing her fingers across the pattern on the lacquered wood of the scabbard. Then she reached out and pulled Jo into an embrace. Dean could see Jaz's shoulders shaking from the sobs and saw tears streaming down Jo's face over her mother's shoulder.

He turned around and gave them some room while he looked at the scattered items on the table next to him. Most of it appeared to be junk, or the items were ruined enough in the fire and building collapse that they would not be usable anymore. Dean looked through all the items on the table in front of him and looked over at the other two tables in the trailer. A thought occurred to him.

"Jaz, what happened to all the guns? I know your family had to have a lot of guns and ammunition in the building."

Jaz pulled away from her embrace with Jo and wiped at her eyes. "We did. Most of them were in the building's armory which largely survived the explosion and fire. It was built with additional structural and security support. There is a large gun dealer we know outside of the city that has taken possession of them until I can get some place secure to store them again."

Dean knew that the Erringtons' national security business had an arrangement with the FBI and U.S. Marshal's office that gave the qualified team members nationwide carry permits. Jaz had once mentioned that the close relationship with the Marshals carried back to just after the U.S. Civil War.

"I still have all the gear from my personal SUV, so I have my full load out. I don't need the rest right now. The other weapons will have to wait for me to go over them. I can't do that until we get local offices set up again. Right now the remaining staff is stretched pretty thin covering all of our existing contracts."

"I know your parents and two cousins died in the blast," Dean said. "Were there many staff members lost in the fire as well?"

"No. Luckily, it happened after regular business hours and all the staff had left. Now I have some new offices rented in a building on the outskirts of town. I have stopped in but haven't set up an office there for myself yet."

"I'm sure it's hard, Mom. You have to take over for everything that both your mom and dad did. Maybe Dad and I can help in some way."

Dean cringed. He didn't know anything about security work and was still uncomfortable with many of the ways that the hunter clan looked at some Unusuals. He realized that Jaz noticed his reaction.

"Sorry, Jaz, I just think that me working there part-time would not be a good fit. I feel like it would be a conflict of interest."

"Actually, Dean, I could use your expertise if you'll give it. We were in the process of refitting our medic bags and gear. Now all of those supplies were destroyed inside the building. None of it is salvageable and I have no idea what my Dad was doing with the project. I could use your help fitting out an updated tactical EMS bag equipment list."

"Oh, I could help with that certainly."

"What about me, Mom? It is a family business after all."

"I didn't have anything planned for you, Jo. I thought that Dean and I were going to find a way to send you back to your own time. You need to go back to the future time frame. I'm concerned that you being here in the past too long could mess up something in the future."

"Nah, the Coven told me before they sent me back it was unlikely that I could do anything to change the timeline as long as I returned before I was actually born. It seems that if I interact with myself at all, even as a baby, I could change something in myself which could really mess up both me and the timeline. They had a huge discussion about it before they sent me back. Some of the members didn't agree because of the risk if I couldn't come back."

"So there is some risk to the timeline?" Dean asked. He was thinking about how Marty McFly started to disappear in "Back to the Future" when he screwed up his parents getting together in the past. "I think we need to focus on getting you back sooner rather than later. It's better to be safe than sorry."

"But I want to stay here. I like you guys as your younger selves. You're not all parenty and stuff."

Dean and Jaz shared a look. Jaz stepped in.

"Dean's right, Jo. We don't know how many things might get shifted in time, even just a little bit, just by you staying any longer than is necessary. Dean will contact the coven right away, and see when they can send you back."

"But, don't you need my help to find the other idols? Who is going to cast your protection spells?"

"There are other witches around, Jo," Dean said. He hated to be more 'parenty' as she put it, but this was important. "No more argument. You have to go back."

Jaz looked around at the tables one more time. "We know the idols are not here and there's nothing else of value beside my mother's sword. Let's go and head back to the apartment. I need to show up at the office today and I have that conference call coming up. They need to see my face and know that everything will be alright." She saw Jo's pouting face. "Jo, you can carry the sword if you want. I promise that when the time comes in the future, it will be yours."

That seemed to perk the teen up a bit, but Dean could see she was still disappointed and her shoulders had sagged a bit as they left the storage trailer. Dean collected the helmets when they got to the gate and took them over to the foreman. Joe waved to Jaz as he took them back, and then returned to his work directing the demolition of the building.

The three of them headed out to the street and started walking back to Jaz's apartment. Dean wondered aloud where the other two idols could be.

"Someone must have picked them up," Jaz replied. "Either it was one of the firefighters, investigators, or one of the construction workers. It should be a small list. I'll have one of the staff at the new office put together a list. Once we have that, we can take some time to track each of them down. These things are powerful enough that we should see some signs of their presence if we end up with the right person."

Dean hoped so, he worried about how some poor, unsuspecting person might react to supernatural bad luck in their life.

Chapter 4

Sam continued his search for the perfect, creepy magic words to use in the weekly Dungeon Masters game with his friends. They had been participating in this role-playing game campaign with him as the Dungeon Leader for the last five years. He, his wife, and a few of his old high-school buds had been playing off and on for years, but this was the longest running game any of them had been involved with.

They had each invested a lot into their characters, and Sam worked hard to make each week's adventure special in some way. This week, he had them invading the lair of a Lich, a supernatural being of the undead variety. This particular Lich he had designed was a real bastard and he was going to enjoy playing his part in the upcoming gaming encounter.

The Google search had turned up several options for old incantations and it was hard to choose from them. He wanted something that was not English and would lend a dark tone to the pretend spell-casting he had planned. In the end, he let random choice make the decision for him, closing his eyes and stabbing at the screen with a finger to pick one of the search engine's choices.

Sam opened his eyes and saw a link to ancient transformation curses. Perfect, he thought. Sam clicked the link and hit the print icon on his computer screen to print out the strange and alien words that came up. He got up to start setting up the dinner table for the game in the small apartment he and his wife leased. A black table cloth went on the table first, followed by the three electric candles from the bookshelf. On a whim, Sam brought the two jade idols over, too. They would add a nice supernatural touch to the Lich's lair.

His friends would be arriving soon, and he went back into the bedroom to see what was keeping his wife from coming out to help set up for so long. He didn't see the faint glow in the eyes of the two green figurines on the dinner table, or the shifting text on the printed paper nearby.

———

A GROAN WENT UP from around the table as Eddie exhibited another of his horrible rolls on the pair of twenty-sided dice. The low result on both dice meant the team would fail to find any traps as they entered the passage that led to the Lich's lair. Sam just smiled and gave a mock laugh "mwa-ha-ha-ha." He was enjoying this night's game a lot. Every one of the four players had shown horrible luck when rolling their dice for the game and several char-acters had come close to dying. Everyone was tense and the mood in the room was both excited and a little annoyed at the string of bad luck.

Sam asked them what they wanted to do next. He knew that there was no real choice. They had come here to play the game and the game led them down into the underground lair of the undead creature waiting for them. The trap had been laid.

"Man, Sam, you've outdone yourself this time," Sandra said. "The whole scenario tonight is super-creepy. The hair on the back of my neck is standing up."

"Thanks, Sandra. Jill and I like it when you guys come over and play. I thought we could go the extra mile for tonight's session. So what do you all want to do next? Eddie detected no traps ahead."

The players all looked at each other around the table. Eddie and Steve had both gone to high school with Sam and even though they had gone off to college, they both had kept in touch with their old friend, rejoining his weekly games when they graduated and returned to Elk City to settle into their adult lives. Sandra was a work friend of Sam's wife, Jill. She was a divorcee and the newest member of their group. He suspected she was using this as a way to get out of her house once a week now that her ex-husband had moved out. She added a lot to the group, though, and she was easy on the eyes, too.

"We will go down the passage to the door at the far end," Steve announced. "It's what we're here for. Let's kill this Lich and steal his treasure."

There were nods of approval and Sam smiled. Now it was time for the fun to begin. Eddie had failed his attempt to find traps and the party of adventurers was about to walk right into the Lich's first defensive trap, laid out just for invaders like them.

"You step forward and hear a 'click' from down the hallway," Sam announced.

"Run away!" Sandra shouted

"I duck to the floor," Eddie proclaimed.

"I draw my sword," Steve said standing up.

"Me, too," Jill added.

"Too late," Sam said. "You are all transported by magic to a large room. There is a pentagram drawn on the floor and you find yourselves within it. None of you can move so much as a muscle. You hear a weird deep voice begin to speak nearby and you can't understand what the words are saying. It is in a language you have never heard before."

Sam picked up the sheet of paper and began to read the words printed there. He was really in the groove and was surprised that he didn't stumble over the unfamiliar word structure he encountered. There was a strange, green glow from the center of the table as he read and he heard the players gasp as he continued reading. He wondered where the glow was coming from, but found he could not stop reading the words once he had started. It was like someone else was reading them through him. He did not hear the spell's final words. He felt his consciousness fade to the background as the being now speaking from inside his mind took over, finishing the dual spells of summoning and transformation. In the small apartment, there was a flash of bright green light and then the darkness came.

"GREAT GAME, SAM," Steve said as he stood up to leave.

Eddie joined in. "Yeah, that was the best one yet. Keep it up."

"Eddie, can I get you to walk me out to my car?" Sandra asked

"Sure, we can all go down together."

Jill closed the door behind them and looked up at him. "You outdid yourself this time, honey. Come to bed. We can clean up this mess in the morning." She walked back to the bedroom in the tiny apartment without looking backward.

Graadu smiled to himself. None of them suspected that Sam was no longer in control of this body. He was still there, but not in control. The demon lord could hear the pitiful screams and protests in the back of Sam's mind. Once the spell had been cast, the four players had been put into stasis while Graadu took some time to acclimate to his new surroundings. He spent two hours deciding what he would do to the band of adventurers in the apartment. In the end he decided to transform each of them in a different way. Each would begin to cause havoc in this small earth city, and each would be unaware of how they had become the monsters of their own nightmares.

The demon turned his attention to the two figurines on the table. Together, the pair had just enough power to help the human fool, Sam, to bring him here in this limited form. He recognized that the idols were actually part of a trio of summoning stones. If he could locate the third summoning idol of the set, it would allow him to fully manifest himself on earth, rather than merely possess this flimsy human body. This fleshy shell was so fragile and delicate. He would have to find the other stone figurine if he were to complete the summoning and enter this world for real. It had been more than six hundred years since he had come to earth. He longed to come back, take revenge on humankind for banishing him away in the first place, and see what this newer, modern world offered in the way of entertainments.

He had been amused by the way the humans of this time and place "played" at the tasks that would have been all too real for individuals just a few hundred years earlier. Had they all forgotten that things really did go bump in the night? Maybe this time, he would be able to remain on earth and create a hold over an entire region. If the humans were all so unsuspecting and unprepared for a true manifestation of evil, this was going to be easy.

Graadu looked at the statues again and asked Sam, cowering in the back of his mind, where they had come from. When he discovered they had been found at a nearby construction site, buried in the rubble after a fire, he became excited. All he would have to do is search the site. He would turn up either the third idol or maybe find the previous owners. They would likely know where the other stone idol was located. It would be child's play to take the last one away from its owner if all the humans of the present time were such fools.

"Sam, come to bed. You've got work in the morning," Jill called from the bedroom.

"Be right there," Graadu said. He could start the search in the morning. Tonight he had other plans. It had been far too long since he had enjoyed the pleasures of the flesh. He had left Jill unchanged so he could savor her fear and terror when she realized her husband was not the man she thought he was. He was not a man at all.

Chapter 5

Two days later, Dean got up and made breakfast. It was his day off and ordinarily he would be getting ready to do some chores around the house and yard for his landlords, the Baxters. They were a nice elderly couple that Dean liked a lot. They offered him a break on the rent if he mowed the lawn for them and did other odds chores around the outside of their house and property as they needed.

That would have been his normal routine for a day off, but this wasn't a normal day off. This was the day they sent Jo back to the future. The local witch coven had to wait until the "stars and heavens were aligned" or some such nonsense. He didn't know how magic worked, though he had benefited from it several times before since he started working at Station U. It did work, though, and if all went well, Joanna would be going back home today. He had mixed feelings about the spell and sending her back.

He and Joanna had become close over the last few weeks. He had come to grips with the fact that he had a daughter, and that she was the future teenaged version of that child. She was a good kid and had turned out alright. He had always wondered what kind of parent he would become when the time came. He had grown up with a single mother and a missing father. It turned out that, for all that he could see in Jo, he was a pretty good dad despite not having a good role model of his own growing up.

He was thinking about this over a cup of coffee and a bowl of cereal when Jo came padding out of the spare bedroom. She was still tired and had a serious case of bed-head hair going on.

"Hey, Jo," Dean said. "There's some more coffee on if you want a cup. Are you ready for today?"

"I guess so, Dad. I'm not sure I'm ready to go back. You and Mom need me to help you out with things. How are you going to find those other two figurines without my help?"

"We'll just have to make do, I guess," Dean laughed. "Seriously, Jo, how did you think we got along and got things done before you got here?"

"I don't know and the two of you didn't get along before I got here. It took me to make you stop fighting and start working together." She had a big grin on her face. She wasn't exactly wrong.

Dean didn't have the heart to tell her that she was not the cause of the friendship between him and Jaz. He considered himself easygoing and he made friends easily. He would have found a way to get along with Jaz even if Jo had not come back and forced the issue while they searched for Ashley.

"Well, you can't keep staying here, Jo. People would talk. I told the Baxters that you're my niece and that you're only here for a short time. No one will believe you're my daughter and it will make me look like some sort of creepy guy with a teenaged girl living with him."

"Eww, Dad. Way to make it weird."

"See, that's just what I mean."

Jo came over and made her breakfast while Dean cleaned up his. The two of them chatted about other things while she finished her food, and he admitted to himself that he would miss her when she was gone. She was a good kid. The two of them cleaned up the breakfast dishes together one last time and then they headed out to drive to the witch coven in Elk City where they would cast the spell to send her back.

. . .

ASHA, the leader of the witch clan met Dean at the door of their large home located in one of the more prestigious neighborhoods of the city.

"Welcome, Dean, and welcome Joanna," Asha said, gesturing for them to enter. "It is wonderful to finally meet you after all that Dean has said about you."

Jo rushed forward to give Asha a hug that startled the older woman for a moment, then she enfolded the teen in her arms and returned the hug. She smiled at Dean over his daughter's shoulder.

"Jo, your father sent us the details you shared about the spell that sent you here and we believe we have the necessary power and items needed to cast the reverse of it to send you back. We must be careful, though, in that we do not wish to have you cross over and alter the timeline in any way. This could be disastrous for all of our futures."

"We are confident that you can do this, Asha," Dean said.

"Don't be so sure, Dean Flynn. The Coven has not always had great success when it comes to casting spells on your behalf."

Dean remembered the magical explosion when they had tried to do a scrying spell to uncover who was at the heart of an anti-Unusual terrorist plot just a few months before. That had been the spell that had required the promise of his firstborn daughter to the coven in the first place. Jo would not have ended up in the hands of the witch coven were it not for the price paid for that spell. It made him think. Nothing came for free.

"Asha," Dean asked. "What is the price for this spell? I know there is always a price."

The older woman laughed as she led them into the communal casting room with its circle of chairs and the waiting women of the coven arrayed around it.

"Payment is for outsiders, Dean. Joanna is one of us, promised to us by you in your past. This spell is for one of our own. We will assume the price for the magic cast here today."

"Well, I certainly hope that this one goes better than the last spell you cast for our family. I do not wish there to be any problems or injuries from such a powerful spell."

"Dad, this is not a spell like the scrying spell where the Coven had to pierce the defenses of another magical being. That was what caused the danger before in that instance. This is more of a magical price to be paid in drained power and fatigue. They can only cast this type of thing once in a while."

"She is right Dean," Asha added. "We will not be up against those types of countering forces today, although, the power of the spell required to pierce the veil of time is significant. We would not try this were it not for the fact that young Jo here is proof that it can be done. The sun, moon, and planets are in a good position to assist our efforts as well. We will have ample power to do this today."

Dean heard a knock at the door behind them in the hallway and turned to see Jaz being led into the room. He heard a sharp intake of breath from several of the assembled witch sisters. They could see that she was a hunter, one who, in another time and place, might have been chasing witch casters down. Asha shushed them with a sharp glance.

"Welcome, Jaswinder Errington," the elder witch leader said. "Your presence here is an important part of the casting and we wish you well while you are within these walls."

Jo walked over to her mother and gave Jaz a hug. Dean was pleased to see the two of them continue to bond, although this would be the last chance for a while.

"Thanks for coming, Mom."

"I was told that my presence was necessary for the spell to work out. Plus it is my last chance to see you before you go." Jaz smiled at her daughter. "Of course I would be here."

"It is time," a voice intoned from the circle behind the family. "Will the spell's focus please enter the circle."

Dean and Jaz turned to watch as Jo walked to her place in the center of the large casting circle. Asha had assumed her place at the apex opposite from where Dean and Jaz stood. Dean could feel something, he wasn't sure what it was, as the low chanting began. He watched as Jo closed her eyes and tilted her head up toward the high domed ceiling, painted with a motif of heavenly bodies and zodiac symbols.

The chanting grew in intensity and Dean looked around as the light streaming in the windows from the sunlight outside seemed to dim. The room grew dark and the chants reached a crescendo, stopping with a sudden shout and then Dean turned to see Jo collapsing in the center of the circle. He started to rush forward, but Jaz's steel grip on his arm stopped him. Dean knew she was right. His entry into the casting circle would only serve to break up or even alter the spell.

The chants began again and the whole process repeated itself as Dean and Jaz watched. This time, there seemed to be an edge to the tone, something that had not been there before. The darkness returned again and this time Dean kept his focus on the casting circle. He watched as the thirteen women leaned in from their seats around Jo as if forcing their wills to push her back to when she belonged. Then there was a collective gasp and the light returned to normal.

Dean heard a whimper and saw Jo struggling to rise from the center of the circle. She was unsteady getting up from where she lay on the floor. This time he could not stop. He broke free of Jaz's grasp and rushed into the circle to Joanna. As he got closer, he could see her crying.

"Are you alright, Joanna?"

"Daddy, it didn't work. I tried to release myself to the spell. I did everything right, I promise."

He embraced the teen and looked around at the circle of watching women. Asha came forward from her chair as the high priestess of the coven. She looked pale and drained of energy. Jaz came and joined him at the center of the circle, too. She rested her hand on her daughter's head where it lay on Dean's shoulder. The girl was sobbing now.

"Asha, what happened?" Dean asked.

"There is something holding her here," the witch leader said. "Some great evil has entered the region and young Joanna is tied to it magically somehow." She looked down at Jo. "Child, have you cast any spells recently? I told you that you must be free of any magical ties to this timeline in order to be sent back."

Jo looked up at the three adults clustered around her at the center of the casting circle. Her brow was furrowed as she considered the question.

Jaz answered for her. "The protection spell."

"What?" Dean asked.

"The protection spell. Jo cast it on you, and the figurine, when you pulled the summoning idol from the box back in my apartment."

"What is this summoning idol you speak of, huntress?" Asha asked.

"It was one of three placed in my family's care for safe-keeping. When my family was attacked and the building burned down, the protection spell and the box for the three summoning idols were both destroyed. We only found one of the idols in the items salvaged from the fire. The other two belonging to the set are still out there. We thought they were at the demolished building site but a search there proved fruitless."

"And young Jo here cast a protection spell over the one idol to keep its effects from harming her father, yes?" Asha asked.

The three of them nodded.

"Well, there is bad news and worse news, then," Asha announced. "The bad news is that Jo cannot be sent back until the other idols are recovered. The worse news is that our spell's failure revealed that the other two must have been used by someone to do evil. That evil is now tied to her. If she does not break that tie before the next time we might cast this spell, the autumnal equinox in three months, she will never be able to return to her correct time."

Jaz spoke up. "I think you're missing the bigger picture, Mistress Asha."

They all turned to look at her.

"Those stone idols are powerful. If they've been used, even

partially, to summon a demon here to Elk City, then the whole city is in danger. The demon lord tied to those figurines is one of the most powerful I've ever heard of. My family's lore masters were clear in their records. His presence here will spell doom for Elk City unless we can find a way to send him back to Hell."

Chapter 6

Dean was still shocked by how quickly the tables had turned with the spell. It seemed his family was doomed to have spells fail when they least expected it. The other members of the spell circle had left the casting room for other areas of the massive coven house. Only Asha remained with the three of them.

"Young Jo here still has much to learn," the witch leader said. She looked from Jo to Jaz and Dean. "You must protect her while she is tied to this spell she has cast on the idol. Once the demon discovers it is she who blocks it from connecting to the other two idols, he will come searching for her."

Dean had a thought. "Wouldn't it make better sense to have her stay with you all here? She'll have the full coven to protect her."

"No, Dean Flynn. The demon will surely come searching here first since he will detect the nature of the protection and realize it must come from one of our number. We can watch over ourselves, but it will soon learn that the protection spell does not emanate from any caster in this protected place."

"If this is so strongly protected, then it would be the perfect place to keep her from harm," Dean protested.

"Nay, Dean. There is stronger protection available. The huntress knows."

Dean looked at Jaz. She was staring at the floor and shaking her head.

"What, Jaz? You know what she is talking about, right?"

"Family," was all Jaz said.

"What do you mean, 'Family'?"

"Dad, she means that the hunter clans have created protections over their family structure during the centuries they tracked and hunted down demons. It is a level of protection that no one else but one of our family can offer. It is called a sanctuary spell and it is very strong."

"But it is also extremely hard to do and I've never done it myself," Jaz added, joining the conversation. "I know the theory and the words to enact it, but I'm not sure how to make it work in this instance. I'm the last Errington. If I'm to provide sanctuary, then who is the one who will go out and hunt this demon down?"

Asha smiled. "You are forgetting that you are not as alone as you think you are, young Jaswinder. Your family is only mostly gone. Dean here is a member of your clan now, too."

"What?" Dean asked. "How can that be?"

"You are tied together by Joanna, Dean. Despite your doubts, you and Jaz will marry someday, and after that, have a daughter. That daughter ties you to the Errington clan. You may provide sanctuary."

"But all of that is in the future. It hasn't happened yet," Dean protested.

"Dean, magic and magical beings aren't as concerned with our human ties to linear time, past, present and future. Magic sees all of it as a whole that exists at once, in the same space. You will marry Jaz. She will bear your child. As far as magic is concerned, that is enough."

"Trust her. It makes sense, Dad," Jo said.

"Jaz?" Dean asked. "Does it make sense to you? You're the one who needs to make this work."

"Yes," Jaz nodded. "I may not have fully admitted it all being true to myself, but it makes sense. If that is the case, then I should be able to lay the sanctuary protection on you so that you can watch over Jo. It does mean that you will have to keep her close to you at all times. She must stay by your side, within a few yards of you or she must stay in your apartment." Jaz shot a look at Jo. "You understand that? You will only be protected while inside your father's home or by his side. You must not go out on your own."

"I understand, Mom. I'm not the newbie here."

Once he learned she had to stay another three months, Dean had hoped to get another place for Jo to stay while she remained here. It seemed, however, that she was to stay with him for a while longer. He'd have to come up with some sort of excuse again that would work for his landlords. She was young enough to still be in school, so he'd have to explain to them why she wasn't going to the local high school like other neighborhood kids.

"Asha," Dean said. "I thank you again for your willingness to undertake another spell on our behalf. We'll keep Jo safe. Please remain safe yourself. We'll see you back here in three months, I guess."

"Be safe as well, Dean Flynn. We shall surely see each other again in three months."

Asha led the small family to the entry of the large home and watched them head outside. The three walked to their two cars, parked next to each other on the street. They were all silent. Dean wondered how he was supposed to protect Jo from a demon. If some creature came up and burst into his apartment, he'd do his best to defend her, but he was no trained fighter like Jaz, or even Jo.

"Dean," Jaz said, interrupting his train of thought. "The sanctuary should be cast in your home. It will tie to you and Jo there and remain with you when you are together. That should be our next stop."

"How does this work, Jaz? I'm not a fighter like you. I will not be as able to defend her from an attack as you would be."

"The sanctuary spell should avoid that necessity," Jazz replied. "If I understand how it works from the family lessons and lore, sanctuary makes it so the target of an attack cannot be found. It is like they don't exist. Some magical beings won't even be able to see Jo when she is under the protection of the spell."

"So how close do I have to be to Dad to make it work?"

"My guess is within his aura, so say about five to six feet, maybe more? But remember that you'll always be within the protection when in his apartment. So just stay close to him whenever you go out and you'll be fine. I'll track down this demon and get the other stones back. You just stay safe."

Jo nodded and the three of them loaded up in their cars and headed to Dean's apartment. Jo rode with him while Jaz followed in her black Ford SUV. It was time to get the sanctuary spell in place.

THE RIDE back to Dean's apartment was quiet. The time travel spell had failed and Dean was back to having Jo stay with him. It was going to be a little awkward with his landlords. They were a nice enough elderly couple but they did have definite notions about how things were supposed to be.

Now she had to stay with him through the entire summer, for three months, until the next heavenly event, the autumnal equinox. They had that long to find the other summoning idols and get Jo back to her own time. If that didn't work, Dean guessed he'd have to enroll her in school and make her attend just like any other fifteen-year-old.

They got back to Dean's apartment and pulled up out front of the small suburban home where he rented the apartment over the garage. He winced when he saw Mrs. Baxter out watering her flower garden. She waved and then saw Jo and got a look of puzzlement on her face.

Dean told Jo to take Jaz upstairs and walked over to his landlady when he noticed her expression. "Hi, Mrs. Baxter. We ran into a bit of a snag with Jo's mom and dad, so she's going to stay with me for the rest of the summer. I hope that's not a problem."

"No, Dean, of course not," the elderly woman said. "I know not everyone has parents as supportive as they'd like. She's lucky to have you and your new friend Jaz to keep an eye on her." She waved at Jaz and Jo as they went by.

Dean and Mrs. Baxter watched as the two women in question walked up the stairs on the outside of the garage up to Dean's apartment.

"How are things going between you and your new lady? I have to say I miss your Ashley, but don't get me wrong. I understand how these things go. We each have to make our own decisions in these things."

"We are getting along alright, just good friends right now I guess. I miss Ashley, too, Mrs. B. She just had to leave suddenly and couldn't tell me when she would be able to return, so we sort of broke things off."

"I understand, dear," the woman said. She laid her hand on Dean's arm. "Don't let an old lady's sense of what is right for you get in the way of your own heart. You're a nice boy. You'll find the one for you."

She said goodbye and went back to her gardening while Dean walked over to his apartment. As he was climbing the stairs, he heard a heated discussion between Jaz and Jo.

"You can't leave me here without some weapons to defend myself, Mom. I am more than capable in handling myself. At least bring me my sword."

"It's not your sword, it's my mother's. You don't get it for at least eighteen years yet, right?"

"That's not the point, it's tied to me, too. I can feel it when I hold it. I will feel better if I have it with me."

"So, you'll settle for just having the sword?"

"No, you should leave me a pistol and AR-15, too."

"Absolutely not. People will talk if you are found toting that kind of weaponry around a residential neighborhood."

"I'm not stupid, Mom. I won't be wandering around outside with them."

"Then you don't need them. The sanctuary spell will protect

you in the apartment, and if you stay close to Dean when you're outside of the home, you should be safe as well."

"C'mon, just a pistol? What could it hurt?"

Dean decided he needed to enter and add his two-cents-worth. Pushing open the apartment door he entered, shushing the ladies as he came in.

"Can you two quiet down a bit? We are lucky Mrs. Baxter is a little hard of hearing so she can't hear you arguing over which assault weapons you'd like to leave in the apartment on their property."

"Dean stay out of this," Jaz said. "This is between the two of us. We know you're not a big fan of guns, so let me handle this." She turned back to her daughter and paused for a moment. "I'll leave you one Glock with a few holster arrangements for you depending on what you're wearing. I'll also leave mom's sword, but it's just a loan. It's not yours yet, no matter what you think or feel. Understood?"

"Hey, I thought you just said the spell would protect her?" Dean asked. "If that's the case, we don't need all the weaponry. I'm not sure I'm comfortable with this."

Jo looked over at him and rolled her eyes. "Dad, you're never comfortable around guns. So what else is new?"

"You two stay here and I'll go get what we need out of the SUV," Jaz said. "It is better to be safe than sorry, Dean. She's right. Jo knows how to handle firearms safely. If I raised her, she's been handling guns since she could write her name. I'll be right back."

Dean watched her head out to her vehicle and shook his head. It was like he wasn't even here when the two of them had these discussions.

"Don't take it so bad, Dad. She didn't like it when you insisted you honor your commitment to the Coven and turn me over to them to be educated as a witch. She didn't like it, but she also accepted that you made the promise in good faith and couldn't go back on your word. She is still working through all that now, but when the time comes in fifteen years or so that you first send me there to live for a while, she gets over it. I secretly think she's proud of how powerful I already am."

"You do seem to have a lot of power for one so young, Jo. Have Asha and the others ever commented on it?"

"They seem to think that the innate hunter magic is part of it. I'm the first of one of the major hunter clans to ever become a witch. So there's that. Some of the sisters seem to think there is something magical in your past, too, Dad. They say that only a unique combination of family powers could explain my affinity for magic." The teen shrugged. "It's no big deal either way. I like it and the magic comes easily to me."

Dean nodded in agreement. He remembered the way she defended herself with no trouble when they were on the rescue mission to get Ashley back. She was able to command some pretty incredible powers on her own. It seemed at the time that she was able to do things that surprised even herself.

Jaz came back up to the apartment then, carrying a small, black plastic case and a long, cloth-wrapped bundle. The bundle must be the sword. He guessed the case contained a pistol.

"First things first," Jaz said, opening the small plastic gun case. Inside Dean saw a black semi-automatic pistol and three magazines. There was also a box of bullets in the case.

Jaz continued as Jo laughed with delight. "The pistol is a standard that you should know very well. I've left three magazines and a full reload for each. They are standard silver frangible reloads which should handle most Unusual types, and at least slow a demon down. You don't have a license to carry these outside of the house so this is just for home defense or emergency situations. You'll be careful, right?"

"I will, Mom." The teen picked up the pistol, checking to make sure it was unloaded and safe. Dean knew she was capable with one of them. He'd seen her handle one like it before. "I still need to get used to the manual safety. In the future, we use biometric grips that sense and recognize the owner when you pick a gun up. It means that it can never be used against you in a fight."

"That's good to know," Jaz said. "The technology exists now, but few gun owners use it."

"That changes with the new licensing laws that go into effect in 2028. All gun owners have to use the technology to deter thefts."

"Hey, no talking about the future," Dean cautioned. "We don't want to know things we're not supposed to know, remember?"

"Sorry, I forgot."

Jaz turned and unwrapped the bundle. It did contain the katana. It also held a belt clip holster with another double magazine clip-on holder for her belt as well. There was also a shoulder holster rig that held the pistol on one side and two magazines on the other.

"These are for emergencies only if you have to leave the apartment. I don't expect you to use them, but I wanted you to have options based on what you were wearing at the time, if you have to leave without your father."

"But she's not going to have to leave alone, right?" Dean clarified.

"Plan for the worst, hope for the best, Dean," Jaz said.

"Yeah, I guess so. So, what do we need to do to enact this sanctuary thing?"

"This is the sticky part," Jaz said. "The spell works because the family members are of one blood. It comes from being blood-related and from physical intimacy, if you get my meaning."

"Wait, you mean we need to …" Dean started. He was uncomfortable.

"Eww, Mom, that's gross…"

"No, I definitely do not mean that. In theory, though, it should work if the blood of one mixes with the other, without the intimacy part."

"Kind of like a blood pact from the middle ages?" Jo asked.

"Yes, or like some of the native cultures around the world. They all understood the nature of blood as a binding and protective agent in magic." Jaz pulled out a pocket knife and flicked the blade open with her thumb. She laid the blade against her palm and drew it toward her while wrapping her hand around it. She hissed in pain and opened her hand to show a long, shallow cut there. She handed the knife to Dean.

"Well, the funny thing is, this isn't the weirdest thing I've ever done," he said. He took the blade and repeated the process that Jaz had done. The pain was sharp and burning but he opened his palm to show a matching wound to Jaz's.

"What now?" he asked.

"Clasp my hand while I say the binding spell. This is usually part of a hunter wedding ceremony to bless the wedding night. Hopefully this works as well."

Dean clasped her hand, palm to palm, their blood mingling. Jaz closed her eyes and started saying something. Dean thought it was Latin but he wasn't sure. After a while, he might have started feeling a tingling sensation between their clasped hands. It felt kind of warm and kind of like there was a small insect buzzing between their clasped palms. Jaz opened her eyes and released his hands.

Dean smiled and observed, "You know, for monster hunters who dislike magic, you sure use a lot of it."

"We use what we need to protect us from the creatures we hunt, nothing more." Jaz's tone was cold and her glare told him not to press the point. She was more than a little uncomfortable with Jo's magical endeavors and he wouldn't make any points following this little jab with more similar observations.

"So did it work?" Jo asked.

"We'll know if the demon shows up here," Jaz said.

"Wow," Dean said. "That's encouraging. Is there anything else I need to do?"

"No, the magic should be working. It felt like the spell completed," Jaz said. "I'm not completely sure. I've never done this before either."

"Okay, then, I should get some gauze and a bandage to clean up that wound. I don't want you dripping blood all over the apartment."

Dean went and got his home first-aid kit out and started tending to Jaz's and his own wounds all the while wondering what would happen if and when the demon showed up here.

Chapter 7

The next day and a half sped by. Dean got Jo settled back in and they prepared for her staying with him for another three months. They even took a trip to the mall to get Jo some more clothes beyond what she had packed to bring back in time with her. Jaz helped out with some funds to help offset the expense since Dean's paramedic salary was not up to supporting both of them in the long term.

Jo had wanted to wear her shoulder holster rig to the mall, but Dean pointed out that while she might have some sort of allowance to do that in the future, she'd end up in jail here in the past for carrying a concealed weapon without a permit. She pouted a bit about not being able to go out armed, but she got over it as soon as they got down to some serious shopping.

Dean didn't much like shopping, he was a typical guy. He went out, bought what he needed and then went home. Jo enjoyed the whole process, though. She wanted to see all the possible outfits in all the stores serving teens with the latest in casual fashion before she made up her mind on which outfits to buy. It was exhausting for Dean but Jo seemed to recharge every time she found something new to try on.

The whole time they were out, Dean kept his eyes open for anything that looked like a threat. He was not sure what the demon would do or look like. Jaz had only said that the creature would come looking for Jo, and Dean had to remain close to enable the protection spell to work. Dean also knew that Jo possessed potent magic of her own, but Jaz seemed to think this demon was going to be more of a challenge for them all before this was all over.

Dean and Jo went home from the mall, one exhausted and the other energized. Both of them had enjoyed their time together, Dean thought. He had to go to work the next morning and Jo was going to have to stay home in his apartment all day with nothing but the internet and his cable TV to keep her occupied. He knew how he would react to being cooped up that way all day. As a teenager this negative reaction would have been even stronger. Still, Jo seemed alright with the restrictions. He wondered how long that would last.

The next morning rolled around soon enough, and Dean got up at five a.m. to shower and get ready for work. Jo had not gotten up by the time he was ready to leave, so he left her a note to have a good breakfast and he'd check in on her later that morning if he got the chance. He grabbed his stethoscope and other gear and headed out to his pickup truck to drive in to work.

BARRY WAS ALREADY THERE at Station U when Dean arrived. Bill and Lynne were just wrapping up their shift work as he entered the squad room and he saw the other three paramedics seated around the small dinner table eating breakfast. Based on the smell, the station's zombie chef Freddy had outdone himself yet again.

"What is that amazing smell, Freddy?"

"I got some supplies in from Kristof Algar at Sabatani's. He got some new spices and herbs in so I was able to whip up some Cajun steak and eggs for breakfast this morning. I hope you like it."

"Freddy, that sounds fantastic. I'm famished," Dean said. He sat down with the other paramedics who, based on their silence, were enjoying the meal as much as he expected to.

His steak was nicely medium rare and the accompanying dual fried eggs were amazing. He knew that having their own personal chef in the station would make them the envy of every other ambulance unit in the Elk City Fire Department, if they had known. Freddy was definitely the best-kept secret in the whole department.

Bill and Lynne finished up their meals and headed home for the day while Dean was finishing up his breakfast. It was excellent and he was eating his last bite of steak when the tones sounded over the squad room speakers announcing the first ambulance call of the day.

"Medical Box 843, ambulance U-191 respond for a behavioral emergency, apartment 24, 8342 Hopewell Ave."

Barry looked over at him and raised one eyebrow in question. "Hey Dean, what do you think? I've never heard of that with our patients before."

"I don't know, Barry. Our Unusual patients are just like normal people, though, aside from their special abilities or circumstances. They can have mental illness, too."

His partner nodded and the two of them headed to the ambulance bay to roll out to the new emergency call. Dean wondered what the emergency could be, too. This was the first such call he'd encountered with his patients. Overall, the Unusual community seemed pretty well adjusted to their lives. If they had cases of depression or schizophrenia, he had never seen it. He hopped in the front of the ambulance to drive while Barry jumped in the passenger side. He got on the radio to notify headquarters they were responding to the call. They drove across town and were almost there before the dispatcher came back on the radio with some additional information relayed from the 911 caller.

"Ambulance U-191, you are responding for an agitated male patient threatening suicide. Use caution when approaching, Police units also responding."

Barry acknowledged the radio message. While Dean considered

the information they had on the patient. Suicidal patients were not just dangers to themselves. They could also cause problems or injury for responders and bystanders as well. The dispatcher didn't say anything about a weapon, but it would make sense for them to pay extra attention to the patient and scene when they arrived.

It didn't take more than three or four minutes for them to arrive on the scene. It was an apartment complex that sprawled around a central courtyard. Dean had been here before and knew that all the apartments' entrances opened up on that courtyard. He pulled up on the scene, noting a police car pulling up at the same time.

"Barry grab the stuff you need. I'm going to go chat with the officers about how we should approach this."

Barry nodded and hopped out to get the bags he thought they would need for this patient. Dean knew there were no injuries so far so their basic trauma bag and their medication kit would suffice for now. Hopefully they could talk their patient down from whatever was going on in his life that caused the present emotional response.

Dean knew the first officer who walked up. Officer Hamm was one of the police officers assigned to their police counterpart to Station U. They handled police emergencies with Unusuals in the community.

"Hey, Craig," Dean called. "We got the additional that the patient is suicidal. I was thinking that if there is no weapon present, we'd take the lead and try and talk him into letting us help out."

"That sounds good to me, Dean," Officer Hamm said. "I'd just as soon as watch you work as have to deal with this on my own. Knock yourself out."

Dean smiled and gave the officer a thumbs up and then went back to join his partner by the ambulance. The two of them then walked into the complex's central courtyard and looked around until they figured that their destination apartment was to their left. Dean took the gear from Barry and let him take the lead, since he was still the probie here.

They heard the shouting and yelling before they got to the door. Someone inside was very upset. Barry knocked on the door and then stepped back just in case someone came to the door with a weapon. Officer Hamm and his partner stood back and watched from about fifteen feet away, ready to jump in if needed.

The door swung open and a woman with a worried expression stood there. "Oh, thank God you're here. He woke up and started talking in a different voice, in a language that I couldn't understand. I freaked out and ran out of the bedroom and called 911. Since then he's come back and started talking like himself again, but now my husband says he has to kill the voices in his head, no matter what. I don't know what to do. He's making a noose and is threatening to hang himself."

"Okay, Ma'am," Barry said. "We will try to help out. What is your husband's name?"

"Steve," she told them. "He's been acting strange for the last few days, but just told me he was not feeling well. Then he woke up like this."

"Let us go talk with him. We'll see if can talk him into going to the hospital to get help," Barry said. He looked to Dean and started to head inside. Dean followed him.

Once inside the small apartment, they heard muttering coming from the next room and found a man standing on a chair fashioning a noose out of a torn-up sheet. He was in the process of tying it to the ceiling fan in the middle of the room. The man did not immediately notice the two paramedics enter the room.

"Steve," Barry said in a calm, even tone. He stood with his hands in plain view so that the patient could see he was unarmed. Hopefully it would be interpreted as non-confrontational.

The patient turned his head to look at them. For just an instant, Dean would have sworn there was a flash of green light in his eyes, then it was gone. The man shook his head and went back to his work.

Barry tried again, taking a step forward. "Steve, my name is Barry. Why don't you tell me what is going on. Your wife is very worried about you."

"Stay back," Steve said. "I have to stop the voice. It keeps telling me to do horrible things, to bite my wife, to drink her blood. I can't stop the voice and I'm afraid it's taking over. I have to end this the only way I know how."

Barry held out his hands palm forward. "Why don't you stop for right now and talk with us. We might have some medicine that will help take the voices away for a time. My partner and I are here from Station U, so you can tell us anything and we'll keep it a secret from your wife and neighbors." The paramedic turned his right hand, showing the back of it to the patient. This would expose the stamp with ultra-violet ink that only could be seen by the Unusual patients.

Steve just looked at the back of Barry's hand and shook his head. "What are you trying to show me? I don't see what you're pointing at. Do you think I'm crazy?"

"We think you're upset, not crazy," Barry said. He looked at Dean. Dean nodded. Whoever this guy was, he wasn't an Unusual. He was acting like an Unusual and that was probably why they got dispatched. Still, even a human patient who was agitated and suicidal could be dangerous to a paramedic crew.

"Steve, why don't you step down from that chair and sit and talk with us for a while? Tell us what is going on and we'll see what we can do to get you some help." Barry took another step forward and extended his hand.

Steve looked at Barry and then to Dean before looking up at the ceiling where he had tied the makeshift rope. He swayed a little bit and then slumped, falling off the chair and to the floor. Barry was able to catch him part of the way down and kept the patient from hitting the hardwood floor head first.

Dean rushed forward to help. Steve was sobbing now, curled up in the fetal position on the floor. Together, the two paramedics started to check the patient for any injury from the fall. There was no sign of anything. Dean did notice how cool to the touch the patient's skin was, as well as how pale he was. If he didn't know better, Dean would have thought he was a vampire, especially since he had talked about biting his wife and drinking blood.

He was pretty sure that vampires didn't spontaneously happen on their own. "Check for bite marks," Dean instructed his partner.

Barry was near the head and looked on the patient's neck. Steve just cried and ignored the two paramedics assessing him. After a quick check around the collar of Steve's T-shirt, Barry looked back at his partner.

"Nothing there."

"This is weird," Dean said. "I'm going to call medical command on the radio and get permission to give him a dose of Haldol to calm him down some. Then we can take him in to the hospital." Haldol was a sedative and hopefully the drug would make it easier to get the patient to go along with them peacefully.

He called Craig to come in the room while he went outside to call in to the hospital on his portable radio. The police officer was standing in the hallway and came in to sit with his partner and the patient. It wasn't a good idea to leave Barry alone with a disturbed patient.

It only took a few minutes to call in and talk to the doctor in the ER. Dean got the permission to administer a loading dose of Haldol to sedate the patient while he was transported to the hospital. He drew up the med in a syringe and took it back in to the apartment.

Dean walked over to their patient. Nothing had changed from when he had left the room. "Steve, I'm Dean, another paramedic. I have some of that medicine we mentioned that would help you out while we take you to the hospital. You'll feel a little pinch where I give you the shot, then you'll start to feel better."

Dean quickly cleaned a spot on the side of Steve's arm and gave the intramuscular injection. He rubbed the injection site when he was done to help the medication absorb a little faster. Steve barely moved the whole time.

Dean knew that many people saw mental illness as nothing more than a weakness of character. He knew better. It was often a chemical or anatomical problem in how the brain worked. It was no less a medical problem than a broken arm. It was just not as easy to see and acknowledge because you didn't put the head in a cast and sling where everyone could see it and understand. It was a problem that all of society needed to address and help build awareness about.

It took about fifteen minutes for the drug to start to have an effect. The crying stopped and Steve started to calm down. Then they ran into another problem.

"Steve, let's stand up and we can walk together out to our ambulance, okay?" Barry asked.

"I can't go outside. The sunlight burns my eyes and hurts me," Steve said.

Barry looked at Dean and shrugged. They had to get him out to the ambulance and take him to the ER. Dean thought to try something.

"Steve, I can understand that. How about if I bring you one of our special reflective blankets to cover up with. The sunlight will bounce right off of it. Does that sound good?"

Steve just gave them a groggy nod in agreement.

"Okay," Dean said. "I'll be right back."

Dean went out and got one of the mylar emergency blankets from the bags they'd left in the kitchen. When he opened it up, it was a large reflective and opaque covering for their patient. That did the trick. With the mylar emergency blanket wrapped around him, Steve accompanied the two paramedics back out to their ambulance.

Dean told the wife to meet them at the ER in her own car as it would take a little time to evaluate her husband before she got there. Then he got in the front of the emergency vehicle and started the drive to the hospital. This was a new one. He had a lot of questions and needed answers. Was there another way to turn a vampire other than biting and feeding on them, then feeding them vampire blood before they died from the blood loss? He needed answers.

If this guy wasn't a vampire, he might be in some sort of transformation into one. That posed a problem if there was someone running around turning people into vampires without going through the normal process. Dean resolved to check in with his vampire expert, James Lee, a vampire himself and the feudal lord over all the Unusuals in the Elk City area.

He and Dean's former partner, Brynne Garvey, were together as a couple. She was no longer working as a paramedic, not since she had been turned into a vampire herself after almost dying from a gunshot wound. Dean had encouraged her boyfriend James to turn her so she wouldn't die. Neither of them had wanted to lose her.

If anyone knew of another way to turn a vampire, it would be James. Dean would call him and meet up with him right after this shift was over. Someone might be up to no good and James needed to know about it, while Dean needed to find a way to heal the problem.

Chapter 8

Dean texted a message to Celeste Teal, James' long-time assistant, to see if he was available that evening. The response came in right away to come over any time. Dean said he'd be there around seven PM after work. He left himself enough time to go home and change first. He also wanted to check in on Joanna. He was sure she was tired of being cooped up in his apartment all day. He wasn't wrong.

"C'mon, Dad. You have to take me with you. I haven't seen James and Brynne in like — well, like forever."

"I'm not sure that is such a good idea. Remember, they don't know you in this timeline yet. Doesn't meeting them now as a teenager mess up the future or something?"

"Oh, you mean the whole paradox thing? The way it was explained to me, once I get back in time, anything I do is already a part of my past. I would have to cause the death of you or mom to change my future."

"Well…" Dean said with a sly smile.

"Seriously, Dad? I get mad at you but I would never do something like that."

"Okay, bad joke. It hasn't been that long since I was a teenager, though. I know how angry parents can make you."

"That's only when they aren't reasonable and make rules that make no sense. You're not going to do that, are you?"

"I'm not getting sucked into that one, kiddo. Alright, you can come, but stay close to me just like your mother said."

"Got it." Jo gave a little salute as she grinned ear to ear.

Dean felt bad for her. He knew he would not like to be shut in the house all the time either. He resolved to make sure to get her out of the apartment with him whenever he wasn't working. It would make it easier to stay in when he couldn't be with her.

Jo disappeared for a bit in her room while Dean changed into jeans and a golf shirt. He came out and only waited a few minutes before she came bouncing out into the living room wearing one of the outfits she had bought at the mall.

"I love this. I feel so retro, Dad. My friends back in the future would think this outfit was awesome."

Dean was surprised at her response. She looked like any other teen he would run into, but maybe that was the point. She had squeezed into skinny jeans and a t-shirt and a jean jacket. She spun around to show off her outfit and grabbed her purse and the katana from the kitchen counter.

"Hey, wait a minute. Where do you think you're going with that?"

"What?"

"The sword."

"I can't go out without this dad. I'll feel naked. Plus, there's a demon out there hunting me."

"That's what the protection spell is for, Jo. Leave the sword here."

"Fine." Jo's shoulders slumped as she set the katana back down on the table in the kitchen. "I hope I don't need it."

"You'll be fine. You still have your magic. I've seen you deal with demons without your sword. I have no doubts that if we run into something during our time out of the apartment that you'll come up with a spell to take care of it. What good is having a witch in the family if she can't use her magic once in a while?"

He could see the beginning of a smile on her face before she remembered she was annoyed with him. "Dad, we prefer 'witch' if you please. Witch is so old fashioned. It's not like I have warts on my nose, like in some Disney movie."

"Hey, there's Glinda the Good Witch. What about her?"

"She's the exception to the Hollywood rule."

"Fair enough. Okay, ready to go?"

Jo nodded and the two of them left the apartment and went to James' building downtown. Called the Nightwing building, it was a high-rise office building with apartments and a penthouse on the upper floors. Dean had stayed there briefly for safety's sake during a recent series of home-grown terrorist attacks on the Unusual community. He was familiar with the layout and felt very comfortable there. Jo was pointing out things that she recognized, too, as they entered the elevators and rode up to the penthouse level.

When they got to the top and exited the elevator car, Celeste came through the penthouse apartment's double doors to greet them.

"Dean how are you? I heard that you had been through quite a lot since we last saw you." Celeste's southern drawl dated back to the American Civil War when James had first met her and turned her into a vampire. She had served as his assistant, and perhaps more, ever since.

"I'm well, Celeste," he said, returning the brief embrace she pulled him into.

"And who is this young lady accompanying you? You didn't mention a guest."

"This is Joanna. She's my, uh…"

"I'm his daughter, Celeste. I go by Jo and I am back from the future to help him and mom out with some stuff." Dean winced as the teen just blurted it all out. He was going to use the whole visiting cousin thing they used with the Baxters.

"Well, well, well, Jo. It is certainly a pleasure to meet you, then. Any family of Dean's is welcome here. I'm Celeste, Mr. Lee's assistant. If you need anything while you're here and you can't get ahold of your dad, you just call me."

"Oh, I know who you are. We've met, or, uh, will meet, in the future."

"Are we friends?" Celeste said with a laugh.

"Oh, definitely. You used to babysit me."

"Babysit, really?" She gave Dean a look. "Well then, we must be close."

Dean shook his head as Celeste led them into the large, open floor plan of the penthouse, shutting the doors behind them. He was trying to envision a time in the future when Jaz would allow a vampire to babysit their child as they walked into the living room area where James and Brynne were seated. It was much like the last time Dean had been here.

Brynne was such a new vampire that she needed to be chaperoned around humans so she wouldn't lose control and feed on them. It was hard on Dean to see her like this, where she was seated all the way across the room with James there to intervene should she forget her humanity. He was told it would be unnecessary soon, though for some it could take up to a year or so. He was anxious for that time to come. He missed his old partner and friend.

"Forgive me if I don't rise and shake your hand, Dean," James said from his seat next to Brynne. He gestured to the large white leather sofa for Dean and Jo to sit opposite them. "Brynne has not fed yet today and it's important I stay close."

"James, I can answer for myself," Brynne said. She was wearing her dark brown hair back in a ponytail and looked pretty good if you avoided the red-rimmed eyes and the very evident canines.

"I'm just a little hungry is all. I will control myself. You said yourself, James that I'm getting better at controlling myself."

"I did say that, my love," James replied. "I just know that you would not forgive yourself if you attacked your friends. Let's just follow protocol, alright?"

Brynne gave a sigh and leaned back in the matching white chair.

James turned back to Dean. "I caught a bit of that conversation on your way in. Is this stunning young lady really your daughter, Dean?"

"She is, James. Believe me, no one is more shocked than her mother and I."

"Her mother?" Brynne asked.

"My mom's Jaz Errington. She and Dean are destined for each other, they just don't know it yet."

"Oh my, the huntress herself?" Celeste said. "I sense a wonderful story here. I think I'll get everybody some drinks and we can settle in and hear the whole tale. I can't wait to hear the background on this one."

"That would be a grand idea," James said.

They made small talk while Celeste went to the kitchen. She came back with a beer for Dean, a can of Coke for Joanna, and three white mugs for herself and the other two vampires.

When they were all settled, Dean, with some help from Jo, told the tale of their rescue of Ashley and discovery that they were a family during that quest. The three vampires all loved the story of how Jo blurted out the relationship during an argument between the three of them.

"So," Dean finished. "She's here staying with me until the autumnal equinox. Once we get all this other nonsense resolved, we can send her back to her own time."

"That is quite the story, Dean," Brynne said. "You're living a tale worthy of the books in the Station U library."

"I'd rather not, honestly. I just want to do my job and take care of patients."

"So, while it was great just catching up, Dean, I sense that there is another reason you are here visiting on short notice," James asked.

"Yeah, James, I'm hoping you can help me out with something. I ran into a patient today who I'd swear was a vampire, or at least transitioning into one, but there were no bite marks, and he had no idea what was going on. I was thinking that there must be something to this but I only know of one way to make a vampire. Is there another way?" Dean gave the three vampires the details on his encounter with Steve earlier in the day.

James listened intently and Dean caught the exchange of glances between his host and Celeste while he was telling the story of his patient encounter.

"Where is this gentleman now?" James asked.

"He's in the psych ward at Elk City Medical Center. Is he really turning into a vampire? I thought it wasn't possible without the bite and the exchange of blood between host and prey."

"Celeste?" James asked his assistant.

"I'll call the hospital right away. We might still have time." She rose and hurried down the hallway to her offices off the main living area.

"What's going on James?" Dean asked.

"There is another way to turn a vampire but I haven't heard of it for a very, very long time. It's almost considered a myth among most of our kind, but I've heard about the process first hand. It was from a very ancient vampire I met in my youth over a thousand years ago."

"I was afraid of this," Dean said. "It's why I came to you first. What can I do? Are we going to have more like him roaming the city?"

"I'm not sure what you can do. This is serious business. To answer your second question, I need to talk to this newly turned vampire myself. Until I can determine how he was turned and who turned him, I can't tell you how many more you might run into."

"But how? Why?" Dean asked.

"Once upon a time, Dean, there were no vampires or werewolves or any of a whole host of Unusuals living among humans. There were only humans, the gods above, and the demons below." James paused and looked at Dean. "Do you know of the concept of free will? Did Ashley ever mention it to you? The idea that both sides, good and evil will keep their direct influence off the world in-between and let the humans decide to act for good or evil in the world."

Dean nodded and James continued.

"It wasn't always that way. There was a time when the heavens above and the hells below actively battled to sway humans to worship them. Both sides created hybrid humans, bestowing magical powers and abilities on them in order to help their side win. It almost destroyed the earth before its time. That was when the two sides decided to let free will determine humanity's fate. They didn't clean up their mess before they left us to fend for ourselves, though. So, after they left us alone, the various Unusuals had to take care of themselves and find a way to live among the humans."

James sat back in his chair as he continued the story. "Vampires in the beginning were made by the influence of demon magic. We didn't propagate as we do today, with the exchange of blood. The seed of vampirism would be planted in a human and over the course of two to three days, the transformation would take hold, often in the family home. Eventually, the new vampire would have to feed to complete the transformation and would destroy his own family in the process. It was a win for evil and the demons would rejoice in the slaughter."

Dean thought for a moment and then looked up in shock. "Oh my God, I just sent a hungry, new vampire to the hospital. He'll kill dozens if they aren't warned." He started to get up.

"Relax, my friend," James said. "That is what I sent Celeste off to do. She is warning the hospital. Luckily, it is night time so the psych patients are locked down in their rooms, right?"

"I think so," Dean said.

"Good, so we have time to get a vampire over there to escort the man out and get him somewhere safe where we can control the transformation. We'll make it look like a standard inter-facility transfer. No one will be the wiser."

"He knows me, maybe I should go, too," Dean suggested. "He thinks he's going insane. Maybe a face he knows will help him understand what is happening. Besides which, I want to try and find out how he was turned. We've got to keep this from happening to anyone else."

"Cool, another adventure," Jo said.

"You are not going," Dean said.

"You don't have a choice, Dad. You don't have time to take me all the way home," the teen countered.

Damn, she was right. "Alright. But you do what I say and stay close."

James looked around at them, "Now if we only had a vampire with nothing to do who's available on short notice."

<hr>

Chapter 9

<hr>

Dean and Jo waited in the underground garage beneath the Nightwing building with Celeste for their ride to show up. A car horn sounded, echoing off the concrete walls as a white conversion van pulled around the corner and up to where they waited by the elevator entrance. The tinted driver's window rolled down and a round-faced figure leaned out.

"So, we're getting the band back together?" Gibbie asked.

"Don't get your hopes up, Gibbie. It's probably just a one-time gig," Dean said.

Gibson "Gibbie" Proctor was a frumpy, middle-aged vampire who Dean and Brynne had trained to be a Community Emergency Response Team or CERT member. Along with a few other members of the Unusual community, Gibbie had learned first aid, disaster response, fire suppression, and search and rescue skills in a twenty-hour program Dean and Brynne taught at Station U over the course of a few weeks. Since then, the Unusual CERT team had come in handy on numerous occasions.

"Aw, darn, I was hoping to get a chance to ride with you again on a regular basis," the vampire said. "So what are we up to tonight?"

"We have a new vampire about to turn in the hospital psych ward," Celeste explained. "He needs to be escorted out and brought back here to the Nightwing building before he starts slaughtering staff and patients when his bloodlust hits. You and Dean will go in and pose as hospital transport paramedics to transfer him to a private psychiatric facility."

Gibbie's face broke out in a big grin. "Sounds like fun. Who's the girl?" Gibbie asked.

"That's my daughter, Jo." Dean held up a hand to forestall questions. "Don't ask, I'll explain it on the way to ECMC." He walked with Jo around to the passenger side and opened the side panel door for Jo to climb in. There was another occupant sitting in the back seat already. Another teen-aged girl with bright pink hair looked out at them with a big grin on her face.

"Hi, Dean. Gibbie wasn't sure if you needed anyone else to help out and I was available, so I came along." The teen, Marian, was a werewolf girl who had also taken the CERT class and had ridden along on some of the emergency calls Dean had shared with the team while he was suspended from the Ambulance a few months before.

"Marian, this is Jo ..."

"I heard. She's really your daughter? That's awesome. I could use someone my own age along on these little adventures." Marian slid over on the bench seat and offered it to Joanna. Both Marian and Gibbie were in navy blue cargo EMS pants with plenty of pockets to stow supplies and small bits of EMS equipment. They also had light blue uniform shirts with CERT patches on their left shoulders. They both looked much more official than they had running emergency calls with Dean before. He noticed the change and said so.

"Marian, Kristof and the rest of the CERT team members decided we should have something to wear that identified us as sort of official responders," Gibbie said. "Marian designed the patches. I like them." He twisted to show Dean a good look at his.

"That is pretty cool," Dean said. It would help to play up their transport ambulance cover when they got to the hospital. James assured them that one of the ER docs who supported the Unusual program at the hospital would have transfer orders written up by the time they got there, but it would not hurt to look the part as well.

Dean wished he had time to go home and change as well. But, since he wasn't on official Fire Department business, that might cause a bit of a problem. Many of the nurses knew him, though, so if he threw a stethoscope around his neck and acted confident, they could probably pull this off without a hitch.

The four of them closed up the beat up white van and pulled away as Celeste turned and headed back upstairs. She would get the accommodations arranged for the new arrival on their return. They were only five minutes from the hospital, so if all went as planned, they would return soon with their patient.

Dean had Gibbie pull the van up next to the ambulance entrance, careful not to block the way since they weren't a real emergency vehicle. Marian and Jo had hit it off on the short ride over and were chatting away in the back seat by the time they arrived. Dean turned and looked at the team.

"Okay, Gibbie and I are going to head upstairs to the fourth floor and the psych unit. It should not take too long. You two ladies move to the front seats and wait for us." Dean looked at Marian. She was older than Jo by a year and he thought she had her license. "Marian, if Gibbie doesn't mind, I'll have you drive the van on the way back to the Nightwing building. Do you have your license with you?"

"It's in my backpack, Dean," she said patting her bag.

"Good, you and Jo keep the van running. I want to move quickly. Every minute counts and we have to get him back to James and Celeste before he turns completely. Gibbie, come on, and keep that vamp strength ready to go in case we need to restrain him."

Gibbie nodded and together Dean and the vampire climbed out and headed into the hospital. Dean grabbed a spare wheel chair staged at the ambulance entrance to the ER and then went inside to get their paperwork from the doc before heading upstairs.

Everything was ready to go, waiting for them, and they were

soon riding up the staff elevator to the fourth floor to collect their patient. Dean hoped they weren't too late.

———

THE ELEVATOR OPENED on the fourth floor to silence. Dean and Gibbie rolled the wheelchair out into an open waiting area situated in a hallway that ended in a large door. Dean had never been up here during his time as a paramedic, but he knew from the description the doc gave them downstairs that he had to be buzzed in to the locked psych ward via that door at the far end of the hallway.

As they neared the far end of the hallway and reached the speaker panel on the wall next to the door, he reached up to press the intercom button to reach the night nurse on duty. That was when Dean noticed the door was not latched closed. He got Gibbie's attention and pointed to the door. Gibbie's eyes got wide but neither of them said a word.

Gibbie pointed to himself, indicating to Dean that he'd enter first. Dean was glad he did. If there was a hungry vampire on the other side of the door, he knew he would be no match for it. The paramedic kept the wheelchair between himself and the doorway as his partner pulled open the door and stepped into the ward on the other side.

Dean was not prepared for what he saw. There was a common room with tables and chairs on the far side. The furniture was in disarray and overturned. The overhead lights were darkened and a few of the fixtures were broken. He followed Gibbie through the common room towards the nurses' station desk situated where the common room opened up, with a hallway lined with doors to both the left and the right.

This was where they encountered the first body. It was obvious that the nurse had died as a result of a vampire attack. The ragged double wound caused by a vampire's elongated canines was evident on her neck. She had been drained of blood, with a great deal of it pooling on the floor around her crumpled body. Gibbie knelt down and looked her over, when he turned back to look at Dean, the paramedic was shocked to see that Gibbie's normally pleasant face had hardened and his fangs were clearly evident. He was in full vamp-mode now.

Dean whispered to Gibbie, his voice sounding loud in the silence that enveloped them on the ward.

"I saw some blood around her mouth. Is she going to turn?"

His vampire partner nodded. "It will be a few hours yet, but yes, she will turn eventually, Dean. I smell a lot more blood and death up here. I think she's not the only new vampire we are going to find. We need help."

"Let's check the rest of the floor before we call, maybe we can stop him from turning anyone else."

"If you say so." Gibbie didn't seemed convinced. He stood up and led the way down the right-hand hallway.

Each of the doors were open. Each patient room contained a body in the same condition as the nurse. The same was true for the left-hand hallway except for the last door on the right. It was locked closed and Dean looked in through the window set in the door so the nurses could check on their patients. He saw a figure on the bed, curled up and rocking back and forth.

Dean checked the door's number and went back to the nurse's station, pressing the corresponding button there. It unlocked the door with a click and he went back to the room. Opening the door, Gibbie entered first and then jumped back with a frightened shriek as the figure turned over revealing the canine face and hairy arms of a werewolf.

"Back, stay back, vampire. I will not let you turn me into one of your minions," the werewolf said.

"I don't want to change you into anything. I can't. You're already a Lycan. We came up here and found everyone dead except for you."

Dean came forward and stood between Gibbie and the werewolf. "Calm down, take some deep breaths." Dean kept eye contact with the werewolf and hoped his smile would help calm the partially shifted werewolf down. "That's it. Keep taking deep breaths, in and out, slowly breathing until you feel more in control."

It took a few minutes, but the shift to werewolf reversed and soon Dean was sitting on the side of the bed talking to a normal-looking man.

"We came up here to take a newly turned vampire from the ward to a safe place. This is what we found. What is your name?"

"I'm Ronald. I've been depressed lately and my wife suggested I come in and get my meds situated here before I came back home to her."

"Do you know what happened up here?" Dean asked.

"About two hours ago, there was some commotion outside of the room. I had gone to bed early. I didn't feel well. My door was locked and I couldn't see much, but I could hear the screaming. Then I saw him. He was covered in blood and he just looked in at me. He smiled. It was a horrible, awful smile with fresh blood dripping from his fangs."

Dean laid a hand on the man's shoulder and urged him to continue.

"He said, 'I can't feed on you. You smell different.' Like he didn't know what a Lycan was. Then he turned and ripped the door open across the hall and fed on the girl in there while I watched. Before he was finished, he forced her to feed on a wound he made in his wrist. Then he drained her, leaving her on the floor like some sort of trash and came out smiling at me. Then he left back down the hallway."

"Okay, Ronald. You stay here. You're safe for now. We'll have someone come and check on you in a little bit." Dean led Gibbie from the room and down the hallway back towards the nurse's station.

Dean looked at Gibbie. "Is he still up here, maybe hiding somewhere?"

The vampire shook his head. "I would have detected him right away. He has left the immediate vicinity. I don't think he can feed anymore, or change any other vampires. He only has so much blood to give and he has tried to turn about eighteen people up here so far.

He has to find someplace to hide out. He'll seek out some familiar surroundings in which to make a lair."

Gibbie looked back out to the hallway and shook his head. "I haven't seen anything this bad since back in the old country. There were a few rogue vampires around that would do things like this. The rest of us would work together to catch them. It was always a messy business."

"Well, we need more help up here," Dean said. "We are going to have eighteen new, hungry vampires in a few hours. They are going to have a whole hospital on which to feed if we're not careful."

Gibbie nodded. "James needs to send us some help or there is going to be some major carnage up here."

"You don't think this is major carnage?" Dean asked. He had never seen anything this bad before, not even when a trio of demons had ripped apart a family of dryads.

"You think this is bad, Dean? Imagine what this hospital is going to look like when each one of those eighteen bodies out there turn and start feeding their way through the building."

"So we've got two problems. We've got patient zero loose in the building, or maybe the city at large and we've got to stop the eighteen new vampires up here from going rogue and killing or turning more people. Great."

Dean's phone buzzed in his pocket and he pulled it out and looked at it. It was a text from Jo. "Dad, we have a problem. Get down here."

"Gibbie, I've got to go down and check on the girls in the van. You call James and Celeste and get what help you need to manage these new vampires as they start to turn."

Gibbie nodded and pulled out his phone as Dean headed back to the elevator to go down and see what the problem was outside.

Chapter 10

After her dad and Gibbie left, Jo moved up to the front passenger seat of the van while Marian moved to the driver's seat. It was cool to meet another teen for a change. She had left all her friends behind when she came back to the past to help her parents out. It took a conversation with another teen girl like herself to make her realize how much she missed kids her own age.

They talked about a lot of things while they waited outside the hospital ER. Marian had just broken up with her boyfriend of six months and was pretty vocal about how guys were all pigs. Jo listened and nodded occasionally while her new friend explained how her ex had cheated on her with another girl at school.

She was still half listening and half looking out the window when she noticed a guy in a hospital gown descending the exterior of the hospital building. Because of her hunter amulet, given to her by her mother years before, Jo could see in the dark nearly as well as most Unusuals and she saw the man clearly despite the darkness of the cloudy night.

"Hey, Marian," Jo interrupted her companion. "Didn't my dad say they were going to the fourth floor?"

"Yeah. Why?" Marian started looking around at the building through the windshield, craning her neck so she could see better.

"Oh, no reason. Other than the guy in a hospital gown, covered in blood, climbing down the side of the hospital. It looks like he came from that open window." Jo pointed. "Should we try and stop him?"

"I think so," Marian answered. "I think I'm strong enough when I shift to outlast a vamp. After all, we just need to hold on to him until your dad and Gibbie get back. You stay in the van and call your dad. Tell him we think we found his guy."

Jo took out her phone and texted a message to her dad while Marian got out and started walking over to where the guy was climbing down the building. She watched her friend's hands elongate into claws while she watched and her face changed and shifted to an elongated wolf's visage.

The turned teen werewolf had just reached the base of the wall when the man dropped the rest of the way to the ground. When he turned, Jo got her first good look at his face and saw the blood dripping from his fanged mouth. The blood stains on the front of his hospital gown were even worse than those on his back and sides. This guy looked like he'd laid down in a wading pool filled with blood.

Jo opened the door and stepped down from the passenger side of the van. She called out to warn her friend to be careful. If this guy had been feeding, he would be a lot more powerful than they anticipated. She was too late. The new vampire turned around as Marian walked up to him. She had her hands outstretched in an effort to calm him and get him to stay where he was. The werewolf teen never got the chance to say another word. The vamp charged her and swatted her aside, slamming her into the brick wall of the building. Her head slapped against the concrete wall. Jo watched in shock as Marian crumpled unconscious into a heap on the pavement.

"Hey, that's my friend," Jo shouted, regaining her composure. "Why don't you come over here and try that on someone who knows how to handle scumbags like you?"

The vamp snarled at her, showing his fangs and then started laughing. "You smell human, like those others upstairs. I guess I get to eat you, too."

"You can try."

The vamp charged her with all the power and speed granted by his blood-fueled, supernatural body. Jo stood her ground, reached inside her jeans jacket and drew out the loaded Glock pistol she wore there. Her dad hadn't seen the shoulder holster rig she had donned with the outfit back at the apartment. With the calmness that comes from long hours of training and muscle memory, she aimed and unloaded the entire clip of fifteen rounds into the charging vampire.

Normal bullets might not have stopped him, but Jaz had given her daughter silver-lead alloy frangible loads. These broke apart inside the target, causing massive internal damage. They also had the additional benefit of hindering the regeneration capabilities of werewolves and vampires because of the silver content.

The charging vamp got no closer than ten feet from her before he fell to the pavement, writhing in agony, clawing at his wounds. Jo switched out a new, fully-loaded magazine for the empty one, releasing the slide on the semi-automatic pistol, loading another round in the chamber. Then, with her pistol trained on her target, Jo circled the vamp at a distance and made her way over to her injured friend.

Marian moaned as she approached and Jo took a moment to look down at her. Thank the Goddess she was alive. She had shifted back to human form when she was knocked unconscious. A noise from the street caused her to look back up and she caught a glimpse of waving hospital gown as the vamp sprinted away around the corner. Damn, should she try and follow him? Her mind was made up for her when she heard voices coming from the ambulance ramp.

"I'm telling you, I heard gunshots out here," the first voice said.

"I'm not doubting you, I just question your judgement in coming out here without calling the police first. We're just security guards," said a second voice.

Jo holstered her weapon and adjusted her jacket to hide her

shoulder-holster rig just as the two security guards turned the corner on the ramp into the ER. The first one pointed to the empty brass cartridges scattered on the ground outside of the van. The other saw her and Marian by the side of the building.

"I told you I heard gunshots. Look." He pointed at the scattered shells on the ground.

The first guard's partner looked at Jo and saw Marian on the ground. "Is she okay. Is she shot?"

"Uh, no. A bunch of guys came around the corner chasing another guy. They knocked her down and one of them shot at the other guy, chasing him down the alley and round the corner. That's all I saw," Jo said.

"What are you young ladies doing hanging around out here by the ambulance entrance anyway? It's not safe out here at night alone."

"Now you tell me," Jo said rolling her eyes at him. "We were waiting for our friends to come back down. They're paramedics and stopped in to pick something up."

"Oh, you're with Dean and Gibbie?"

"Uh, yeah. You know them?"

"Yeah, Dean just went with Gibbie upstairs to pick up a psych patient to take him somewhere. I don't know why they would bring teenaged girls along with them on this type of thing, though."

Marian was starting to come around. Jo knew that her regeneration capabilities would have her back on her feet in just a few minutes. She had to stall and keep these guys from calling for help until her Dad came back down and got the situation straightened out.

"We are high school students on a career day ride along. We thought we might want to be paramedics one day."

"Well, you got an eyeful already tonight, haven't you. How's your friend? Does she need a nurse or a wheelchair to go inside?"

Marian sat up, rubbing her head. "No, thank you. I'm fine. Just a little scared."

"We'll be alright, you two should go and see if those guys are hanging out around the front of the hospital. We will stay here," Jo suggested.

"Hey, she's right, Ed," the closest security guard said. "Come on, we should look and see if we can still catch up to these guys and then call the police."

"Yeah, but we should be careful. They've got a nine millimeter pistol with them."

Jo waited until their attention was turned away from her and focused down the alley to the front of the hospital before she waived her hands in the air and muttered the words of the spell. The two men froze in place, staring down the end of the alley in the position they had taken just a moment before.

"Hey, what did you do to them?" Marian asked.

"It's just a stasis field. We need to keep them here until Dad and Gibbie get back and decide what we should do."

"What we should do about what?" she heard her dad's voice coming down the ramp from the ER. "Hey, what is wrong with those guards?"

"I had to put them in stasis, Dad. I think your vampire escaped and he attacked Marian and me."

"Are you both alright?" Gibbie said as he came around the ramp and followed Dean down to the street. He saw the werewolf teen getting to her feet. "Marian, honey, what happened?"

"We saw this guy, covered in blood, climbing down the outside of the hospital," Marian said. "I thought I could stop him, but he overpowered me and knocked me out. I'm okay now. Jo managed to fight him off, somehow, and distracted the guards while I healed up."

"You're lucky this guy didn't tear your heads off," Dean said. "He killed eighteen people upstairs and Gibbie thinks he turned each of them into vampires. They are going to wake up soon. I have already called James and he is sending over every vampire he can contact to contain the new vamps until he can smuggle them out of the facility and to a safe house to complete the transformation. This is going to cause all kinds of trouble. Now the guy is loose in the city and will do this all over again if we don't stop him."

"Dad, you need to call Mom. She's the best equipped to track and stop this guy. She is the hunter after all."

"I don't want her going all vigilante on this person. He is not responsible for what happened to him. He can't control his urges right now, he's too young in the change."

"I hate to say this, Dean," Gibbie said. "But she's right. We are only going to find him by following a trail of bodies. The Erringtons have been doing this for centuries. I hate to send a hunter out to go after any vampire, but if she can track him and will let us join her in the hunt, we can find him a lot faster."

"So what do we do about the two security guards? I know these guys, they don't deserve to be frozen like that," Dean said.

"All we have to do is clean up the spent shell casings and I can make a post-hypnotic suggestion. They'll forget, and go back to work as if nothing happened. They will have no lasting effects from the spell, I promise." Jo met her father's gaze to reassure him.

"Wait, what shell casings? Are you armed?" Dean asked

"Did you shoot at the vampire?" Gibbie said, alarmed.

Dean and Gibbie both blurted out the questions in a rush of words. Dean looked angry while Gibbie looked a little scared.

"I had to shoot him. He would have killed me otherwise. And yes, I'm armed. Why did you think Mom left me the Glock if it wasn't to make sure I could protect myself? I shot the vampire full of silver frangible bullets, so he's not going to be attacking anyone anytime soon. He can't heal while the silver is in his body. He'll have to seek out medical help of some sort. That gives us time to track him down."

She could see her father sorting through the options facing him, glancing at the two frozen security guards, noticing the shell casings littering the ground around the van, and looking back to Marian and herself. He was angry, but also stuck with a list of priorities that took precedence. He must have made up his mind as he crouched and started picking up the spent brass shell casings off the pavement by the van.

"Gibbie, help Marian back to the van and get loaded up, we've got to get out of here before an ambulance pulls up and wonders what is going on here. Jo, do what you need to do to these guys and get back in the van. Be careful with them, they are decent guys, okay?"

"Of course, Dad."

"We'll head over to Jaz's apartment and see if she has any thoughts about tracking this guy before he harms anyone else."

Joanna nodded to her Dad and turned to help Marian walk over to Gibbie. Then she walked up to the two guards and whispered in their ears. She gave them a series of instructions. She told them to go back inside and tell everyone that they were mistaken about gunshots outside. She also suggested it must have been some kids with firecrackers.

She snapped her fingers as she said the words to release the spell and the two of them turned and walked back inside without even looking at the four companions by the van. Jo turned and smiled at her Dad while she climbed into the back seat with Marian and shut the van door. She knew that this was not going to be the last she heard about it, and she probably should have told him that she was armed when they left the apartment, but she knew he would have told her to leave the gun behind.

Her father was never comfortable around firearms. He tolerated the extensive training in their use her mother had given her because of the Errington family background and traditions. It was just one of the strange opposing positions between her parents that made their relationship so strange. They were opposites in so many ways, and yet, in the future – her future, they were totally committed to her and each other. At least they would be eventually. She watched as Gibbie and her Dad climbed in the front of the van and they sped off into the night.

Chapter 11

Dean thought about what he was going to say to Joanna when they were alone again. He was conflicted in his feelings. He was both angry that she brought the pistol with her, and thankful she had it. It was a weird juxtaposition between his two sides in this issue. He cared about what happened to the girl, his daughter. He also didn't want her to grow up thinking she could shoot first and ask questions later.

He glanced back over his shoulder while Gibbie drove across town to Jaz's apartment. Jo met his eyes and smiled at him. It was like she knew what he was thinking. He turned back to the front and hid a small chuckle. She might know him better than he thought. She had grown up with him in her lifetime. He was the father she had known since her birth and he realized he had to have taught her his feelings about guns and their place in society. He believed in the right to bear arms, but he also didn't like the way there were so many readily available guns on the street.

Jo must have grown up with two parents who had wildly different views on this subject, Dean knew. Her mother had trained her well. That much was evident based on her handling of the situation back at the hospital. She had survived an enraged and blood-crazed vampire attack. He wasn't sure he would have been able to do as well, in fact he was sure of it. If it had been someone else in that alley by the ambulance entrance, they would be dead right now. That was thanks in no small part to her being armed and trained to defend herself.

Dean thought about all of these things as Gibbie stopped in front of Jaz's apartment building. He found a parking spot and pulled his van into it, in front of the building. Dean and the girls got out but Gibbie wanted to stay in the van.

"I think I'll pass on meeting the Errington heir in person, Dean," Gibbie said. "She's dedicated to killing people like me."

"Oh, nonsense, Gibbie," Jo said. "Trust me. You and mom are good friends where I come from."

Gibbie snorted out a strange noise that Dean realized was half laughter and half crying.

"Come on, Gibbie. It's just Jo's mom," Marian said. "How bad could she be?"

"Ask Dean that question. He told me how she single-handedly took on a revenant demon lord in a sword fight."

Marian laughed. "That just makes her awesome, not scary. Come on."

They waited and the middle-aged vampire climbed out of his van, locked the door and joined them as they went up to Jaz's apartment. Jo must have texted her to let her know they were coming. She opened the door as they arrived greeting them with a grim look on her face. She was dressed in full hunter mode, with black BDU pants and a black t-shirt. Her pistol and Bowie knife rested in the shoulder holster rig she wore. She reached over and pulled on her black leather jacket to complete the outfit as she gestured to them.

"Come in and tell me what the problem is," Jaz said. "I have a few vague texts from Jo, but nothing that makes a lot of sense."

Dean filled her in on what he discovered about his patient's recent change to being a vampire, the attack at the hospital, and the incident in the alley between the girls and the vamp. He expressed his belief that this was the act of a young vampire, out of control and without support.

"So, what, Dean?" Jaz asked. "Are you asking me to go easy on this guy? He's killed or turned eighteen people that we know of right now. How many more have to die before he is stopped?"

Gibbie muttered something under his breath and Jaz shot him a glance that caused the vampire to shriek and throw up his hands in apology.

"Oh, be quiet," Jaz said. "I'm not going to hurt you Gibson Proctor. Everyone in the hunter community knows you are harmless. In fact, I have seen notes to that effect going back over a hundred years."

"Really?" Gibbie asked. "You know, I really don't want to hurt anyone. I don't."

"See, Gibbie. I told you. Mom and you are going to be friends."

"I don't know about that, Joanna," Jaz said. "I don't have vampire friends."

"You must mellow with age then, Mom. You let Gibbie and Celeste both babysit several times when I was little."

Marian laughed aloud at that statement, and Jaz shot her a look. She raised her hands in defense. "I'm sorry Ms. Errington. I just find that so funny. It's like the beginning of a joke."

"Well I'm not laughing, Marian. It's not a joke and I don't approve. Just like I don't approve of my daughter having a werewolf as a friend. You seem like a nice enough girl, but you can't change who you are underneath."

"Mom, that is just rude. Take it back."

"I won't, Joanna. You may know me as a different person in your future, but I'm not that person. I only know who I am right now and I'm the hunter who has seen a lot of situations that are a made more dangerous because of Unusuals out of control. That is the reason you are all here, after all."

Dean had to diffuse this situation. He stepped between Jaz and Jo. "Maybe the two of you could work together to track this guy down before he kills anyone else. He's been shot with silver bullets so he can't heal, right?"

Jo nodded and Jaz explained, "The silver inhibits healing and regeneration within about one inch of every fragment in the body.

Based on Jo hitting him with fifteen rounds, he'll need surgery to remove the bullet fragments before he can start healing again."

"So where would he go?" Dean asked.

Gibbie cleared his throat and everyone looked his way. He paused and swallowed hard before continuing. "I was just thinking what I would do. If I was hurt like that, I'd go home and lair up while I tried to heal. He's new, though so I don't know where he'd lair up. He wouldn't have a lair yet, would he?"

"But he's human so he does have a lair, Gibbie," Dean said. "He would go back home, the only place he would feel safe and secure." He looked around the room. "We've got to hurry. His wife will probably let him in, but that will put her in incredible danger."

They all nodded and Dean led the group back downstairs to Gibbie's van. Jaz grabbed her katana sword on the way out the door. Once outside she settled in the center of the van's middle back seat, forcing Jo and Marian to sit behind her in the rear seat. Gibbie hopped into the driver's seat and Dean gave him the directions to the apartment building where he had picked up Steve, the new vampire, earlier in the evening. They sped across town, hoping they would get there in time to save the man's wife.

BY THE TIME THEY ARRIVED, Jaz had laid out her plan to approach the apartment and assess the situation. Dean knew she had the most experience with this sort of take-down. It was why they had sought her out. She and Jo, as the only trained hunters in the group, would stand on either side of the apartment's door while Dean knocked to see if anyone answered.

Gibbie would be next to Dean and if he could, would use his superior speed and strength to tackle the vampire if he answered. Marian would stay back, behind Dean and help lend first aid if anyone needed it. She would carry the EMS bags Gibbie kept in the back of his van.

Dean approached the ground floor apartment's door from the inner courtyard of the apartment complex. Everyone else was in place, Jaz to the left with her sword drawn in one hand and her pistol in the other. Jo was on the right, pistol at the ready. He looked at Gibbie who nodded he was ready.

Knocking on the door, Dean took a step back to give the team some room should the vampire come charging out. The door opened a crack and he saw the wife's face appear.

"Yes, who is it?"

"Ma'am, I'm paramedic Dean Flynn. Do you remember me? I was here earlier with your husband."

"I remember you. You should go. My husband doesn't want to go back to the hospital."

"Oh, so he's here?"

She nodded, looking back behind her somewhere. Dean could hear another voice inside but not what it said.

"Ma'am, tell your husband that we mean him no harm." Dean raised his voice, knowing the new vampire's sensitive hearing would be able to hear him. "Steven, we can help you. We know you are hurt. Unless we get the bullet fragments out of you, you will not heal, no matter how much blood you get. You need surgery. We can help."

The wife squealed in alarm as she was pulled back from the door and then it opened, showing Steven standing there. He was a mess. His hospital gown was covered in dried and crusted blood. The bullet holes where Jo had shot him were evident. His eyes were red-rimmed and his pale skin color was even more alarming now than before.

"I have to drink more. The master instructed me to feed and share blood with as many as I could. It was the only way to heal me. Now you tell me I have to go back to the hospital?"

Dean held his hands out to try and show he was no threat. "I have a friend with me who is like you are now. He can help you with what is happening to you."

Gibbie waved, "Hi, Steven. I remember when I was new like

you. I know there are so many distractions and urges that you don't understand. If you'll come with us, we can help you."

"Then why do you have more people with guns nearby? I can smell them, you know. It's faint, masked somehow, but I think they're closer than their smell would indicate," the new vampire said.

Dean was alarmed. If he decided to fight, someone was going to get hurt. Jaz and Jo had hunter amulets that both enhanced their vision into the infrared and ultraviolet spectrums, as well as masking their heat signatures and scents. It seemed that it could only mask so much when they were just a few feet away from their target.

"Of course we brought some protection, Steven," Dean said, trying to soothe the man. "You have caused many injuries tonight. We have to be sure that you don't hurt anyone else. If you come with Gibbie and me peacefully though, there is no need for anyone else to get injured."

It was a standoff. Dean knew it. He was at a loss as to what he should do to defuse the situation. Gibbie took a step forward and tried to take matters into his own hands and that triggered something in Steven. He charged forward with a snarl, aiming for Dean. What happened next seemed to go in slow motion.

Dean saw Jaz raise her katana up to strike as the vampire passed through the door. Jo pushed her free hand forward and he saw her lips begin to move, casting a spell, no doubt. He started to call out for everyone to stop, but Gibbie was already moving. Dean had never seen the frumpy, middle-aged vampire move so quickly.

Gibbie dove forward, intercepting the charging vampire and knocking him to the sidewalk in front of his apartment door. They both fell to the ground and Jaz's heaven-blessed sword blade swished through the air just above them. At the same time, Jo finished her spell and a brief flash of light caused both vampires to cry out, covering their eyes. Gibbie didn't let go, though, and had the younger vampire wrapped up in a bear hug. Steven struggled, but Dean could see that Gibbie had him under control.

The elder vampire, looked up at Dean from the ground, rolling his eyes. "Well, that was close."

Chapter 12

It was an hour later when the five of them turned Steven over to a pair of vampires sent by James to collect him. Then they returned to Jaz's apartment. The whole evening had not gone as Dean, or any of them, had expected. A text query to Celeste had come back with the listing of the carnage. Twenty-one people in all, counting Steven, had been turned into vampires. Two more were dead and would not rise again. It was unlike anything most of them had seen before.

"What concerns me is something Steven said before we captured him," Jaz said. "He said something about his master telling him to feed on blood and let others feed on him in turn."

"They are simple instructions, but they would be enough along with the vampire instincts to create a small army of hungry, new vampires in the city," Gibbie observed.

"Does this mean we have more vampires to look forward to?" Jo asked.

"It means that this is not an isolated incident," Dean said. "James told me that in the earliest days of man, vampires and some of the other Unusuals were created by netherworld demon lords to fight with the humans and other forces of good in the world at the time."

"That matches up with the lore of the hunter clans. We learn a lot about Unusual creature origins growing up," Jaz said. "It's said we gained some of our abilities during those ancient times to help us battle the enemies of mankind. It would make sense that the Gods of good would make some changes of their own to counter those of the other side."

"But both sides eventually determined to back off direct intervention in the world thousands of years ago," Dean mused. "What would have changed that brought a demon lord back on the scene here in Elk City to start the process all over again?"

"The better question is, what other types of Unusuals have been created?" Jo said, jumping into the conversation. "If demon lords can create vampires, what else can one create?"

"Werewolves, and other Lycans and shifters, maybe more," Marian said. She said the words in a whisper as if she were afraid of them. "We need to warn my dad and the other pack leaders. The next full moon will be in two days. If there's a new werewolf out there, we can expect him or her to strike then."

"I'll have Celeste warn Rudy and James," Dean said pulling out his phone to send a text. Rudy was James' second in command. He was also the Alpha werewolf pack leader in the Elk City area.

"The thing I'm most concerned about is finding the source of the new vampire," Jaz said as she crossed the room and looked out the window of her apartment. Dean noticed that Gibbie flinched a little when she passed close to him.

"You think this all has something to do with your missing summoning figurines?" Dean asked.

Jaz turned and shot him a look. He knew she didn't like sharing information openly with anyone, but how else were they supposed to get to the root of the problem if they didn't include the whole team in the information chain?

"Jaz, you have to let people help you," Dean urged. "You don't have the whole clan to back you up like you used to. I know that's a hard pill to swallow, but if you'll let us, we can help you out and take some of the burden the rest of the clan used to before the explosion and fire."

The huntress looked around the room and Dean wondered what she thought of the group assembled there. It wasn't exactly a hunter's dream team. She had the future father of her child, the daughter who was also a witch, a teenaged werewolf, and a middle-aged vampire who was scared of the dark. She used to think of most of the group as second-class citizens simply because of who they were. For all Dean knew, she still did. This was the team she was stuck with, however. He was trying to help her see that.

He watched her shoulders slump a little in resignation and then she said one word.

"Okay."

She turned to look outside and Dean took that as permission to take the lead and fill the team in on what they were up against. He told them of the missing summoning idols and the fact that it was likely, based on current events, that there might be some sort of demonic force involved in the recent outbreak of vampires in the city. If there were other, similar outbreaks of dangerous Unusuals, they would have to take the lead on tracking them down and containing the situation.

"I can tap us into the dispatch network for Station U. If there are suspicious calls, I'll make sure the paramedics on call at the station each shift alert me so we can follow up on it afterwards." Dean looked at the assembled group and they all nodded. They were in on the plan so far. "Ideally, we can find out quickly what is going on and respond with our team simultaneously, assisting the paramedics and other responders. Our goal is to find the source of the outbreak and then track that back to the demon lord behind it all."

"We'll have to work in shifts of some sort," Jo interjected. "I'm available all the time, but Marian has school during the day, and Gibbie can only come out at night."

"We could bring the rest of the CERT team in on this," Gibbie suggested. "Kristof would be available during the daytime before his restaurant opens. The Dryad twins, Wim and Dora, are around most of the time, too, so they can fill in as needed."

Jaz spun around from where she stood looking out the window. "I don't think you all understand the danger we are facing here. Demon lords are not to be underestimated. They are ruthless and very powerful."

"But, Mom, this demon lord is limited some way. He has to be. He can't be here fully, can he? We have the third figurine, so the demon must be here in some other form and that gives us an advantage." Jo looked from her mom to Dean and he picked up the thought.

"Jo's right, Jaz. We have the advantage of that weakness and the surprise that it doesn't know we are chasing it yet. The faster we work, and the bigger the team, the more likely we are to find the demon before he creates too many more rogue Unusuals to run amok in the city." Dean watched as Jaz looked from him to the rest of the assembled team.

"We only have one hunter, Dean. I can only be in one place at a time and I have to sleep at some point. We can't staff a response group twenty-four hours a day, seven days a week."

"You're wrong, Mom. We have two trained hunters."

Jaz started to protest but Jo held up her hand.

"I handled myself fine tonight. I stopped the vampire and kept him from injuring me and my companions, and I helped cover up the incident from mundane eyes and attention. I can pull my weight." Jo looked to Dean for help.

Dean looked back at her. He was torn. He was thinking of her like a daughter more and more. That meant he wanted to protect her. The other side was that she was right. Jaz needed help with this, and Jo had exhibited the skills needed on more than one occasion. She could take care of herself. He knew that Jaz was aware of that, too.

Jaz met his eyes and then gave him a slight nod. Jo saw it, too, because she gave a quiet fist-pumped yes from where she sat on the couch next to Marian. They had a team and basics of an idea on how it would work. It was time to get down to business on who would do what and when.

Dean sent Gibbie home and had him drop Marian off. He and Jaz would work out the details, with Jo's help, and he told the vampire that they would be in touch about setting up their response team. Gibbie smiled a little, nodded at Jaz and left. He told Dean that he'd alert the rest of the CERT team to await instructions.

When he closed the door after Gibbie and Marian left, Dean heard Jaz mutter something under her breath.

"What was that?" he asked.

"I was just saying 'what have I gotten myself into.' This has got to be a first for a hunter clan and my father and mother must be rolling over in their graves."

"Maybe it's time for more cooperation between the clans and the good Unusuals in the community," Jo interjected. "Most just want to live their lives without being judged for who they are. Only a very few are doing things that require the hunters or others to intervene. Why hold all of the group accountable for the actions of a minority?"

"Because that's the way it's always been, Jo. Because old habits die hard and I'm not sure I can overcome the prejudices of centuries, even millennia."

"Does that mean you don't accept me? I am, a witch. Do you accept me for who I am?"

Jaz looked at her and Dean saw her eyes soften as she looked at their grown daughter. He wondered what conflicting feelings she must have. They must be much more complex than his own. He didn't have the preconceived notions about witches that she did.

"I accept you, Jo. You've given me no reason not to. I'm sorry if I haven't had the chance to tell you that. This whole situation with you and the revelation of who you are is still very new to both me and your father." Jaz looked at Dean and he took his cue.

"Same here, Jo. It's been slow, I know, but we've come to accept you for who you are, and know that we are some sort of family, dysfunctional as it may be."

Jo got up from the couch, rushed over and gave Dean a hug, then turned to look at her mother. Jaz paused only a moment and then held open her own arms. Dean watched as their companionship gelled into the bond of a family. Jo and Jaz hugged there, tears streaming down both of their faces. Jo had needed this for a long time. Come to think of it, so had Jaz. Her family had been ripped apart by the explosion that killed her parents. She thought she was all alone in the world. This realization of what Jo and Dean represented for her must have given her back something she thought was lost forever.

Dean wiped some moisture from his own eyes, trying to do it without the two women noticing. He was unsuccessful, as they both turned and laughed at him. He started laughing, too. This was going to be alright. Whatever else happened, he too had a family again. That was something he had not felt part of for a long, long time. It felt good.

Chapter 13

Graadu, formerly Sam the construction worker, searched the construction site as he went about his mundane work. He would not ordinarily allow himself to do such labor as it was beneath him, but this time it formed a useful ruse to allow him to search for the other idol. He first went back to where Sam's frantic mind told him he found the other two idols. There was nothing there, and when Graadu searched in the magical spectrum he found no trail leading to the location of the other missing figurine.

That was strange. He expected to find a clear trail to the third summoning idol if he didn't find it near the same spot the other two had been found. That was not the case and it meant that someone had discovered the other one and knew what it was they had found. Knowing this, they would have taken pains to cover their tracks and cast a protection spell over it to prevent discovery. At least that was what he would do.

The demon lord knew the story of the destroyed building. He rather liked the idea that an entire hunter clan had been destroyed in the explosion and fire. Perhaps someone related to the hunters had discovered the idol. He decided to ask the foreman who was paying them to do their work here, clearing the property of the debris from the fire. He walked up to the foreman's trailer and entered without knocking.

The foreman looked up at him as he entered. "Sam, what's up? It's not break time yet."

"I need to know who is paying for this construction project. I need to know, right now."

"Sam, I don't like your tone. You know, you've been acting pretty strange since we started this job. I think you should go back out and get back to work. If you do that, maybe I can forget what an ass you're being right now." The foreman went back to work, ignoring the presence of his employee.

Graadu took a step towards the desk and pointed his finger at the insolent man. "I don't like your tone."

The foreman's head jerked back and his eyes widened as he realized he could no longer breathe. His hands clutched his throat, then fell to his stomach as his diaphragm muscles spasmed and froze, stopping the process of inhalation.

"I think you should do a better job of recognizing your employees for the work they do. You should pay attention to their unique abilities, Mr. Foreman. Do you think you can do that?"

The foreman's eyes looked at him, pleading with him to be allowed to breathe again. One hand reached out in supplication and the man dropped to his knees in submission.

"That is much better." Graadu waived a hand and the muscular paralyzation spell stopped. "Now would you like to answer my question? I want to know who ordered this construction project and where I can find them."

The foreman gasped, his hands clutching his throat while he drew in air. Graadu waited for a moment while the man gathered his senses again. These humans were so weak compared to what he remembered.

"There was a daughter of the family that owned this building. She survived the fire and is staying in an apartment building nearby. I don't have the address, but she's walked here in the past, so it can't be that far away. The bills are all being paid by the insurance company and the paperwork is being handled by a law firm."

"So, the hunter clan is not dead after all," Graadu said to himself. "That explains the protection spell."

"I'm sorry. I don't understand?" the foreman said.

"You are very sorry. A very sorry example of humanity indeed. I don't think I need to come here anymore. Please give me a raise, say double my current pay, and forward my checks directly to my home. I will not be coming by to pick them up."

"Uh, yes, certainly. I'll do it right away."

"You will notify me immediately the next time this huntress, the daughter, comes here to the construction site. I must find her new abode. She has something that belongs to me. That must be where she is hiding my property."

"As you say, I will call you on your cell phone as soon as she arrives."

"Very good, puny man. If you continue to serve me well, I may spare your life when I arrive in my true form to take over this city."

The foreman bowed from his position kneeling on the floor, pressing his head against the trailer's floor in supplication. He did not see his former employee, now his lord and master, leave. He stayed there for several minutes more then got up and began the paperwork to approve the pay raise and forward the checks to his master's address.

Outside the trailer, the demon lord cast about with his inadequate human senses to try and get a sense of who had cast the protection spell. If he could track down the spell caster, he could get them to remove the spell, or destroy them, whichever was most efficient. Either would suffice, but a powerful spell caster could be a strong ally. It was important he take care not to anger this one, unless there was no other choice.

Graadu thought for a moment, standing outside the foreman's trailer. Then he made up his mind. He would return home. Sam's wife, Jill, was still at home where he had left her. She would not leave, he controlled her completely. She was an entertaining plaything, but perhaps her life force would be useful in helping to track down this spell caster. He would have to think on that while the rest of his plans went into effect.

The vampire he created should have started feeding the previous evening. It would have taken two or three days of the transformation to be complete. The feeding frenzy and subsequent turning of dozens of other vampires would be a welcome bit of chaos to start off his conversion of this city to his will. It was time to activate his other creations and see what havoc they could create in this weak and modern human world.

Chapter 14

The last several days had passed in a daze for Sandra. She had gone home from Sam's Dungeon Masters game feeling a little ill. Because of that, she had called in sick for work in the morning and spent the day in bed. One day led to two and then three. Her boss called, asked how she was doing, and said that he was going to need a note from a doctor since she had missed so many days in a row.

Sandra rolled out of bed on the fourth morning after the game and decided to go to the urgent care center. That was when she noticed the changes. While she had never considered herself fat, she knew she was a little overweight. It was something she had battled all her life. It had a lot to do with her sedentary lifestyle and her job as a computer programmer. She sat behind a computer all day long and had little opportunity at work to exercise.

That was why she was so surprised when she stumbled into the bathroom on that fourth morning to take a shower and saw what stared back at her in the mirror. It was such a startling change she checked behind her for the stunning naked woman staring back at her in the reflection. There was no one there.

Staring downward, she looked over her body. Sandra noticed her breasts were higher, firmer and maybe a little larger. Her waist was more defined and she had definitely lost some weight. Her legs even looked a little longer and she loved the shape and definition she saw. She was so stunned she stood there for five minutes, running her hands over her body and curves, trying to understand the transformation that had occurred.

She had to go see a doctor now. She had lost way too much weight, and lost it too fast. While she liked what she saw in the mirror, she was confused by it and a little scared what it meant. Without thinking about it, Sandra showered, applied make-up, put on a tight-fitting red dress she hadn't fit into for years, and headed out to the urgent care center. She had the strange feeling that she had to always look her best whenever she went out.

The ride on the Elk City Metro Bus from her apartment to the urgent care center by the hospital took the usual twenty minutes, but for Sandra it was anything but usual. She could feel everyone watching her, taking in her every subtle movement. The bus driver kept checking her out in the mirror above his seat and she resisted smiling at him after the first time. He had nearly driven the bus into a line of parked cars. If she weren't so frightened by all of this she would have enjoyed it. She was a beautiful woman, with all the assets she could want in this sexist world.

The bus dropped her off at the medical center complex and she walked to the next block to get to the urgent care center. Several times, she saw men, and women, stumble or trip on the sidewalk as she passed them by. They should pay more attention to what they were doing.

The receptionist at the urgent care center didn't look up as she walked up. The bored woman just pointed to the clipboard on the counter and told Sandra to sign in and wait for her name to be called. Sandra scrawled her name and walked over to the seating area to sit down. Four different men stood up and offered her their seats in the packed waiting area. That had never happened before. She had to admit to herself, she could get used to this kind of treatment.

She nodded to the closest of the men and sat down there. He stood there smiling down at her and she smiled back. When he didn't move from where he was standing after she sat down, she told him to sit down over there, waving her hand toward the other side of the waiting room. Without skipping a beat, he spun around and went to where she had indicated with a wave of her hand and sat on the floor, staring back at her as if he were thankful for the opportunity to follow her commands. How odd, she thought.

Sandra waited for her turn, aware of the attention from every adult in the room. She noticed the children paid no attention to her, or at least not any undue attention. The adults, however, all watched her every move and those who had their names called, seemed to be reluctant to leave and get their medical needs attended to, looking over their shoulders as they left the room. The staff had started to notice her as well. The nurses who came out to call in new patients acted disappointed when they called a name and it wasn't hers.

Finally one came out and called her name. She stood and walked as fast as her heels would allow to follow the nurse holding the door for her. She was led to a room and the nurse took her vital signs, her hands lingering whenever they touched her skin. It wasn't unpleasant and Sandra found that she was enjoying the physical contact with the woman. Sandra wasn't gay, but she found herself thinking about what it would be like to take this woman to bed. After the vital signs were finished, Sandra just told the nurse she hadn't been feeling well and needed a note for work. The nurse said the doctor would be right in to see her. She kept her gaze on Sandra until the moment the door closed.

Sandra looked up a few moments later as the doctor entered the room staring down at his clipboard. She noticed how attractive he was and as soon as he shut the door, she stood, took the clipboard out of his hand and pulled him into an embrace, kissing him with passion she had never felt before. He protested only briefly before becoming almost limp in her arms, succumbing to her attack. She continued the prolonged kiss until his body weight was too much for her to hold and he dropped to the floor.

She leaned back on the exam table, feeling energized and full of life. She could count the pores on the doctor's face, her senses had sharpened so much. Part of her was concerned about what was wrong with the doctor, but only a part of her. Mostly she wanted more. She wanted more of whatever she got when she kissed that doctor.

Sandra walked to the door and opened it part way and stuck her head out in the hall way. "Hey nurse. Could you come in here for a moment?" She ducked back inside.

"Yes Ma'am, what can I do for you?" the nurse asked as she entered the room. She stumbled over the doctor slumped on the floor and started to scream, but was cut off by Sandra's embrace and kiss. After a moment, the nurse's eyes rolled back in her head and Sandra let her fall to the floor.

"Wow," she said to herself. "I feel juiced. I could do this all day." The thought intrigued her and she pulled the nurse out of the way of the door and repeated her request for help.

DEAN AND BARRY were back in the station still cleaning up from their first call of the day when the radio tones sounded again on the overhead speakers. It was Dean's first day shift back on duty since his two days off, helping Jaz and Jo set up the Cert team to track down the demon. Now he was back on duty and trying to clear his head and get his focus back on doing his job. The next ambulance call was another opportunity to do that.

"Medical Box 822, syncopal episode, Elk City Urgent Care Clinic," came the dispatcher's voice over the radio.

Barry looked at Dean and winked. "This sounds like an easy one, boss. Maybe this will help you shake off the funk you've been under since you came in for work this morning."

"You just want me to take over patient care for a change. Well, no chance. You're still the probie here, albeit not too much longer." Dean planned on notifying headquarters after this shift that Barry was ready to come off his probationary status as a new Station U paramedic. That would make them essentially equals and offer

Dean the opportunity to get back to direct patient care, rather than observing his partner at work all of the time.

"So, you're finally ready to let me off the leash?" Barry asked.

"You've earned it. I was going to contact the Chief about it today."

That put a bounce in his partner's step and Dean watched as Barry got a big smile on his face while the two of them walked into the ambulance bay to load up and head downtown for the emergency call.

While he was making the brief drive downtown, Dean wondered why the staff at the Urgent Care Center didn't take their patient over to the hospital themselves? They were located right next door. It didn't make much sense and it set his Unusual cautionary radar off, if that was a thing. A syncopal episode was a fainting spell. It was often caused by a blood pressure problem or other cardiac problem that affected the blood pressure. This should have been relatively easy to stabilize and take next door to the ER.

Dean pulled the ambulance up and looked at Barry as he slid the gear lever into park. "Be careful on this one, Barry. I've got a feeling there is more going on here than we're getting over the radio."

"What do you mean?"

"I'm not sure. Call it a hunch. Just be on your guard, okay?"

"Got it. Be ready for anything."

The two paramedics gathered their gear and walked through the double doors into the waiting room of the Elk City Urgent Care Center. There was no one in sight. The waiting room was empty and there were no receptionists or nurses behind the counter at the far end of the room.

"Hello?" Barry called out. "Paramedics here. Does someone need assistance?"

The door leading back to the examination rooms opened and out walked a stunning woman in a tight red dress. "I need some help, gentlemen. I think you two are just what the doctor ordered."

Dean felt the voice pull at him, while her stunning looks fixated his eyes on her approaching form. She was beautiful and he had to be close to her. He would do anything she wanted, do anything she asked. He was disappointed when the woman went to Barry first. She walked right up to him and pulled him into a passionate embrace. Her hands reached up and pulled Barry's face to hers so they could kiss.

Dean watched fascinated as his partner exchanged a very intimate kiss with this woman. It went on for a long time. Something tickled at the back of his brain. Why was she kissing the paramedics? This wasn't some scene out of a porn flick. Life didn't happen this way. Without thinking why, Dean dropped the bags he was carrying and ran over to his partner, tearing him out of the woman's embrace.

The woman screamed as if in pain, and she stumbled backward. The pained noise broke through whatever spell had overcome Dean's senses, at least for the time being. He steadied his partner who stood on wobbling legs, weakened by whatever it was that had just happened. Barry nodded that he was okay and he sat in one of the waiting room chairs. Dean turned back to the woman but kept his eyes down and tried not to make eye contact with her. She had some sort of charm ability, that much was sure. It wasn't just her voice, though. It was something else and Dean was betting that her eyes held the power. They were the windows to the soul, after all.

"Ma'am, I need you to stay where you are. Don't come any closer. Just tell me what is happening here." Dean found that taking control back for himself helped to clear the cobwebs from his minds. His ability to focus was returning.

"How can you resist me? No one can resist me."

"Just tell me what your problem is. What kind of Unusual are you?" Dean asked.

"What kind of what? Things are certainly unusual this morning, but they've been strange for the last four days. That's why I came in here this morning instead of going to work. Now I found that I feel better when I get close to people, really close. Can I show you?"

Dean felt her turn on the charm again. It seemed as if she almost had no control over it.

"Stop," he shouted. He kept his eyes lowered, but he saw her halt out of the corner of his eye. "Barry, don't look up. Keep your eyes on the floor. I'll tell you when it's safe."

Dean turned his attention back to this woman. "Tell me more about what happened when you got up this morning. What was different about it?"

"I don't know. I have been in bed, sick for several days. When I got up this morning, my body looked different. I was still me, but I was the 'me' I always wished I could be. I mean, look at me, paramedic boy. Come on, look at me."

She was turning on the charm again. He could break her out of it but he had to take charge.

"Stay back," he cautioned. He held out his hand again, forcing himself to resist her. The more he did so, the easier if became, he found. "Just answer my questions and we'll find out what's wrong with you. So, you've never had any strange powers or been able to get people to do what you wanted before?"

"No, I don't usually like hanging around people that much, come to think of it. Huh, that is strange." She paused. Then Dean heard sobbing. "Oh my God. I think I've become some sort of monster. What is wrong with me?"

"You're not a monster. Something has happened to you, that's all. What is your name?"

"I'm Sandra."

"Okay, Sandra. You listen to me, and stay where you are, and we'll get through this together."

"First off, where is everyone? Did you do something with the staff and patients?"

Dean heard Sandra begin sobbing and she brought her hands up to her face. "I don't know what happened. When the doctor came in to check me out I thought he was attractive and I just stood up and started kissing him. It felt really good and energizing in a way but it faded and he passed out and couldn't kiss me anymore. Then I called in the nurses and then the registration people, one by one. It was all the same, whether they were men or women. They would make me feel better for a while, but then I needed more. Are you sure you don't want me to show you what I mean?"

"No," Dean felt the pull on his mind and he fended if off again. "Sandra, I need you to focus. Stop trying to do that to me. This is a power that has come to you. I don't know how or where you got it, but you have to learn to control it. You need to know how to turn it off."

Whatever kind of Unusual she was, she appeared to be human, or at least she used to be before whatever had happened to her. Now she was some sort of — Dean searched for the word — succubus. That was it. He again thanked whoever had started the library at Station U containing all the stories of myths and legends they could find. Succubi, and the male counterparts, Incubi, were a special class of Unusuals that fed off of sexual energy. Unless he missed his guess, something had transformed Sandra into one.

Dean wondered if that something had to do with his family's current demon hunt. If it did, that was all the more reason to help this woman get some sort of control over herself. Once she was tended to and safe around others, he needed to check on the rest of the staff and patients here at the clinic. He hoped she had not killed anyone. It didn't sound like it, but he didn't want her to bear that burden, on top of the changes that had already occurred to her.

"Okay, Sandra, I think I have a handle on what might have happened here, and to you."

"Really? I thought I was going insane or something."

"Yes, my name is Dean and I'm part of a special paramedic unit that helps people with strange situations like yours. Do me a favor. Look at the back of my right hand. Can you see anything there?" Dean held up his hand to show her his Station U tattoo with the special UV ink only his patients could see.

"Sure, it's kind of hazy but you have an ambulance emblem or something there."

"Okay, so that means that you have had some sort of change placed on you. I don't like to call it magic. Let's call it a special virus or infection."

"So you can cure me? I can go back to normal?"

He could hear the pleading in her tone, even if he avoided seeing it in her eyes.

"I'm not sure yet. Sometimes, if the transformation is very new, these things can be reversed. But if we cannot reverse it, I'll make sure you get the help you need to learn to control it and maybe look upon it as a gift of sorts."

"So here's what I want you to do, Sandra. I want you to go over to that restroom." Dean gestured to the waiting room bathroom in the corner. "I want you to go in there and stay there with the door closed and locked until I come back for you. I have to check on the people in the back, and I can't do that if you're out here using your new abilities on people without control. Can you do that for me?"

"I guess so. You'll make sure and come back and tell me what is going on?"

"Yes. Let me just check on the doctors, nurses, and patients in the back to make sure they are all okay. Then I'll come back and tell you what we're going to do to help you."

He could see her nod out of the corner of his eye as he focused on the area past her and not looking right at her. She turned and walked to the restroom, closing the door after she went inside.

Dean turned and looked at Barry. "How's it going partner?"

"I feel like I've run a marathon or something. I'm drained, Dean."

"Okay, you stay here. Use your radio and call headquarters. Tell them we have a mass casualty incident. Some sort of gas leak. Tell them the gas has dissipated but the patients are going to need transport from here to the hospital. I'll have the number of patients for them soon."

Barry lifted his portable radio mic and nodded. Dean heard him start talking while he went back into the treatment area to see what was going on with the staff and patients back there.

Chapter 15

Dean breathed a sigh of relief as he checked a pulse on the last of the unconscious people he found in the back of the clinic. They were all alive. All of the staff were in one exam room, stacked on top of each other where they fell. The patients waiting for their turn were all found slumped in the hallway leading back to the exam rooms. He wasn't sure what Sandra had done to them but they were breathing normally and had a pulse. If he didn't know better he'd have thought they were all asleep.

He left them, all shifted to laying on their sides in the recovery position so they wouldn't choke on their own saliva or, worse yet, vomit, if they started throwing up for some reason. He had nothing to go on for how they would recover, or even if they would recover. He didn't know exactly what a succubus fed on when she drew off the sexual energy of a victim. It could be just a shift in neurotransmitter chemicals in the brain and after a while they would all return to normal once the body reproduced enough brain chemicals to replace what was lost.

He heard voices in the waiting room and went out to see several nurses and docs who had come over from the hospital's ER next door to help out. He recognized that these were all those who were trained to treat Unusuals just like himself. He saw his medical director, Doc Spirelli, and walked over to him after directing the rest of the arriving help to the back patient care areas.

"Hey, Doc. I think we have our first succubus attack in the city. The good news is I don't think it was intentional. In fact, I think she was recently transformed into a succubus and came here just to seek some medical attention."

"Is she still here?" the old, grey-haired doc asked.

"Yep, I had her stay locked in the rest room over there until I could figure out what to do with her. I found that I could resist her charm effects if I didn't make eye-contact. I could still feel it, but it was bearable and I could get my work done."

"Good job, Dean. I don't think many boys your age would have been able to resist a succubus."

"Well, maybe it was my previous experience being charmed by a siren when I first got started in this job." Dean shrugged. "I don't know. She seems nice enough otherwise. The problem is that since she's brand new at this, she never learned to control it or turn it on or off. The power is just there, all of a sudden."

"Let's go over and you can introduce me, Dean," the doc said.

"Can you help her?" Dean asked. "I wasn't sure what to do but isolate her from anyone else who came in."

"You did the right thing. Don't second guess yourself." Doc Spirelli laid a reassuring hand on Dean's shoulder. "I happen to know a succubus who lives outside of town. She is a licensed therapist specializing in sexual dysfunction. I will call her to come down and take this young lady in until she can be trained to control herself. We'll get her the help she needs."

Dean led the doc over to the restroom in the corner of the waiting room. After introducing the doctor to Sandra through the closed door, Dean went to check on his partner.

Barry was still sitting in the waiting room chair, looking around. The activity increased as more people came in to help and hospital stretchers were wheeled out and over to the ER with the unconscious victims. He watched one of the stretchers go by and looked up at Dean.

"That could have been me."

"Yep, and it wouldn't have been your fault," Dean said, trying to reassure his partner and probationary paramedic. "Look at it this way. If you had stumbled into a home with a carbon monoxide leak in the furnace, you wouldn't have known it was there until you got inside and started checking the family. If you spent too long in there with them, you could have become a casualty as well without ever knowing what the problem was."

Dean gestured to the now steady line of patients being rolled by the ER response team. "We got a call to come here for a fainting spell, a syncopal episode. We didn't know this was a mass casualty incident. I didn't pick up on it from what the dispatcher told us. The lesson we need to learn here is that in the realm of Unusual emergency medical care, always assume something supernatural is to blame until proven otherwise."

"I guess so, Dean. I know I shouldn't blame myself, but it's hard." Barry shook his head in resignation. "Maybe I'm not cut out for this kind of specialized EMS work."

"Nonsense," Dean countered. "You have learned a valuable lesson. Don't give up now. Take that lesson and learn from it. Let me tell you about my encounter with a siren who tried to kidnap me and turn me into her own private paramedic."

Dean and Barry gathered their bags while he told the story of the siren, who charmed him with her melodic singing voice early in his tenure as a probationary paramedic at the station. They finished stowing the gear in the ambulance and had put themselves back in service when the first of the news vans rolled up. Dean saw the fire department public information officer walk over to the reporter and he overheard her tell the reporter that it was an anesthesia gas leak in the urgent care center. Clever, he thought as he climbed up into the driver's seat and pulled away from the increasingly busy scene outside of the clinic.

As he drove back to the station, he thought about Sandra and her sudden transformation into a succubus. He didn't know much about that variety of Unusual, but if they were like most others, they reproduced just like humans did. Most didn't come into their full powers until they reached puberty. Sandra's sudden change from human into a succubus pointed to another source, one that was similar to Steve from their vampire encounter earlier in the week.

Dean made a note to call Jaz about it when he got back to the station. She might have more information about how succubi were created and she would certainly want to follow up on this lead into who had the other figurines.

JAZ WANTED to meet up after he got off work to talk over what she had been able to discover so far about the vampire Steve. He reminded her that he had to check on Jo back at his apartment, and get her some dinner after work. Dean checked with the station chef and resident zombie, Freddy. Maybe he could take home some leftovers. The zombie suggested they all come over and have dinner at the Station. He was cooking up some fresh pasta and a garlic pesto sauce to go with it. He told Dean there would be plenty for everyone.

Dean sent a text to Jaz to pick up Jo and come by the station for dinner. They could talk freely here without worrying about other diners in a restaurant overhearing their strange conversations. He told her what was on the menu and she sent a text back right away saying she'd be there just after six.

He spent the rest of the shift making sure Barry was okay and getting the station chores done in between running the few other ambulance calls that came in. They were all routine sick calls that required standard medical knowledge. Most Unusuals were basically human when it came down to it. They had the same incidence of heart disease, diabetes and respiratory illnesses that other humans did. Often it was just a case of treating the immediate problem and directing them to seek treatment with one of the Unusual-friendly doctors scattered around the city.

By the time the end of the shift rolled around, the station

smelled of fresh pesto sauce cooking on the stove and Dean's mouth was watering. Barry took his dinner to go, and Brook and Tammy arrived early to grab a plate and eat before their shift started. They were just finishing up when there was a knock at the door and Dean went over to answer it. It was Jaz and Jo. Jaz nodded to Dean and looked around before she entered, as if she expected to be attacked at any moment. Jo just bounced in as if she belonged there. Seeing as how she probably grew up around the station in her youth, it made sense.

"Don't worry, Jaz," Dean said. "Nobody here bites, I promise. You play nice, they'll play nice."

She looked great, wearing a pair of tight blue jeans, knee-high black leather boots, and a white t-shirt. She had her characteristic short-waisted black leather jacket on, too. He was sure that was there to hide the shoulder holster rig she had to be wearing underneath. He sighed. Once a hunter, always a hunter.

"Come on, Mom and Dad, get over here. Freddy has made the most spectacular meal." Jo already had a plate in her hand and was holding it up to show them.

"Yeah, Mom and Dad," Tammy said. "Listen to the kid. Get in here and eat. It's good." She was just finishing up her meal and she got up to make room at the small station table. "I still can't believe you have a teenaged daughter Dean. This whole time travel thing isn't fair. You didn't have to change any diapers or anything."

Dean laughed. There were few secrets between the Station U paramedics. "Don't forget, Tammy. I have all of that fun to look forward to at some point in my future."

"True. True. Still, it might be nice to fast forward through some of the harder times growing up," Tammy mused.

"Yeah, because suddenly being the parent of a teenager is easy," Dean replied.

"Hey, I'm right here," Jo protested through a mouthful of food.

"Don't talk with your mouth full," Dean and Jaz said simultaneously. The other paramedics in the room burst out laughing and Dean and Jaz looked at each other, blushing in embarrassment, then they laughed too.

Dean sat down at the table next to Jo. Jaz took a seat across from him. He dished up a generous helping of pasta and grabbed a slice of garlic bread. Freddy's food was excellent, but this meal was among his best. He marveled at what the zombie chef could do with only a few simple ingredients.

It was quiet for a while with the three of them eating their dinner. Brook and Tammy were in the Ambulance bay doing their chores for the beginning of the shift. It was pleasant to eat together, Dean thought. He could see the three of them gelling into a family unit of sorts. Jo had it the easiest he figured. She was used to following their lead. She had grown up with them as her parents. He and Jaz had the most to struggle with, but that had started to resolve into something else. It might not have been a parental relationship, but it was a sort of shared responsibility for another person that approached being parents.

He caught Jaz watching him as he ate and he smiled at her. She gave him a smile in return that made him wonder if she had been having similar thoughts. His rumination on their small family unit ended as Jaz cleared her throat and leaned back in her chair, her plate wiped clean.

"I've been doing some backtracking of Steven's movements before he started acting strange," Jaz started. "I also went back and interviewed his wife to see if she had anything to offer. The only thing I've been able to find out is that his strange behavior started two days before we picked him up. He woke up looking a little pale and seemed to be bothered by the sunlight. She told me he took off work that morning, staying in bed most of the day. It was on the evening of the next day that she called 911 for help."

"That time frame matches up with what Barry and I found today. A woman was turned into a succubus and she nearly wiped out an entire urgent care clinic downtown before we figured out what was going on. We've isolated her for now but I was able to find out that she started feeling strange four days ago too. It took several days to complete the change and alter her physiology."

"Mom, these have to be related, right?" Jo asked. "Could our demon be randomly changing people into Unusuals?"

"I would say that in this case there is no such thing as a coincidence," Jaz answered. "I don't think it is random. There has to be some connection between these two situations. The time frame has to link them somehow. Based on what I've been able to research, the demon would have to be in pretty close proximity for hours to enact the change."

"So this isn't a case of someone causing this to happen just brushing up against someone on the street?" Dean asked.

"No, it would have to be done in a secure location based on the time required." Jaz leaned forward and rested her elbows on the table. "I think we have to interview the two subjects again to get anywhere further."

"There is the amnesia to account for," Jo interjected. "They don't remember anything strange in their recent past, so there must have been that spell on them, too. That takes a while to cast if my teachers were correct. It takes a half hour or more to correctly lay on the memory blocks in a person's mind. To cast it on more than one person would take over an hour."

"The question is how many more are out there?" Dean asked.

Chapter 16

Eddie had been itchy all day. It felt like there was something moving just under his skin. He'd scratch and scratch and then it would stop, for a while. When he had to go to work at his telemarketing job for the bank that afternoon, he hoped it would stop. At least there would be air conditioning. It didn't stop. It got worse.

The latest bout with the elusive itch was right between his shoulder blades. His growl of frustration caused some of his work colleagues to peek over their adjacent cubicle walls to see what he was doing. What they saw was him, contorting his arms and body to reach the middle of his back with a pencil, trying to scratch there.

Finally, he couldn't take it anymore. He looked at the clock. It was almost ten PM. He only had one more hour on the phones. They called until it was eight PM on the west coast. The three hour time difference put the end of his shift at eleven o'clock. He got up and headed to the bathroom to splash some water on his face. Walking down the hallway, he found he couldn't stop staring at the full moon out the windows lining the corridor. He almost walked right into a co-worker, the woman dodging out of his way with a startled shout. Eddie muttered an apology.

Stumbling into the restroom, he was glad to see the stalls were empty. The itch was moving all over his body now. He could barely control himself as he scratched. He made his way over to the sinks and looked in the mirror. He almost screamed when he caught a glimpse of the yellow-irised eyes staring back at him.

He reached up to touch his face, and stopped as he saw his fingernails start to lengthen and sharpen into talons, his fingers and the back of his hand sprouting thick brown hair. Eddie shouted for help but all that came from his lengthening snout was a howl of pain as the shift consumed him, tearing apart his clothing, leaving shredded strips of cloth hanging from him. The last thing he remembered was the door opening and inquisitive voices calling to see what the noise was.

DEAN'S PHONE buzzed in his pocket with a text message as he drove Jo back to his apartment. He was almost there, so he didn't bother to pull over and check the message. Jo's phone buzzed, too, immediately afterward. He glanced at her as he pulled into his parking spot on the street in front of the Baxter's house and detached garage. She turned from looking at her screen with a huge grin on her face.

"We've got a lead. A wild animal is running around the inside of the Elk National Bank building."

"What?" Dean pulled out his phone and looked at the screen. His text was from Gibbie and said the same thing.

"It's the full moon dad. Look," Jo pointed toward the night sky. The bright white orb hung there, a harbinger of busy EMS nights and ER overcrowding. It also pulled at the adolescent Lycans, causing the youngest and the newest to shift against their will. It likely had the same effect on any newly created werebeasts, too.

"Get the address from Gibbie. We'll meet him there."

Dean put the gear lever back into drive and pulled away

heading back downtown. He waited until Jo was done texting and asked her if police units were responding.

"Apparently, the police are backed up and have called the ASPCA animal response unit. Their ETA is over an hour away."

"Are you armed, Jo?" Dean asked. "I suppose I shouldn't assume you are, but …"

"Of course I'm armed, Dad. I've also got an idea for a spell that might work. We don't want to kill this guy, right?"

"No, we don't want to kill anyone," Dean confirmed. He took out his phone as he drove and used the voice recognition feature to call Rudy, the Elk City werewolf pack leader.

"Hey, Dean. What's up?" Rudy answered.

"Rudy, I've got a lead on a potential newly turned Lycan downtown. I'm headed there now. I don't suppose you're available to meet me down at the Elk National Bank building in say, ten minutes or so?"

"I've got several new pack members who just aged up to start the change tonight. I'm booked up. If you can contain this one for a few hours, I can probably catch up with you later this evening."

"I was afraid that would be the case. I'm meeting Gibbie there. I think he has Marian with him. Will she have enough pack seniority to back a newbie down?"

"Maybe," Rudy answered. "It's hard to say. You could try, but don't let her do it alone. Her dad will have my hide if anything happens to her. I vouched for you guys when she started riding along with you all on these CERT team calls."

"Don't worry, Rudy, I'll make sure we don't put her in any unnecessary danger. We're prepared to do what we need to, to protect the team and the public. I'll let you know how it goes." Dean hung up the call. He glanced at Jo as he drove.

"I hope your spell works, or that Marian has the ability to calm this person down, Jo," Dean said as he drove onto the freeway. "We can't let this one bite a bunch of people and have a whole crop of new Lycans next month when this happens all over again."

It took them just under ten minutes to make the drive and Gibbie's beat up, rusty white van was pulled up out front of the bank building when he and Jo arrived. The two of them got out and walked up to the van, tapping on the tinted windows. The passenger side window rolled down and an excited teenager's face topped with bright pink hair popped out.

"Good, you're here. Hey Jo, ready for some fun?" Marian asked.

Jo nodded and Dean decided he needed to nip this in the bud right away.

"Scene safety and team safety first, ladies. Remember that, okay?"

"Yes, Dad," they both replied, followed by a string of giggles.

Gibbie climbed out of the driver's side of the van. He was wearing his non-uniform uniform. It looked like a typical EMS uniform for the city's fire department, matching Dean's in every way except for the lack of official patches and a badge. Still, he sort of looked official.

"Come on, let's see if we can even get inside the building," Dean said, leading the way for his group of four responders.

The distraught security guard seemed relieved that someone else, anyone else, was here to take over for him and his colleague.

"Man, am I glad you guys are here. I called nine-one-one a half hour ago." The guard unlocked the front door and let them in.

"The city is busy tonight and thought we might be able to help," Dean lied. "My partner and I are here to treat any injuries and these two ladies are interns from the zoo." The last was a sudden inspiration for the young ladies accompanying them. "They have some experience with wild animals and might help us contain the creature."

"I don't care who you are, honestly. I have twenty people cornered up on the fourth floor in the call center. They've barricaded the door, but the animal is between them and the hallway leading to the stairwell and elevators."

"Are there any injuries?" Dean asked.

"I believe there are a few bites, but nothing too serious."

Dean looked at Gibbie. "Do you have anything for that?"

"I have a basic med kit that we can use. It has what you need,

Dean. I'll have Marian and Jo go back and get it. I should have made sure we carried the bags in with us."

"No worries, Gibbie. Have them get the gear. We needed to see what we were going to need anyway." Dean turned to the guard and had him show them where the stairwell was.

Without saying it aloud, Gibbie had told Dean he had wolfsbane extract that could be administered as an antidote for the bites, counteracting the Lycanthropy virus that caused the change from human to were-form.

It only took a few minutes to gather the gear they would need. Dean learned that the other on-duty guard was waiting for them on the stairwell landing outside the fourth floor. The first guard had to remain here by the front desk and doors.

Dean and team went into the stairwell and started up to the fourth floor. By the time they got halfway there, Gibbie was out of breath, or whatever a vampire ran out of when he got tired. He was sweating and muttering quiet complaints by the time they arrived at the landing where the other guard awaited them.

The guard shook Dean's hand with enthusiasm. "I'm sure glad you all are here. I don't know what to do. I can hear the - the whatever it is - prowling on the other side of the door. Sometimes I can hear it snuffling at the door like it's smelling me."

"Well we are here now. We'll take it from here," Dean said. "My team and I need to get set up. Your partner said he might need your help downstairs if you don't want to be here when we open the door."

The guard seemed relieved. "Yeah, that might be a good idea. I should go down and help him out."

Dean waited until the guard was out of sight around the bend in the stairwell before he turned to the rest of the team and began to lay out his plan in whispered tones.

"Marian," Dean asked the teen werewolf. "How aware is this guy likely to be? Can we talk to him in his Lycan form?"

She shook her head. "If this is his first shift to animal form, he won't be able to control himself. I might be able to shift and get him to listen to me. It's all about seniority in the pack and I've been in the pack longer but it's not a sure thing since this one's not officially a pack member yet."

"Okay, you try and get control and I'll be right behind you, then Gibbie and then Jo."

"I should go in second, Dad," Jo spoke up.

"No, absolutely not."

"I'm the only one here who is armed and has the firepower to put this creature down if that is the only other option. Plus, I have that spell I'd like to try if Marian's idea doesn't work. I think I can create a local time-shift around them that will cause a shift back to human form."

Dean thought about it. He knew she was right but he felt like he was supposed to protect her from risks. Wasn't that what a parent does?

"Dean, I can go in second, right behind Marian. My vampire strength and speed should be enough, at least for a little while, to hold the creature off if it attacks any of us. Its bite can't affect me or Marian. You and Jo can go in last."

Gibbie had a point, too. "Okay, Marian and Gibbie, then Jo and I'll bring up the rear. Marian, do you need time to prepare or anything?"

The pink-haired teen shook her head.

"Alright, then let's open the door and see what we can see." Dean nodded to the door on the far side of the landing. The team got in the correct order and Dean watched in amazement as Marian partially shifted to her wolf form. Her face elongated into a wolf-like shape and fur sprouted from her head and arms. He noted the talons on the ends of her fingers and the stripe of bright pink on the top of her head amidst the brown wolf hair there.

Marian tried to grasp the door knob but her talons got in the way. Her wolf hand could not operate the mechanism properly and she whined in frustration and turned to look back at them. Gibbie smiled and reached around her, turning the knob and pulling open the door. She darted through and the vampire followed her, with Jo and Dean close behind.

They were in a normal office hallway. It was L-shaped with

them at the top and the hall turned the corner to the left about twenty yards away. That would be where the elevators were and the entrance to the bank's call center, where all the hostages were holed up. The quartet of responders started forward towards the bend in the hall ahead of them.

They stopped when they heard snarls of rage and some muffled cries of fear from around the corner. Marian peeked around the corner and pulled back looking over her shoulder and nodded. Then she stood up and stepped out into the corridor and growled down the hall in the direction of the snarls and human cries.

The snarling stopped for a moment, shifting to growling in return. It sounded like it was getting closer. Marian increased the intensity of her growls and Dean watched as she stood up straight and tall, stretching up on her tip toes. She must be trying to assert her dominance on the other Lycan.

Dean looked at Gibbie and Jo in front of him. The vampire was standing on the balls of his feet, ready to leap forward if needed. Jo had drawn her pistol from the shoulder holster rig under her jeans jacket, holding it in one hand, the other, empty hand outstretched towards her friend and the turn in the hallway.

The snarling of the other Lycan got closer and closer until they finally saw him. It was vaguely man-shaped. It was still wearing the shredded remains of men's khaki pants and a dress shirt. Other than that, it was fully changed into a werewolf. Gibbie tensed as it walked into view. The creature turned to look in their direction with yellow-irised eyes. A low growl began as it saw fresh prey.

Marian let out a ripping snarl and tried to draw attention back to herself, but this werewolf was too far gone for the teen to command it to stop. She leapt forward and tried to knock it back away from her friends. A single back-handed blow from the larger werewolf knocked her back against the wall. Gibbie jumped towards the creature but Jo shouted "Stop" and she threw herself forward, her open hand beginning to glow.

Dean wanted to cry out and halt her forward motion, but it was as if time stood still for a moment. He couldn't move. She stopped in front of the snarling creature as it loomed above her and she said one word as she slapped the werewolf on the chest.

"Tempos."

The wolf had started to swing back a taloned hand to strike her when she struck him with the spell, and Dean was sure she would be killed or at least injured by the attack. Then, there was a nimbus of golden light that outlined the form of the werewolf. It froze in place and then seemed to fold in on itself, falling to the ground.

When Dean looked to the floor, there was a man in tattered, shredded clothing lying there. He didn't move and seemed to be unconscious.

"Huh, it worked," Jo said, looking at her hand.

"What?! You weren't sure it would work?" Dean asked rushing forward.

"Jeeze, Dad. It's not like this is something they teach in witch school. I figured the theory was sound. I just had to try it out."

"Try it out?" Dean was furious. What if the spell had not worked? Even Gibbie's enhanced speed wouldn't have kept her from getting hurt. "We are going to have a long talk when we get home young lady. That is not how this team works."

"Dad, it's fine. See? It worked." She pointed to the man lying on the floor.

"Now is not the time, Joanna. Later, we will talk and I think we should include your mother in the discussion."

"Wow, Jo, you're in trouble now," Marian joked. She had shifted back to human form and was getting up from where the werewolf had knocked her down. "The double the parent, double the fun treatment is classic parent-speak for you're up shit creek."

"Marian," Dean said. "I'll ask you to stay out of this and also watch your language. Otherwise, I'll have a word with your father and make other arrangements for the CERT team."

The teen werewolf, closed her mouth and looked at her friend with a shrug. Joanna just gave her a grim smile and then shot Dean an angry glance.

He was not an expert on teens in any respect. He had only been a father for a little more than a month now. That look, however, told him that he was in for a fight over this when they got home. He thought he was the one who was angry, but now he was sure she was just as angry at him because she had been embarrassed.

Gibbie broke the tension. "I hate to bust up this family conversation, but we've got untreated patients to take care of at the end of this hallway. Maybe we should focus on them?"

Dean shook himself and reassessed the current situation. He had to take care of the former hostages and he also had to get this werewolf somewhere he couldn't hurt anyone else.

"Okay," Dean ordered as he settled on the plan from here on out. "Gibbie, you get the bags and come with me to see to the injured. Marian and Jo, stay here and keep an eye on our friend here. See if you can find a room where you can get him out of sight so we can get the people in the call center downstairs without seeing anything."

The girls nodded and Gibbie picked up the trauma bag and med kit. It was time to treat the injured and clean up this mess.

It turned out that two of the call center employees had been bitten before the others were able to close and barricade the door. Dean and Gibbie started the process of treating them for the early stages of the Lycanthropism infection. The injection of an extract of wolfsbane would halt the process temporarily until they could have definitive infusion treatments in the ER at Elk City Medical Center.

Once he had the names of the two injured employees, he called the dispatch center directly and told them to send a station U ambulance to the scene. He would turn the two injured folks, one man and one woman, over to Brook and Tammy when they arrived. Dean told the employees that the animal was likely rabid and those two would need additional shots and treatment at the hospital.

Gibbie started to chat up the woman as he wrapped up her injured hand. She was smiling and flirting back while the vampire first responder bandaged her wound. Dean shook his head as he went back out into the hallway. Gibbie always found a way to get the most out of any situation. He'd likely have the plump woman's phone number before they left the building.

Dean headed down the hall to see how the other patient was doing. He found no sign of the two girls or the unconscious man when he turned the corner. They must have found an unlocked door and dragged him out of the way. He called for Jo and Marian and was rewarded when Jo popped her head out of a doorway and waved him over.

"Come on in, Dad. He's starting to wake up," Jo said as he entered the small conference room they had appropriated for a holding area.

"Is he going to shift back again?" Dean asked.

"I don't think so," Jo replied. "I time-shifted his body, well the cells in his body actually, so they think it's yesterday. It should hold him for twelve hours or so. After that, he'll definitely shift again with tomorrow's moon. We'll need your friend Rudy and Marian's dad to hold him until he gains more control over the change."

A groan from the floor of the conference room drew their attention and Dean walked around to the far side of the conference table. The man in the shredded clothing had rolled onto his side and was pushing himself up into a sitting position. He seemed disoriented and looked around the room and at the faces he saw there. Then he looked down at his shredded clothes and at his hands, touching his face, then buried his face in his hands and began sobbing.

Dean crouched down and laid his hand on the man's shoulder. He waited while the man gathered himself.

"I'm Dean. I'm a paramedic and I'm here to make sure you come out of this situation alright, okay?"

The man looked up at him. "I know what happened. I saw myself change in the bathroom mirror. I hoped it was a bad dream, but look at my clothes. It's true. It's all true." He began crying again.

"Look, you are correct. Something happened to you tonight. But I know a lot of people who are just like you and they live normal lives. You can learn to control it," Dean said.

Marian came over and knelt down in front of the man. "Mister, I'm just like you. My whole family is, as far back as anyone can remember. I go to school. My mom and dad work normal jobs. There's no reason you can't go on with your life."

The man looked up at Marian then over at Dean, who nodded. "But how did this happen? I wasn't bitten by anything recently. Isn't that the normal way a person becomes a-a-a werewolf?" His voice trailed off to a whisper as he said the last words.

"That is something we are investigating," Dean explained. "Can you tell me your name?"

"Eddie. It's Eddie. I was having problems all afternoon here at work. I went to the bathroom because I wasn't feeling well. Then this all happened."

"Were you feeling all itchy? Kind of like bugs were under your skin?" Marian asked.

"Yes. That is it exactly." Eddie exclaimed.

"Yep, I felt the same way for a day or so before my first change. I was thirteen. Of course, I knew I was a werewolf and my parents were expecting it."

"So you don't just turn into a monster whenever the moon comes up?" Eddie asked.

"Oh, no. Not anymore. After the first few shifts, you learn to override the change. You can also learn how to initiate it if you want to, eventually. That usually takes a couple of years to master, though."

"Well, I guess that's a relief." Eddie seemed to relax a little after Marian's explanation.

"We can get all of your questions answered shortly." Dean pointed to his daughter. "Jo here made sure you won't shift again tonight. You'll probably change again tomorrow night, but we'll have others like you to help you through the change. You won't be alone in this anymore."

Marian nodded and pointed to a chair nearby, next to the conference table. "Do you want to try to get up and sit in a chair? You might be more comfortable."

Eddie looked at the chair and smiled. Dean and Jo helped him up and over to the seat. He was still a little unsteady on his feet.

"I would like to ask you a little about the last few days, if you don't mind," Dean said. "You said you weren't bitten by anything recently. Can you account for your last four or five days? We have reason to believe that there might be something going on that affected you in that time frame."

Eddie looked at each of them. Dean thought he might finally get a clue to go on, giving them all some way to track down the missing summoning idol and the demon creating all the problems in Elk City.

"The last few days have been pretty normal until today. I don't know. I mean, I haven't done anything out of the ordinary for a while." Eddie looked perplexed and he seemed like he wanted to help.

"It wouldn't have to be anything unusual," Jo offered. "Maybe we're going about this the wrong way, Dad. Maybe they ran into the demon in the course of a normal activity. We know that things started going strange four days ago, right?" She turned to Eddie and asked him, "Eddie, tell us what you were doing five nights ago at this time?"

The man thought back and then remembered. "Oh, nothing strange. I was at my friends Sam and Jill's apartment. We were playing our normal game night of Dungeon Masters. We've been playing with that same group every week for over two years."

Dean thought Jo might be on to something here. "Eddie, tell me the name of your other game night friends."

"It's just Sandra and Steve. Why?"

Dean looked at Jo and nodded. This was it, their link between all of the recent, mystery Unusual patients. He was proud of Jo. She had figured it out and come up with the perfect question to get the answer they needed.

Jaz had said that she didn't believe in coincidences and he had to agree with her in this case. The names matched. The time frame matched. They had found their source. The question for the team now was what to do next?

Dean had to admit that he figured they'd find the demon, fight the demon, and take the idol back. This was different. They had the names of a couple and would get the location of their apartment. The problem was there were too many questions left unanswered. They couldn't go and kick the door in like a bad police show on TV.

"Eddie, you've been really helpful. This could be the information that helps us get to the source that changed you into a werewolf."

"You mean you could find a way to change me back?"

Dean looked at Jo and Marian and back to their patient. "No, Eddie. There's no going back. You'll have to find a way to live with how you are right now."

"You won't do it alone, Eddie," Marian said. "The pack supports their own and I can vouch for you as a new member. We'll get you through the next few months. Don't worry."

Eddie looked overwhelmed, and Dean didn't want to give him anything else to worry about. He told them he needed to check on Gibbie, without talking about the two co-workers who were bitten. Telling Eddie he'd hurt his work colleagues would only upset him more. Dean left the conference room and pulled the door shut behind him. As he walked to the call center room at the other end of the hall, the elevator door opened and Brook and Tammy walked out with a stretcher full of EMS gear.

"Hey Dean," they called out in unison. They laughed and Brook deferred to Tammy.

"We heard from dispatch that you were here ahead of us. Did you find anything useful about our outbreak of Unusual problems?" the older medic asked him.

"I might have a lead or two. We've got two Lycan bites down here in the call center. I've already administered the first dose of wolfsbane."

"Hey, thanks," Brook said. "That makes it all that much easier for us. Two patients, no waiting. Lead the way."

Dean took them into the call center part of the office and he and Gibbie turned patient care over to the Station U paramedics on duty. While Brook and Tammy checked out the patients for themselves, Dean and Gibbie escorted the rest of the people out to the elevators and got them all started down to the first floor.

The last to leave the floor were the two paramedics with the two bitten patients. Both walked next to their caregivers, careful of their bandaged arms, and loaded onto the elevator down. Dean waited until the door was closed before he and Gibbie went back to the conference room and checked on Eddie and the two teens. He was ready to go too, and stood up when Dean and Gibbie entered the room.

"Okay, Eddie," Dean said. "We got all your co-workers out of the office safely and you're the last one. We'll take you to meet some of your new pack mates tonight and get you settled."

"I guess so…"

"You'll do fine. I already texted my dad to expect you. He and Rudy, the pack leader, are going to meet us at my house. Gibbie and Dean will drop us both off there."

"Don't sweat it, Eddie," Gibbie said with a big smile, showing his fangs. "Some of my best friends are werewolves."

Chapter 18

Dean contacted Jaz that night after he got home. He had the address for the couple mentioned by Eddie. She could run the names through her security databases and do a complete background check on them, which was more than he could. It helped that the Errington clan had a longstanding relationship with the U.S. Marshal's service dating back to the U.S. Civil War. She'd dig up anything on them that needed investigating, before the three of them paid Sam and Jill a visit.

He chuckled to himself as he drove back to his apartment with Jo. He always considered the three of them as a unit now. It had been that way since they had returned from the rescue mission to free Ashley from the demon kidnappers, though he hadn't realized it at the time. They might not be the perfect family unit in most people's eyes, but they were gelling in their own unique way.

Jo was listening to her tunes on her smartphone. He wondered if she was listening to current music or some future techno-pop from her own timeline. The phone looked like anyone else's nowadays and all she would say about it was that retro was in where she came from. He didn't know how she had service either. He'd asked and she just smiled and made a comment about parents and new technology. Dean was getting enough of the teen attitude, that was sure.

The residential street was dark and quiet when he pulled up out front and parked. He got out, and he and Jo walked up the exterior stairs to their apartment over the Baxter's garage. The elderly couple had accepted his explanation of Jo being his cousin and told him they'd look in on her when he was working to make sure she was alright. They were great people to have as landlords. He liked living here. It was just the kind of place that made a nice retreat from the things he saw in his work as a paramedic on the street.

Jo went straight back to her room. She had cast a pretty powerful spell back at the bank building. She didn't make a big deal out of it, but he knew from his talks with Asha at the local coven, that anything that influenced time required a lot of energy. Jo had to be exhausted from her casting that night. He hoped she slept well.

Dean went to his room and set out his uniform for the next shift, then went about his nighttime routine. Five in the morning came all too early and he was in bed and asleep within a few minutes of arriving home.

Neither Dean nor Jo noticed the man step out of the shadows next to the garage when they went upstairs to the apartment. They didn't see him levitate to peer in at them as they readied for bed, before his form folded in on itself and blinked out of sight without a sound. Graadu had found them.

DEAN'S DAY went by fast with a series of routine calls for sick Unusuals. They had the same issues with heart disease, diabetes, and other chronic illnesses as normal humans did. Throughout the day, Dean and Barry did what they could to help their patients manage their disease and return to health.

Jaz called in around lunchtime and said that nothing had come back on the background check.

"They're clean as far as I can tell, Dean," the huntress said. "Either they've got some sort of solid background cover I can't penetrate, which is not likely unless they work for some foreign government or something, or they are just normal mundane people without so much as a speeding ticket against them."

"Well, you're the one who said there are no coincidences, so they've got to have something to do with this."

"I agree, it only means that they aren't on anyone's radar, which is probably why they got away with snatching the idols in the first place. Sam works for the construction company that is demolishing the Errington building," Jazz paused as if she was checking her notes. "He also hasn't been to work for a few days and the foreman was very cagey when I asked him about the guy. This has to be the connection to the summoning idols."

"So, what's the plan?" Dean asked.

"I think we head over and introduce ourselves this evening after you get off work."

"And by 'we' you mean …?"

"You, me, and Joanna," Jaz said, her matter of fact tone making it seem like she, too, considered them a unit and maybe even part of the family.

"Okay, I'll pick her up and meet you at your place. We can drive over to Sam and Jill's apartment building in your SUV. It's a lot more roomy and impressive than my beat up pickup truck," Dean suggested.

The radio tones alerted overhead and Dean took the phone away from his ear for a moment listening to the dispatcher.

"Medical Box 811, Ambulance U-191, respond for an injured subject, in the area of 8834 Red Pump Road."

"Hey, Jaz, we've got a call. I've got to go. I'll see you later, around seven, at your place."

"Sounds good. Stay safe, Dean," Jaz said and then disconnected the call.

Barry called from across the squad room. "Coming, Boss?"

"Yep, I'm on my way."

. . .

\---

IT WAS late in the afternoon as the ambulance turned down the back country road on the outskirts of Elk City. Dean looked at the battered mailboxes scattered along the winding, wooded road until he found the one they were looking for.

"Eighty-eight thirty-four," Dean said, "That's the one. The dispatcher said in the vicinity of this location. Put us on location, Barry."

Dean slid the gear shift lever into park while his partner contacted the dispatch center to let them know they had arrived on scene. He looked around. The sun was low in the sky and the surrounding trees deepened the shadows further as he scanned the area for their patient. He was about to ask Barry to have dispatch contact the caller again when he saw movement in the woods nearby. He had to stare into the shadows for a moment before he saw the tall figure standing there.

"I think that's our patient over there," Dean said.

"Where?" Barry asked looking in the direction Dean indicated. "I don't see anything."

"Right between the two tall trees, next to the road on the left."

"Oh, there he is. The guy sort of blends in to the surroundings doesn't he?"

"Keep your wits about you. There are some strange sorts of folks who live out here on the edges of the city," Dean cautioned.

The two paramedics exited their ambulance and gathered their gear and walked through the woods at the road's edge for about fifty feet until they had arrived at the side of their patient.

"Hi, I'm Dean, this is my partner Barry. What seems to be the problem?"

The bearded man was wearing bib overalls, over a plaid shirt, and, when Dean looked down, no shoes at all. Not that shoes would have been an option. The man had the largest feet he had ever seen. They were weathered, dark and dirty and the toes stretched out as far as his fingers did.

"I'm Jim," the man said in a deep bass voice. "I stepped on something back a ways and I can't go any further until I get it looked at." His words were slow and measured, almost as if he didn't use them very often.

"Okay, Jim," Barry said. "Why don't you have a seat on this log over here and we'll take a look at your foot. Which one is it?"

Jim pointed to his right foot as he settled his large form on the log. He lifted his foot up and rested it on his left knee to show the two paramedics a large gash on the bottom of his foot. Dean noticed that the foot's callouses were thick and leathery, like one would expect of someone who went barefoot everywhere.

"Can you tell us what happened?" Barry asked.

"I rushed crossing the road. I know I should be more careful, but there was a car coming and I didn't want to be seen. I don't like to be seen. People make fun of me. I think I stepped on a broken bottle or something on the road's edge. It hurt a lot, but I couldn't stop to check because of the car."

Dean nodded and looked around. "Do you live around here? That cut is pretty bad and you're going to need help getting back home. I assume you don't want to go to the hospital."

"No, no hospital. A dryad told me I could call you. She let me use her phone." The bass rumble of Jim's voice reminded Dean of distant thunder on a summer evening.

"Do you live close? We could bandage this and then give you a lift home," Barry offered.

"I live here and there. Or there and here. It depends on what I want to do," Jim replied. He stared at the ground, avoiding eye-contact with the paramedics.

Barry looked at Dean with a shrug. He understood his probationary partner's indecision. This guy couldn't get far on this foot, but he was clearly homeless and didn't want to leave behind what little he had, to go to the hospital. He probably had a tent and maybe a backpack nearby that were all the possessions he had in the world.

Dean took the lead. "Alright, Jim. We don't have to take you to the hospital if you don't want to go. Barry's going to bandage that foot up for you. We'll use some butterfly bandages to close up the cut after we clean it out first. Then we'll wrap it up for you to keep it clean. Okay?"

The large man nodded and Dean and Barry settled in to providing what care they could for their patient. Barry got some sterile saline out of the trauma bag and some gauze to clean up the foot while Dean opened the med bag. Most paramedics didn't carry basic vaccines, but the Station U paramedics did have a few options most did not.

He had to call in for permission administer the tetanus shot, but the doc on call agreed with Dean's assessment. Given the refusal of transport to the hospital, it was the best option they had to avoid him developing lockjaw. The doc also ordered a broad spectrum antibiotic injection, too.

By the time Dean was finished giving the injections, Barry had completed the wrapping of the feet. Dean noticed he had used his trauma shears to cut down a padded board splint and fashion a padded sole for the bandage. This guy didn't wear shoes but he might tolerate this much of one until his foot healed.

"Jim, I want you to try and keep that dry and as clean as you can," Barry instructed. "If it gets dirty or too loose to stay on your foot, you have the dryad call us back. If it's not us, it will be two of our friends. They can re-wrap your bandage and make sure you're doing alright. Okay?"

"Okay," the large man responded. His voice was slow and deliberate as always and Dean knew that often, the homeless had other underlying mental health issues that made them choose to live alone and isolated from the rest of society.

"Remember that you can call us any time you want," Dean reminded the man. "Even if you just want us to come and talk with you sometime. We'll have someone come out and check on you. Just ask."

The tall man nodded and stood up from the log where he had been sitting. He towered above Dean by a foot or more.

Dean and Barry gathered their gear and carried it back to the ambulance. They stowed what they carried out back into the proper compartments, and turned to check on their patient one last time. He was nowhere to be seen. Dean scanned the trees, peering into the deepening gloom of evening in the forest, but he could see nothing there.

He shrugged and looked to Barry who returned the gesture. They climbed into the ambulance cab and Barry got on the radio to put them back in service while Dean drove away.

"Hey, Dean. Was that guy a …"

"A what? A Bigfoot? I guess. He, or those like him, might be the source of that particular legend. It's as good an explanation as any." He drove as Barry fell silent again, thinking about the answer Dean gave him.

Dean hoped Jim did alright with that wound. He doubted the man would call them or their colleagues back unless it got really bad again. So many of their Unusual patients felt isolated from the rest of society. When you were both homeless and an Unusual, the isolation must be severe. Still Jim seemed to do fine avoiding human contact as much as possible. That was what Sasquatches did after all.

Chapter 19

Dean got off work and went to get Jo from the apartment. The plan, according to Jaz, was to head over to this guy Sam's apartment. She used her resources to get some information on the guy and she told him there was nothing on the surface that was unusual or alarming, but that didn't always mean anything either.

Jo was ready to go as he pulled up in front of the garage. She came bouncing down the stairs in an outfit that looked a lot like her mother's hunting gear. She was wearing black skinny jeans, a red top and a black leather jacket. He couldn't help but notice the sheathed Katana and shoulder strap she carried in her right hand. Apparently it was time to go into full on hunter mode.

Dean guessed she was right. He had seen, first hand, the carnage a demon could cause. It was better to be prepared to fight than to have to wish you had protection later on. Still, he wondered why she didn't rely more on her magic. She was a strong spell caster. He had seen her take down a demon with a literal ball of the sun's fire. What did she need a sword for, he wondered?

She climbed in and saw him looking at her.

"What?" she asked, getting defensive.

Dean held out a hand. "Don't get bent out of shape. I was only

321

wondering why you decided to bring that blade with you. Don't you have your magic to back you up?"

"Magic has its place, sure. I'm pretty strong, but the more I use magic here, in this place and time, the more tied to this timeline I become. I've tried to use it only when nothing else would do the job." She patted the blade. "Sometimes, there's nothing like cold steel to solve your problems."

Dean saw the broad grin on her face and shook his head. If there was any doubt who her mother was, this was the proof in his book.

"You are your mother's daughter," he said with a chuckle.

He shifted the pickup into gear and started downtown to meet Jaz and switch over to her black SUV. It was more unobtrusive he knew, and it could easily hold all three of them, something his truck could not do.

Parking on the street and pumping some coins into the meter, Dean and Jo went up to Jaz's apartment. She was waiting for them and popped open the door before walking back inside. Jaz was putting her blonde hair up into a ponytail, then pulling the hair through the hole in the back of her black baseball cap. It sported an embroidered version of the Errington Crest. She wore her black duty pants, a white T-shirt and a black leather jacket.

"Did you pick up anything else on this dungeon master guy, or his wife?" Dean asked.

"No, there's little record of them. I ran a credit check and while they have some credit card debt, it's not enough to warrant them to call on a nefarious source for help. I find no evidence of demonic influences in either of their backgrounds." Jaz picked up her Katana and turned to face them. She noticed Jo carrying hers as well, though the teen had slipped the sword's strap over her head so that the sword hung down diagonally across her back with the hilt sticking up over the left shoulder. She held her daughter's gaze for a moment, but said nothing. The huntress just gave a nod and looked to Dean.

"Feel up to driving? That will give Jo and me a chance to discuss tactics and check over each other's gear on the way there."

"Sure, where are the keys?" Dean asked.

Jaz reached into her jacket pocket and pulled out the keys to her SUV, tossing them to him. Dean caught the keys in midair with his right hand. "Cool. Shall we go, ladies?" He gestured toward the door with a slight bow. Jaz snorted in amusement and passed him to head out the door. Jo followed her mother and Dean pulled the door closed behind him, checking to make sure it was locked before following the other two to the elevator.

The ride over to the subject's apartment was short. It lasted only about five minutes. During that time, Dean listened as Jaz laid out a quick action plan for their confrontation with the demon lord. She'd take the lead, Jo would be second right behind her, and Dean would bring up the rear. She tasked the witch with trying to sense the location of the missing idols with a spell once the door was open, if she could do it without drawing attention to what she was doing. Jo assured her that she could keep it all on the down low. No one would know she was casting a scrying spell.

Dean would prepare to help if anyone was injured. It was likely that if the demon lord was inside, there would be some type of injury to others living in the apartment with it. He was concerned that she might be a "shoot first, ask questions later" kind of person in this situation. Jaz was under an incredible amount of stress, with her family's recent demise and now this hunt to recover essential and dangerous items stolen from her family's home and offices. He would keep an eye on her when the time came to check for shooting and other victims.

When they got close, Jaz told him to park around the corner from their destination. She wanted to sneak up on Sam and Jill, and avoid having them see the trio getting out of the SUV with all their gear before they had a chance to get upstairs.

"I can't help but get the feeling that we are treading on the wrong side of the law here, Jaz," Dean said. "We don't have a search warrant or anything like it to go after this guy."

"We are just going to ask him questions, and be prepared to defend ourselves if anyone or anything decides to attack us. That is all we are doing. The members of the Errington clan have all been deputized to deal with these special investigations by the Federal government. Let's just say I have broad latitude in how I handle things like this."

"Dad, let Mom handle this. This is something she knows. Trust her."

Dean looked from one Errington hunter to the other. If he didn't know them and ran into them in a dark alley, he'd think they were two very dangerous women. Heck, he knew they were two dangerous women. He nodded and got out of the SUV. When the ladies had exited as well, he keyed the locks on the vehicle and stepped into position behind Joanna and Jaz.

There was no doorman on the building, but the front door's lock was broken and they were able to gain entry to the apartments upstairs. Their target was on the third floor, and they walked up the three flights of stairs with no signs of other residents.

Soon they were standing outside the door of apartment 3-F. Jaz checked that Jo was in position by the door jamb before she stepped up and rapped on the door with her bare knuckles. She stepped to the side and slipped what looked like a billfold from the pocket of her black leather jacket. She reached out, opened it and held it in front of the door's peep-hole. Dean could see a brass or gold badge on one side and a picture ID on the other.

"Who is it?" came a man's voice from inside the apartment.

"Special investigator, Mr. Aker. Would you please come out and answer a few questions for me?" Jaz sounded professional and confident. She had done this before.

"Just a moment." Dean heard the rattle of a chain lock and the click of a deadbolt. The door popped open a crack and a face peered out.

"May I see that badge again?"

"Certainly, sir." Jaz stepped into view and held up her badge ID again.

The man, opened the door a little wider and put on wire-rimmed reading glasses to examine the offered identification.

"You're U.S. Marshals?"

"We're special investigators with the Marshal's office, sir. We just had a few questions for you," Jaz replied. "May we come in?"

"Uh, yes, certainly." The small, wiry man stepped back, opening the door. "I'm not certain I know of anything that could possibly help you. Is it about one of my neighbors? I don't like to be the one to tell tales."

Jaz entered first with Jo and Dean following. She continued to take the lead.

"It is just a routine investigation into some unusual events recently in the city. Your name came up in the course of the investigation, and we had to follow every lead. These are my colleagues, Ms. Errington and Mr. Flynn."

Dean nodded to acknowledge his name as he looked around the room. He supposed it was too much to hope that the missing idols would be sitting in plain view. He saw Jo craning her neck to see back down the hallway to the rear of the apartment. It must be where the bedrooms and bathroom were located.

"May we sit down, Mr. Aker? It won't take us long, but I find that it goes even faster if we're all comfortable."

"Certainly. And please call me Sam." He gestured to the oval dining table with six chairs in the center of the main room.

Jaz, Dean and Jo all sat down with their host at the table. Dean wasn't sure what he expected to happen when they came up here, but this cordial exchange and mundane conversation in the apartment wasn't it.

"How may I help you?" Sam asked.

"Is your wife home? I understand you're married, from my records." Jaz took out a note pad from her jacket pocket and flipped it open. She clicked the pen that had been clipped to the note pad and jotted something down.

"No, Jill is not here right now. Why, is she in some sort of trouble? She's been acting most strange lately."

"Strange how, if I may ask?" Jaz leaned forward as she asked the question.

"About four days ago, she started talking to herself. It was like she was having a conversation with someone who wasn't there. It went on for several days. Yesterday, when I got home from an errand, she was gone. Her suitcase was missing, along with some of her clothes. She took our car, too. I tried calling the police but they said to call back in forty-eight hours. I thought maybe you were here in response to that."

"And your wife had never acted that way before?" Jaz pressed.

"No," Sam said with a wry chuckle. "Everyone says she's the normal one."

Jaz, made a few notes and there was an uncomfortable silence. Jo voice broke the quiet.

"Mr. Aker, may I use your bathroom?"

"Certainly, young lady. It's down the hall. First door on your left." He returned his attention to his questioner.

"Thank you." Dean watched as she got up and walked down the hallway behind the man. She turned right instead of left and entered another door. Sam was watching Jaz and never noticed.

"Mr. Aker, do you work for A-Plus construction?" Jaz asked.

"Yes, though I have not been at work for a few days. I've been ill."

"It has come to our attention that several personal items were found at the construction site at the old Errington building. Some of these items seemed to have gone missing."

"Is this about those green bookends? I'm sorry. I know I shouldn't have taken them. I put them on the shelf over there." He gestured to the bookshelf in the corner.

Dean turned to look, half expecting to see the summoning idols sitting there. They were not. That would have been way too easy.

"Where are they now?" Jaz queried after glancing at the shelf herself.

"I don't know. They disappeared when my wife did. I guess she took them with her when she left. I'm not going to lose my job over this, am I?"

"Right now, we just want to recover them. That will be a matter for you and your company to discuss."

Dean saw Jo come out into the hallway again. She shook her head at him and went into the bathroom door on the left. Dean heard a toilet flush and she came back into the hallway as if she had been in there all the time.

"If you find my wife, you're not going to hurt her are you? You are rather strangely armed for police investigators, aren't you?" He gestured to the sword hilt poking up over Jaz's shoulder.

"We're special investigators, Mr. Aker. I can't speak about our operational methods or equipment. I do thank you for your help with this investigation. We will do all we can to keep your wife from harm." Jaz handed Sam a card from her pocket. "If you think of anything else, or you hear from your wife, please call me. I will answer that phone line day or night."

She stood up and Dean took that cue to stand as well. Jo stepped over to join them as they headed towards the door.

"Please don't hesitate to call us if you think of anything else that may be of help to our search and investigation. We'll fill in the local police on your wife's missing person's report. Contact me directly if you want an update on the search efforts, alright? I can break through the red tape for you."

"Thank you, I will."

The three of them stepped into the hallway and Sam closed the door behind them. Dean heard the click of the deadbolt and the rattle of the chain lock sliding into place as they stood in the hallway. This had been a dead end. He followed the two women downstairs in silence.

GRAADU WATCHED in his mind's eye as the three so-called investigators left the building. He knew hunters when he saw them. They were so foolish. Their swords alone gave them away. He had hated to cower and put on the act the way he did, but it was useful. He had gotten closer to the witch who had cast the masking spell on the third idol. She was powerful for one so young.

The day before he had tracked her to that garage apartment in the suburbs. Due to some protection spell, he had not been able to approach too closely and had not been able to gauge her ability before this time. Now, with her only an arm's length away from him across the table, he had been able to see just how powerful she was. He would have to proceed carefully if he was to get close enough to her to kill her and break the spell.

It was strange. She carried a sword as well. He had not heard of a witch who was also a hunter. Perhaps it was just a coincidence. The other woman, this Jaswinder Errington, was clearly a huntress. He was not sure he had fooled her completely, and he would have to tread carefully moving forward with his plans. She would be watching him, he was sure.

Their companion, the man, was bothering him, too. He appeared to be human, but he could not penetrate his defenses to read him as he could other humans. That was something he had not encountered before. There was no detectable protection spell on him. The huntress and the witch had their protections, but he could still read their auras to see what they were. The human, Dean Flynn was different somehow. His aura was confused and masked by something. It bothered him, and he would have to be careful around this one too, if he ran into him in the future.

He thought about Jill, in the prison he had created in their storage unit on the outskirts of town. It was the perfect place to do the things to her he wished to do without the screams bothering the neighbors. He had left the summoning idols there, too, for safekeeping. It had been a prudent move on his part.

The misdirection of the hunters from him to her should keep them busy for a while. They would have to follow up on that before they could be sure if he had been lying to them or not. He could be patient when he needed to be, for a little while. In the meantime, he needed to find a way to dispatch the witch. If he could kill her, the spell she cast to mask the last idol would be removed and he could locate it and complete the set, allowing him to come to earth in corporeal form. Once he accomplished this, he would be the first demon lord to manifest on earth in centuries. He would be the envy of his brothers in hell.

The humans of this time had become soft. They no longer believed in the old ways and religions as much. They thought of evil with a lowercase "e" and not as something that could be literal evil personified. He would rule this land and all the people in it.

Graadu planned to go to visit Jill in the storage facility. He could use some of her life force to bring a lesser demon here to track and kill the witch. She would have some protections, but he sensed she was young and impetuous. That would work to his advantage, he was sure.

Chapter 20

Jo had expected to become embroiled in a battle with the demon when her mom knocked on that door. She wanted a little action again. It was hard staying cooped up in her father's apartment all day. The mousy little man who answered and the subsequent conversation with him had not been all that exciting. Clearly he was not the source of their problems. His wife was the one they were looking for.

She had taken the initiative to pretend to need the bathroom and did a quick search of the bedrooms in the back of the apartment. There had been no sign of the idols there or anything else out of the ordinary. It was a definite bummer.

The teen followed her parents back to the SUV parked on the street and wondered what they were going to do next. Jo was sure they were going to ask her to do a scrying spell and search for the wife. She was ready for that. She had found a hairbrush in the bathroom with a few longer brown hairs in the bristles that could not have come from the husband. She had pocketed a few of the strands just in case.

The scrying spell would not be that hard to accomplish if she was given the time to set up the casting correctly. They should be able to track the wife now. It would take some time to put in place but Jo was confident they would find the woman at the root of their problem. The hardest part of what Jo needed to do was to get her parents to spend more time together. She was pretty certain that the reason the spell failed to send her back was because she had changed the timeline somehow so that she no longer fit in the future from whence she came. The reason for that had to do with her parents' relationship, or lack thereof.

As she climbed into the back of the SUV she looked at them sitting up front. It was strange. She saw the parents she had grown up with and loved more than anything. And yet, they weren't those people either. Like how they were sitting there, in the front seats as two very separate individuals. Her memory of the two of them had her mother and father always needing to be touching each other, holding hands or shoulder to shoulder. She used to think it was gross, but now that it wasn't there anymore, she missed it.

Was there something she was supposed to do to spur on the relationship? The two had become friends over the last few weeks, but not anything close to the loving couple she had grown up with. Maybe it was time for some more direct action. She had tried that once before, back in the rescue mission to save Aunt Ashley. Putting the two of them in a situation where they had to be in close physical proximity to each other had been fun to watch, but it had not made them any closer. If anything, it had made them uncomfortable being too close together.

That could mean they felt something during that time when they had to lay next to each other and hide. If she could replicate it, maybe it would bring those feelings to the surface again. It was worth a try. Jo set her mind to coming up with a way to force more physical contact between the two of them. She'd bring them together, somehow, someway.

· · ·

DEAN LOOKED over at Jaz as he drove the SUV away from the apartment building. He hadn't known what to expect exactly back there, but it wasn't the encounter they ended up having. Sam was not the threat they had assumed he was. He stole the idols from the job site, that was for sure. But his wife had been the one who succumbed to their evil influence and now she was on the run. He wondered what the hunter next to him had in store for them next on the list of things they were to do.

He saw Jaz look over her shoulder at Jo in the back seat and Dean checked on her in the rearview mirror. He saw her brow furrow in thought. She's probably wondering what they would do next too.

"So, Jaz," Dean said. "What is the plan now? Is there a way to track the idols now that Jill is in the wind?"

"I'm not sure. I was going to ask Jo that question. I know there are some mundane things I can do to track her. I can track her credit cards and ask for access to automated toll booth records, thing like that. There might be a way to magically track her down, though. Jo?"

Dean looked at her in the backseat via the mirror again and saw her startle out of her concentrated expression.

"What? Oh, sorry. I was thinking of something else. What did you ask me, Mom?"

"Is there a way to track Jill magically? She's using the idols to turn people into Unusuals. There's got to be a magical signature for something like that."

"I'm sure there is, but it would be difficult to track even if I knew what to look for." Jo reached into her pocket and pulled out the strands of hair. "Now, if only someone had something personal or a few strands of hair. Then we could do a proper scrying and search."

Dean saw the big grin on her face and he was filled with pride. She was resourceful as well as smart. She'd make a good paramedic and she was his daughter.

"Kid, you remind me of me sometimes," Jaz said. "Good job. How long to get the scrying spell set up?"

"I need a day or so to come up with the supplies. I should be able to get them from the coven. I can do the spell at Dad's once I have it all in place. If she's within, say, a hundred miles or so, I'll be able to locate her."

Dean thought for a moment and asked the question that had been bothering him most. "Once we find her, then what? She's possessed or something like it. It's not her fault so we can't just run a sword through her and be done with it. That's murder."

"Dean, we may not have a choice," Jaz said and held up a hand to stop him when he opened his mouth to protest. "I don't want to do that either, but we have to be prepared for the option, even as a last resort."

"What about some way to save her life and separate the demon from her?" He looked from Jaz to Jo as he pulled to a stop at a traffic light.

"You mean like an exorcism?"

"Yeah, some way to separate the two without killing her," Dean suggested. "There has got to be a way."

"Perhaps," Jo said. "But it would be risky and would require all three of us, working together."

"I feel like we have to try," Dean said. He didn't want to be part of a summary execution. It was not this woman's fault her husband brought the idols home. It was not her fault that she became possessed by a demon lord.

Jaz turned around and looked at her daughter. "Jo, can you do this, too?"

"It's a lot of magic to cast. It will take a lot of energy, but yes, I can do it. It's going to require you two to come up with a part of the solution, too. The demon lord needs to be confronted and distracted, then we need some way to break the physical connection to the body. I'm not sure how to do that. If we can do it though, I can pull the demon out into corporeal form. Then we can send it back to the netherworld where it belongs."

"It's a lot easier to just put a sword through her," Jaz said.

The simultaneous shouts of "Mom" and "Jaz" had the huntress put her hands up in surrender which made Dean laugh aloud.

"Don't shoot the messenger. I'm just saying what has been done in these instances in the past," Jaz explained.

"You know, we make a pretty good team," Dean said.

"Yes we do." Jaz looked back at him, smiling.

He had to admit, she was a remarkable woman. She was unlike any woman he had been with before, except for maybe his former partner, Brynne Garvey. When he realized he and Jaz had some sort of destiny together, he wanted to deny it. The fundamental differences in their approach to handling Unusuals was a deal breaker, he had thought. As he had gotten to know her though, he found there was a complexity and depth to her he hadn't allowed for in his initial assessment.

In the beginning, Dean had assumed all hunters must be assassins and murderers. He saw Jaz as a killing machine, hell-bent on killing anything she thought was a monster. Since some of those monsters were his friends, he was predisposed to disliking her, even hating her.

That had changed as he realized she had a moral code, a strict one, that she followed without fail. Jaz was prepared to kill, but only those who had endangered others through their actions. Usually this was limited to demons from the netherworld, but it could be aimed at anyone who preyed upon the innocent.

He could understand that motivation, and it wasn't that different from his calling to help those in need as an emergency responder. Their methods were different, but they served the same public need for protection and rescue. Dean had come to admire her for her devotion to her clan's calling. Could that become more, someday? Perhaps, he thought. Perhaps.

Chapter 21

Jo and her dad got home late that night after they dropped her mom off and switched to Dean's pickup truck. She was tired but had enjoyed going out. It was exhausting being cooped up in the apartment when her dad wasn't home. She knew the family protection charm her mother used was a strong ward against evil. It was keeping her safe, she supposed.

Jo thought they were both overreacting. She had proven time and again that she could take care of herself. Maybe she could convince her dad to let her go on a few errands for the supplies she needed for the scrying spell tomorrow afternoon while he was at work.

"Uh, Dad?" she asked when they got to the apartment over the Baxter's garage.

"Yeah, Jo, what do you need?"

"I was thinking. You're so busy all day, and you're tired when you get home. Maybe I could go out tomorrow during the day and pick up the spell supplies I need. I really don't think anything will happen to me in just a few hours of shopping." She put on a smile and tried to make it all sound as natural as can be.

"Jo, you know you have to stay here or near me. Your mother

explained that to us both very clearly. You don't receive the protection of the charm without it. You can wait until I get home. We'll go out after dinner."

"But if I go out it will be in broad daylight, and most demons are weakest in the day time. Nothing is going to happen. You know it."

"I don't know it, Joanna. I don't know anything of the kind."

"You and Mom need to stop treating me like a baby, a child. I've pulled my load in this family. I came back in time on my own and I can go shopping on my own, too." She was getting angry and the tone had slipped into her voice. Her father noticed.

"Look, Jo," he said. "I am not going to argue with you. You need to stay here and sit tight until I get home from work. You can always call your mother and see if she's available."

"She's busy all day with her international security empire." Jo put air quotes around it. It wasn't much of an empire anymore since the central part of the family had been killed in the explosion.

"Jaz is doing the best she can. You know she's barely had a chance to mourn her family's passing. You and I never got to know them, but these were her parents and cousins. Stop being so selfish, Jo. It's not a very attractive feature and it doesn't become you. Go to bed. Get some rest. We'll go shopping tomorrow evening when I get off work."

Jo watched him and realized he wasn't giving in so she nodded and went off to her room. She'd go to bed and get some rest, but only because she wanted to. In the end, she was in charge of herself, no matter what her parents thought. She went into her room and shut the door without saying goodnight. Let him stew on making her upset.

Her dad was gone by the time she got up the next morning. It was nearly noon. She checked her phone and there was a text from Marian.

It's Saturday. Let's do something.

She texted back about her shopping plans and asked if Marian wanted to come along. Jo hoped she'd say yes. Marian had a car and Jo didn't. She'd have to walk to get anywhere without one.

I'll pick you up in 1 hr.

Jo texted back an enthusiastic yes with a few thumbs up emojis and went back into her room to get showered and dressed for a day out shopping.

MARIAN PULLED up in a beat up silver Nissan. Its motor made a little more noise than it was supposed to, but it ran and that was all that was important. Jo came down to meet her and jumped in the front seat.

"Hey, thanks for coming to get me. I was getting so tired of being cooped up in there."

Marian looked over and offered a high five. "No problem, Jo. What are friends for if we can't rescue each other for a shopping trip? Where are we going, the mall?"

"We can hit the mall later, I have to go to the Coven house first. They will have some of the things I need for this spell I'm working on. The rest we can get around town and then go to the mall for some real shopping."

"Excellent."

Marian pulled out of the parking spot and headed down the residential street. Neither she nor Jo saw the other car pull away from the curb and start down the street after them.

THE DAY WAS PRODUCTIVE. The Coven had some of the things she needed, and Asha told her where to look for the other items on the list she had made. There were a few stops at various shops in the downtown area and then she announced to Marian they were free to hit the mall. All the essential shopping was done.

It was about two thirty in the afternoon when they arrived at the mall parking lot. Marian wanted to shop for a new outfit to wear on a date with her boyfriend later that evening. Jo figured she could use some new clothes, too. Her Mom had given her some cash to use to help with groceries at the apartment. Dean had told her to keep it when she offered to pay and she still had most of it left, even after the earlier purchases.

They decided to shop in one of the bigger department stores first before they hit the smaller mall shops. There were several sales going on and the stores were crowded. They did find some choices that matched what each of them were looking for, and they collected their options to try them on in the changing rooms.

Jo and Marian got checked in with the sales girl to go try their outfits on and went into the small changing area to get started. There was a small hallway with a row of doors along one wall. All the rooms were occupied but two at the very back. Each teen took a separate room. They were too small to share.

Starting with the dress she wanted to try out, Jo stripped down to her underwear, piling her shoes, jeans, t-shirt and jacket with her shoulder holster wrapped up inside on the bench seat. Slipping the dress over her head, she admired herself in the changing room mirror as she straightened the dress. It was simple in cut but looked great on her. She decided to show her friend.

"Hey, Marian, check this out," Jo said as she exited the changing room. She stopped as she noticed the body of the sales girl who had been monitoring the changing rooms. She was laying on the floor in the narrow hallway. Her throat had been slashed open. There was a bloody hand and arm showing from one of the other changing room doors.

She heard a snarling noise from the room next to hers as the door was pushed open and two figures slid out to stand in the hallway. One was Marian. The other, holding a wicked looking hooked blade at her friend's throat, was dressed in black, wearing a khaki trenchcoat. The face was pale and misshaped with one eye set lower than the other. If the lack of symmetry in the face didn't clue her in to the true nature of the demon in front of her, the mouth full of needle sharp teeth would have.

"Hello, witch," the creature snarled. "I've been following you all day long. Have you been enjoying your last day on this miserable earth?"

Jo glanced back over her shoulder at the pile of clothes containing her pistol in its shoulder holster. She'd never get to it before the blade finished off Marian.

She thrust her hand in front of her instead, and turned her head so that she was looking right down her arm, aiming at the demon's head. What she had planned was not something she wanted to miss.

"Let my friend go and I'll just send you back to hell." A ball of blazing sunshine the size of a golf ball appeared in front of her outstretched palm. "Otherwise, beast, I'll end you. You'll not regenerate, you'll not be able to return in a hundred years, you'll just be gone. Your choice."

The demon met her eyes, then focused on the spinning ball of white hot plasma Jo held in her palm. She wanted it to make up its mind. Holding sunfire like this hurt like hell. She didn't want to release the spell so close to her friend but she might have no other choice.

"How do I know you'll keep your word if I let your friend go?"

"You don't. Five seconds and you won't care." Jo began counting down from five, wanting to scream in pain as the ball of the sun's plasma started to cook the flesh of her palm.

The creature in front of her hesitated and then she saw the decision in its eyes as the arm holding the blade tensed and started to draw the hook towards Marian's throat. With a scream of rage and pain, Jo released the spell and the ball of fire shot forward, creating a miniature explosion that encompassed the demon's head. Lifeless fingers dropped the blade and the corpse with the smoking head and shoulders collapsed to the ground as if a marionette cut the strings to a puppet.

She ran forward and patted the flames out that had started in her friend's hair. There were second degree burns to Marian's scalp and neck and the shirt she had tried on was smoldering around the shoulders from the proximity of the plasma. Jo turned and uttered a word of power and her purse flew from the room behind her to her outstretched hand. She reach inside and grabbed a bottle of water, opening it and dumping it on her friend's head and neck. She knew that she had to diffuse the residual heat in the burns and this was the best way to do it.

Marian was crying in pain, along with a few curses and choice words for her friend. "Dammit, Jo, did you have to set my hair on fire? This hurts bad."

"He was going to kill you. I gave him a choice. That's something he never gave you. Besides, you'll regenerate and be good as new in a few days."

"Yeah, but how do I explain this to my parents. I told them you and I were just going shopping, not hunting demons." Marian's mom and dad were very strict with her. "When they find out I took you out against your dad's orders I'm going to get grounded again."

There were shouts of alarm coming closer and a sales girl and security guard ran into the end of the short hallway into the changing area. The guard saw the body extending from the first room, and turned and puked in the corner. The sales girl just screamed and ran away.

Jo needed to get a handle on this right away. Pulling her phone from her purse, she steeled herself for the yelling that about to commence and called her mom.

"Jo, what do you want?" Jaz said on the other end of the line. "I'm following a lead to find Jill."

"Uh, Mom, how close are you to the Elk City Mall?"

"Jo, please tell me you're not at the mall right now. I just heard a radio report of an explosion and fire at Marker's department store. It came in over the scanner."

"Okay, so don't be angry, but Marian and I went out to do some shopping."

"You what?"

Jo had to hold the phone away from her ear, the shout was so loud.

"I know I should have waited for Dad to get home from work,

but I couldn't wait and I didn't know that there was a demon following me."

"I'm turning around now. Is everyone alright?"

"Marian's injured but she'll be alright. The demon killed a bunch of people in the changing area, though. I killed it, but now people are showing up and I don't know what to do," Jo said as the tears came and she began sobbing.

"I'll be there in five minutes. Just cooperate with the police until I get there but don't admit to anything." Her mom cut the connection and Jo looked up to see two police officers turn the corner with their guns drawn.

"Hands up where we can see them," the first cop shouted.

Jo and Marian raised their hands up as they leaned into each other, crying.

Chapter 22

Jaz had to turn on the black SUV's emergency hazard lights and put her police light on the dashboard to get into the mall parking lot closest to the Marker's department store. There were fire trucks, a dozen police cars and an ambulance was just pulling in. She glanced at the number on the side of the ambulance. It read U-191. That was Dean's unit. Good, he was here, too.

She had tried to impress upon both of them the severity of the danger facing them. Demon lords were resourceful and powerful. While this one couldn't manifest itself, it could summon lesser minions to do whatever it wanted to do here on earth if it wanted to. Jo had discovered that first hand.

She pulled up behind the ambulance and jumped out of her vehicle to catch Dean as soon as he got out of the ambulance's cab. He was driving. Jaz ran up to him and poked him in the shoulder.

"Jo's inside," she said, trying to keep her anger under control. "I thought you were going to keep an eye on her? She went out shopping on her own and now she's been attacked by a demon."

"Whoa, hold on there. Jo's inside?" Dean asked, grabbing her arm to slow her down. "Is she alright? Why didn't she call me?"

"I don't know why she called me instead of you, Dean." Jaz shrugged her arm out of his grasp. "Maybe it was because she needed her mother to handle this particular problem. I want to know why you didn't make her stay in the apartment as we agreed."

"Hey, I told her to stay, but I had to go to work. I can't be there all the time."

Dean's partner, Barry came around the front of the ambulance holding some EMS bags, took one look at the heated discussion and turned around, disappearing again behind the front of the ambulance.

"Look, Jaz. We'll have this discussion later. Right now, I have patients to tend to. If you want to help, I'll let you carry some of our gear in with us."

Dean pushed past her and started unloading a monitor and another EMS bag from the back of the ambulance. He also grabbed the stretcher and called Barry. The two paramedics piled their bags on the wheeled stretcher and started pushing it towards the mall entrance. Jaz followed close behind.

A police officer tried to stop her at the curb, but she flashed her special Marshal's badge and he let her pass. People were still streaming out of the building as the responders rushed in. Dean asked another cop for directions and started toward the back of the department store.

When they got closer, they smelled the distinctive smell of burnt flesh. It intensified as they reached the changing room area and Jaz got her first look down the hall of the changing area, with its half doors. The body on the floor was missing most of its head, but a look at the clawed hands and the wicked dagger still clutched in one of them told her it was the demon.

"Mom, Dad, over here," sounded from behind her and turning around, she saw Jo and Marian waiting on a small couch in the seating area outside the changing rooms.

Dean and Barry left the stretcher where it was, but grabbed a few of the bags and moved over to the two girls. Jaz followed them. She saw Jo clutching her hand and saw the circular burn there.

Sunfire. It was the same burn she got from casting that spell before. She must have held the spell for too long again. The girl was going to have to work on that.

Marian showed signs of burns on her head and neck on her right side and Jaz's investigator's brain started piecing things together given the state of the demon's body. Jo must have had to make a hard decision regarding how to take this demon out, knowing she was going to injure her friend.

Part of her respected what it must have taken to make that call and she wanted to rush over and talk to Jo about it and tell her it was alright. The other part of her was still furious with her daughter for leaving the protection of the apartment. If she had stayed home, no one would have been hurt.

She noticed that Jo was dressed in a pull-over dress that still had the tags on it. Where were her clothes? She would not have left the apartment unarmed. That would have been even more stupid than leaving unattended had been. Jaz turned and, flashing her badge to another officer, stepped into the changing room hallway, seeing the bodies in the each of the rooms as she approached the back. Three bodies of the women the demon had killed on the way to Jo lay where their throats had been slashed open. She noted the wounds but kept walking.

Reaching the last room, Jaz found Jo's clothes. The Glock and shoulder holster rig were wrapped up in her jeans jacket. Maybe the detectives would miss it, but not likely. Jaz slipped into the room and pulled off her leather jacket once she was out of sight. She picked up the shoulder holster rig and put it on over her own. Jo was left handed, so it worked out with one pistol hanging on either side. She felt like some sort of video game heroine as she slipped the leather jacket back on, hiding both pistols again.

She stepped back into the hallway and over the body of the demon, returning to where Dean and Barry were treating Jo and Marian for their burns. Jo's hand was wrapped up now. Jaz shook her head and chuckled. She was going to have to learn how to control the use of that sunfire spell or else come up with a solution to deal with the burns it caused to its wielder. Barry was tending to Marian, wrapping her head and neck in gauze to hold the burn dressings in place. She'd be alright after a few days' rest. It was handy to be able to regenerate like that.

"Excuse me, Ma'am, may I ask who let you back here?" a voice from behind her spoke.

Jaz turned and saw a man in a sport coat and tie standing there. He must be a detective sent to process the crime scene.

"I'm a special U.S. Marshal, detective." She pulled out her ID and badge, showing it to him. "I had been tracking an individual suspected in the killing of women in the area and I think our suspect is laying on the floor right there."

The detective looked at the badge and smirked. "You sure you're not here to cover up what your daughter did to that guy?"

"I don't think I know your name, detective …?"

"Ricketts, Ms. Errington, and yes, I know who you are and your relationship to this young lady. I also know that she has some special abilities that might make her a danger to others if not used appropriately."

"She defended herself and her friend," Jaz said. "If you examine the body on the floor and his knife, I'm sure you'll find that he had just killed three other women in that changing area and was working his way down to my daughter. If she had not killed him, he would have surely killed her. There would be five dead women in there, not just three."

"I'm sure your assessment fits the scene as it presents itself," Detective Ricketts said. Jaz noticed he didn't say her assessment was correct. That annoyed her and she decided she didn't like this guy very much.

"I'll ask you to include me in any questions you have for my daughter. She is not to be interrogated without me present, detective. Is that clear?"

Ricketts snorted a laugh. "Very clear, Ma'am. I'm sure I'll have some questions for you, too, when the time comes." He nodded once at her and then went to survey the crime scene himself.

Jaz turned back to Dean, Barry and the two girls. Barry and Dean had finished treating the wounds and had brought the stretcher over for Marian to sit on. They intended to take her in to the hospital it seemed. Maybe the injuries were more severe than she thought.

"Is she going to be alright, Dean?" Jaz asked.

"I'm worried the burns might need further treatment," Dean replied. "The sunfire spell cooks the demons so quickly that their soul can't flee to the netherworld. I think it might also be bad enough that it hinders the regenerative process in Lycans. It's better to be safe than sorry in this case."

"What about Jo? Does she need to be seen, too?"

"No," Dean chuckled a little. "She does need to find a way to stop getting herself burned when she casts that spell, though."

"I know, right?" Jaz said with a short laugh of her own. "So I can take her with me?"

"That would be great. I don't have the time right now to figure out what she could possibly have been thinking, coming out in public like this. Can you wait to ream her a new one, for me to come and join in?"

"I think making her wait for both of us to confront her about this might be a good way to make her think about what she's done here," Jaz said. "Can you come by right after work? I'll get something for dinner and we can have a family pow-wow."

"Sounds like a plan, Jaz. I'll see you then." He turned and helped Barry wheel Marian out to the ambulance.

Jaz watched him go. He was a nice guy and he took this fatherhood stuff seriously, she could see. He took responsibility when he needed to. Maybe it was time for her to start taking up her part of the load. Jo was standing watching as they wheeled her friend away. Jaz went over and decided it was time to start parenting this impetuous teen.

"Come on Joanna, I've got to get back to work on the lead I was following. You can come and help me since you have nothing better to do."

"Mom, I told you this wasn't my fault. How was I supposed to know there was a demon chasing after me?"

"Because I told you there would be." Jaz stopped and looked her daughter in the eyes. "Did you think I was kidding? You keep saying I helped raise you. Did I really raise you to take such warnings so lightly?"

Jo looked back at her. The teen's eyes were defiant. After a bit, though, she lowered her gaze. Jaz shook her head and decided that wasn't good enough.

"I didn't hear you. I asked you a question. Did I raise you in a way that you would ignore warnings about things like this?"

"No," Jo said in a whisper.

"I didn't think so. This is all on you, Jo. You need to come to grips with that. Those women lying in there, lifeless. That happened because you didn't pay attention to the warning. Marian, your friend, is going to the hospital because you didn't pay attention to the warning."

"So, I guess I'm grounded or something?"

"Oh, grounded doesn't cut it, Joanna. This is something you are going to have to think and make some hard decisions about. You need to decide who you going to be, what you are made of inside. Dean is coming over for dinner tonight and we are both going to have a long talk with you about how your actions have far-reaching effects. Until then, you think about all the lives you affected with the deaths and injuries you caused today. You can share what you've learned about this at dinner tonight."

Jaz took her daughter out to the SUV in the parking lot and loaded her inside. Detective Ricketts caught up with her there.

"I don't have to tell you to keep your daughter around. I'll need to ask her some questions about what happened here."

"I can do that, but we need to have a family discussion about this tonight. I'll bring her by the station tomorrow morning. Is that acceptable?"

"That will do, I suppose. One question for you, though. Is there anything else we need to be ready for? Is this an isolated event or should we prepare for another attack like it?"

"I don't know, Detective, I don't know." She climbed into the SUV and drove from the mall. That question had occurred to her as well and she didn't know the answer. It bothered her, and gave her something else to worry about as she drove her distraught daughter home.

Chapter 23

Dean and Barry returned from dropping Marian off at the ECMC burn unit. She did not appear to be regenerating like a Lycan should after an injury. The docs and nurses were good at the burn unit, though. They'd be able to help her. Dean was more concerned about why Jo had endangered her friend's life by going out with her in public that way. Jaz had explained to them both the need to stay close to Dean to take advantage of the family protection spell.

The three dead women in the mall changing rooms would never know the real reason they all died. The demon had been quick as it worked its way down the row of doors, silently slitting the throats of each one as it searched for its prey. That Jo had been able to defend herself was a moot point. She had to be more aware of the collateral damage of her actions. Three people were dead and her best friend was seriously injured as a result of her decision to go shopping.

He received a text message from Jaz asking him to pick up a few items for the dinner at her place after his shift. She called it a family meeting. It felt strange to him to think of it that way. He knew they had become a family. It wasn't a traditional family, that was certain, but it was a family nonetheless. Dean replied back to the text message, saying he'd be there sometime before seven, as soon as his shift was completed.

Duty called, though, and soon his mind was occupied with resupplying the ambulance while Barry completed his report on the call at the shopping mall. He was just packing up the last restocked bag when the alert tones sounded over the speakers in the station and he and Barry were off on their next call. There'd be time to worry about Joanna and what to do about her later.

The dispatcher was sending them to a private residential home for the mentally ill. There was a call for an agitated behavioral patient. Dean wondered aloud to Barry what type of Unusual call this could be.

"Maybe it's an Unusual with a mental health problem?" Barry suggested.

"Maybe it's another newly turned vampire or werewolf," Dean replied.

They'd find out soon enough. The location was only a short drive from the industrial park that housed Station U. Barry pulled into the driveway and the two paramedics got out and gathered their gear to take inside.

As they walked up to the two-story home in an older section of town, a gentleman in blue jeans came out of the home's front door.

"Boy am I glad to see you guys," he said. "I'm Gary, the dayshift caretaker here at Heaven's House. We have a situation inside that I couldn't handle on my own."

"Okay," Dean said. "Take it easy and tell us what we're dealing with here." Dean showed the back of his right hand to Gary and the man looked at the invisible UV tattoo there. Dean didn't know what kind of Unusual this guy was, but he was a supernatural being of some sort.

"I don't know if you know what Heavenly House is or what kind of patients we deal with here?"

Barry and Dean looked at each other and shrugged.

"We don't know anything about it," Barry said. "I assume it's a half-way house for the mentally ill to help get them integrated back into society?"

"Partially correct," Gary replied. "Our patients are, uh, unique in that they can't be returned to society. We have the funding to keep them here in this residential community until the church can schedule an exorcism. You see, these patients, they are possessed by demons."

"So we're back to the old school definition of mental illness," Dean said. "I thought we were past all of that."

Gary waived his hands in front of him. "No, you misunderstand. I know mental illness is a real thing. These people aren't technically mentally ill. They are just possessed by demons. The Catholic church in Rome has homes like this set up all over the world to hold them until such a time as an exorcist can make the journey to perform the exorcisms."

"Today for some reason, one of the patients is more agitated than normal. He said he felt his brother die and has been inconsolable for the last hour or so. I don't know what to do with him. I was hoping you could help me calm him down."

"We can try," Dean said. "Could you answer a question for me, though? Are you human or Unusual? You said you work for the church, so you're a catholic priest?"

"I'm a monk actually. There are several orders devoted to helping the sick and injured. Ours is the order of St. Antony of the Desert, the patron saint of all those who battle demons. At our ordination, all of us are given the power to talk with and resist the influences of demons. While we cannot command them or banish them, that is the purview of the divine, we have the ability to enable those who are possessed to resist while awaiting the exorcism of the demon. In this case, though, I'm unable to communicate with the human side anymore. The demon has subverted him completely, which is concerning to me. I'm unsure of what to do and the priest of our order who performs the exorcism won't be here for six weeks."

Dean looked at Barry and his partner nodded. "Well, Dean, we can try and sedate the person. That should help keep the demon under control. Let's go inside and see what we can do."

Gary smiled and seemed a little more relaxed as he took them inside. Dean noticed a foul smell immediately on entering the foyer of the home. There was a man tied to a kitchen chair in the living room to his left. A group of five men and two women, all dressed in pajamas or sweat pants, stood in the hallway to the right. He made a point to keep an eye on the rest of them. If one demon possessed patient could lose control, so could the others.

Dean and Barry approached the man in the chair. He was about forty years old and was pale with a serious case of bed head hair. Dean let Barry take the lead while he kept an eye on the others in the room.

"I'm Barry, what's your name?"

"My name doesn't matter puny human. I'm not giving you back this one until I exact revenge on the bitch who killed my brother." The man in the chair spewed spittle as he yelled at Barry.

Barry stepped back and pulled out a pair of clear-lensed safety glasses. No sense risking getting spit in the eye. Dean did the same, but remained in his position of watchfulness. He needed to have his partner's back in case any of the other residents decided to get involved.

"Okay," Barry said to the demon possessed man. "I understand you're upset. I would be upset if my brother was killed, too. But you can't stay tied up like this forever so why don't you let us talk with you and try to help?"

"There is no help, there is only my getting loose and having my revenge on the witch who killed my brother. It is one thing to destroy our human forms. We return to the netherworld and await our opportunity to be reborn for the final conflict here on your pitiful earth. That bitch killed him, destroyed him utterly. I saw it all happen through his eyes in the end. She burned his soul from this existence and he is gone forever."

Barry looked at Dean and mouthed the word "Haldol" to him, mentioning the potent antipsychotic drug and sedative that could, maybe, calm this guy down a little. Dean started to assemble the syringe and draw up some of the medication for the patient.

He came forward and handed the syringe to Barry and then took hold of the patient's restrained arms while his partner pulled the waistband of the man's sweatpants down to expose a portion of the buttocks to inject the medication into the muscle there.

They didn't get the chance. As soon as Dean touched the man's arm with his bare hand he craned his neck to look into Dean's face. He saw raw hatred in those eyes as they stared back at him.

"You. You are related to the witch who killed my brother. He had a mission to accomplish and she killed him before he could complete it."

Dean made the connection then. This demon, who possessed this patient was the brother of the demon from the incident with Jo earlier. This man, or demon, or whatever, knew about it and wanted revenge on his daughter.

"Hold up, Barry. Don't sedate him yet."

"You're the boss, Dean."

"How do you know I'm related to the one you seek to harm?" Dean asked the demon-possessed man.

"I feel the tie that binds you, and something else, too. You are not what you seem either. You pretend to be a man, but you're no man. But it doesn't matter. Whatever you are, know that I will hunt down and kill your offspring, making her beg me to end her as I slowly tear her skin from her body."

Dean felt a sudden surge of anger. He would not let this guy, demon or not, threaten his family. He reached up and grabbed the man's head in his hands as the anger took over. He felt his mind losing control, but he could not stop what was happening.

"You will not touch one hair on her head, creature of the netherworld. Damn you. Go back to your hole in hell and never return to this earth again. If I run into you again, I'll end you just like your brother, do you hear me. Go back to hell and never return." Dean found himself shouting at the end of it, his fingers digging into the man's skin as he pressed in on his skull. The man's eyes went wide and then he slumped in the chair, limp and unconscious.

The room was silent when Dean stopped yelling and he was embarrassed by his lost temper. He had not truly lost his temper in years. The adrenaline was coursing through him and he felt the tremors in his extremities from the natural drug coursing through his system.

"Dean, what the hell was that? What did you do?" Barry asked rushing forward to check the patient. He reached over and took the man's pulse. Then wrapped a blood pressure cuff around his arm to assess him fully.

"Is he dead?" Dean asked, fearful about what had happened.

"No, he has a pulse and his blood pressure is good. Everything is normal and it appears he's just sleeping. That was weird, though. You'll have to teach me that one sometime," Barry said.

"I don't know what I did. I got angry at him when I realized he was talking about hurting Jo and I just lost it."

Gary came forward and laid his hands on the man's head. He closed his eyes and muttered something under his breath, ending with an audible amen. The monk looked at Dean when he opened his eyes. They were filled with a look of wonder.

"How did you do that?" the monk asked. "The demon, it is gone from him."

"Gone, you mean it escaped?" Dean started to pull out his phone to warn Jaz and Jo.

"No, I mean gone as in, sent back to hell. Even the exorcist must use his powers to call upon God himself to intervene and banish the demon. You didn't invoke God, you did it yourself, as if you possessed the power to do it on your own. That's impossible and yet I saw it happen."

"I didn't do anything," Dean said. "I just yelled at the guy. He was threatening someone I cared about and I was scared for her."

Gary crossed himself and pulled a rosary from his pocket. "I have never seen anyone other than an exorcist banish a demon back to hell, and that with much prayer, invocation and difficulty. You did it like the apostles in the Bible, like Christ himself."

"Okay, hold on there. I think that you're blowing things out of proportion here. I just said some things I shouldn't have said to a patient." Dean wondered what the Chief would say if he heard that he was telling patients to go to hell. He'd lose his job. He tried to defuse the situation and settle the man down a bit.

"Look, Gary, whatever happened, it looks like it solved your immediate problem," Dean said. "Barry and I can come back if you need us, but I don't think there's anything else we can do here."

"Nothing else you can do?" Gary protested. "There are seven more people here who can use your help. Can you not banish their demons, too? Would you deny them the service you provided this man?"

"Look, it's like I told you. I didn't do anything other than lose my temper and shout at him. I'm nothing special. I'm just a paramedic. Call us back if you need help again, but I am not the guy to help you out with the rest of your residents right now. You have a priest for that."

Dean picked up his bag and motioned for Barry to grab his. He started towards the door as Gary called after him.

"I will not forget what you have done here, today, paramedic Dean. You have a gift, a gift from God himself. You cannot deny that for long. Your chance to save yourself and those close to you is near."

Dean heard the words but chose not to acknowledge them as he left the home and walked back to the ambulance. He caught Barry looking at him out of the corner of his eye and ignored it. He knew that something happened back there. It was something he couldn't explain or begin to understand. He was not sure he wanted to understand it. He didn't want to acknowledge it or do anything that didn't involve being a paramedic. He and his partner loaded up and drove back to the station in silence.

Dean had a lot on his mind as he wrapped up his shift. He had a teenager who needed a lesson in foreseeing consequences of her actions. He had to come to grips with his apparent ability to dispel demons from possessed individuals. The ability to control or influence demons was scary and he needed time to do some research and try to identify why he had such a gift, if that was what it was. For all he knew, it could mean he was part demon himself.

At least with the first problem he had some help. Jaz would be there to participate in their family discussion about Jo's disobedience and rash actions earlier that day. He was angry at her, but he was also angry at himself for not foreseeing the possibility that she would not want to stay cooped up in his apartment all day long. This was something he should have seen coming. Maybe he should have let her come to the station with him a few times and hang out with Freddy there while he was on ambulance calls.

Jo had said it was just to do some shopping. He knew it had more to do with hanging around kids her own age. It was tough being fifteen. Lord knows he never wanted to be fifteen again. The pimples, the awkwardness around girls, and his frequent run-ins with school administrators and teachers all made him glad to be past that time in his life.

He could only imagine what Jo must be feeling, thrust into the past where she knew no one, with parents who didn't know her, no friends, and no connections. She had planned to return back to her own time and place in the world after helping him and Jaz rescue Ashley. She had never planned on getting stuck here for an extended period of time. It was like going on a trip that never ended, never allowing you to go home.

Dean shot Jaz a text message to see if she needed him to pick up anything else on his way there. He was planning to get the loaf of bread and other items she had requested earlier. She suggested a nice bottle of red wine for the two adults. She even added a smiley face emoji. He laughed when he saw it, in spite of how he was feeling. She was starting to let her guard down. It was good to see there was a person under that tough hunter exterior.

He texted her that he'd pick something up for them to take the edge off before their parenting conversation with Jo. There was a small liquor store near the station that was owned by a nice family. They even had some grocery items so he'd be able to shop all in one stop. He knew very little about wine, but the proprietor of the shop would help him select something that was nice but not too pricey. Paramedics could not afford expensive wine.

It was a quick drive to the store and then ten more minutes afterward to get to Jaz's apartment building downtown. Dean grabbed the bottle and other groceries, along with his duffel bag with a change of clothes, and headed upstairs. He hoped Jaz wouldn't mind if he changed out of his uniform after work and put on some civilian clothes. He pressed the call bell at the exterior door to her building and she buzzed him up, the door opening when he pulled it.

Jaz answered as soon as he knocked on her door and he was surprised to see her in plain blue jeans and a red blouse, no BDUs or tactical pants and leather jacket.

"Good, you remembered the wine," she said as she took the bottle from him. "Make yourself comfortable. Jo is in the spare bedroom sulking or something. I told her if she couldn't be nice and help out in the kitchen she should stay in there by herself."

"Sounds reasonable," Dean said. "It's likely a good parenting move when dealing with sulky teens. Hey, is it alright if I change out of my uniform? I always feel grimy after work and need to change."

"Absolutely. Feel free to take a shower, too, if you want. Dinner isn't going to be ready for forty-five minutes or so anyway. I'll crack open the wine and have a glass waiting for you when you come out. There are spare towels in the hall closet opposite the bathroom."

"Thanks," Dean said. "I think I'll take you up on that."

He went down the hallway and found the linen closet just where she told him it would be. A quick shower would hit the spot. He took his bag and towel into the bathroom and turned the water on.

When he came out of the shower ten minutes later, the smells of the cooking food had permeated the whole apartment. It smelled delicious. He got dressed in his civvies, and since he didn't have a comb, just ran his hands through his short hair to straighten it out a little. Jaz was standing at the stove when he went into the kitchen.

"Can I help with anything?"

"No, I've just got to stir the sauce a bit and then I'm going to take a break and let it simmer."

"What are we having?"

"I'm not much of a cook. It's spaghetti. My mom was Italian so I at least know how to make a gravy. That's tomato sauce to you uninitiated in the ways of the famiglia. Your glass of wine is already poured over on the dining room table. I'll be right out."

He walked from the small kitchen and saw the two filled wine glasses on the dining room table. It was already set with plates and silverware for three. He picked up one of the glasses and took a sip. Not bad, he thought. He'd have to stop in the liquor store again and thank the manager for his recommendation.

Looking around the apartment, he thought that Jaz had done a good job of creating a place that was her own in such a short time after the explosion destroyed her family's office building and home apartments. There were even a few pictures around on the walls and shelves. Good for her.

Jaz came out of the kitchen and picked up the remaining glass of wine.

"Sit down," she said, gesturing to the couch in the adjacent living room. She followed him in and sat down across from him on the same sofa. "How was the rest of your day?"

"You have no idea. More strangeness in a job filled with strange things." Dean told about getting called to the possessed man in the halfway house.

"I know Heaven's House well. We drop the occasional possessed person off there if their particular demon is not a real danger to others. I assume you met Brother Gary?"

"Yeah, nice guy. He kind of freaked out when I managed to banish the demon from the patient for him."

"You what?" Jaz said, leaning forward in her seat. "That's impossible. It takes a full exorcism ceremony and a trained priest to do that. What happened?"

"When I touched him to hold him still while Barry gave him a shot of Haldol to sedate him, he freaked out. He said he knew who I was and what Jo had done to his brother. I assume that was the demon Jo killed at the mall. He threatened her and that's when I lost my temper with him." He met Jaz's eyes. "I just grabbed him by the head and told him to leave her alone and never come back."

"Dean, this is important. Tell me exactly what you said."

"I don't really remember. It was something like, 'Damn you. Go back to hell and never come back.' When I said that the guy initially struggled with me, then he kind of fell asleep. Brother Gary looked him over and Barry checked to make sure he was okay. Gary told me the demon was gone and seemed really impressed that I could do it. He called it a gift from God."

"It might be exactly that, Dean."

He laughed. "I can think of a lot of things I'd rather have as a gift from God than the random ability to banish demons."

"Dean, this is not a normal ability that just crops up in humans. Casting out demons is a function of connection with divinity. Our enchanted hunter's swords do it through being blessed by an ordained priest or other holy person during their crafting. We need that holy blessing on our blades to accomplish the task. We can't just lay hands on a person and throw the demon out."

"What are you saying, Jaz? It's not like I'm some sort of god on earth."

She rolled her eyes with a laugh. "Lord knows that is true. No, you're not that, but maybe you're something close. Remember when we rescued Ashley, and you handled her heavenly blade, even though you should not have been able to touch it without getting injured or burned or something?"

Dean nodded. He remembered how unusual she and the others there thought it was at the time. "I still don't think I have anything to tell you now that I didn't then. I'm just a normal guy who is a paramedic. I'm nothing special."

"I think you need to stop saying that, Dean. This is not something I've ever seen or heard of before. Maybe if Ashley or Ingrid were here, we could ask them what it means, but Ashley is not coming back anytime soon. Plus, I'd rather not invoke Ingrid right now. She's a bit too chaotic to have around given current events here in Elk City."

Dean agreed with her about Ingrid. She was a shoot first, ask questions later kind of person. She wasn't a person exactly, though. She was a Valkyrie, a type of angel just like Ashley was another kind of angel. He thought about how much he missed Ashley and sighed.

"I'm sorry, Dean. I shouldn't bring up Ashley like that. I of all people should understand that we all need time to grieve our losses. Forgive me?"

"Jaz, there's nothing to forgive. I lost my girlfriend, but she's not dead. You lost your whole family. I don't think it's the same thing." He reached out and touched her hand where it rested on the back of the couch. She didn't pull it away but instead turned her wrist so that her fingers clasped his.

"Thank you for thinking of me, Dean. I'm doing alright most of the time, if I stay busy. Honestly, it's been the connection to you and Joanna that is helping me get through this." A buzzer sounded from the kitchen and Jaz pulled her hand back as she finished the last swallow in the wine glass. Then she got up.

"I think the sauce is almost finished. I'm going to start the pasta. It's fresh so it won't take too long to cook. Do you want to go and fetch our daughter?"

Dean nodded. He stood up and headed down the hallway to get Jo. While he walked, he rubbed the fingers of his right hand together, remembering the touch of Jaz's hand. It had been nice. He thought about what it might mean, for him, for her, for the two of them. It wouldn't be awful being with her, he thought. He wondered if that was just the knowledge that they had a daughter together in the future, or if he really felt like it would work out on its own merits.

He knocked on the guest room door. There was no answer. He knocked again.

"Jo, it's Dean, I mean Dad. It's time for dinner."

He opened the door when Joanna didn't answer. He looked around the room. There was no one there. He noted right away the open window opposite the door. He went over and looked out. There was a fire escape and he looked down to see if he could spot Joanna. She was nowhere in sight. Damn. Rushing back out to the kitchen, he looked at Jaz.

"She's gone."

"What do you mean gone? She just went back there an hour ago."

"I mean gone, not there. The window's open. She must have gone down the fire escape. Where do you think she's gone?"

"She's our daughter, Dean. I'd be willing to bet she's gone to fix the problem herself, just like you or I would do." She went over to a wooden chest by the door. Taking a key from her pocket, she opened it and started pulling out weapons. She slipped into her shoulder holster rig with the pistol on one side and dual magazines and a drop down Bowie knife on the other. It was strange how natural he thought she looked. He was not comfortable around guns in general, but he didn't feel strange with her being armed.

"So, I guess we go figure out where she would go?" Dean asked. "I hope you have an idea, because I have no clue."

"My guess is she's going to cast the spell to find Jill on her own and track that demon down for us. It's what I would do. If I make a mistake, all I want to do is make things right again. I think she'd react the same way."

Dean turned and went in to shut off the stove and oven. He placed a lid on the pot of sauce so it would stay warm. Hopefully they wouldn't be gone that long. His stomach was growling with hunger. He came back to where Jaz was standing by the door. She had put on her leather jacket, covering her weapons from casual view.

"We can finish dinner when we get back. It will keep. Let's go get our daughter before she does something really stupid without us," Dean said.

Jaz nodded and pulled the door open for him. They were back on the road again and he thought they made a pretty good team, like a family.

Chapter 25

Jo let go of the iron ladder at the bottom of the fire escape and looked up at the open window above her. She had heard her father come in and knew how disappointed in her he was. She had killed people. Maybe not with her own hands, but she had killed those women in the department store all the same. She had nearly killed her new best friend, first because the demon had attacked her, and then by launching the sunfire spell without thinking about the harm it would cause Marian, too.

She felt her eyes welling up again and wiped the tears away with the back of her hand. This whole situation was her fault. She had to make it right. If she could find Jill on her own and banish this demon back to hell then she could make everything better. She could look her mom and dad in the eye again and they would be proud of her.

The plastic shopping bag stuffed in her oversized purse held all the scrying supplies she needed for locating Jill, but she needed a few more things. She could now find Jill, but then she also needed to be able to magically send the demon lord back to the netherworld without harming the woman whose body it occupied. She thought she had come up with a way to do it. The challenge was going to be getting the extra items she needed to do the second spell. It was more complex than anything she had tried before.

Asha, the coven leader, had told her she was the most powerful witch practitioner she had ever tutored. The priestess had also told her that power could be her downfall, if she wasn't careful. Time to see if she could carry the load or not. Jo set off down the street, hoping the location she looked for existed in this past world.

The long walk across town gave her time to think about what she was doing, and to organize her thoughts and plan for how this was going to work. She knew the demon lord could track her in some way. That was how the demon attacker at the mall had located her. That meant she had to move quickly in order for her plan to work.

The building she sought was on the same street as the police headquarters downtown. If her parents had discovered her missing, they might have put out an alert to find her. It would be just like them to use the mundane police to pick her up and hold her. She stood on the corner across the street from the police building and watched the police officers and cars come and go. It was only eight o'clock, and there was still a lot of hustle and bustle in front of the building as people went about their evening activities.

She decided to walk across the street and down the sidewalk as if she were just another city resident on her way home. Mom had always told her you could go anywhere, enter any building most of the time, if you acted as if you belonged there. It was all about attitude. She hoped she exuded that attitude as she walked down the street now. Surely no one had the time to pay attention to one fifteen-year-old girl.

Jo was sure everyone was looking at her, wondering what she was up to as she passed the front of the police building. Still, nothing happened, and she passed by unmolested. She felt her shoulders relax a little as she passed a few more buildings, until she arrived at the one for which she was hunting. She breathed a sigh of relief as she realized it was there in the past just as it was in the future.

She stood in front of the Elk City Historical Society offices and the local history and lore museum. She walked up the red stone steps to the front door and let herself inside. There was a man at the desk in the vestibule. He was packing up his briefcase, putting files and a few books inside as she approached him. He was balding, with wisps of grey hair on the sides of his head above his ears. It gave him a comical look that only accentuated his scowl when he noticed her standing in front of him.

"I'm sorry, young lady. The museum closed at eight. You'll have to come back tomorrow."

"Oh no, Mister. I've got a project for school and I have to look at one or two things in the museum to finish it. Couldn't you open up for just a few more minutes?" Jo tried to look innocent and even batted her eyes at him.

"If I had a dime for every child or parent who came in here at closing time for the last minute school project, I'd be able to retire early." He looked at her and shook his head. "The answer is no. Call it a lesson in being properly prepared and planning ahead. You'll thank me someday."

His answer made her angry. Why did he have to be such a douche? Why did older people always think everything bad that happened was meant to be a lesson to some young person in need of one? Jo muttered one word, "stop" as she reached up and tapped the man between the eyes with her left index finger. His eyes widened and then he stopped moving. His eyes darted left and right and then stared back at her. She could see the fear in them.

"It's alright sir," she told him as she swung her purse around and reached to pull his keys from his hands. "You'll be fine. It will wear off in a few hours and you'll be good as new by morning. Next time, maybe you should be nice when someone asks you for a favor. I only needed a few minutes in your museum after all."

Jo left the man frozen in position behind his desk. He'd be sore from the muscle stiffness he'd have from standing still for so long, but nothing else. She went over to the glass doors of the museum and started trying keys from the caretaker's key ring in the lock. It took her several tries. What did he need so many keys for anyway?

Finally she found the right one and the glass door swung inward to allow her entry into the museum area.

She had come here with her parents when she was younger and remembered the things they had pointed out to her that had Unusual or occult connections. The normal humans had no idea of the true nature of these artifacts held in the museum's collection, or if they did, it wasn't on the description cards on the displays.

There was one particular item she looked for and she wasn't sure if it would be here or not. If she remembered correctly, it was in a small display of Native American artifacts found in various excavations around the city. Like most of the east coast American cities, Elk City was built on or near the location of former native villages. That meant as the cities expanded in modern times, excavations uncovered artifacts from the past on occasion.

She rounded the corner and saw the display she sought. It was just where she remembered it. Rushing to the glassed-in enclosure, she looked over the items inside. There were pieces of pottery, a few flint arrowheads, and a flint knife with a carved bone handle. It was the flint knife she wanted. Her mother had told her it was the enchanted blade of a shaman and was used to fight demons the tribe would encounter from time to time. Jo really hoped this wasn't just one of those stories parents told kids to make it seem like they knew more than they did.

Inspecting the glass box that covered the items on the table, Jo looked for signs of an alarm or other security device. When she ran her hands around the base of the enclosure, she found what she was looking for. There were two wires extending from the base into the wall. This would be some sort of sensor switch that would alert the alarm company if anyone touched something or tried to remove the enclosure.

Jo looked around and tried to think of how she could do this. She needed that knife. She had to have it, or tonight's whole plan would fail. In the end she decided on the direct approach. She would break the glass, snatch the knife and leave the building before anyone could respond.

It looked like no one else was in the building since the man out front was planning to lock up things for the night. That meant that any response would have to come from somewhere else. With the police headquarters just a few buildings away down the street, that might be closer than she wanted. Still, she had to take the chance. She had to make this right.

Taking her pistol out of her shoulder holster, she turned it and gripped it by the barrel, wielding it like a hammer and brought it down hard on the top of the glass box over the artifacts. It bounced off. She hit it again and again, striking the glass harder each time. On the fifth strike, the glass shattered inward and she was rewarded by reaching inside and pulling the knife free.

The alarm started sounding almost right away. She stuffed her pistol and knife into her purse and rushed out to the front foyer. The man was still standing there. His eyes looked angry more than fearful now. She waved as she passed.

"I'll return it, I promise."

She remembered to slow down and walk at a normal pace as she exited the building. The alarm bells were muted once she was on the street but they were audible to anyone who passed by. If they didn't automatically call the police, someone walking past would. Time was of the essence now. They would be looking for her in earnest, and if her parents found out what she took from the museum, they would be able to piece together her plan.

Her next destination was to find a place in the city park where she could cast the necessary spells to enact the scrying to find Jill. Once she had a location for the possessed woman, she could figure out the next steps. It would depend on how far away she was. If Jo needed a car to get her, she was pretty much screwed. She couldn't drive and didn't know anyone else to call for help in this time and place.

She was a few blocks away when she heard sirens and, looking over her shoulder, she saw several police cars pulling up in front of the historical society building. She picked up her walking pace and looked for a place to turn off the main street onto a side street. She needed to get out of sight. There were probably cameras in the museum and within a few hours, they'd have her photo in every police cruiser in the city.

Jo turned down the first side street on her left and crossed over it while she broke into a jog. It was time to get to the City Park as soon as possible now, she had both her parents and the police looking for her. She wasn't sure which option would be worse if they found her first. She suspected it would be her parents. The police would just lock her up. Her parents were going to lecture her if they found her. That thought jolted her into picking up the pace and she ran the rest of the five blocks to the park.

Chapter 26

There was no moon and it was very dark in the central, wooded portion of the park. There were streetlights spaced along the paved paths through the trees, but Jo had chosen a secluded area where one light was broken. She knelt in the grass and laid out the materials for the scrying spell on the ground in front of her. The small bowl, a bottle of water, the plastic zipper baggie that contained Jill's hair, and the small collection of magical herbs she would need.

She poured the water in the bowl and added a pinch or two of the selected herbs while she murmured the incantation. The last thing she did was to lay the strands of hair across the pool of water and herbs in the bowl. She was rewarded with a satisfying glow from the bowl and then she saw the city from above. Jo had been prepared for this, and had her phone open to the maps app, choosing the satellite angle to see the same view.

It was disorienting at first, but once she had the phone turned to match the view in the bowl, she began to focus her mind on the locator spell. With two fingers on her phone scrolling across the map, matching what she saw in the bowl, the witch teen narrowed her search until she had zoomed in on a small storage unit complex on the outskirts of town. She glanced back and forth between the bowl and phone until she was sure she had the same location on both and then tapped her phone to save the location.

Jo heard voices nearby and she closed and darkened her phone screen, dumping the bowl of glowing water over, dousing the light there as well. She slipped back into the bushes beneath a pair of nearby trees, pressing herself against the trunk of one tree as she willed herself into the shadows.

"I saw the light coming from somewhere over here," one voice said.

"I didn't see anything. It's probably just some kids fooling around after dark," said another.

"Well, they are not allowed out here after dusk. We should run them off. Besides, someone reported a girl running into the park. She could be the one we're looking for based on that all-points bulletin we heard over the radio," the first voice said.

Jo froze in place as two police officers with flashlights came down the path to her left. They walked along until they found her scrying bowl, the empty water bottle, and scattered plastic baggies of herbs. The two officers stopped and looked at the strange collection of items on the ground.

One of them laughed, "See, I told you it was just kids. They were getting stoned and we scared them off. They left their drugs behind."

The other officer stooped down, poking at the baggies and the bowl. "This doesn't look like weed. I'm not sure what it is, but it's not marijuana."

"Who knows what weird internet plants the kids are using nowadays? Every week we get another alert from the poison center about new drugs on the block. Just clean it all up and we can test it back at the station."

The kneeling officer pulled a larger zipper bag from his pocket and put the scattered trash in it before closing it and standing up. He turned and played his light around the clearing causing Jo to pull deeper into the brush and shadows. He didn't see anything else worth investigating, and he and his partner continued on their patrol. Their conversation turned to what they were going to eat for dinner later as they walked away.

Jo breathed a sigh of relief. She relaxed and stood to move out of the bushes. She looked at her phone as she did, pulling up the maps app to get directions to the storage facility. As she took a step towards the path, a scaled hand closed over her mouth from behind, pulling her back into the bushes. She felt a blow to her head and she lost consciousness before she could even cry out. The last thing she remembered was dropping her phone to the ground.

THE POUNDING WOULDN'T STOP. It just pounded and pounded in her ears until it drove her mad. Jo tried to cover her ears with her hands but she couldn't. Her arms were secured and she couldn't seem to free her hands. Why couldn't she do this? She tried again, struggling both to free her hands and to clear her mind. That was when she realized she was bound, seated and tied up in a chair or something like it. She tried to open her eyes but the bright light overhead seemed to pierce directly into her brain and the painful pounding got worse.

Jo realized the pounding sound she heard was the blood pulsing past her ears in her arteries. It matched the throbbing pain in her head. She remembered being captured in the park and being struck from behind, and she stopped struggling. She turned her energy inward, listening for anyone else around her. Trying to open her eyes again, slowly this time, she again was forced to shut them after the bright overhead light caused waves of pain and vertigo to course through her head.

Damn, she thought, I've got a concussion. That would explain the light sensitivity and pain she was feeling. She slowed her breathing and tried to say a few healing incantations under her breath but the words were muddled and she couldn't concentrate enough to direct the magic. It was the brain injury from the concussion that was muddling her thoughts and concentration so that she couldn't cast the magic. She would have to try something else.

She needed to get a sense of her surroundings and she decided she had to look around, despite the pain the bright light caused her. She tried opening her eyes only far enough to let the tiniest amount of light in, and looked around through slitted eyelids. It still hurt, but it was bearable and she could see her surroundings.

There were boxes and assorted items of furniture in this room. The floor was concrete and the walls, where she could see them, were made of corrugated metal. The room appeared to be about twenty feet long by ten feet wide. She looked down and saw that she was secured in what appeared to be an old, metal desk chair on wheels. Her arms were duct-taped down to the arms of the chair. She couldn't see her feet. They were pulled up under her with the souls of her feet facing behind her and the toes of her shoes resting on the floor.

Turning her head and looking around carefully, she could only see one part of the room. She thought she'd try something and attempted to push against the floor with her toes. She was rewarded when she started to swivel a bit in the chair. She tried again and again until she managed to turn around one hundred eighty degrees. That was when she found Jill, or what was left of her.

Jo forced herself to look even though she wanted to scream in terror. The woman's body was stretched on an old wooden bed frame, fully assembled but without a mattress. Her body laid on the wooded slats that rested across the side rails, usually to support the mattress and box spring. In this case there was just the bare wood. The woman's arms and legs were secured with ropes to the four bed posts.

Her lifeless eyes stared back at Jo, unseeing, glazed as they were with the film that covered them in death. She had bloody gashes in her chest and abdomen and what looked like burn marks on her arms and legs. The wound that probably killed her was the gaping slash across her throat. Jo noticed the metal basin on the floor set beneath her head and neck to catch the blood. She could see the dark pool of fluid there.

Wait, this didn't make sense, Jo thought. Jill was the demon lord. Had some other hunter gotten here first? No, they wouldn't have tortured her like this, they would have just killed or captured her. Could there be another demon in competition with the first one? Maybe it was the other demon that killed her, some sort of internal power struggle between the netherworlders?

Her mind was foggy, but she forced herself to puzzle it out and the realization struck her like a thunderbolt. Jill was never the demon. It had been Sam all along. He was the possessed one. He was the demon lord's host. He had fooled them into looking for his wife and they had missed their chance to get him when they had him in their hands.

She knew where she was now. She was in the storage unit where she had scried for Jill. Something or someone had brought her here. This must be one owned by the couple and where Sam could commit his horrible rituals on his wife without anyone hearing them. If you came in here, on the outskirts of town, late at night, it was unlikely anyone else was checking their storage rooms. You'd have all the privacy you'd need to do whatever you wanted.

Jo pulled at her bonds again and tried to look around for a way to get free. She vaguely remembered a scaled hand clamping over her mouth. That meant that Sam had summoned another lesser demon to do his bidding, maybe more than one. That they had captured her and not merely killed her meant that Sam needed something from her - and the thought chilled her to the bone. She stared at Jill's body in front of her and renewed her struggles to get free. If she were going to get out of this, she had to do it herself. No one else knew where she was.

Dean was losing patience, but he didn't let it show. Jaz was doing the best she could to track Jo's phone signal. Jaz revealed that she had given Jo a sim card for her phone that worked on her family's network plan when they got back to town after rescuing Ashley a few weeks before. The teen's own device from the future didn't work here in the past on its own, and had served only as a media playing device, serving up whatever music it was that the teen listened to when she retreated into her earbuds. With the addition of the sim card, Jo had been able to access the local phone network.

The new sim card meant that Jaz was able to track it, sort of. The phone's GPS system had localized them to the park but they had been unable to narrow their search down to less than a one hundred by one hundred yard square wooded area at the center. Now the two of them were scanning the ground, a step at a time, playing their flashlights back and forth as they tried to find some clue, and hopefully their daughter.

They had tried to call it at first, hoping they would hear the ring as they walked around. They soon realized it must have the ringer set to silent. Now they had resorted to a step by step search of the entire area after a quick sweep had shown them nothing. Dean took his time, trying to keep his emotions under control as he searched.

There was evidence that Jo had been involved in a break-in at the Elk City Historical Society building. They had heard the report over the police scanner in Jaz's SUV. He was not sure what Jo had been looking for at the museum. The police did not report anything about what was missing over the radio. They only reported on video in the security cameras showing a girl matching Jo's description.

Another report had come in saying someone had seen a girl running into the park, but police officers on the scene had searched and sent back that they had found nothing. Now that Jaz had tracked Jo to the park, it confirmed those reports were probably accurate. His thoughts swirled through the events of the night over and over again as he searched for the missing phone and his daughter.

He was thinking through this jumble of thoughts when his flash-light caught a glint of a reflection on the ground ahead. He ran forward and shouted with relief when he reached down and picked up the phone. He called to Jaz, waving the discovered phone over his head in triumph. He spun around as Jaz came over to him. He shined the light in all directions, trying to pierce the gloom around him. Jo had been here, she must be close by.

"Jo. Jo," he called. "Where are you? Are you out there?"

Jaz joined him and called out as well. Their only answers were the resumed chirping of crickets in the darkness surrounding them. Dean's shoulders slumped as he looked at the phone in his hand. He pressed the button to activate the screen and saw all their phone calls to her listed on the notifications there.

"Here, let me take a look," Jaz asked. Dean handed her the phone and she tapped a security code in to get past the lock screen, opening up the phone's access.

"How did you know her password?"

"I didn't. All the phones in our plan for Errington Security have an override to wipe the phones in case they are stolen. It works on the sim cards, too. I used that to open the phone." Jaz gave him a grim smile. "It pays sometimes to be paranoid security types."

She tapped around on the screen, opening different apps. "I'm trying to see what she was doing before she dropped it. It looks like she was looking at the maps app on the phone."

"Could she have cast the scrying spell on her own and found Jill? She wouldn't have gone after her on her own would she?"

Jaz cast him a sideways glance. "You were a teenager not that long ago just like me. What would you have done?"

"I get your point. So where was she searching for on the maps app?"

"It looks like she was looking for this address on the outskirts of town. Do you recognize it?"

Dean looked at the screen when she turned it to him and shrugged. He watched as Jaz took out her phone and entered the address into a search program and the address popped up right away as a self-storage facility.

"That could be where Jill is hiding," Jaz said.

"But we have no way of knowing if Jo went there. She wouldn't have left her phone here. Could she have been taken and dropped the phone?" Dean was starting to get anxious.

Jaz took his hand in hers. "Look at me, Dean. We need to work together and stay calm. We'll find her. This is the best lead we have right now."

He gave her hand a squeeze and looked around in the darkness. He felt responsible for yelling at Jo and making her feel guilty about the attack at the mall. His reaction to her going out on her own may have forced Jo's hand to run off like this. Jaz was right, though. He had to keep his head on straight and not overreact. It was time to take action.

His phone buzzed in his pocket and he took it out to see a number he didn't recognize. He tapped the screen to answer and put it on speaker so Jaz could hear. The voice on the other end was garbled as if it were being run through a computer program to alter it.

"Hello Mr. Flynn. I have your witch girl and know you have found her phone. I left it so you would know that I have her."

"Don't you hurt her," Dean blurted out.

"That is entirely up to you and Miss Errington. Can she hear me?"

"I am here," Jaz answered. "What can we do for you? I assume you want something,"

"You know very well what I want. I want the idol. It belongs to me. It belongs with the others like it." Dean listened to the voice, trying to decide if it was a man or a woman. He couldn't tell. The computer voice alteration was too good.

"If we bring you the idol, what guarantee do we have that Jo is still alive and will remain that way?" Dean asked.

"Say something to your friends, witch," the voice said.

There was a pause, then Dean and Jaz heard Jo's voice clearly over the phone. "Mom, Dad. I'm in a storage shed or something …" Her voice broke off suddenly with a yelp.

"Jo, are you there?" Dean called out into the phone.

"She is quite alright, for now, Mr. Flynn. Whether she stays that way is up to you. You have one hour to come up with the idol. I will turn this phone number back on in sixty minutes and leave it on for exactly one minute. If you don't call me in that minute for instructions, I'll assume you want your friend to die and I will oblige you. Is that understood?"

Dean looked at Jaz. She gazed back at him and nodded. "I agree. You'll get my call in one hour."

"Very well," the altered voice said. "I look forward to your call in sixty minutes from now."

The call disconnected and Dean saw Jaz take out her phone and set a timer for sixty minutes.

"What do we do now?" Dean asked. He paused and continued. "We have to get the idol from your apartment and get it to him."

"Whatever happens, Dean, we cannot let Sam get his hands on the third idol. It will enable him to fully manifest on this plane. You have no idea what a demon lord can do if he is able to walk physically on this earth."

"So we let Jo die?" Dean was astonished with her callousness.

"I didn't say that, Dean. We have to try and rescue her. I agree. I just want you to understand that we cannot let the idol fall into his hands. No matter what else happens, that cannot occur. If we have to kill Jill, or me or you, or even Jo, we cannot let that happen. Do you understand?"

Dean thought about it. He had seen what kind of carnage even lesser demons loose on the earth could cause. It made him cringe at the thought of what a demon lord would do with all the power to summon lesser demons at his command. He met Jaz's eyes and nodded. "I understand. We can't let that happen. So what's the plan?"

"We have an advantage that Jill doesn't know about. We know where she is. At least, I think I know where she is."

"The storage facility?" Dean asked.

"It has to be where she's taken Jo. That's where she is if the scrying spell worked at all and Jo's map query is correct." Jaz looked around. "We need to be careful, Dean. I think we're being watched. She knew when we found Jo's phone."

Dean realized she was right and looked around in the darkness, too, scanning the brush and trees with his flashlight. The thought of being watched caused the hairs on the back of his neck to rise and sent a chill down his spine.

"Let's go back to the SUV and finish talking while we drive," Jaz said. She started in the direction of the paved path through the woods in the city park, heading back towards the parking lot.

Dean looked over his shoulder once more as he followed her. It took them ten precious minutes to return to the parking lot and climb into the vehicle. Jaz sat in the driver's seat and looked at Dean next to her. He closed his door and returned her gaze.

"Alright, Dean here's what we're going to do."

Dean listened and nodded as Jaz's plan for Jo's rescue unfolded. She had done hostage rescues before with her security team background so he had faith in her planning. She also had a whole lot more experience with demons and their ilk than he did. It was not without its risks and a lot was going to rely on him since he was the only team she had to work with.

She finished laying out the plan, then started the SUV and drove off into the night. They had a lot to do in one hour.

Chapter 28

Dean watched as Jaz plugged a laptop into the case open on the dashboard in front of her. He was driving so she could get the gear set up in time. She reached over and toggled a switch, then looked at the result on the computer screen. The resulting nod seemed to indicate everything was working correctly. In theory, she had told him, this equipment would be able to track the incoming call from the caller to his cell phone.

They hadn't had much time, with only an hour to get the summoning idol and the gear Jaz said she needed. Now as the final minutes counted down to the deadline, they sped through the night towards the storage facility they found on Jo's phone. It was a gamble, but Jaz was convinced it had to be the location of the demon lord's hideout. That was where they would find Jill, and it was likely they would find Jo there as well.

The tracking system would help them localize the caller. If they were right, it would target the source of the call in the storage facility. That gave them the advantage of surprise, since Jill wouldn't know they were close by at the time of the call. It would all work, if their hunch on her location was correct.

Dean pulled the SUV over to the curb one block away from the location. He looked at Jaz and she returned his look with a grim smile. He knew she couldn't give him any guarantees Jo would be safe. He wanted them anyway.

They were both startled when the timer on Jaz's phone went off signifying the end of the hour. Dean tapped the phone to redial the number. Dean's phone buzzed as the call rang through to the other side. It was plugged into the box on the dash and they each had a set of ear buds to hear the call while it was patched through the system. Dean waited for their mysterious caller to pick up on the other end.

He tried to sound calm and took a deep breath before he spoke, "Hello, Dean here."

"Well, well. Your call is prompt. I like that," the electronically altered voice responded. "Do you have the idol?"

"Let me talk with Joanna," Dean said. "I have it, but we go no further until you prove to me she's alive and unharmed."

"You are in no position to bargain, Mr. Flynn."

"Neither are you. Let me talk to her," Dean said as he flinched. Jaz had gone over the need to continue to request proof of life throughout the process. They had to keep Jo alive through the exchange. It was an important part of their plan.

"Very well. I will fetch her." There was a pause and Dean looked over at Jaz who was leaning over the computer in her lap, tapping keys and watching the screen. She saw him looking over at her and she made a stretching and pulling motion with the fingers of both hands. He needed to keep the caller on the phone longer for the trace to work.

There was some noise of someone fumbling with the handset of the phone on the other end and then he heard Jo's voice.

"Daddy, are you there?"

"I'm here, Jo. We're going to get you out of this. Just hold on. Alright?" Dean said.

"Alright, I will," Jo answered. There was more fumbling on the phone again and then the garbled voice returned.

"There, you have your proof she's still alive. Now you are going to do exactly what I say. You will bring the idol, alone, to the site of the Errington building fire. Wait by the construction entrance gate for further instructions. You have ten minutes to get there. Your time starts now."

"If you don't bring Jo, we don't give you the idol," Dean blurted out to try and keep them on the line. There was nothing but a click as the caller hung up.

Dean looked over at Jaz and breathed a sigh of relief as she pumped her fist and gasped "Yes! We've got her."

"Really?"

"Yep, they are here in the storage facility, just ahead of us," Jaz said. "Pull the SUV up next to the fence. We can get on the roof and climb over to get inside. We've got to hurry. He will have to leave soon to get to the construction site in time to make the exchange. We have to catch them outside of the unit."

"Can you tell which unit they're in?" Dean asked.

"Not exactly, but I can localize it to one row of units. That should get us close enough." Jaz hopped out as he pulled up next to the fence around the storage facility, grabbing her katana and slipping it over her shoulder. She settled the sword so the hilt popped up over her shoulder. He knew she was also armed with a pistol and her Bowie knife.

He got out. He had no weapon, and for the first time, he felt like he needed one. Too late to worry about that now. He knew he needed some training before he was ready to carry even a pistol into this situation. He'd lend Jaz what assistance she needed as best he could.

The two of them climbed up on the roof and then over onto the top of the brick and wrought iron fence surrounding the lot filled with storage sheds. Jumping to the ground, they took a moment to get their bearings. The storage sheds were arranged in rows with about twenty units on each side of the row.

"By my count, they should be somewhere in the sixth row down," Jaz said. "Let's hurry up, but try to be quiet."

Dean followed her as she jogged in the direction specified. She stopped at a corner and peered around it as Dean caught up to her. She pulled back and turned to look at him.

"There's a minivan parked in front of one of the units. There's light spilling out from inside. It has to be them." Jaz glanced around for a moment and then pointed up. "Boost me onto the roof. I'll get the jump on them from above when Jill brings Jo out."

Dean nodded and cupped his hands together, interlacing his fingers to form a step for Jaz to put her foot in. She stepped into his hand and she straightened up as he stood and lifted upwards. She reached up and pulled herself onto the roof, disappearing from view. Dean looked up for a few seconds until he realized she wasn't coming back. He inched forward towards the corner of the end unit and looked down the row.

He saw the minivan and the light from the open unit door about fifty feet down the row from where he stood. He didn't see any movement, but Jaz was right. This had to be the right place. He looked upward to the roofline but could see no sign of his companion. Jaz was staying out of sight.

Dean continued peering around the corner at the scene until he thought that Jaz had to have made it to her position above the unit, then he stepped around the corner. He flattened himself against the doorway of the first unit and slid along its length to the wall with the next one. Stopping, he looked to see if anyone was moving around the open unit. Seeing no one there, he stepped around the walls separating the units and back into the slight cover and shadows of the door alcoves.

He continued moving up, unit by unit until he was only one away. He could hear voices now and stopped to listen to them. The first voice he heard was Jo's and his heart leapt in relief. She was still alive.

"You know my parents will never give you what you want, right?"

"It's not up to you, my dear. They're your parents, of course they'll do whatever it takes to get you back."

Dean started at the sound of Sam's voice. Was Sam in on this, too, or were they wrong and the Demon was Sam all along. He wished he could see Jaz right then. Had she heard and recognized the voice as well? If Sam was here, was Jill here, too?

Jo started speaking again. Dean listened to try and gauge if she was hurt or not. "They want the other two idols from you so they can seal them away safely again and prevent you from ever entering this world again. That is more important than my life. They know this."

"I'm counting on it actually," Sam replied. "They will likely come up with some rescue plan to save you and not realize that merely having the idol nearby will strengthen me. I don't have to have it in my possession right away. Close is good enough."

Dean saw a shadow on the pavement that showed a person coming out of the storage unit. He flattened back into the shadows. Sam stepped out into the open doorway of the storage unit, turned and looked right at him.

"Hello, Mr. Flynn. So good of you to come and bring the object of my desire close enough to enable my final transformation."

Sam stretched a hand upward towards the roof and swatted at something as if at a bug. Dean heard a grunt of pain from the roof and was shocked to see Jaz flung from the roof top to bounce onto the roof of the van, rolling from there to the ground. She groaned and struggled to rise. The huntress let out a brief yelp of pain as she put weight on one leg. Dean saw it buckle under her and realized she must have broken it in the fall.

Their adversary laughed out loud when he saw her struggling to rise and walked over toward her. She reached for her pistol but Sam, moving inhumanly fast, was on top of her in an instant and Dean heard the snap of her arm and her grunt of pain when the demon-possessed man twisted the gun from her hand.

"Nice of you to join us Ms. Errington." Sam dragged the broken but still struggling Jaz around the van into the pool of light spilling from the storage room.

Dean saw he was pulling her by her good arm, keeping it from reaching for another weapon while the other arm dangled uselessly at her side. He could see the tears welling in her eyes from the pain in her arm and leg but she did not cry out.

Sam reached over and pulled the katana from her back and tossed it into the storage room where Dean heard it clatter on the floor. The demon-possessed man turned to Dean and gestured to him.

"Come over here, Mr. Flynn and keep your hands where I can see them. One wrong move and I'll snap this woman's neck."

Dean felt his feet move against his will and he stepped out from the shadows and walked into the light, seeing inside the storage unit for the first time. He took in the grim scene in a glance and knew that he was in something that was way over his head. There was a table set up in the center of the open space with the two stolen summoning idols sitting on it. He saw Jill's body stretched out on the bed frame in the back of the unit, and Jo tied to the chair in front of it. Her eyes were wide with fear and worry. She didn't know what to do and was looking to him to come up with a solution. He could not do anything about it, his feet were now rooted to the floor by the demon lord's will.

He was struggling with his helplessness and trying to come up with some sort of answer when he heard a crash of glass and then the sound of a car alarm coming from behind him. He looked back and wondered what it was.

"Don't worry, Mr. Flynn," Sam said with a laugh. "That is just my minion bringing me the other idol from your vehicle."

"Aren't you afraid the alarm will bring police or other help?" Dean asked.

"No one pays any attention to things like that in this out of the way neighborhood," Sam said. "If the police show up, I'll kill them like I'm going to kill you. The more sacrifices and blood involved in my ultimate summoning, the greater my power on this earth will be."

A few moments later a scaled humanoid demon stepped around Dean and walked over to Sam holding the third and final summoning idol. Sam nodded with a feral grin and directed the creature to set the idol down on the table in the storage unit forming a triangle with the other two matching idols. There was a flash of green light when the idol was set in place and the jade eyes in each one glowed a pulsing, sickening green.

Dean had to try something, anything to get someone out of this.

This was approaching the moment of no return. He had to at least free Jo from this mad demon's plans.

"Let Jo go free, Sam," Dean said. "You have the Hunter and you have me. You don't need her as well."

"No I suppose not," Sam said, looking at Jo where she sat tied up. "But, I don't have my wife anymore and I will still need something to satisfy my more carnal appetites. I think I'll keep her around after I sacrifice you two. It will be enjoyable to see the look in your dying eyes to know that she'll suffer far more than you will."

Dean felt anger rising inside him. He was trapped by this demon lord and he realized in this moment that two of the people he had come to care about more than anything in the world were in imminent danger of death or worse. He watched as Sam dragged Jaz over to the table with the glowing idols. Their pulsing green light intensified as the possessed man neared it with his intended sacrifice.

The struggling paramedic could not even lift a finger or take a step to help and his failure to rush over to help Jaz weighed down on him more than anything he'd ever felt before. He didn't know what to do other than offer a prayer for help to whoever might be listening. Demons were real. This evil was real.

He knew the gods existed, too, but where were they? Ashley the angel, had once told him of the struggle for control of the earth. Humans were given free will in the earliest days of that struggle in order that they might determine the fate of the world around them. What good was free will if the gods were not willing to intervene in those instances when the other side stepped in with their own direct hand?

The more he thought about it, the angrier he got. His fist clenched, and in that moment of defiance, Dean felt his right foot slide forward on the pavement. He looked down and saw his foot lift and take another step. He pushed against the will of the demon holding him still and found that he could push back against it.

Dean was winning this battle of wills over control of his body, but he still might lose the war. Jaz was now lying helpless in front of the table and the glowing idols. She was pinned to the ground, likely by the same unnatural force of will that now struggled to control him. She was glaring upward at Sam in angry defiance as the demon lord in human form reached down and pulled the Bowie knife from its sheath under her jacket. He held the knife up letting the blade catch the light and shifted his grip so that he could plunge it downward into his victim.

Dean had to stop this. This abomination of suffering and death could not be allowed to manifest on earth. A voice that was both his and something more rose up from within him and Dean shouted at Sam as he forced himself to take another step forward.

"Stop."

The blade, raised up over Sam's head, wavered as it started to come down, halting after only a few inches of movement. Sam whipped his head around to gaze at Dean, curious fury in his eyes.

"You will not interfere in this, human. You cannot stop me."

"I said stop," Dean said again in the voice that was both his and something more. "You will not harm that woman or anyone else further, Graadu." Dean uttered the demon lord's name, though he knew not where that knowledge had come from.

"How do you know my name, human?" Sam said. "That is hidden from this world."

"I know your true name, Graadu," Dean felt himself say. "That name gives me the power to command you, in both this world and beyond it. Stop what you are doing to these agents of good on this earth." He took two more steps forward and felt the control of the rest of his body returning as well. He raised his arm and pointed at the demon-possessed man.

"You are an abomination that has no place in this world. You will return to the place from whence you came."

Sam uttered a curse and snapped an order to the humanoid demon. It rushed at Dean, its clawed hands raised to strike him down. Dean should have been afraid, but his being felt a new confidence. He felt, what? Invincible in this moment. He swung to face the onrushing demon with a raised arm, palm outward. When his hand contacted the head of the scaled demon, there was a flash of white light and the creature crumpled to the ground, its form turning to ash and then crumbling to a pile on the pavement.

"What are you?" Dean heard Graadu utter the question as he turned back to face the demon lord, continuing his advance.

"I've been getting that question a lot lately," Dean said. "I'm not sure who or what I am, but in this time and place, I am the one who is going to send you back from whence you came."

Graadu swung the knife towards Dean as he stepped up next to him. With a backhanded blow, Dean swatted at the hand wielding the blade and the knife spun away to clatter on the floor. He reached up and gripped the possessed man's head in his palms, staring into the depths of the man's eyes. Dean felt like he was peering into Sam's soul. Maybe he was. He said two words to end this once and for all.

"Be gone."

Sam's eyes rolled up in his head, his body spasmed at Dean's words, then he collapsed to the floor at the paramedic's feet.

Chapter 29

Dean stood for what seemed like an eternity looking at his hands and at the man crumpled on the floor of the storage unit at his feet. He didn't know what he did, or how he did it, but somehow he knew it was over. He was still lost in thought when a voice broke through his introspection.

"A little help here?" Jaz said through gritted teeth.

He looked down, shaking himself back to the here and now. There was still work to be done.

"Jaz, I'm sorry. Let me take a look at that."

She was cradling her broken arm, clutching it close to her body as she tried to sit up. He knelt down and helped her to a sitting position while he looked at the arm. Her forearm bones were clearly broken but she was able to move her fingers a little and he sensed a pulse in her wrist when he gently felt for one. Those were both good signs that is was a clean break and would likely heal well. He helped to straighten her legs, careful of the obvious break in the right one. That one was going to need some help sooner rather than later. He could see blood soaking her pants leg and he suspected it was a compound fracture with the bones breaking through the skin causing the bleeding. He didn't have any gear here but Jaz always kept supplies in the SUV. He was going to need some help, and he needed to check on Jo and Jill at the back of the unit.

"Wait here while I go check on Jo."

"I'm in no condition to be going anywhere, Dean," Jaz said with a grim smile as she gritted her teeth against the pain.

He got up and walked across the storage room to where Jo was duct taped to the desk chair. She was looking at him as he approached, tears welling in her eyes. He had been angry with her when she first left the apartment. That anger had softened to worry in the intervening hours and now he was filled with joy, glad she was found safe and alive.

He pulled out his penknife, flipping it open with his thumb and, being careful not to cut her, sliced away the duct tape binding her arms and legs. When she was free, Joanna jumped out of the chair and wrapped him in a huge hug.

"I'm sorry, Daddy."

"That's alright, Jo. Let's get all this sorted out and take care of your mother. We can talk about what happened later," Dean said.

The girl nodded as she released her grip.

"We need to get her to the hospital," Dean said. "We also need to get some police here to close off the area. With Jill's body here, this is a crime scene." He had noticed right away that Jill was beyond his abilities to help.

"Will Sam be charged? He was possessed?" Jo asked looking over at the dead woman's body stretched out on the bed frame.

Dean saw her lingering glance and redirected her attention away from the woman's body. She didn't need that image in her mind any more than she already had.

"See if you can find something to splint Mom's arm and leg," Dean asked her. "There's a BLS bag in the back of your mother's SUV. There might be a SAM splint in there."

"Got it, Dad. I'll be right back."

"Here, take these and shut off the alarm." Dean tossed her the keys for the truck.

Dean followed Jo to the front of the unit and watched her turn the corner towards the sound of the SUV's car alarm. He knelt back down by Jaz and using his knife, carefully cut away her blood-soaked pants from her injured leg. It was as he feared, a serious compound fracture of the two bones in her lower leg. Reaching into his pocket, Dean dialed 911 and spoke to the dispatcher that answered, identifying himself and requesting the Station U ambulance and police to the address of the storage facility.

The alarm stopped with a final chirp and Dean knew that Jo would be back in a minute with the basic life support bag. It should have an IV fluid bag in it and the bandages and splints they were going to need to start treating this leg. A few moments later Jo returned and the two of them started to work treating Jaz's injuries.

Jaz looked up at him as they worked on her. "Dean, what did you do to Sam? You shouldn't have been able to do that. Was that what you did back at Heaven House?"

"Sort of. Once I was able to move against his compulsion to remain standing there to watch you die, I figured our only chance was to try and banish this demon like I did the one earlier today."

"Your voice changed, too. Did you notice that?"

"It was weird. I felt like I wasn't alone, that I could do almost anything in that moment. I stopped that scaled demon who rushed me without flinching. Then a name appeared in my mind and I knew it belonged to the demon lord inside Sam. I just had to compel the demon to leave. The rest sort of happened on auto pilot, as if something or someone else took over."

Jaz laid her hand on top of his as he was wrapping her leg in the splint. He stopped working and looked at her.

"I'm glad you are whoever or whatever you are Dean Flynn. You saved me and the only family I have left. If I had lost you and Jo in this. I don't know what I'd have done." Tears welled in her eyes and he felt his own eyes misting up, too. He felt a rush from beside him and soon he and Jaz were clutched in a three way embrace with Joanna as she burst into tears hugging the two of them. He smiled and thought about the family he had found for himself in the last month or so.

The sound of sirens sounded in the distance and Jaz let go of the group embrace. The three of them settled back to sit on the floor of the storage unit.

"Jo, go over to the idols and cast a misdirection spell on them. Can you do that?" Jaz asked.

"Easy-peasy, Mom." Jo stood up next to the table and placed the idols into a cardboard box there. She closed her eyes while she muttered a few words over the box of idols.

Something happened. What, Dean wasn't sure. All he knew was that one minute the box was there and the next, it was not. Except, if he really forced his attention on it, it would fade back in for a moment. He knew that for anyone else who didn't know about the box beforehand, it would simply not be worth noticing, for lack of a better way of putting it. They would see it, but it would be so unremarkable they would dismiss it as unimportant.

Jo had cast the spell just in time. Two police officers came around the corner of the unit with their hands on their guns. They looked around at the room, took in the condition of Jill's body at the back of the unit, and Sam's unconscious body on the floor, and told Dean, Jaz and Jo to remain where they were.

Jaz already had her special U.S. Marshal's badge out, explaining that she was tracking a dangerous cult. They had attacked this man and killed his wife. She indicated Sam on the floor. The perpetrators attacked the three of them, injuring her before they fled. The officers were dubious, but accepted the badge as an excuse to let another higher authority take the lead. Dean relaxed once they took their hands off their guns.

They would be here for a few more hours at least, answering questions from the detectives and crime scene investigators. The good news, if you could call it that, was they had recovered the idols. Dean decided to check on Sam and see if there was anything he could do for him while they waited for an ambulance to pick him up. Jaz seemed to think that he would remember very little of his time possessed by the demon. That was merciful, at least. Dean wished he could forget, too.

As the first detective arrived, Dean was giving a report to the recently arrived paramedics. It was Tammy and Brook. He told them, in a roundabout way, what had occurred to Sam and helped them load Jaz on the stretcher. She needed help first. Tammy called for a second unit to transport Sam. If he didn't wake up before they arrived, they could take him to the hospital. Maybe Doc Spirelli at the ER had some sort of med for the recently possessed.

Dean walked beside the stretcher with Jo until they loaded Jaz up to take her in to the orthopedic surgeons at the trauma center. She was going to need surgery to set the bones in her leg and maybe her arm, too. Jo climbed in with her mom, handing Dean back the keys to the SUV. He'd bring it along after the police were done here.

It was dawn before he was able to leave, having answered all the police questions and making sure Sam got sent to the hospital for evaluation. As he headed back to their SUV, Dean picked up the box of idols from the table without a word. None of the police paid any attention. He left the scene of the night's carnage behind him, looking forward to a brighter future as part of a new family.

Epilogue

Dean looked at the large circular pattern on the floor of the Coven's main room, then at the two women nearby who were so important to him. One was the daughter he only recently discovered. The other was the woman he now knew for sure he'd marry someday. They had spent the last three weeks getting to know each other better than ever before. Jaz was in her wheelchair. She was confined to it until she could put weight on the leg extended out in front of her with all the pins sticking out of it. He and Jo had spent the week in the apartment with her, helping her recover from the surgery and getting her strength back. Dean had already decided he'd take some leave time and tend to her until she was on her feet again.

Now the time had come, though, when Asha and the sisters of the witch coven announced the planets were once again aligned. It was time to return Joanna to her own time and place in the world.

He saw his daughter from the future standing talking with her mother, his future wife. He shook his head. It wasn't a mistake to think of Jaz that way. There was something between the two of them. It had already started to develop. The last few months had caused the relationship's spark to come to life.

Jaz and Jo both looked his way and caught him looking at them.

They both burst out laughing and he wondered what they were talking about. He would probably never know.

"It is time," Asha, the high priestess of the coven announced.

The women of the coven took their seats around the circle of thirteen. Jo pushed Jaz in her chair over to him and Jo wrapped her arms around his neck, pulling him close.

"Bye, Daddy," the teen said. "You'll see me again. I'm born just about five years from today."

"See you, kiddo," Dean said. He struggled with unfamiliar emotions as he said his goodbye. "Try to stay out of trouble when you get back home. I know my future self will be perturbed with you if you don't listen."

Jo laughed a little at that and pulled away from him, looking one more time at Jaz before walking to the center of the casting circle. Dean pulled Jaz back behind the circle of chairs so they were behind Asha's high-backed chair. The high priestess began the incantation with a low droning murmur of words. The chant was taken up by the others in the circle and Jo smiled at him once more. There was a flash of white light and she was gone.

Dean looked around and stepped forward to stand next to Asha's chair. "Did it work? Is she okay?"

"It is done, Paramedic Dean. She has returned home."

He felt a hand and arm slip through the crook of his elbow and he looked down to see Jaz sidling up next to him. He was shocked by how right it felt all of the sudden. Looking back to the center of the casting circle, he was sure now that he'd see his daughter again, in about five years.

━━

Read on for Book 6 - The Paramedic's Nemesis

The Paramedic's Nemesis

BOOK 6 IN THE EXTREME
MEDICAL SERVICES SERIES

Chapter 1

Paramedic Dean Flynn walked into work ready for another night on the ambulance at Station U, the team of paramedics that served the creatures of myth and legend making up the Unusual community in Elk City. No sooner had he dropped his backpack on the break room table when the tones sounded from the overhead speakers for the first ambulance call of the night. He sighed. Dean had been a little late getting in today, so there'd be no time for dinner tonight before the shift. It was a shame, but that was the life of the working paramedic. Their live-in zombie chef, Freddy, would keep dinner warm for him until he returned in a few hours. His partner, Barry, had arrived early enough to wolf down what looked like an amazing Pasta Bolognese before their shift started. Dean waved at the departing day shift and headed to the ambulance bay with Barry.

"Do you want me to drive?" Barry asked.

"No, I'll drive. You can have the first run tonight." As full partners now, Dean and Barry divided the workload for their ambulance calls. They'd alternate who took the lead all night so they'd each get an equal chance to manage individual patients. Even with their unique and Unusual patients at Station U, most 911 calls were routine. Even the creatures of myth and legend got regular chest pain and had trouble breathing after an asthma attack.

The dispatcher's voice sounded from the speakers as the two paramedics climbed inside the ambulance. "Paramedic U-191, respond to 1327 Central Avenue for multiple victims of an assault. Unknown at this time if the assailant is still on scene or not."

Barry picked up the mic from the center console and keyed it to answer. "U-191 responding. Confirm if the police are responding as well?"

"Police units are responding but may be delayed due to an additional incident across town," the female dispatcher's voice replied.

There were special police units assigned to respond to Unusuals who needed law enforcement assistance as well. If there were some mythical creature rampaging and attacking people, it'd be good to have knowledgeable police officers there to back them up while they took care of any victims. Most of the human residents of Elk City were unaware of the true nature of their Unusual neighbors. Most Unusuals kept a low profile preferring to live quietly among the humans of the city.

Dean pulled the ambulance out of the bay, checking to make sure the garage doors were closing behind him before he pulled out onto the street and headed off to the scene of the incident.

"We need to stay on our toes, Barry. It could be anything."

"Agreed."

Dean had been Barry's training officer until a few months ago, and he still slipped into instructor mode. The new Station U paramedic had lots of experience with human patients, even more time on the street in total than Dean did. But Dean had gained a lot of knowledge about their special class of patients in his short time on the Station U ambulance, and he had worked to bring the more experienced medic up to speed. Barry was a quick study, and he quickly passed his Station U probationary period, graduating to equal status with Dean.

It took them seven minutes to get to the address the dispatcher gave them. Dean pulled the ambulance into the parking lot of a funeral home. People were streaming out through the doors into the lot. Some of them were clutching bleeding wounds. Dean looked around for signs that police had arrived but saw no flashing blue and red lights that signaled law enforcement units were on the scene. He should have checked before they got to the location so they could stage at a safe distance. It was too late now, though. The injured funeral home visitors saw the flashing red and white lights of the ambulance as Dean pulled into the parking lot and started moving in their direction.

"It looks like the assailant is still inside from the way they are all running out of there. Let's set up here, and we'll start treating the ones in the parking lot until police arrive," Dean suggested.

"Sound's like a plan," Barry agreed. He unlatched his seatbelt and popped open his door to jump down and start pulling out supplies to treat whatever traumatic wounds the victims had.

Dean knew that often, in the case of an Unusual attack, it would be bite or claw wounds. Usually, they were not too serious as far as wounds went. The problems came from the magical side effects such bites tended to have. Every creature that bit humans could cause different problems. That made it necessary to identify the type of attacker as soon as possible so they could initiate counter-measures. There were herbal extracts and simple vaccinations that could treat most Unusual bites if they caught the victims in time.

Hopping out of the driver's side, Dean turned and reached back inside the cab and switched on the perimeter floodlights that lit the area all around the ambulance. It was just getting dark outside, and they were going to need the light to assess any significant number of patients tonight. It would also help them spot any potential attacker mixed in with the retreating human victims. On the way to the rear of the ambulance, Dean got out their emergency bites kit from a compartment on his side of the unit which had all the vaccines and herbal extracts he might need for whatever was attacking people. He jogged around to the back of the unit to open the back doors and prep for receiving their first patients. Judging from the people streaming across the parking lot, it wouldn't take long.

A woman walked up assisting a middle-aged man in his early fifties. They were the first to arrive. Dean smiled at her, all while watching around and behind her for signs of any disturbance that could signal the arrival of the assailant. He wanted to be ready to defend himself if needed. He and Barry had both been inoculated against most of the infectious magics that Unusuals carried. That didn't matter much if you didn't survive the initial attack. The woman started talking as soon as she entered the pool of light thrown by the floods on the ambulance.

"Thank God you're here," she said in a rush. "I've never seen anything like it."

Dean raised his hands, palms outward, to calm her down.

"What happened, ma'am. Just go slow and try and tell me what we're dealing with here," Dean said in an even voice. He needed to set a tone of calm from the get-go. It might help to manage the crowd that was coming towards the ambulance's lights. Setting the tone of the response early was important.

"It's Grandma," the woman exclaimed, her eyes going wide. "She sat up in the casket and made this horrible groaning noise. Someone screamed, and she turned her head, saw all of us attending her funeral and said 'fresh brains.' Then all hell broke loose. It was like something out of a horror movie."

Dean nodded as he started examining the bite marks on the man's arm. Grandma had torn all the way through his coat and broken the skin underneath. He was bleeding a bit and would need a stitch or two to close the wound. Dean slapped a four by four gauze pad over it and had the gentleman hold it in place applying some pressure while he thought about what the woman said. Zombies, in his experience, were just normal people except for the fact they were dead and slowly decaying. This case, though, seemed to match up with the more classical Romero "Night of the Living Dead" style zombie. He scratched his head in thought. Maybe there were different varieties. He'd have to ask his Zombie expert, Freddy, when he got back to the station.

One thing he was sure of, all these zombie bite victims would need to get a shot from his emergency bite kit. He called out to Barry as he opened up the black pelican case he'd grabbed from the side compartment behind the driver's door.

"Barry, I'm not sure what this is, but everyone here with even a nick of a bite gets a shot of Sodium Benzoate dilution." It was a common preservative used in milk and other dairy products that also sometimes interfered with digestive enzymes. The docs that backed up Station U had also discovered it was pretty good at counteracting zombie bites or other undead exposures, even as rare as they were.

Barry looked at the people crowding in around them seeking medical attention. Grandma sure did get around the crowd at her funeral. "So you're thinking Z-bite?"

Dean nodded, appreciating the abbreviation of zombie. No need to alarm all these folks that their family's matriarch had been turned into some sort of raving undead creature. He was still trying to understand her strange behavior. He wished he could contact Freddy back at the station for some zombie lore, but he'd have to wait. Freddy never answered the phones since he wasn't technically supposed to be staying there. That station U had a professional chef in residence was the best-kept secret in the department.

"Are you going to try and help our grandma, too?" Another woman asked. "She's still in there. I think she stopped biting people when her dentures fell out."

"I can't believe we all thought she was dead," said a teenaged boy of about seventeen.

"She can put the dentures back in," a girl of twelve or so beside the boy mentioned. "I saw them fall out more than once. She would just scoop them off the floor and then pop them back in before she kept chomping. It was totally bizarre."

Dean tried to reassure the people. "We'll go and check on her once the police get here to give us a hand. In the meantime, I want everyone to line up behind the ambulance if you've been bitten. Even a small bite or nick should be tended to so it doesn't get infected. We'll check you all out and give you a shot for the infection, and you'll be good to go."

He watched as the folks started to sort themselves out while he and Barry herded them into a manageable group. Dean kept looking back up at the doors to the funeral home for signs of

Granny, but apparently, she was either still occupied inside or couldn't open the heavy glass doors. She could have some more victims trapped inside with her, though. Turning away from the group of patients and onlookers, he keyed his lapel mic and called headquarters.

"U-191 to dispatch. Expedite PD en route and notify the health department of a possible Z-bite incident."

"Received, U-191. Can you repeat and confirm Z-bite scenario?"

"I have not laid eyes on the assailant yet, but based on crowd accounts, I think it's accurate. The health department should send follow-up units to track all attendees for possible infection."

"Received. We will advise." There was a pause then the dispatcher came on again. "We have PD about two minutes out."

Dean acknowledged the dispatcher's update and went back to helping Barry treat the patients. "The police will be here soon, folks. We'll get to the bottom of this."

IT TOOK a while for the police to gather enough force to go inside and check on grandma's whereabouts. In the intervening half-hour, Dean and Barry were able to give diluted Sodium Benzoate shots to all the folks who'd been scratched or bitten by the rampaging corpse. They were able to deflect questions about the shots by telling them it was a broad-spectrum antibiotic for those nasty human bites. Both paramedics avoided answering questions about how a corpse could get up in the first place. They said things about how the docs might have pronounced her dead too soon. It seemed to keep them from asking too much more.

By the time they were finished giving all the shots, the health department team had shown up and taken over getting information from all the folks who'd been involved. With that taken care of, Dean walked over to the police officer in charge. It was one of the police's Station U type officers.

"Hey, O'Malley. What's up inside? I assume you guys managed to subdue the old lady responsible for all of this."

"We got her cornered in a utility closet. It took three of us with riot shields to keep her off us. We pushed her back until she was in the room and then we shut the door. I was kind of hoping you and Barry would know what to do with her."

Barry laughed and then stopped. "Wait. You're serious."

"Sure I'm serious. We can't take her to jail. She'll just turn all the jailbirds to zombies," O'Malley said.

Dean considered the situation for a moment. "I don't understand why she's so different from other zombies we've encountered. Usually, a zombie bite is an accidental thing or a self-defense reaction. Plus, how did she turn anyway? You'd need a voodoo priestess or some other magical source if there's not a bite involved to begin with."

"That's above my pay grade," O'Malley said. "You paramedic types are the ones who know how all the biology stuff works, not me."

"I don't care if it's above your grade or not," Barry said. "You're not using that as an excuse to make us go in there and deal with her alone. You've had the same inoculations we've had. At the least, you can help us secure the woman so we can escort her to the hospital."

"I guess I can come in with you and help with that. You're dealing with all the nasty stuff, though. I don't do blood."

Dean shook his head as the three of them started walking up to the funeral home doors. Dean pulled on some purple exam gloves then he reached out and opened the door, holding it for the others and following Barry and officer O'Malley inside.

They could hear the woman snarling and scratching at the inside of the closet door as soon as they got inside. Dean was able to figure out which door it was right away. He walked up and tried talking to the woman through the door. He saw a sign at the entrance to the larger funeral parlor room with an announcement printed on it. It had her name and dates of birth and death. He tried to call out her name to get past her current bloodlust.

"Gladys, I'm Dean Flynn. I'm a paramedic, and I'm here to

help you if you let me." He waited. The scratching and snarling stopped. He put his ear up to the door to listen and jumped back as the woman on the other side slammed into the opposite side hard enough to pop the door open and knock Dean over backward. Before he knew what happened, he had a bundle of snarling grandmother on his chest, snapping at his face with her mouth.

He was screaming in alarm and trying to fend her off. He couldn't understand why Barry and O'Malley weren't coming to his aid. Then he realized the sounds coming from the opening and closing mouth above his face weren't quite right. He looked up at the face inches above his and realized that she didn't have any teeth. The sounds weren't teeth snapping together but rather a dull squishy sound of drooling gums rubbing together. That was when he heard the laughing coming from his partner and the police officer.

"Will you guys get control of yourselves and come over here and get this woman off of me?"

"I'm sorry, Dean," Barry said, wiping tears from his eyes. "You look ridiculous there screaming for help with that ninety-pound dead woman on top of you. You're able to hold her off you with one hand, but you're screaming and yelling like it's a tiger or something."

O'Malley stopped his belly laughing long enough to chime in, too.

"Didn't you tell me not to worry because we all had our shots?"

"That doesn't mean she can't hurt me," Dean shouted over the snarls. The drool was starting to spray all over his face. "Come on, guys. Help me out here."

The two of them came over and hooked the weight of the woman off of him by grabbing her under the arms and lifting straight up. They were easily able to manage her struggling by themselves. Dean got up and wiped his face with a gauze pad he had in his pocket.

"I can't believe it took three officers with riot shields to manage this woman. I was expecting much worse." Dean shook his head and continued, switching to treatment mode. "You two hold her here," Dean announced. "I'll go and back the ambulance up to the doors, so the family doesn't see her like this. Hopefully, we can figure out what's animated her corpse and maybe get her back to some semblance of herself before we tell the family what happened. I'll talk with the health department lead and see where they want us to take her."

He headed outside and looked around the parking lot at the surrounding bystanders and remaining funeral visitors who were still lined up and had to talk to the health department teams. He thought about the woman being restrained inside. Something about this didn't make sense. He had the nagging feeling that grandma's turning wasn't a spontaneous accident. Shaking his head while he tried to work it out, Dean walked over to bring the ambulance up so they could transport their patient to Elk City Medical Center or wherever else the docs wanted him to take her.

Artur watched Dean Flynn climb into the ambulance from his vantage point across the parking lot. The vampire lord had been able to conceal himself amidst the initial rush of people out the doors of the funeral home once the ambulance arrived. He had not counted on such a rapid response to the attacks. It had been his plan that the woman would attack all the people and they would disperse so that the local authorities would be unable to locate all of them. That would give them all time to start the turning of a larger zombie horde in the city and surroundings, creating a final confrontation between the humans and Unusuals here in Elk City. Unfortunately, that wasn't going to happen tonight.

He reached into his overcoat's pocket and felt the withered finger he held there. The artifact had been hard to locate and even more difficult to obtain once he'd discovered its location. The relic was the detached finger of the great Occulus, the Eldara warrior from the earliest days of the conflict between good and evil on earth. He had lost his right hand during a battle with the demon lord Asmodeus somewhere on the Assyrian Plains around four hundred B.C. The people of the time had divided the appendage up into individual relics that were used to do everything from heal mortal wounds and fatal diseases, to endow warriors with nearly endless endurance. This particular appendage, the ring finger, imparted on the user the ability to control the dead, either turning away and controlling Unusuals of undead types or creating new ones from the freshly dead.

Artur had used a substantial amount of the power stored in the relic that day to animate Gladys tonight. It had nearly worked out. Now he had to let the finger recharge for a day before he could use it again. He'd have to plan more carefully in the future if his plans were to work. There was also the challenge of avoiding the young human paramedic who seemed always to be there to counter him at the worst possible time. Mr. Flynn needed to be dealt with at some point, too.

The plan had been simple. Artur had shown up at the viewing and funeral with the intention of setting the woman loose on the visitors. He pretended to be a family member and mingled with the crowd. He blended in, playing the part as a distant cousin of Gladys McKellin. Even the closest family had not seen through his ploy, so there was not even need to use his vampire powers to charm anyone. They had invited him to visit the deceased in the casket, and he had accepted, waiting until he was alone to pull out the relic and touch the fingertip to the woman's forehead and heart three times as the ritual demanded.

Then it was merely a game of waiting for the ceremony to begin. He was offered a seat in the front row with the surviving family members. He graciously accepted. It would be enjoyable to have a front-row seat for the coming festivities. He was not disappointed. He muttered one word under his breath while gripping the relic in his pocket.

"Rise."

The gasps of alarm from those seated around him when she suddenly sat upright in the casket had been delightful to him. When she vaulted from the raised platform to attack the minister, who was delivering a tiresome sermon on living a virtuous life, the alarmed gasps turned to shrieks and screams of fear. He particularly enjoyed the memory of one little girl who sat crying through the whole attack, asking the same thing over and over again.

"Grandma, why?"

He had to admit it started out as one of the better schemes he had ever implemented in his long un-life, but that all changed when he ran outside with the others in the crowd to find the ambulance pulling into the parking lot. Once again, the cursed Station U paramedics showed up, plied their trade, and saved his victims from their fate. Artur contemplated more than once racing over to snap the necks of the paramedics, ridding the world of at least two of them once and for all. He thought better of it, though. He remembered the shocking touch he'd received before when contacting the Flynn boy.

The last time he'd tried to lay hands on that one, the contact had nearly undone him, though he covered it well. He wasn't sure if Dean was under that protection anymore. He had managed to dispose of the Eldara bitch, even if only temporarily. There was no telling, though, if she had bestowed some lasting benefit from her presence on him. Over the past few centuries, she and her infernal Valkyrie sister, Ingrid, had done many things that had surprised him and foiled his plans. Artur would be more careful and bide his time on this go around. He had plans for paramedic Dean Flynn.

He was distracted a moment later from his contemplation of what he would do to Dean Flynn some day. An attractive brunette woman in a reflective orange and yellow vest that read "Health Department" walked up to him in the parking lot. He had been careless standing in the shadows so close by. She had noticed him standing on his own and came over to ask him to join the others.

"Sir, excuse me, but have you been inoculated against the infection from the outbreak?"

She laid a hand on his arm, and he spun on her in anger, gazing into her eyes. He was frustrated by his failed plan this evening. Perhaps this young cutie would offer him some entertainment for the night, as well as a meal later on. He bared his fangs at her in a broad grin as he poured the power of his charm ability over her like a deluge of water. She had a moment's fear in her eyes, and then her face went blank.

"What is your name?" The ancient vampire asked.

"Felicity. Felicity Richards."

"Well, Felicity, do you live alone?"

"I do, sire."

"Did you drive here on your own or did you ride with a group?"

"I came in my car, sire," she answered in a monotone.

"Excellent. I would like to leave here now without anyone noticing. Bring your vehicle over here so I may enter from the shadows. Then you may drive me to your abode."

"Yes, sire. It will be as you ask."

He watched as the young woman walked back through the parking lot to where a small sedan was parked. She had a wooden, awkward gait. The charm worked on the surface mind, commanding the body and muscles. Inside she was trying to fight. She wouldn't win that fight, but it pleased him to see her fighting so. Perhaps she had promise as a disciple with a fire inside like that. Felicity soon returned, driving the car around the outskirts of the lot until she had pulled up next to the shadowed area in which he hid.

Stepping from the shadows, Artur pulled the passenger door open and slid into the seat in a single fluid motion. Once inside, he gave her instructions to drive back the way she had come, around the perimeter of the lot to avoid as many people as possible. Most would not notice him leaving or remember the old cousin from all that happened the midst of the chaos that evening. He would remain in the shadows exactly as he wished so that all his plans could be put into motion. This was only a minor setback, nothing more. There was still plenty of time to succeed in this town and take control from the existing vampire lord of Elk City, James Lee.

Artur's hand strayed to the relic in his pocket as Felicity drove them away from the scene of his crime. He knew the sphere of control over Gladys would fade as he drove off. She would remain a zombie, a true undead one, but by morning she would regain her human memories and no longer be the mindless creature that attacked the family at her funeral that night. That was all right.

These fragile humans died all the time, so there was no lack of bodies to animate. He'd find another to animate or perhaps use the powerful relic to control a higher form of undead. It would be fun to exert even limited control over a fellow vampire with the mummified Eldara finger.

Felicity drove from the parking lot and turned right onto the main avenue in front of the funeral home just as the struggling figure of Gladys was carried from the building and into the back of the waiting ambulance. Artur smiled at the way the paramedics and policeman fought to retain a hold on her as he drove away. Maybe she'd manage to bite one of them before she was done being his unwilling tool for evil that evening. One could hope.

Chapter 3

Being undead sucked. Brynne stared at the ceiling in the darkened room and thought of all the glamorous stories that made it into powerful immortality or something out of a gothic romance.

Bullshit.

You lost everything when you changed. You missed half of every day. You lost your friends and family. You even lost control over your own body. You can't turn off the massive sensory input you get all the time. As a vampire, she was bombarded by all the information from her enhanced senses needed to make her the apex predator she was. She could hear human heartbeats through walls now. That wasn't a good thing when you couldn't look at a normal human without wondering how they'd taste. She was thirsty all the time, thirsty for warm blood.

Brynne thought she knew a lot about. She had studied them for her work as a paramedic at Station U. Hell; she had dated a vampire in an exclusive relationship for over five years. Then, when everything was finally working out for her, she was almost killed in a nightclub shooting by a crazy ex-mentor who secretly coveted her for himself. To save her life, her boyfriend, James Lee, had changed her into a vampire moments before her heart beat out its last pulse of life. It wasn't like she wasn't thankful for what he did. She was grateful. She appreciated what had gone into that choice. It had not been an easy decision for James or her human paramedic partner, Dean.

Still, here she was. She was spending another sunny day in this sunless un-life, resting as she stared at the ceiling in the room she shared with James. It was like she had nothing to look forward to anymore. She was a virtual prisoner in their apartment. She knew she shouldn't complain. It was a beautiful apartment, sitting on the penthouse level atop the high rise Nightwing building in downtown Elk City, Maryland. The place had every amenity she could hope for, and she knew James would install anything she wanted if she asked. The fully stocked kitchen gave her access to blood of every type and almost every nationality. There were some who would say she had everything she could need in life, except it wasn't a life at all, not anymore.

She forced a breath into her lungs and let out a long sigh. It was for effect only. She didn't need to breathe except to talk and for dramatic emphasis, like now.

"Brynne, dear, is something bothering you?" James asked from where he lay next to her on the bed.

"I'm bored, James. I need something to do. I need a real life and job to give me purpose. I'm just a caged tiger here in this apartment, pacing the enclosure, longing to run in the forest and have a real life again."

"It's almost time," James said, rolling over onto his side so he could look at her. "You've gained a lot of control in these last few months, Brynne. It won't be long now. Soon you'll be able to go out and mix with people again, I promise. Think about how it would devastate you if you lost control and injured someone because you couldn't control your bloodlust. Imagine what you would feel like if you killed some poor innocent just because they cut their finger on a thorn when you walked by." He shook his head. "You have to give it time."

"You've had centuries to adjust to this type of life, James. I've had just a few months. I'm not suited to being cooped up, kept from doing anything useful. I need to be working, helping people. It's who I am. I don't stop being the person that became a paramedic just because I'm a vampire now. I have to have something to give my new life purpose."

"I understand, my dear. I really do. Consider this merely a convalescence after an illness. You're almost well, and we will find something constructive for you to do. You can have any job or role you want here in my business ventures; in our business ventures. I noticed how frustrated you are. I've had Celeste pick out a few likely opportunities for you. Would you like to begin trading in securities based on your medical and health care knowledge? That can be very exciting if you give it time."

Brynne snorted a laugh at his last statement. "I don't want to be a stock trader, James. There is nothing exciting about that life. I've been on the streets. I've seen excitement firsthand and know what it feels like. I know that stock trading is how you make most of your money these days, but that is not what I'm supposed to be. I'm a person of action. I need to do something constructive and active with my time. I want to go back to being a paramedic."

"That is impossible, Brynne. You'd cross over and give in to the bloodlust the first time you ran a call for a person with a simple cut." James reached over and turned her head towards him so she could see his eyes.

She looked at him and realized he wasn't kidding. He really thought it would be impossible for her to return to her former job as a paramedic.

"You have no faith in me, then." Brynne knew she was pouting and she hated it. She also hated how set in his ways James could sometimes be. He assumed things couldn't be done if he'd never seen it done before.

"Brynne, it's not that. It takes years to master yourself to the point that you could even consider returning to a career in the medical field, let alone the unpredictable chaos of emergency medical services."

Brynne sat up and turned away from him. He kept telling her

the same thing. He said it would take years until she was ready. She was determined to prove him wrong.

"Let me take the test, James. I'm ready now." Brynne turned to look down at him laying next to her. She couldn't believe she'd said it. Was she really ready for the test? It was a series of challenges for a new vampire to determine if they had gained enough control over their predatory nature to avoid killing humans when they encountered them. The test was a relatively new process for a race of Unusuals who had, only a few centuries before, routinely fed on humans without regret, killing without remorse the people who lived in this world alongside them. It had bred an adversarial relationship between humans and their Unusual counterparts in the world, the vampires, werewolves, shifters, fairies and other creatures of myth and legend.

That was different now in the modern world. The Unusuals lived in secret alongside their human neighbors, known only to a few humans in the government and some local businesses. They lived in peace because the Unusuals policed themselves and made sure humans weren't harmed by anyone whose powers could be used to overwhelm or take advantage of them in some way.

That was the world Brynne had been changed into when James turned her. She couldn't just go out and hunt as she might have five hundred years before. In another time, James would have taken her hunting with him from the very beginning. Now, in the modern world, she had other sources of fresh blood and even willing live donors if she wanted them. She shuddered out of both disgust and longing. The thought of feeding on a live human caused her to stomach to growl and her canines to elongate into fangs in her mouth. Could she control herself around normal humans if the mere thought of feeding did this to her? That was what the test would determine.

She had been able to meet with some of her old friends and paramedic colleagues after her change. They were the paramedics who went on the nine-one-one calls that served the Unusual community. It was an outstanding service making sure the Unusuals had access to modern health care, too. That had made it easier to tell them about the transition she had undergone to become a vampire. They also accepted the need for her being chaperoned by another adult vampire when they came to visit.

Her old partner, Dean, had been by most often. She knew the decision to let James turn her haunted him. He couldn't save her himself, no matter how hard he tried. Brynne was dying after she was shot in the chest that night in the club. He, even with all his life-saving skills learned through many long hours of training and experience, could not keep her from bleeding out. She was a paramedic, too. Brynne had been unconscious at the time, but she learned from him later what he had seen and tried to do. She knew how bad her injuries were and knew that no one could have saved her life. She would have died even if he could have teleported her to a trauma center's operating room. Brynne had tried to assuage his guilt. It had not been his fault. Changing her, making her this creature of the night, was the only way to save her. She told him as much every time she saw him. She would never tell him how much she regretted it now.

Brynne remembered the first time he came by the apartment. He was seeking advice regarding a situation he was involved with having to do with his girlfriend at the time, an Angel, one of the Eldara. She barely remembered the conversation at all. She could only remember hearing his pounding heart, seeing the pulsing arteries lying just under the surface of his skin. She didn't want him to keep talking; she wanted to leap off her spot on the sofa next to James and bury her fangs in his neck. He wasn't a dear friend. He was food. James' vice-like grip on her forearm and his orders to her as her vampire sire were the only things that kept her from feeding on Dean that day.

With time, though, it had gotten better. James was patient with her. He let her have all the bagged blood she wanted. She tried every variety he could get. It was strange how nuanced individual blood could be between donors. She found she had a taste for A-positive blood, didn't care for humans who ate a lot of garlic, and liked female blood more than males. That last part was strange because she preferred men otherwise.

Along the way, the bloodlust lessened. In the beginning, she grabbed the cup of warm blood James brought her and gulped it down, spilling blood around the corners of her mouth in her haste to ingest it. Now she could sip politely and savor the blood's flavor as well as the life-giving nature that was essential to her existence. It was still hard to fight down the predator instinct when in the presence of humans, but she found she could control herself and overcome the distraction of their heartbeats, their pulses, and their blood, most of the time.

The last time Dean had visited, she didn't need James to sit right next to her. He was in the room with them, but she had resisted the urge to rip open Dean's neck and feed on him. She even remembered their conversation this time. He talked about his new probationary paramedic in the Station U program, Barry. He had graduated to full status paramedic and was working out very well in the program. Dean told her it was due to everything he had learned from her and the patience she had with him during his probationary period. She said she was proud of her protégé and it was true. He had come far.

Thinking of Dean made her want to get back out in the community even more. She wanted to make a difference again. The first responders of the world considered themselves a fraternity, a group of brothers and sisters with a common bond and goal to save lives. That commitment didn't go away with her change. Even as a vampire, she wanted to give back and help save others. She had to find a way to do something like she had done before.

"I want to go back to work, James," Brynne said. She met his eyes and saw him looking back at her. She guessed he was searching her face for some sign of intent. "I'm not asking for permission, James. I'm telling you that I'm going to be a paramedic again. I can do things now no other paramedic can do. I can see and hear things that I could never even fathom doing in my time before as a human paramedic. That gives me an advantage and the ability to save even more lives out there."

"That's a tall order, Brynne," James said. He sat up in bed and turned to sit facing her, legs crossed. He leaned forward and laid a hand on her arm. "It's one thing to say you're ready to pass the test. It is something else entirely to say you're ready to deal with situations where there is blood all around you and a patient in distress. As a predator, you will find it hard not to take advantage of a weakened human, especially if they are injured and bleeding already. I'll say it again. I think it might be an impossible goal to set for yourself, my dear."

"I'm a paramedic, James. I didn't stop being that in my soul, in my core, just because I became a vampire. I still want to help people, and that desire is stronger than my desire to feed on my patients. I'm sure of it."

It was James' turn to take in a breath and let out a sigh. She knew he was conflicted. He would do anything for her; she was confident of that much. The challenge he was facing now was that he didn't believe it was possible for her to do this. He couldn't read her determination or her desire to reclaim some part of who and what she was before the change. She was used to this. She had been in a position to prove her commitment to doing the job before. Many instructors in the fire academy doubted her ability to do the job, to live up to the physical and psychological demands of the job because she was a woman. She had proved them all wrong. It was time to prove James' fears wrong, too.

"Prepare me and give me the test. You'll see."

Chapter 4

Brynne felt the sweat beading on her forehead as Celeste came into the building's clean room. She discovered that every modern vampire coven had at least one of these set up in their stronghold. It was the place they tested the newly turned to see if they could be trusted out among the human community unchaperoned. Brynne looked around the tiled room taking it in again as she had the first time she was here a week before. It was about ten feet square and tiled like a bathroom would be. There was a drain in the center of the floor, and the tile on the walls extended up to cover the ceiling. She wondered what the human contractors must have thought such a room was for when they were building the place.

"Ready to try again?" Celeste asked in her smooth southern drawl. Brynne thought the redhead laid the southern belle act on a little thick since it had been over a hundred fifty years since James turned the young southern girl in the midst of the Civil War. She became James' assistant since soon after that, and she now managed most of his substantial assets around the world.

Brynne nodded. "I guess so."

"There's no guessing about this, honey. If you don't think you're ready to try again, don't force it. Every time you backslide, it becomes harder to come back in here and go through the process of acclimation to blood again. Some vampires never quite get the hang of it and have to be watched whenever they are around humans and other sources of fresh blood."

Brynne shook her head. "I'm ready to try again," she affirmed. "I just don't understand why it's so hard for me to move past this."

"There's no shame in it. It takes time to gain control over all the changes your body has gone through. You're stronger and faster than you've ever been before, certainly stronger than any human out there. Your new vampire self knows you're the predator in the room and wants to assert that position."

"But I'm not like that. I'm a healer, not a killer." Brynne said it even though her recent string of failures in this room every day for a week proved otherwise. Lord, she could still feel the rush of pure joy she felt when she pounced on that poor lamb when Celeste had opened a vein in its neck. Brynne couldn't help herself. She had to have the blood, even though it wasn't human. The fresh coppery smell and taste in the air overwhelmed her control. When she leaped on the poor animal, she threw the metal chair in which she was sitting back against the wall behind her so hard it chipped the tiles.

"Brynne, honey, this is a process, a journey to reach a point of control over your inner nature. You can't rush it. Every one of us had to overcome it in our early days after our transformation."

"I know that I can master this, Celeste. I just need to force myself to remember who I am."

Celeste's voice turned uncharacteristically stern. "What you are is a vampire, Brynne. You're not the same Brynne Garvey you were before the incident at Sensations. That version of you died the night Mike Farver shot you. You have to look at it like the former you died there. It is best to put all of it behind you and move forward in your new life." Celeste's voice softened again. "I understand how you feel, I really do. You just have to remember that you can't go back to your past."

"I've never failed at anything I've ever tried to do before. I won't accept failure here."

"Don't think of it as a failure. It might just be too soon to try this. You wouldn't try to run a marathon back when you were a human without the proper training and preparation, would you?"

Brynne shook her head. She knew where Celeste was headed with this.

"Look, Celeste, I see what you're saying. The problem is I think I'm ready to push through this. I can't keep spending every day locked up in the penthouse here without going out and doing something constructive with my life. I have to live my life, even this life."

"You don't want to rush this. That's all I'm saying. I don't think you'd do well if you had a relapse and killed someone."

"But I won't, I can't kill someone. It's not in my nature."

Celeste's voice became stern and hard as ice. "That's a lie. It's not only in your nature; it's your only nature now. I know. I've had more than one relapse since I was turned. What would you do if you killed Dean or one of the other paramedics? What if you managed to turn them into a vampire like yourself by accident?"

"That won't happen. I …"

Celeste interrupted her. "You don't know that. I didn't think I'd attack the people I loved either. In the end, I not only killed my older brother, I also turned him, and he didn't take well to the transformation. He never got over his bloodlust. Eventually, James had to put him down." Celeste held her gaze for a moment before continuing. Brynne could see tears welling up in her eyes. "They had to put him down like a rabid dog because he couldn't stop killing people and it risked exposing all of us."

Brynne had never heard that story before. She thought about what would happen if that happened to Dean, or Brook, or Tammy, or any of the paramedics at the ambulance station she had called her family for so long. It would devastate her. She thought back to the last failure here in the testing chamber. She thought she had mastered the feelings that overcame her the last time a few days before. Brynne stared at the redheaded vampire.

"I'm ready to go again. I have figured out what went wrong."

"Alright, honey. We'll start just as we did each time before. Building slowly on small successes until we get to the point where you can't go any further by your admission, or you fail in your control over your predator urges."

Brynne nodded, and Celeste went to a metal table in the corner. Lifting a white towel covering the table, she saw the other vampire pick up a white ceramic mug and a bag of warm blood. The bag was still sealed, and Brynne could smell nothing from it but disinfectant and the ever-present perfume that was Celeste's favorite fragrance.

Celeste came over and handed Brynne the mug. She took it and held it while Celeste pierced the bag's port with a large sixty-milliliter syringe drawing a substantial amount of blood into the chamber. Withdrawing the syringe's needle from the rubber port, Celeste set the bag down and then removed the needle from the syringe with a twist, dropping the needle in a sharps container there for that purpose. As soon as Celeste removed the needle from the end of the syringe, Brynne caught a faint scent of blood just from the tiny amount exposed to the air at the opening of the syringe. She felt the familiar urge to feed but fought it down. Brynne was determined to do this.

Celeste returned to where she still held the white mug and, depressing the syringe, she deposited about half of the contents into the mug. The warm blood splashed in the mug and the detection of the stronger scent cause Brynne to feel the hair on her neck rise.

The redhead stood for a moment watching Brynne struggle not to drink the blood in the mug. She had not fed since the night before. The test was more robust and reliable when the subject was hungry, Brynne knew. She wanted to drink, just a sip, but she fought back the urges again. She looked at Celeste and managed a smile. This was working.

Celeste smiled back and brought the end of the syringe up to her mouth, her tongue flicking out and taking a drop of fresh blood from where it perched on the end of the syringe. Brynne felt every muscle in her body tense.

"Mmmmm, A positive and a woman, too. Your favorite, right?" Celeste said holding the end of the syringe out to Brynne, only a few inches from her mouth. "Want a taste? It's delicious."

Brynne suppressed a growl starting deep in her throat. She cursed silently. There was no doubt that Celeste heard it. She saw the smile spread across the other woman's face. Did she have to enjoy this so much? Brynne cursed again and then met her examiner's eyes.

"No, thank you. I'll wait," Brynne managed to say with only a slight quaver in her voice.

Celeste shrugged. "Suit yourself. But you really should experience how good it smells."

Taking the syringe, she squeezed a drop of blood on her finger and reached out to dab it on Brynne's cheeks. Some of it dripped down past the corner of her mouth. God, she wanted more than anything to flick her tongue out and catch the drip as it went past the corner of her lips. Somehow, with a supreme effort, Brynne resisted. To do so would be to fail the test. She would not fail this time. She knew it with every fiber of her being.

"Excellent, Brynne. I thought that would get you. Someone did that to me during my testing, and I failed several times to avoid the dripping deliciousness passing my lips. Maybe if I turn around so I can't see, you'll cheat a little." Celeste turned her back but then spun back to watch her. Brynne smiled an actual smile this time. She hadn't fallen for that little trick, either.

"Alright, honey, let's try out the big guns, shall we?"

Brynne nodded. She watched as Celeste took her phone out and tapped a message into it. The redheaded vampire turned and watched Brynne while she idly sipped on the blood from the syringe, pressing the plunger a little each time to squirt a bit onto her extended tongue the way a child might catch icing from a cake decorating tube. She smiled as she swallowed the blood. Brynne was starting to hate that smile. It meant she had more ideas to tempt Brynne in that devious mind.

The door opened, and a woman led a small goat on a rope into the room. The woman was a vampire, too. Her chosen name was Coda; at least that was what everyone called her.

"Here's the next stage. How's she doing?" Coda asked Celeste as if Brynne wasn't even there.

"Surprisingly well, considering yesterday's failure. We'll see how our dear Brynne does next. Are you still alive in the office pool?"

"Yep. I have nine days before she gives up. Don't let up on her, okay?" Coda said.

Had they created an office pool on her success or failure? That wasn't fair. The thought of people betting against her angered Brynne. She felt the beginnings of the loss of control and fought to get ahead of her feelings again. Any strong emotion could undermine her determination to get through this, causing an opening for her inner nature to escape. She'd have to take the matter of the betting pool up with them later.

Celeste took the goat's lead rope from Coda and smiled. "I never let up. You know that. No one gets a pass from me, especially this one."

Coda shot Brynne a wicked grin and left them, pulling the door shut behind her. Brynne steeled herself for what came next. She didn't want to hurt anyone or anything with her newfound hunger. The presence of the goat told her what was to come next and she thought she was ready for it.

Celeste picked up a small surgical steel blade from the table and held it up to the goat's neck. Brynne watched as she held the knife next to the creature's external jugular vein. With a small flick and a bleating yelp from the goat, Celeste cut a quarter-inch gash in the animal's neck.

Blood flowed freely in the room from a living, beating heart for the first time today. Brynne felt the powerful urge to charge across the room and drink the blood, to savor the coppery smell and taste as she sank her fangs in and opened more vessels deeper in the creature's neck. Her fists clenched and she held her back rigid as she forced herself to remain in the chair this time. After a moment, Brynne regained enough control to allow herself a tiny smile. She had done it. She had resisted.

"Very well done, Brynne. You did it," Celeste congratulated her.

"I did, didn't I?" Brynne was filled with pride as she contemplated the hard work and control it took to resist the bloodlust that filled her, even now. The blood was still flowing in a trickle down the goat's neck and splashing on the floor. Brynne felt the pull to drink but resisted and pushed it down even deeper. She could do this. She looked up at Celeste.

"Thank you, Celeste. I couldn't have made it without your help and advice." Brynne got up and crossed to her examiner. She'd done it.

"Oh, think nothing of it, honey. It was the least I could do."

The older vampire never broke eye contact as she spoke. Her hand swung down and slashed open the goat's entire throat. A splash of fresh arterial blood from the animal's deep carotid arteries sprayed across Brynne's chest and face. Before she was fully aware of what happened, the new vampire was on her knees with her mouth latched onto the broad gash in the struggling goat's neck. Brynne buried her fangs in the hairy flesh, and her tongue worked to suck the life-giving fluid pumping out of the creature's failing heart. She couldn't stop herself no matter how she tried to regain control.

Brynne felt Celeste looking down at her pupil, the pupil who knelt at her feet in a pool of goat's blood. The red locks of hair swayed as she shook her head.

"So close, honey. So close."

Chapter 5

Dean checked his watch at the end of his shift as he restocked the ambulance's drug bag with fresh medications to replace those he'd used on the runs that day. Barry was emptying the trash and wiping down the interior before Brook and Tammy's arrival to take over for the night shift. It had been a long week since the first zombie attack. There had been one or two new zombie attack calls each night requiring their rapid response and a health department quarantine until all those affected could be inoculated with the Sodium Benzoate solution.

The police were still no closer to discovering who was creating the new zombies or how it was being done. O'Malley had been at the scene today for their call. This one was different in that it took place in the daytime; though it was likely the zombie was turned sometime the night before. Someone had killed and then transformed the night watchman at the local library branch overnight. No one found him until they opened up the branch for the toddler story hour the next morning. That had been chaos. The security guard-turned-zombie bit many mothers and young children.

Officer O'Malley had it right when he asked, "What kind of creep targets little kids and their moms?"

Dean agreed with the portly officer. This one was pretty scary. He never wanted to treat a child zombie, but they had come too close to that today. The whole Unusual community was upset about it. If the zombie threat became widespread and word about the rest of the Unusuals living among them got out to the general public, it would be pandemonium and possibly the start of a new race war between humans and their Unusual neighbors. That couldn't happen.

Their shift was almost finished, and then he was supposed to pick up Jaz at her new offices downtown at police headquarters. She was his almost girlfriend though they still hadn't gone on a real date. They'd been forced together when their future teenaged daughter returned to the past to help them on a quest. Now the daughter was back where she belonged, and the two of them were trying to see if their destined romance was going to happen.

Jaz was at the police headquarters because she'd been doing consulting work for the Elk City Police Department on the attacks. Her family had a specialty in tracking this sort of thing down, Dean admitted. She was the last in a long line of Hunters, and the Errington clan was very well known in the Unusual community. He hoped she didn't have to go on some hunter rampage when all was said and done. His few Unusual friends had almost gotten used to having her around with him on a regular basis. Maybe they'd forgotten she was the leader of a Hunter Clan. That would all change if an open war between humans and Unusuals started.

If nothing else, that was reason enough to work hard to find a way to stop it from happening. Things were progressing on that front. James had called a briefing for all his various resources in the Unusual community for later that evening, and he had invited Dean. He had been surprised when the Elk City vampire lord extended his invitation to Jaz.

"Bring the Errington woman if she'll come along. I'd appreciate her input on this, as well," James had said.

Just as surprising to Dean was Jaz's answer when he told her about it over the phone.

"Of course I'll come along. This is serious business, and we all have to work together to figure out the source of the problem before it's too late for all of us."

This was kind of like dogs and cats living and playing together in his eyes, but he was glad to see his two groups of friends willing to get along for the greater good. Still, it wasn't likely to go too far. He pictured James and Jaz playing a round of poker together and laughed aloud. Barry poked his head from the back of the ambulance.

"What's so funny, Dean?"

"Oh, nothing. I was just thinking about how weird the proposed partnership between Jaz and my friends at the Nightwing building is going to be. They are starting off surprisingly well."

"That's a good thing, right?"

"I guess so," Dean concluded. "We'll see what happens if things escalate with the zombie attacks. How's the restocking coming in there?"

"Almost finished," Barry answered.

"Good." Dean checked his watch. "I'm going into the break room. Put this bag away for me." He handed up the drug bag, now fully stocked with another shift's worth of supplies.

Dean got into the break room just in time to see Tammy walk in. Brook had already arrived and was logging into the computer system to check her inbox for the beginning of their shift.

"We had another attack today. This one was at the public library branch on Elm downtown," Dean told the two of them. He relayed the story of what happened while he gathered up his belongings.

"Wow, that must have been a mess. I hate having to treat kids," Tammy said. "It reminds me of my own kids too much."

"I don't have children yet, and I don't like it either," Dean replied.

"What about that teenage daughter of yours? Doesn't she count?" Brook asked.

"She doesn't count because she is from the future so technically she hasn't been born yet. I think I'll feel a lot differently about it when I have little ones like Tammy does."

Dean slid on his coat and shouldered his backpack. "I'm going to scoot. Barry is finishing up things in the ambulance."

"Ooo, gotta hot date tonight?" Brook jeered.

"More work is more like it, Brook. James wants a full report on everything we all know. He even invited Jaz to come by and lend her advice."

"Wow," Tammy said. "He must be worried about the current situation to invite the Errington heir in for this planning session. I know he's more comfortable with her since the two of you connected but the rest of his management team must be pretty wary of her."

Dean nodded. "They are. I don't think they'd come into the same room with her at all if James didn't order them to do it. I keep hoping they'll get over it. Jaz has promised not to go after anyone without James' say so while the zombie thing is happening. That should be good enough."

"Do you believe her?"

"I do, though I get your meaning. I guess there's a lot of cultural bias and history to overcome before everyone plays nice together," Dean said.

"Well go and pick up your date for the big summit tonight," Tammy ordered. "Make sure you fill us in on what you learn in the morning when you come back for work tomorrow."

"Will do," Dean replied. He headed out into the parking lot to get his truck and go pick up Jaz.

HE PULLED up in front of the police headquarters building downtown about an hour later. He had gone home and showered and changed before going to get Jaz. He saw her standing on the steps of the station talking to a few officers. Her long blonde hair was pulled back into a ponytail and threaded through the back of her black Errington baseball cap. She was wearing a pair of black jeans and a white t-shirt with the Errington Security logo on the chest. Over that, she wore a black leather jacket that surely hid her

Glock and extra magazines she always carried with her in a shoulder holster. Given the nature of the current attacks, he was surprised she didn't have her Katana with her. She must have guessed a sword across her back would draw too much attention when she walked in and out of the police building and past the reporters gathered for the daily press briefings.

She looked over as he pulled up and smiled at him across the plaza before she waved goodbye to the group of officers. Jaz jogged down the steps and across the broad pavement to where Dean was pulled up. He watched her every move, appreciating how beautiful she was in a girl-next-door kind of way. They had agreed to go slow with their budding relationship despite the fact that they found out they were destined to be together. Having contact with an unknown daughter from the future did that to a couple. He shook his head and gave a wry chuckle. Nothing like a little pressure about having children early in a couple's courtship to make things awkward.

Jaz jumped in the passenger side of Dean's pickup truck and gave a sigh of relief.

"I'm glad to be out of there."

"Rough day at the office, Jaz?" Dean asked shooting her a smile as he drove across town towards the Nightwing building.

"The police chief and all his senior commanders kept looking at me as if I had some sort of magic bullet to fix everything. I have tried to tell them from the beginning that actual police investigative work was going to be essential to getting to the bottom of this zombie crisis. They all think it's just a matter of me giving them the mythical answer to their problems."

"You do remember we are heading over to James' penthouse to have a dinner meeting about all those same questions, right?"

Jaz waved a hand, dismissing his question. "That's different. James and Rudy know my capabilities and don't expect me to solve this thing overnight. Heck, they don't necessarily want me in the middle of this at all."

"That's not true. James extended a personal invite for you to attend," Dean explained. "I didn't ask for you to come along."

"You're right. I should relax," Jaz said. She blew out a long breath. "James has been surprisingly understanding. He has invited me, a Hunter Clan leader, into his home. That's a level of trust that means something, I guess."

"I think so, too, for what it's worth. Besides, you're not the same hunter who showed up here six months ago. I like that."

Dean reached over and gave her hand a squeeze where it rested on the seat next to him. She returned the squeeze, and he got a sudden warm feeling inside. He liked Jaz a lot, and he was hoping to start going on some regular dates for a change rather than attending war-room sessions and demon-hunting raids with her.

"There's good news. I'm done with physical therapy. I might have a slight hitch in my step for a while longer, but if I keep doing my exercises, the therapist said I should be back to normal."

"That's excellent news," Dean agreed.

Jaz had been recovering from a long convalescence after she was nearly killed by a demon lord in human form. The demon-possessed man broke her leg in several places in the process of incapacitating her while they were trying to rescue their kidnapped daughter. Only Dean's surprise discovery that he had the power to command demons had ended up saving them at all. He still didn't know why he had those powers or from where they came.

"Yeah, I'm glad to be rid of the wheelchair, the walker, the cane, and all the doctor's visits," Jaz said with relief. "I'm not used to having to stay on the sidelines like that."

"The good news is, you used the extra time on your hands to restart your family's security business and start rebuilding your headquarters. I know you were thinking of hiring some new opera-tives. How's that going?"

"Better. The family has always had good connections with the Feds and the Marshal's Service in particular. We always have a few from their Unusual investigations and apprehension division that want to come work for us after their twenty years of government service. In fact, I just hired the soon-to-be former assistant director from that division to be the Errington chief operating officer. He starts in a few weeks when his retirement is official."

"That's excellent news. Is he being brought in on this case?"

Dean asked. Having that level of former deputy marshal working on the situation would bring some big time national attention to the problem here in Elk City. He wasn't sure James would like that, though.

"No, I've already got him focused on building up our international operations to the level they were when my dad and mom were running things. Our contracts fell through soon after they died. I just couldn't manage things as well as they did after it all fell apart. I've always been a field operative, so it's better to have him run the day-to-day operations and let me focus on CEO stuff."

"Oh, like our little problem here in Elk City?"

"Hey, it's my home now, too. Call it my civic duty."

They both laughed at the irony of that as he drove up to the gate to the underground garage beneath the Nightwing building. A quick swipe of his keycard on the panel and they drove beneath the raised gate and headed inside to park. The rest of the gang was waiting for them upstairs.

Chapter 6

Dean and Jaz stepped off the elevator on the penthouse level and almost bumped into Celeste as she was stepping on. She seemed preoccupied with something on her phone.

"Oh, sorry, guys," she said, stepping back to let them exit first.

"No worries, Celeste," Dean answered. "Hey, is everything alright? You look concerned about something."

"I'm good," the redheaded vampire replied. "Just something came up that I need to take care of. I'm sorry I'm going to miss the meeting. James will fill me in when I get back."

Dean and Jaz stepped aside as she jumped on the elevator just as the doors were closing. He had never seen her distracted like that before. Celeste always seemed so composed and on top of things here at Nightwing Enterprises. He shrugged and went over to ring the bell at the double doors to the penthouse apartment. They swung open to reveal Rudy, James' head of security and the were-wolf pack leader in the Elk City region.

"Hey, Dean. Hello, Ms. Errington. Please come in."

"Please, Rudy. Call me Jaz. We have to have a good working relationship. We're on the same side here," Jaz said as she and Dean walked into the apartment's foyer.

"Uh, yes," Rudy stammered. "I guess that's true, Ms - uh - Jaz." Rudy gave half a smile. "I guess I need to work on that."

Dean shrugged and looked at Jaz. He supposed that was the best it was going to get for now.

"Where's dinner. I'm famished," Dean stepped in to relieve some tension as he walked into the large open floor plan that was James and Brynne's apartment. It sat high atop the Elk City skyline, looking out over the city below when the sun went down. The sun had already started setting so soon the blackout shutters would be opened, and they would have a spectacular view of the city's lights around them. He saw the dining area table set up for six, but only James was in sight.

"It's on its way up from the restaurant kitchens downstairs," James said as he came over to shake Dean's hand. "I'm afraid it's just the four of us for dinner. Brynne had a setback today in her training and won't be joining us. She is downstairs working on something else according to Celeste."

Dean wondered what that was all about. He knew something about Brynne's training to overcome her bloodlust, but he thought she was past the point where she couldn't be around humans unrestrained. He pondered it a bit while James took Jaz' extended hand and bowed low over it, brushing the back of her hand with his lips. Dean quirked an eyebrow at that greeting.

"Ms. Errington. I'm very glad you were able to join us tonight," James said in a formal greeting. "I am very interested in seeing what you have to say about the matters we are currently dealing with here in Elk City."

"She prefers to be called 'Jaz,' boss," Rudy corrected. "I mean, it's not like she's the head of an entire clan trying to kill us all."

James shot Rudy a stern glance. "That will be enough of that, Rudy. She is a guest in my home, and I'll not have any insult perpetrated against her." He returned his attention to his special guest. "I apologize for the conduct of my friend. If you prefer to be called Jaz, then Jaz it is, as long as you call me James in return."

"Agreed, James," Jaz said as she looked around. "You have a

lovely home here. It's surprisingly modern. I would have expected …"

"What? You thought I'd have old-world style antiques and creepy relics and weapons everywhere?" the vampire lord replied.

"Well, yes. That has been my experience with, the other ancients I have, uh, encountered," Jaz responded.

"I came to the new world a long time ago to get away from all that. I pride myself on staying up with the times, as well as current fashions and trends."

"It shows. I like it," Jaz complimented, nodding as she looked around the professionally decorated home.

Dean was curious about what everyone had discovered about the problem they faced with the zombies. He wanted to get down to business, but he understood the need to observe the pleasantries, as superficial as they were. This session was to share that information so everyone could be on the same page about how they responded to the threat.

The doors behind him opened and a team of waiters and waitresses came in rolling carts with covered serving dishes. James pointed to the table.

"I'm hungry, how about we sit down and start our meeting while the food is brought up," he suggested.

"You don't have to ask me twice," Dean said. The others laughed and joined him as he sat down at the table. It was set for six, which reminded him of Brynne's absence and Celeste's departure on their arrival.

"I hope Brynne is alright, James." Dean gestured to the empty place settings. "Will we see her at all?"

"I don't think so. To be honest, we are all a little frustrated with the things going on right now, Brynne included. She wants to get back on the street as a paramedic and has been pushing her training beyond normal limits in an effort to do that. That causes some tension when she fails one of the tests Celeste planned for her."

"You have Celeste doing the training?" Dean asked.

"Yes. It makes more sense to have her do it. Then it doesn't seem so personal," James explained. "Brynne had another setback today. Celeste went to see what she could do to manage it with her. I know she's sorry she can't be here to see you, but I'll convey your thoughts on her behalf to her."

There was an awkward pause following James' explanation of Brynne and Celeste's whereabouts. Rudy cleared his throat and changed the subject.

"I'm interested in what you might have discovered through your interactions with the police investigation into the zombie situation, Jaz."

She gave him a startled look as she was dishing up a plate of food from the buffet line staffed by the waiters. "I would have thought you had your own resources inside the police station, Rudy. You are James' head of security after all."

"I do, but I want to compare notes with what I'm seeing and I'm also interested in seeing what your take on the whole situation is."

Jaz settled herself in a chair with a plateful of food. "To be honest, I'm not that impressed with the local authorities' response to the current threat. They are in reaction mode only and haven't implemented more than the most basic investigation so far."

Rudy nodded. "That's been my impression. It's like they want us to come up with a solution solely on our own and not in concert with them. I keep telling them this is a joint problem but they do not see it that way. My sources say that internally they're calling this an 'Unusual problem' which bothers me on several levels."

"I've heard that response from several top officials in the department," Jaz said. "I've also tried to point out to them how this could spell out a bigger issue than just a few zombie bites. I don't think they realize the threat to public safety and health if just one of these attacks breaks containment."

Dean was intrigued. Containment was something with which he and his paramedic colleagues at Station U were involved. He saw the danger there, too. It brought up a question of his own.

"Have they gotten any closer to finding a source for the zombies? From everything I've been able to piece together from the patient care reports, none of them are related in any way so it's not like this is some infectious disease outbreak or something."

Jaz shook her head. "That is where they are dropping the ball in my estimation. Some things need doing, and it looks like I'm the only one doing them."

"Like what?" James asked.

"Like taking video surveillance footage from around the scenes where all the incidents occurred and running some basic facial recognition software on them. It would help to identify any potential known threats or individuals associated with the outbreaks. A person is doing this somehow, maybe a patient zero, and we need to identify them. We can also cross-reference the faces after the software completes its cycle. That way we can see if the same face shows up multiple times, which would also be a key indicator if there was such a person involved."

Rudy put his fork down and looked at Jaz. "That all sounds like pretty sophisticated stuff. Maybe the local police department doesn't have the resources to do it."

"They haven't even tried," she replied. "I finally got fed up and located all the videos myself. I downloaded all the videos to my laptop. I'm hoping to get a match from the databases our company has put together. That said, it's not as complete or sophisticated as the software the FBI uses. That requires the local law enforcement team's involvement. They must send in a formal request for a resource allocation. Given the challenges associated with an outbreak like this, I think it would be approved immediately by the FBI."

"I agree," Rudy said. "I can't see the feds wanting this to spread beyond Elk City if it can be helped."

"I'm not sure they know about it," Jaz said. All three of them looked at her in shock. They knew that local news wasn't covering anything, but that was normal when it came to incidents involving Unusuals. "I get the feeling that the mayor and the chief are both trying to keep a lid on this getting out beyond the city's resources for some reason."

"So we are literally on our own here," James said. "The police won't do a real investigation, and the leaders won't call for help. That's just peachy."

Rudy asked Jaz a question.

"Where did all the video you're testing come from?"

"It all came from the locations associated with the outbreaks. The first is from the funeral home's internal security cameras. I have other footage from the city's traffic cams, too. It's all in there."

"How long do you think it'll take to run through the whole process?" Rudy asked. "Celeste might be able to help. I think she could speed it up with the resources here at Nightwing if you wanted to share the data."

"I have my laptop running initial facial comparison first from all the videos. That's to see if the same person pops up at more than one of the locations. It's in my bag over there. I never leave it alone. It's running even when closed up and will ping my phone when completed. Which reminds me, James, may I plug in and keep the battery charged up while we eat?"

"Certainly," their host said. "Just use the power strip under my desk over there." He pointed to a work area setup on the other side of the room.

Jaz took another bite the pasta dish she was eating and got up to plug in her laptop.

Dean looked at Rudy.

"What about you guys?" Dean asked. "Have you any ideas about what could be causing the outbreaks? We've been reading all the lore in our library at the station but can't seem to come up with anything. They all start the same. A recently deceased corpse animates and goes all 'Night of the Living Dead' on people nearby, usually at a funeral or medical facility like a nursing home. Then once we contain things, they seem to come around and act like the sentient zombies we're used to. They're a little surprised at their change in circumstances but otherwise acting normal."

Both James and Rudy shook their heads. James lifted his cup of fresh blood and sipped before he answered. "We're as stumped as you are. For a zombie to act the way we've seen, there usually needs to be a sorcerous individual around controlling them to override their normal human natures. From everything we've been able to determine, there's nothing connecting the various victims to any common source. They're all different."

A chime sounded from across the room where Jaz was looking at her laptop screen. Dean looked over in her direction.

"What was that, Jaz?"

"The program stopped running because it found a match. There's a video match between the same guy at both the first funeral home video recording and on the library's internal cameras from earlier today."

"Really?" Dean and James said as one. They got up and went over to the desk. Rudy beat them there. He saw the face on the two images first, captured side by side.

"Well, shit."

James walked around and looked over his second's shoulder. "An apt exclamation, my friend," the vampire lord said as he saw the images. "This explains a lot. It opens up a lot more questions as well."

Dean saw the screen last of all and gave a curse under his breath, too. Jaz looked at all three of their faces and then back at the screen. She looked puzzled.

"Obviously you all recognize the guy," she said. "Care to fill a gal in?"

James gave her a surprised look.

"I'm surprised you don't recognize him. Don't you all have your own database of most-wanted or something like that?"

"I haven't run the second recognition software algorithm on the database; just the video comparison program has run so far."

"There's no need to run the other software," Dean said. "That, Jaz, is Errington public enemy number one. That's Artur Torrence."

Chapter 7

Jaz stared at the laptop screen for what seemed like an eternity. She was oblivious to the others in the room, focusing her entire attention on the screen. She wanted to take as much time as she needed to memorize every feature and nuance of that face so she'd recognize it again. This wasn't just the creature who had destroyed so many Errington clan lives over a thousand years before; he was the one who had ordered her entire family killed in the bombing of their headquarters less than a year before. He'd succeeded in killing everyone but herself. The Errington database probably had a picture or some sort of representation of him in the files some-where. She'd never paid much attention to that aspect of her investi-gation, instead of trying to track him down in her free time via a paper trail of some sort. Now he had come back to Elk City to operate his schemes again, right under her very nose.

She let loose a feral growl low in her throat that got a reaction from both of the Unusuals in the penthouse, though it was too quiet for Dean's human ears to pick up. She knew that both Rudy and James heard it because they both shot looks in her direction when she did it. This was the man responsible for so much hurt, not just in her life, but in countless other lives over the years. Erringtons had been tracking and hunting this individual for centuries, ever since the newly turned vampire had rampaged through their village, killing people for sport and not just to feed. It was then that their earliest hunters were commissioned and given their task of tracking the one true enemy of their clan.

She knew that Artur had been involved in so much here in Elk City over the years, especially in the last few. He had tried to overthrow James as the overlord of the Elk City region time and again. Most recently, he'd opened a portal to hell itself to take and destroy the Eldara angel Ashley Moore who had also long been a thorn in his side if Jaz' ancestors' journals were correct. Now he was back to do what?

"What the hell's he doing back here?" She had said it before she realized she'd spoken aloud.

"He's one who doesn't take well to those he considers lesser beings defying him," James suggested. "I suspect he's back to take revenge against you and Dean for your efforts to oppose his plans."

Jaz turned and looked at the vampire lord. "Dean says you let him stay here the last time he was in town even though he had actively worked to overthrow you in the past?"

James nodded. "You must understand. There are protocols to be followed in our world."

Rudy jumped in to deflect Jaz from his boss. "Better to keep him close where he can't do any overt harm, right? Keep your friends close and your enemies closer."

"If I had him that close, I'd stake him," Jaz said. Dean saw her hand absently pat the pocket of her leather jacket. He had assumed she was carrying her usual firearm load. Did she also have a sharpened stake in that shoulder holster rig somewhere? He was sure Rudy and James noticed the unconscious gesture as well.

"Look, this isn't all bad news," Dean said trying to defuse the situation.

They all turned to look at him as if he were crazy.

"Bear with me here," he said. "Think about it. If we know he's behind all of this then we can start looking for him. We can also make some assumptions about his motives and methods. Let's try and make this an advantage and not a negative. Knowledge is power, right?"

James smiled at him and nodded. "Dean's right. Let us go back and sit and enjoy the rest of our meal while we ponder this development. The presence of Artur back in our city is concerning but, as Dean pointed out, now we know. Come sit."

The four of them returned to the table and sat down. No one did much eating, though. James did finish his mug of blood, but he didn't get up to fetch more. Dean figured he didn't want what he had to get cold. After a few minutes of silence, Jaz pushed back from the table and rose.

"James, I thank you for your hospitality. I hope this continues to be a fruitful collaboration for us all. I need to go and work on some things. This news about Artur has implications I didn't expect."

Dean got up when Jaz did. He was her ride after all. He shrugged at the other two as James and Rudy rose as well.

"You're welcome here anytime, Jaz. I have enjoyed your company and your input into our current problem. Let's work to make sure this collaboration is not just a one-time thing."

Jaz shook hands with James and then Rudy, as well, and started toward the door. Dean shrugged again and waved at the two Unusuals as he followed her out.

THE RIDE back to Jaz's apartment was quiet. Dean put the radio on to fill the void as he drove. Jaz stared out the side window and didn't say anything for the entire ride.

Dean pulled up in front of her building and found a parking spot on the street. He knew what this new revelation must mean to her. Artur was responsible for the deaths of her parents and brothers. The return of the vampire lord opened up wounds for him, too. Artur had been responsible for turning his mentor against him, the deaths of countless people in the Barrens fire, and eventually even took his Ashley away from him. He had moved on from the latter, sort of, but the hurt was still there. This monster had a lot to answer for.

"Jaz, we'll get him. He's made a mistake, and he'll make more. I know it's possible to stop him. We'll use his own overblown self-confidence to catch him, just as we've done in the past."

"You don't understand, Dean. He always gets away. We've been tracking him for centuries through countless encounters where we thought we were close and he's always slipped through our fingers. We've stopped his infernal plans, but in the end, he always manages to get away. What's going to make this time different?"

"Because he's lined up too many enemies in one place this time. He's a fool to come back here and confront us all like this."

She turned to look at him, and he saw the tears welling in her eyes. He reached out for her and pulled her close. She buried her face in his shoulder and returned his embrace. The two of them stayed like that for a while, and Dean savored the closeness, noticing things like the floral scent of her hair and the soft sound of her breathing.

Jaz released the embrace, and Dean let go, too. She wiped her eyes with the back of her hand and twisted the rear-view mirror to look at her reflection in the glow of the streetlights.

"Damn, I don't need to go in there with puffy, red eyes. The doorman will be all curious about my wellbeing, and that's so awkward."

"We can sit out here as long as you like. I've got nowhere else to be right now," Dean offered.

She fished around in her purse and pulled out a pair of aviator's mirrored sunglasses. Dean laughed, and she looked at him.

"What?"

"You're not going to wear them, are you? It's nine o'clock at night."

"If I wear these when I go in, no one will notice I've been crying."

Dean chuckled again. "You're worried about what they'll think about you if you look like you've been crying but you'll go in there looking like some movie star diva, and that's okay. You slay me, Miss Errington."

"You don't think I'll do it?"

"No, I don't," Dean answered.

"Fine. Put this thing in park, and you can come up with me. You'll see. No one will say a word to me as I walk by if I wear these."

Dean turned off the truck and unlocked his door. He climbed out and walked around to her side. She climbed out as he arrived and slid the sunglasses on. Dean could see the reflection of the overhead streetlights in them as she walked past him towards her apartment building's entrance. He fell in behind her and tried hard to look like her security escort. Might as well play it up for their audience, he thought.

The doorman pulled the door open for her as she walked up and nodded without a word as she passed him to enter the lobby. Dean followed with a nod of his own to the man holding the door for the two of them. Jaz had already pushed the elevator button, so there was only a few seconds' wait before the doors opened.

Once they arrived upstairs, Jaz unlocked her apartment door and stepped inside before she flung off the sunglasses and laughed. He liked the way she could be so mercurial. One minute she was a ball of negative emotion about finding the man who'd killed her family, and the next, she was strutting past her doorman like some Hollywood starlet, loving every minute of it. Dean walked the rest of the way into her apartment and shut the door, smiling at her.

"That was fun," Dean admitted.

"I needed that," Jaz replied. She pulled off the baseball cap she wore and let down her ponytail, sliding the elastic hair band over one wrist. Her blonde locks fell past her shoulders.

Dean watched her take off her jacket and hang both it and her ever-present shoulder holster weapons rig up on a coat rack by the door. Dean was struck again by his attraction to her. They were opposites in so many ways, yet that opposition seemed to be part of the appeal. He felt like she filled the gaps in his strengths when they were together. He wondered if she felt the same way.

She started towards the kitchen and looked over her shoulder.

"Do you want something to drink or eat? I thought we could hang out and go over the rest of the video footage tonight and see if Artur pops up in any of the other scenes."

Dean smiled. "That would be great. How about a beer?"

"I've got an excellent local microbrew pale ale, will that do?"

"Perfect."

He followed her into the kitchen and helped her pull together a quick cheese and cracker plate with some grapes to sweeten things up. Jaz handed him a bottle of beer and poured herself a glass of wine. Soon the two of them were seated on the couch with the video surveillance footage air-streaming to the big flatscreen TV via an app on her laptop.

Dean watched as she sipped her wine and scrolled through her footage based on the timestamps from the facial recognition software. At one point a camera showed a woman approach a man they thought was Artur in the parking lot of the first funeral home. She was wearing an orange reflective vest. Dean remembered the health department nurses wearing those same vests as they screened the people at the scene. They watched as she went to a vehicle and drove around to pick Artur up. Then they drove away.

"I wonder who she is?" Dean asked.

"I think I remember a report that one of the health department workers was reported missing a few days after the first event," Jaz said. "There were some who thought she might have become infected."

She started tapping on her computer, searching through her files there. She snapped her fingers as she found what she was looking for.

"Felicity Richards," Jaz said. She tapped a key on her keyboard, and a woman's face, framed by long brunette hair popped up on the flatscreen.

The photo widened out as Jaz manipulated the image and Dean realized it was a picture of her work ID badge. Dean read the accompanying report, now on the screen next to her picture. She was a health department RN who had responded to the first scene that night at the funeral home. Two days later, her co-workers reported her missing after she didn't come to work. A search of her home provided no useful information to the investigating detective. The report said there was no sign of foul play.

He snorted as he read that. Jaz looked his way with an eyebrow quirked up in question.

"I think we found evidence of foul play," Dean replied to the unvoiced question. He pointed at the TV screen. "I've seen the way Artur uses his powers to charm and control his victims. My guess is, she's either dead or undead at this point. The bastard probably got hungry and took a snack home with him."

Jaz went back to tapping on her keyboard. "That's a good thought, Dean. If there's a fresh vampire out there, he'd have to feed her, and he's not shy about leaving bodies behind. If we can find evidence of recent vampire kills, it might help us find a location where he's hiding out."

Dean pulled out his phone. "I can help with that. I'll have Brook run a query on our 911 calls on the Station U ambulance to see if the crews saw any signs of recent victims. She's pretty good at querying the system. I haven't seen anything on my shifts, but I've been on dayshift since the funeral home call. The others might have run into something pertinent without knowing it."

"Excellent idea. You check that while I log into the police database and see if they have seen anything like that."

Dean settled in and sent a few text messages to his work colleagues while Jaz tapped away on the laptop next to him. While it wasn't much of a date, he was enjoying her company, and the feeling seemed to be mutual. Things were progressing in their own strange way, but that appeared to be normal for the two of them, and he didn't want to upset the delicate balance between work and personal attraction that seemed to be happening between them. He was happy at this point to take things slow.

Chapter 8

Artur swallowed a last delicious mouthful of fresh blood as he rolled off the naked woman beneath him. Her sightless, dead eyes still had the startled look in them from when he first started feeding. Across the room, he heard a satisfied sigh as Felicity finished off this victim's boyfriend. The ill-fated college couple had blundered into their little trap when he and Felicity ran into them in a local tavern.

The two vampires had struck up a conversation with the couple and after a few drinks, offered to take them to find some "truly awesome weed," as Felicity put it. She was turning out to be a valuable asset as she was so much better at negotiating this modern world than he was. Where he took things by brute force, she had shown him how a more circumspect approach made more sense.

Felicity also showed remarkable control over her urges for a young vampire, as long as she had fed recently. He liked that sign of strength. He had been tempted just to kill her outright after he fed off her but decided to turn her instead. It had been a while since he'd had a new protégé. So far, it had proven to be the right decision. She had taken to being undead very well and was reacting correctly under his thrall.

Artur looked over at her as she stood up and wiped the blood

"

from around her mouth with the back of her hand. She was a messy eater, but then most youngsters were. It took a certain sense of control and finesse not to rip into a throat but rather to gently puncture the vessels beneath the skin and open them just enough to ensure a constant flow. That would come in time. Artur shrugged. In the meantime, let her have her fun.

Felicity giggled, standing there naked as she looked at the torn mess in both of the boy's thighs where she had fed.

"I never thought of taking blood from there," she giggled. "It feels so much more naughty that way."

"Yes, my dear. But then, that's what makes what we do so much fun, right?" Artur asked.

Felicity nodded and padded across the room to pull on her robe.

"Are we going to dispose of these two the same way we did the last one?"

"I think that's best. Eventually, the authorities will start finding the bodies and search for the source of the attacks. Once the dolts realize what it is they're seeing and realize it's a collection of freshly killed bodies that keep showing up, that is."

"Tell me again why we're leaving them in a dumpster close to that big building downtown?"

"Because, my dear, if fresh bodies start showing up just outside of our esteemed local leader's humble abode in the Nightwing building, the humans will have to start asking if he's harboring a killer," Artur said. He paused a moment and savored the deliciousness of his plan to destroy James Lee once and for all. "Couple that with the rest of my plans and you end up with the perfect crime. We'll hurt both James Lee and Dean Flynn at once by implicating someone they both care about."

Artur started towards the bathroom. He needed a shower.

"Come, join me and if you're lucky, I'll tell you more secrets about what I have planned for the humans of Elk City."

Felicity cooed and shook off her robe as she followed her master into the bathroom. She pulled the door closed behind her leaving the two corpses alone in the darkened bedroom with a catatonic Brynne Garvey seated in the corner.

. . .

———

BRYNNE AWAKENED and didn't immediately know where she was. She looked around at the concrete walls and exposed pipes running along the ceiling overhead and assumed it was some sort of basement or underground room. There was an open door leading out, and Brynne stood up, pausing a moment because she felt a little unsteady on her feet. Brynne leaned against the wall for a moment until she regained her balance.

Taking a few steps, she walked through the door and into an underground garage. As soon as she turned the corner, she recognized which garage it was. She was in the basement of the Nightwing building, though she couldn't remember coming down here. In fact, the last thing she remembered was failing her latest test with Celeste and going back to her rooms in the penthouse. While she spent most of her time with James, he had set up a personal space for her within the apartment so she could have some time to herself. Somehow, she must have blacked out and ended up down here. She had a massive headache, too. Maybe it was an allergy to goat's blood. That stuff wasn't the best-tasting blood she'd ever had. It was gamey and, coupled with the animal's smell she wondered why she'd drunk it all.

As she approached the elevator to return upstairs, she noticed her blood-covered T-shirt for the first time in her reflection in the polished steel elevator doors. That thing about vampires and not having reflections was a myth, though Brynne now wished it were true. She looked down in horror and scrubbed a hand across her shirt. It had dried which meant she'd fed somewhere and ended up back here before falling asleep. But what had she fed on? Brynne pulled out her phone and looked at it. It was almost morning. She shook her head again at the lost time and tapped in a number. The person on the other end picked up right away.

"Celeste, I think I'm in trouble."

"Where are you?" The other vampire asked her. "I've been looking for you all night, ever since the nighttime guard called upstairs to say you'd told him you were going out. He tried to stop you, but you pushed him down and left the building."

"I left the building?" Brynne thought of the implications of that considering the blood all over her and being unable to remember anything of the night before. "OhmyGod, OhmyGod, OhmyGod, Celeste. I think I've killed someone."

"Where are you, Brynne? I'll come get you. Don't move."

"I'm downstairs. I'm here in the building, in the garage."

"Alright honey, don't move," Celeste said. "I'm coming right down."

The phone disconnected before Brynne could finish saying, "I'm not going anywhere."

A few minutes later, the always well-dressed Celeste stepped off the elevator and stopped in shock as she took in Brynne's appearance.

"Great," Brynne said. "I was hoping I didn't look as bad as my reflection said I did."

"Brynne, honey, where have you been? You look like you've been in a slaughter house."

"That's the problem, Celeste. I don't know." She pointed to the storeroom in the corner. "I woke up in the room over there dressed like this and with literally no memory of the last twelve hours."

"What's the last thing your remember?" Celeste asked.

"I remember being in my room upstairs. I was pissed off about failing the test earlier. I changed my clothes and lay down on my bed. I remember staring at the ceiling and feeling out of sorts that I couldn't do better." She looked down at her bloody shirt and shrugged. "The next thing I remember, I woke up looking like this. Just tell me I killed another goat and not something worse."

Celeste shook her head with a grim smile. "That's human blood, honey. I can smell it from here."

Brynne started shaking with tremors as she realized what she must have done during her blackout. Tears welled in her eyes. She felt like a monster.

"We have to find out who it was," Brynne said, casting frantic glances around the underground garage, searching for signs of a body or a bloody trail - anything. "Maybe they're nearby. They might not be dead. We could save them."

"Nope, you're not going anywhere but straight upstairs to clean up," Celeste said.

"I can't go up to the apartment like this. James will know something is wrong."

"Exactly why you're coming up to my apartment first. We'll get you cleaned up and try and clear your head. Maybe you'll remember something about what happened."

The older vampire led Brynne to the elevator with a helpful arm around her shoulders. Brynne tilted her head to one side and laid it on Celeste's shoulder. She was devastated by what she had done and followed along with the other woman's instructions without thinking.

Soon she found herself in Celeste's shower, scrubbing the crusted and caked-on blood from her face, neck, chest, and arms. Celeste had come in to take her bloody clothes from the bathroom floor. Brynne assumed she'd dispose of them somewhere. It wouldn't surprise her if James had a medical grade incinerator in the building somewhere.

When she finished in the shower, Brynne got out to find a pair of jeans and a clean black T-shirt. She toweled off and got dressed. While dressing, Brynne heard Celeste talking on the phone in the other room, but she couldn't make out the conversation. She walked out of the bathroom and saw the other woman talking on her cell phone. Celeste held up a hand forestalling Brynne's question while she answered whoever was on the other end of the line.

"Tell the officer I'll be right down to assist him. Thank you for alerting me." She tapped the phone to hang up the call and looked at Brynne.

"You look much better. Do you feel better?"

Brynne nodded. "Who was on the phone?"

"Oh, just a routine investigative request from the police. I have to head downstairs and meet with the officer about it after I take you upstairs."

"What will I tell James?"

"Tell him you and I were out last night together for a girl's night. He won't pry beyond that. James is uncomfortable around feminine topics so leave it at that."

"I don't want to lie to him, Celeste. I have to tell him the truth."

"We don't know the truth. We don't know anything other than you drank blood last night and made a bit of a mess. Let's not borrow trouble. Just do as I say while I do some searching around."

Brynne nodded, but she didn't feel right about the decision. She knew something more had happened than just a messy feeding. Unless someone upended a bottle of fresh blood over her, she'd attacked someone. It was the only explanation for the way she looked when she woke up in the basement.

The two of them left Celeste's apartment and rode up to the penthouse level. When they entered the apartment, James was watching the TV and had on the morning news. He looked up as they entered.

"Nice of you both to make your way home. I hope the evening was fun."

"Um, yeah, it was," Brynne stammered.

James pointed to the TV. "I'm glad you two were together last night. We've got to do some investigating and see if any of our current residents were out alone last night."

"Why?" Celeste asked as she directed Brynne to head back to her rooms.

"Because," James said. "Apparently, someone dumped two bodies in the dumpster in the alley behind our building. It looks like they were attacked by a vamp or maybe a shifter of some sort. We'll know more when our investigators get a look at the bodies. Look into this Celeste. With everything else going on, we need to nip this sort of thing in the bud. If there's a vampire rampaging out there killing people, we need to find them and put them down now. This is our problem to solve."

Brynne froze for a moment as James was talking when she heard about the bodies. Celeste gave her a gentle push between her shoulder blades, and she started moving again.

"I'm already on it," Celeste answered. "There's an investigator from the police downstairs now. I was just coming up with Brynne, and then I was going to head down and follow up on it."

Brynne kept walking as she listened to the conversation receding behind her. She knew what was happening now. They didn't need to look or investigate anything. She was the rampaging vampire that James was talking about. Stepping through her door, she shut the room, blocking off the sounds from the rest of the apartment. Tears started rolling down her cheeks as Brynne contemplated what she'd done. She didn't want to believe it, to believe that she was even capable of such a thing. Brynne thought of herself as a healer, not a killer. She kept telling herself that over and over again. Except it wasn't true.

She sat down in a chair and stared at the blank, white wall, pondering for a long time how she could tell James what she'd done and whether he'd take the actions he said he'd take back in the main room. Would he put her down like a rabid dog? Her sobs overtook her as she drew up her knees to her chest and rocked in the chair while the tears flowed.

Chapter 9

The next morning came early for Dean. He stayed up late the night before at Jaz's looking through video feeds and trying to track down any sign of the missing Felicity Richards. Both he and Jaz spent the night side-by-side working on solving yet another Unusual mystery. It was nice being close to her, but it wasn't leading them any closer to any romantic encounter in Dean's eyes. He needed to remedy that. He knew they had to work on solving the problems of the zombie attacks, but he also had to work on getting Jaz to see him as more than a partner in her investigations. He knew how he felt about her. He wondered if she felt the same way.

All of this rolled through his mind as he drove through the dark, early-morning streets towards the station. The shift started at six, and he always thought it was a good idea to be early, especially since Freddy prepared a fantastic breakfast every day for the crews, both coming and going. He'd never been a fan of breakfast before this job, but that was before he had a four-star chef cooking a fresh meal for him whenever he came into work early.

Dean wasn't disappointed. The smells of Freddy's gourmet breakfast wafted out the squad room door as soon as he pulled it open. Barry was already there. He was seated and looked like he was digging into a freshly made omelet with a side of home fries and a cinnamon roll.

"Freddy, you made cinnamon rolls again?"

"I thought you all deserved it since you've been pulling extra shifts to handle the overload," the shambling zombie chef said in his usual gravelly voice. He gave Dean a big, toothless grin when he sat down at the squad room table. "What'll it be, Dean?"

"I'll have a big ham and cheese omelet, please."

"Coming right up." Freddy headed back to the kitchen to whip up his culinary magic.

"Barry, where are Brook and Tammy?" Dean asked.

"Freddy said they'd been out on calls almost the entire shift," Barry answered. "They must be beat."

"I hope that doesn't translate to a similar shift for us," Dean suggested.

"Don't jinx us."

Dean heard the ambulance bay doors begin to open next door and he got up to check through the windows that overlooked the garage. Sure enough, the ambulance was backing in, with Tammy stepping out and helping guide it in while Brook drove. Dean pushed open the door just as the ambulance came to a stop. Tammy walked over to plug in the overhead extension cord that powered and charged all the equipment on board while the ambulance was parked in the station.

Brook climbed out of the driver's side and reached back inside for her jacket. She looked tired. So did Tammy.

"Hey, ladies. Go on in and get your paperwork finished, I'll go over the bags and restock for you."

Tammy waved him off. "Let us do it, Dean. If last night and the early morning was any indication, you and Barry are going to have a hell of a day ahead of you. Eat your breakfast. We'll be in soon enough."

Dean shrugged and went back into the squad room just as Freddy was setting his plated omelet down at his seat. He went over and added a cinnamon roll from the platter at the center of the table to his plate. Sitting down, he dug into the food in front of him the way he always did. It was a necessary skill to learn to eat fast whenever the opportunity presented itself since you never knew when the next dispatch alert could come in.

Brook and Tammy came in after restocking the ambulance. Tammy sat down at the computer and started working on her report on the most recent patient. While she did that, Brook went over to Dean.

"You guys should have Freddy pack a bagged lunch to take on the unit with you. If you end up running as much as we did, you might not make it back to the station to eat."

"What kind of things did you run into last night?"

"There was another zombie attack, this time at a bar downtown. A recently buried guy showed up and started biting and clawing at folks. We had the usual bites, along with more than a few twisted ankles and bumps and bruises from people trying to get away while drunk." She gave a chuckle. "It probably would have been funny if it weren't so deadly serious."

Dean fished his phone out of his pocket and pulled up a photo of Felicity and Artur to show Brook.

"Did you see these guys on the scene by any chance. They might have been lurking on the periphery."

Brook looked the pictures of the missing woman and Artur Torrence over and shook her head. "I didn't see them if they were there. Who are they?"

"We had a breakthrough last night while we had a meet up at James' apartment. Jaz had some software running and discovered a link between them and the attacks. The guy in the photo is Artur Torrence."

Brook shot him a look of alarm. "The vampire who caused all our problems from before?"

Dean nodded. "If you see him, be very careful. He's ancient and quite powerful. Call the police and maybe drop me and Jaz a line, too. Artur needs special handling, and there are a few of us who have some personal scores to settle with him."

Dean filled Brook and Tammy in on Jaz's family history with the vampire lord as well as his own issues with the guy from Ashley's kidnapping. He wanted this guy almost as badly as Jaz did. Whatever they did, though, it had to be done carefully since he had eluded their efforts to capture him before.

The conversation turned to more mundane topics, and Dean listened while he pondered the circumstances that brought Artur back into his life again and again. He wanted to end this cycle of madness and seek some sort of normal life where he could have a chance at getting Jaz to pay attention to him as more than just another partner in her efforts to hunt down Unusuals who attacked humans.

Brook and Tammy ate breakfast and soon left while Dean and Barry started the routine beginning-of-shift chores around the station. In the meantime, Freddy cleaned up from breakfast. Despite the flurry of calls for the shift before theirs, the early hours of their shift went by without incident, and they were able to get all their regular chores finished as well as a few other things that just needed doing around the station.

Their first ambulance call didn't come until almost noon, which was unusual, but Dean wasn't complaining. Having the downtime was good. He even had time to grab a catnap. He was dozing in one of the recliners when the tones sounded on the overhead speakers. It startled him, but he shot up, ready to go as soon as he heard the radio.

"Ambulance U-191, respond for a subject with a headache. 61 Trenton Drive."

The dispatchers always sounded so calm, cool, and collected on the radio. He knew that was the point. They had to be the voice of calm in the chaos of an emergency for everyone involved. He also knew they were often just as stressed out as he was because they were stuck in a call center trying to help someone, with nothing but a phone line between them to lend a hand.

Barry's voice cut through his thoughts.

"You coming, partner? The patient's waiting."

"Yeah, I'm coming."

Barry drove since it was Dean's turn to take the lead on patient care. They usually swapped days so that every other day was his turn. He didn't mind taking his turn. It was why he did this in the first place.

As they pulled out of the garage and headed onto the street, Barry asked.

"Headache, huh? I wonder what that could be?"

"You know the drill. Could be a stroke. Could be a fall with a head injury. Could just be a headache. We'll see when we get there."

Dean operated the siren while his partner drove. It didn't take long until they were on the scene in a residential neighborhood with small, attached townhouses arranged in neat rows. They figured out which unit it was after driving around the parking lot for a few minutes. Dean spotted the correct house number and notified dispatch they were on scene.

Dean hopped out and grabbed the trauma and med bag. He knew Barry would get the heart monitor and oxygen bag and follow him inside. Jogging up the concrete steps, he started picking up a buzzing sound from ahead of him. As he got closer, the sound had turned into a head-jarring vibration. It gave him a headache, and he'd only been there a minute.

He reached up and knocked on the door. A few minutes later a tall, thin man of about thirty came to the door. As soon as he opened it, Dean was hit with a wave of sound. It was a sad, keening cry that nearly knocked him off his feet. He looked at the man who answered the door. He was wearing headphones, with a strip of cloth tied around the ear cups so as to press them more firmly onto his ears. Focusing his mind over the din of the crying, he could begin to understand why.

Dean was starting to get tunnel vision from the intense waves of sound overwhelming his hearing and pressing in on his mind. Waving the man to come outside, Dean reached up and pulled the door closed. The keening could still be heard in the background, but it was better now that the door was closed.

"Come with me, sir. I need to back away from the house for a bit," Dean said.

"I'm sorry, I couldn't think straight when I called nine-one-one," the man said. "I couldn't get her to stop, and I didn't know what else to do."

The man followed Dean back to the ambulance where Barry was just getting ready to come up the sidewalk.

"What's up, Dean? Is this our patient?" Barry glanced at the man with a quizzical look, taking in the strange headgear.

"I think so, but there's also something else going on here." Dean turned to his patient, able to focus now that he was farther away from the sound of the crying.

"Sir, I'm Dean Flynn. I'm a paramedic. Can you tell me your name?"

The man removed his headphones, settling them down around his neck.

"I'm Wilson, Will is fine, though. I'm sorry to call you for this. I just didn't know what else I could do. She won't stop crying, no matter what I do. At first, I thought it was something I did, but now I'm not so sure. It's been going on for hours."

"She's been crying, like that for hours?" Dean asked.

The man nodded.

Barry, who hadn't really heard the full brunt of the sound, seemed puzzled about what all the fuss was about.

"So this is your, uh, wife, girlfriend, what?" Barry asked.

"It's my girlfriend. But we've been together for six years, so I know what she's like when the crying starts. It's never been this bad before or lasted this long, though."

Dean was still trying to figure out what they were dealing with.

"Will, who or what is your girlfriend? I know she's not technically human, not with a cry like that."

"Oh, Wendy, she's a ban síde, a Banshee in common terms, but she's not evil or anything." He held up his hands, palms outward in her defense. "She can sense impending or recent death. Usually, she starts crying when a neighbor or relative is about to die. That usually only lasts a few minutes to an hour, depending on how nearby they are to us. This is something entirely different, though. It's like she's predicting the whole neighborhood is dying or something."

Dean scratched his head. They had to do something to get her to stop. He could feel the effects of her cry even out here. It was putting him on edge and making him want to lash out. He could imagine what prolonged contact with the sound would produce in an unprepared, normal human over time. He had read where a banshee's cry could make a whole village kill each other off over time. They didn't want that here. He had to get her to stop.

To do that, though, he and Barry had to get inside and deal with her. He thought about what he had on the unit and decided to look in the emergency kit in the compartment behind the driver's door for a solution. That was where they kept the magical and non-magical workarounds for dealing with this sort of thing.

"Wait here. I'll be right back," Dean told his partner and Will.

Soon he was back with the large black Pelican case and had flipped it open. Inside, nestled in little foam cutouts were a number of vials and containers. There was also a collection of various holy symbols and a large flask of holy water that was re-blessed by their resident chaplain on a regular basis. Looking through the supplies, Dean finally found what he was looking for. Picking up a small plastic case, he opened it and pulled out a small pale, yellow-brown brick.

"What's that?" Barry asked.

"Beeswax," Dean replied. "It's got a mild enchantment on it, either because it came from magic bees or because it's got a spell on it. I'm not sure which it is. It doesn't matter to us. What does matter is this will allow us to get closer to Wendy in there. The wax holds the residual buzzing of the entire hive. Supposedly, it drowns out magical sounds so we can talk normally inside without going insane from the crying. I know from personal experience it works against sirens. I don't know why it wouldn't work here, too."

"Wow," Will said. "I need to find me some of that."

"I'll hook you up with some after we get this resolved. It's available from the local witch coven, I think."

Dean pinched off two pieces of the soft wax and handed the block to Barry.

"Twist the wax into a small cone and push the cone into your ear canal."

Barry did as he was told and extended the wax block to Will who did the same before handing it back to Dean. Dean replaced the remaining wax in its container and closed the emergency kit. He hoped this worked. He knew it should work in theory, but that was different than testing something you had never done before in real life.

Dean picked up his two bags again and started up the steps to the townhouse's front door. He noticed as soon as he put the wax in his ears that the annoying sound disappeared. Time would tell if it would work close up, though. This time he didn't hear anything at all until he opened the door. Then the crying came through. It was different this time, though. It was muted, and he could think and coordinate his thoughts. He didn't feel like he was shutting down. Taking that as a good sign, Dean stepped inside and tried to locate the source of the crying.

In the living room on the first floor, he found a woman of about thirty years of age with long red hair. She was dressed in a white cotton nightgown, and she was sitting on the sofa with her knees pulled up and her arms wrapped around her legs. The woman was rocking back and forth while she cried out as if in agony or severe grief. Dean approached her carefully, trying to remember his lore on Banshees. He didn't think they had any other magic that might make them dangerous, but it didn't hurt to be cautious.

"Wendy," Dean said, trying to use a soothing, even tone. "I'm Dean Flynn, a paramedic with the Elk City Fire Department. I'd like to see if I can help you, okay?"

He was startled and almost fell over backward when she looked up at him with red, glowing irises in the center of her eyes. She opened her mouth and let out a cry even louder than the rest. This one began to penetrate his beeswax earplugs. He had to do something to calm her down so he could try and get to the root of her problem. He could sense Barry behind him, struggling to reach him in the midst of the renewed assault of sound.

Dean unzipped the med bag and started digging around, trying to find the drug he was looking for in the midst of his shrinking tunnel vision. He found it, the Haldol, which should help her calm down if he could manage to inject her with it. He fumbled with assembling a syringe and needle, something he'd done hundreds of times before. This was not good. He needed to hurry. Drawing up a dose of the drug, he lurched forward and quickly swabbed and then injected Wendy in the thigh. She looked at him in shock and this time screamed at him.

The last thing Dean remembered before he blacked out was staring at the syringe in his hand and feeling like he should be putting it somewhere. Then there was nothing.

Dean awoke to someone putting a cold compress on his forehead. He had a massive headache, and the cooling cloth helped soothe it, for which he was glad. He opened his eyes and saw a familiar redheaded woman, now with green eyes, looking down at him with a smile. Turning his head, Dean saw he was lying on the sofa in the townhouse owned by Will and Wendy. Barry sat slumped on a chair nearby, holding a bag of what looked like frozen peas to his forehead. He saw Dean watching him and gave his partner a half a smile.

"It's good to see you awake at last, Dean. I was about to call for another ambulance, but Wendy and Will said you'd wake up soon."

Wendy put a gentle hand on his chest.

"I'm sorely grateful for your help, Mr. Flynn." Dean heard a hint of an Irish accent in her voice.

He levered himself up on one elbow and looked around. Will sat on a chair across from Barry. He looked as pale as a ghost. Dean suspected they all did.

"How long was I out?" He asked Wendy.

"I think only about ten minutes. Whatever it was you injected me with took the edge off my banshee state, and I was able to switch back and regain control."

"It was Haldol, an antipsychotic drug that we use to sedate people," Dean replied. "I'm surprised you're up and walking around."

Wendy smiled, "I'll admit, I feel a little woozy, but I was the only one who was awake when I shifted back. Someone had to tend to you three."

Dean sat up. He was feeling better, and he wanted to get Wendy to sit down. That was a powerful drug, and she could stumble and fall if the full effect of the Haldol hadn't hit her yet. He told her as much.

"I'll sit once you three are all on your feet. I'm so sorry for what happened. It's been years since I was overcome by my banshee side like that."

"You sense death and impending doom, right?" Dean asked trying to understand what had set her off to begin with.

Wendy nodded. "I do, but this time was different. I could sense something else. I saw in my mind an artifact controlling the dead nearby and being used to do great evil. It has the potential to be devastating to the community here in Elk City. I know it."

Dean could hear how she said the last sentence. She believed it as a statement of fact. He had learned to trust the instincts of Unusuals with predictive powers like this. If Wendy thought there was some sort of artifact affecting the dead in Elk City, Dean was inclined to believe her. He knew that Artur was doing something to control the recently dead. It made sense that he had some sort of magical artifact to help him do it. He couldn't wait to make a few calls and spread the word to Jaz and James about it. They might be able to come up with some more information now that they had this new clue to go on.

Rising to his feet, Dean paused for a moment to get his bearings. He pointed to the sofa where he'd been lying.

"Wendy, why don't you have a seat. You shouldn't be up and walking around without help until that drug wears off in an hour or so."

She sat down, and Dean got out his blood pressure cuff and stethoscope. She was his patient, and he needed to do his job. He looked at Barry.

"Barry, call in to headquarters and notify them we are going to be on scene for an extended time but that everything is otherwise alright." He turned his attention back to Wendy and started to take her vital signs. While he did this, Dean decided to try and get more information from her about what she had seen in her vision or whatever it was. If he could get her to localize the artifact she had sensed they might be able to locate Artur.

"Wendy, can you determine where the thing you detected is located?"

The woman shook her head. "I don't think it works that way. I usually only sense death's presence in those close to me. This was something completely different. I've never sensed anything like it before, and when I reach out now, I can't sense it anymore. Maybe it's the drug, but I don't think I can help you find it if that's what you're thinking."

"It was, but that's okay. I was only asking so we could keep this from happening to you again." He unwrapped the cuff from her arm and put it back in his bag. Her vitals were normal all the way around. He could leave as long as Will was able to keep an eye on her until the drug wore off.

"Will, if you're feeling well enough again to take care of Wendy and make sure she doesn't fall for the next hour or so, Barry and I can get out of your hair. I think the episode has passed." He looked at Wendy. "If it feels like it's coming back, please don't hesitate to call us back and we'll see if we can't do something to stop it again. I'll let the other paramedics in our station know about what we did so they can be ready to help. You might also want to see your own doctor. They can get you a prescription for Haldol in pill form or something like it to take if this happens again."

"I don't think it will. I usually only get one premonition for each death," Wendy said. "I don't think I'll react to the artifact or whatever it is again. I'll call if I feel it coming back, though, you can be sure of that. I never want to be like that again, believe me."

Dean nodded, and he and Barry packed up their gear, heading out to their ambulance to reload the bags in the unit. Once they were finished, Dean climbed back in the passenger seat and paused a moment, looking around at the townhouse neighborhood. He felt like he was missing something, something important. He shrugged and shook his head when he couldn't figure it out. Pulling the door closed, he got on the radio and put the ambulance back in service as Barry drove away from the small residential community on the outskirts of town.

ARTUR WATCHED the ambulance drive away, seeing Dean as he got back inside before it left. He wondered what the paramedic was doing here, so close to his hideaway in the home of one of his victims. He and Felicity were leaving, though so maybe it was nothing, just a coincidence. The ancient vampire shrugged and let the curtain fall back into place, blocking the painful sunlight from coming in, even on this shady side of the street. He went back to the woman restrained and gagged on the bed behind him to continue feeding.

Chapter 11

Dean and Barry's shift ended much busier than it started. They ran the ambulance in one continuous loop it seemed, going from the hospital to the next call and back to Elk City Medical Center again. Dean supposed he shouldn't complain. He remembered a time not too long before when their patients were afraid to call for help, and he had to go out and find them to get work to do on his shifts.

When they finally made it back to the station, they found only Brook waiting for them. Tammy's 12-year-old daughter had collided with another player in an afternoon soccer game and broken her wrist. Tammy was going to be late coming in to work. Dean offered to stay late so Barry could head home. He was taking his wife on a date night, and Dean didn't want his partner to miss that important evening out. Even though he was tired, it would be fun to run some calls with Brook for a change of pace while they waited for Tammy to come in. She was planning on coming after she and her husband got back with their daughter from the visit to the urgent care center.

The call volume let up a little and allowed him to catch his breath, at least. For that, Dean was thankful. He and Barry hadn't even had a chance to stop for lunch while on their runs that afternoon and evening, so he was glad he was able to take time and enjoy the excellent meal Freddy had prepared for them: sirloin steaks with a demi-glace sauce and a side of a roasted veggie and orzo salad. Dean dug in, letting his hunger take over for the first few bites as he wolfed down the food without really tasting it. After the initial two or three bites, he slowed down, noticing Freddy's disapproving stare. He took the time to savor the next bites and was glad he did. The zombie-chef was a true genius with food.

"My compliments to the chef," Dean called out between bites. "This is truly awesome, Freddy."

"Agreed," Brook said through a mouthful of steak.

Freddy smiled and nodded his thanks before returning to the kitchenette area to clean up and put the leftovers in containers for them to take home after work. Dean watched the shambling shadow of a man and thought about the other recently dead people who'd been added to the local zombie community after they'd been raised from their rest by whatever unknown force or artifact Artur was using to create his zombie hordes. He knew they'd been lucky so far. The health department had been able to isolate the outbreaks and then transition the recently dead to what would pass as a normal life after their turning.

He was thinking about this when his phone chirped and he checked to see a message from Jaz. Tapping the screen, Dean opened the text message.

I HAVE *a lead on what might be causing the outbreaks. It's happened before, in the past. It's in our family archives. Can you come over after work?*

DEAN TAPPED a quick reply telling her he was working late. She replied immediately.

I'LL BE UP LATE. *I think this is big. Come by when you're done.*

· · ·

DEAN TOLD her he'd let her know when he was on his way. Dean ran out to his truck and brought in a change of clothes before returning to his meal. Once Tammy got there, he'd take a shower at the station. He hated showing up in his uniform after a hard day's work. It would be better to look like a normal guy for a change.

He tapped out a quick response to Jaz and was returning to his excellent dinner when the radio tones sounded overhead announcing the next ambulance call. Such was the life of the paramedic. He left the half-eaten plate of food sitting on the table and jumped up to grab his coat before heading into the ambulance bay, following after Brook.

FOUR HOURS LATER, well after ten o'clock at night, Dean backed the unit into the station's ambulance bay and shut the overhead garage doors with the remote on the visor. The initial call had turned into three back to back patient transports and, even though Tammy had shown up at nine o'clock, it had taken an extra hour to finish up and get a break in the action long enough to swing back to Station U to drop him off.

He was exhausted. Climbing down from the ambulance's driver's side, he plugged in the shoreline power cord and shuffled into the squad room. Brook was already at the computer completing her last report. Tammy came over as he walked into the station's living area.

"Thanks for covering for me, Dean."

"No worries," he replied. "How's your daughter?"

"In a little pain. It's a clean fracture and not near the growth plate so it should heal in four to six weeks. We've got to meet with an orthopedic surgeon just to be sure, but the ER doc said it should be fine."

"I'm glad she's going to be okay." Dean hooked a thumb over his shoulder to the ambulance bay. "I need to hit the shower, but when I'm done, I'll go and restock for you. We didn't use much in the way of supplies, but I'll make sure the unit is ready to go for the next call."

Tammy waved her hand in the air. "Don't worry about it. I've got it. You go home. You look beat."

Dean nodded. "Thanks. I'll do that. I have to try and catch up with Jaz if it's not too late."

"Ooh, a late night date? How's that going?"

Dean scowled at the reference to a date.

"Pretty well. We're taking things slow, but I like her a lot. I think the feeling is mutual. I mean, she keeps inviting me back, right?"

"It sounds promising," Tammy said, shooting him a big grin. "Of course, I'm not one to give away a girl's master plan. Where would be the fun in that?"

Dean laughed and went to get his clothes and grab a quick shower. While in the bunkroom getting dressed, he heard the tones drop over the speakers and knew Tammy and Brook were headed out again. When he came out wearing blue jeans and a T-shirt, Freddy was waiting for him with two plastic food containers.

"What's this?" Dean asked.

"It's not nice to show up at a lady's home at this hour without something to show for it. Take a nice dinner. This will all heat up well in her microwave. I jotted down instructions on the sticky notes on the lids."

Dean looked down as he took the containers from Freddy and noticed the scrawled instructions. He gave the chef a broad grin.

"This will hit the spot, Freddy. Thanks."

Freddy shrugged and returned the grin with a toothless smile of his own before going back to work puttering around the kitchen and dining area. Dean grabbed his coat and went out to head over to Jaz's place.

Twenty minutes later he was in her apartment zapping the meal in the microwave while Jaz gathered the plates and poured both of them a both a glass of wine.

"I can't tell you how excited I was when you texted that Freddy had sent dinner with you. I was so wrapped up in my research; I forgot to get anything to eat tonight."

"Sometimes, I think Freddy has a sixth sense when it comes to knowing when folks are hungry," Dean said with a chuckle. "It's like it's his super-power."

"It's a good one to have," Jaz laughed. She handed him his wine and held out hers in a toast. "To friends with superpowers."

"Agreed." Dean tapped the lip of his glass to hers and then took a sip. "How's the work coming along? Find anything new?"

"I think I've found a new track to run down regarding a few similar outbreaks in the past. I need a break, though. I've been at this since this morning."

The microwave beeped, and Dean took the container of food out and set it on the counter, taking the lid off as steam rose from the contents.

"What did he send us?" Jaz asked.

"Pasta Carbonara."

"Oooh, my mouth is watering already. Let's go sit and eat."

The two of them dished up bowls of the pasta dish containing fettuccini, egg, bacon, cheese, and fresh cracked black peppercorns. They sat in silence for the first few bites, savoring the gourmet meal Freddy had sent for them. Jaz spoke up first.

"My compliments to the chef," she said as she took a sip of her wine. "When do you work next? You have to tell him how much we enjoyed it."

"Thankfully, I'm off for a few days. That's something for which I'm very glad, believe me. It's been a long week of shifts. I'll make sure to say something when I go back, though. He's outdone himself yet again."

Jaz smiled and started to say something but stopped and took another bite of food instead. Dean cocked his head to one side waiting for her to say what was on her mind and finally asked her when he could wait no longer.

"You looked like you were about to say something that amused you. What was it?"

"It's silly," Jaz said. Her face colored a little as she smiled.

"You're blushing," Dean laughed. "Now you have to tell me."

She paused and smiled some more before she spoke.

"I was just thinking about how Freddy always seems to pull out all the stops when he makes food for you and me. It's almost as if he's taken it upon himself to make us nice romantic dinners every chance he gets. Do you think he's trying to set us up?"

"Of course he is," Dean blurted out with a laugh. "Honestly, Jaz, I think everyone wants us to get over ourselves and get together. Brook and Tammy are practically dying waiting for news that we are finally and officially a couple."

"It's good you have friends pulling for you like that, Dean. It must be nice."

"They're your friends, too, now. Look at it from their perspective. They've met Joanna. They know we'll end up together eventually. They just want us to get past the awkward phase and get on with things."

Jaz leaned back in her chair and looked him.

"What do you want?"

Dean was taken aback by her directness although he shouldn't have been. Jaswinder Errington was a very direct sort of person. He thought for a moment before answering.

"I want us to take the time we need to do this right, Jaz. I don't want to make any mistakes and take the risk of losing you and what we could have together someday down the road. If that means we need to go slow and take it one step at a time, I'm okay with that."

"Me, too," she replied.

"'Me, too,' what?" Dean asked, hoping she'd clarify some more.

"Me, too, as in I don't want to risk losing you and our future together either. I think I see us together for a long time, Dean Flynn."

Dean felt warm all over again, and now he feared he was the one blushing. Their eyes met, and then both of them were laughing together and the tension broke. It was good for them to get this out in the open. He felt like they'd been tiptoeing around the subject practically ever since Jo blurted out she was their daughter.

Jaz, still chuckling a little, stood up and reached out to take Dean's bowl along with her own.

"Let's clean up these dishes and then I'll show you what I've found."

Dean stood and grabbed the wine glasses and followed her to the kitchen. She rinsed out the bowls and set them in the sink while he poured them more wine. He handed hers to her as she passed by, heading for the couch where her laptop sat open, surrounded by stacks of papers and files.

"You have been busy," Dean noticed. "I've never seen you with so much clutter around before. You're always so neat and organized."

Jaz moved a stack of files so that there was room for Dean next to her on the sofa.

"I've been digging into the remaining archive files that survived the fire. Luckily most of the oldest hunter journals from my family were already scanned into a database in the cloud. That's what I've been referencing for the most part. These other files are from the police station and pertain to their previous investigations when we thought Artur was involved."

"So, where did you dig up the new information?"

"It's not new. It's very old." She opened her laptop and typed a query into a search bar and opened a file from the selection that popped up.

"This is a reference from one of my ancestors about an outbreak of the recently dead in a village in what is now Ukraine. It's from the eleventh century, but it describes what we see here almost perfectly."

Dean leaned in to look at the scanned image of a hand-written page. He couldn't make out any of it. Part of it was his difficulty reading the old world calligraphy of the person writing the journal. The other part was it was in a language he didn't recognize. Jaz laughed when she saw his expression.

"Don't let your brain explode trying to read it," she told him. "It's a form of Old High German. We Erringtons all learned to read and speak it from the earliest age. It's one way we keep our secrets to ourselves in this modern age. The language is a sort of pigeon version of the language spoken only in a small region near the Black Forest a long time ago. I don't think there are more than a handful of scholars in the world today who'd even recognize it, let alone are able to decipher it."

"Will you teach it to Jo someday?" Dean wondered aloud.

"Of course," Jaz replied. "She has to be able to carry on the legacy of the clan."

"So what does this ancestor of yours have to say that relates back to what's going on in Elk City now?"

Jaz turned back to the document on the screen and scrolled down a few pages. "This section here describes some sort of relic used by a local witch to get revenge on the villagers who cast her out. She caused those who were recently dead to rise from their graves and attack their former neighbors. The mayor of the village called for a hunter clan and my ancestor responded to their call for assistance. Here's the part I think is pertinent. I translated it for you."

She handed him a sheet of paper from a pile on the coffee table. He looked at the paragraph written on it.

"I tracked the witch to a cottage in the woods where I observed her from a distance. She pulled a small object from her pocket and began to mutter incantations over it. Using my amulet, I could see the glow of magic emanating from what she held. It was small and withered but obviously a finger. Who it belonged to and how it became ensorcelled to control the undead before this woman obtained it, I do not know. I knew only that she must be stopped. I leveled my crossbow and shot the crone as she cast her spell. There was a flash of light that overcame me for a time. When I could see again, the witch was dead on the ground with my shaft in her breast. I could find no trace of the relic she used in her spells against the village…"

Dean looked up at Jaz after reading the passage twice.

"A finger?"

"That's what it said. I read on in his journals, but there is no account of him finding it or destroying it, which he surely would have done."

"He mentioned it was a relic. Could it be some sort of holy relic from the church? I know some old churches and cathedrals in the old world purport to have the bones of saints which contain miraculous powers."

"That's what I as thinking," Jaz responded. She sounded excited. "I believe this is just that sort of relic. Which led me to another archival source."

She went back to her computer and pulled up another series of files.

"This is a database of known magical relics and their powers either verified or suspected. I did a search for fingers and hands to see what popped up. That's when I found this."

She pointed to the screen, and a scanned parchment drawing of what was unmistakably a finger removed just below the second knuckle.

"This is the finger of Saint Azriel," Jaz announced.

"I've never heard of him."

"Well, he's not a human saint. He's almost certainly one of the Eldara. Legend has it he was slain by a horde of demons while in command of a quest of holy knights in the tenth century. His last act before he died was to animate the fallen corpses of his knights to help him hold back the onslaught. During the fight, his finger was bitten off by a demon and fell to the ground where it was recovered by his surviving followers. We know Eldara bodies return to the ether or heaven or whatever when their mortal bodies are killed here on earth. For whatever reason, this part of him didn't go with the rest of the body."

Dean looked at the story on the screen that accompanied the parchment drawing. He was still unsure where she was going with this. How was a finger responsible for what was happening here and now? He asked as much.

"After this account of Azriel's fall, there are numerous accounts of others using the finger for the next hundred years or so to control all sorts of undead creatures. Apparently, the finger still contained the trapped Eldara magic Azriel used to raise and command his dead companions. It can be used to not only raise the dead but also to control any undead Unusual."

"And you think this is what Artur is using to raise and control the dead here in Elk City? How can you be sure and how did he get ahold of it?"

Jaz went back to her computer and scrolled down. "The final account of the finger being used is sometime in the eighteen fifties around Constantinople to control local attacks by newly turned vampires plaguing the area. Then it disappears from the record. Only one passage remains. That account says it was stolen from an ancient Christian church outside the city. No one's heard of it since, until now. I double-checked with my family journals. That was just before we came to the Americas. Our family was called to the region to help with the rise of the new vampires there. We confirmed that Artur was behind those attacks, too. He was there, in the region, when the finger went missing from the church. This has to be what's causing the trouble here. It has to be."

Dean looked at the screen and again at the translated journal passage in his hand. A thought occurred to him.

"Jaz, your ancestor said it could raise and control the recent dead. But earlier accounts you just read also claimed it could control all undead. Does that mean vampires and others like them?"

Jaz nodded. "But, I think it would have to be a relatively young vampire. Older vampires are extremely powerful and can resist most mind control after a few centuries as undead. I would think James is in little danger directly from this relic's powers."

"What about Brynne or another young vampire?" Dean asked.

"Oh," Jaz replied. "I hadn't thought of that."

"We have to get over there right away."

Chapter 12

Brynne was tired and frustrated. She was overcome with grief over the possibility that she'd killed the humans found outside the building. But she was never the type to give up on something she wanted. She'd been like that when she was a human and she wasn't going to let that change as a vampire. Despite the setbacks and the period when she blacked out the week before, she was determined to get back on track with her work on overcoming her bloodlust. She had to find a way around this. She wasn't going to be a monster for the rest of her long undead life.

So, after she recovered from the blackout, Brynne resolved to make up for her lapse and the people she had killed. She contacted Celeste and soon found herself back in the clean room with the redhead. They started from scratch. Celeste had insisted they return to the very beginning of the process to see if any ground had been lost in their limited progress when Brynne had blacked out, recovering in the basement of the building. Brynne started by taking a sip of warm blood but not swallowing it. She held the warm and delicious fluid in her mouth for a count of ten then turned and spat it out into the bucket next to her chair. It was a disgusting exercise, not only because of the cleanup but also because it was a waste of good blood. She didn't know who had to clean up the mess. Brynne hoped James was paying them enough.

She could resist drinking in this situation, though Brynne understood the need for the process. She could remember a time when she would have gulped the entire mug of life-giving fluid down without hesitation and begged Celeste for more.

"Good, Brynne, honey," the Celeste said. She used an insulated coffee carafe and added more blood to her mug. "Now, I want you to drink some of the blood, but stop before you finish all of the blood in the mug, understood?"

Brynne nodded and picked up the mug staring into the dark crimson depths of the blood before she brought it to her lips. Then she felt every muscle in her body freeze. She stopped there, without taking a drink. Brynne sat frozen in that position. She didn't understand what was happening, but she couldn't move. It was as if she was paralyzed in that position. She couldn't drink the blood or put the cup down.

"Go ahead, Brynne," Celeste said. "You may drink. Just don't finish all the blood. Let's see if you can stop yourself."

Brynne tried to move her hand, to blink, to do something but she'd lost all control over her body.

Celeste's expression changed to one of concern. "Brynne, what's wrong? Put the cup down and talk to me. What's happening?"

Celeste came around the table to stand next to Brynne and laid a hand on her shoulder, leaning over her. To Brynne's horror, her arm moved raising the white ceramic mug high and smashing it against Celeste's temple. The other vampire's eyes rolled up in her head and she collapsed to the floor next to the chair. Brynne, an unwilling passenger within her own body, watched as she stood up and looked down at her unconscious friend. Then she felt a tugging on her whole being and even control over her thoughts was taken away from her. The last thing she remembered before it all went black was watching her hand reach for the doorknob that would lead her out of the room.

DEAN AND JAZ had taken one of the Errington black SUVs and raced over to the Nightwing Building. Dean had called James. He was out of town on a business trip and said that Celeste was watching Brynne. The vampire lord told Dean he and Rudy were hurrying back but wouldn't be able to get back until close to dawn. Dean's next call was to Celeste, but there was no answer on her phone at all. Brynne didn't answer his calls either.

Jaz had a police light bar mounted on her dash, and she switched it on. She used the lights to blow through traffic as she wound her way through the few cars on the road this late downtown. It wasn't long before she was pulling down the ramp of the Nightwing Building's underground garage. Dean jumped out before Jaz had even come to a complete stop. She yelled at him to slow down as she raced after him. The elevator doors opened just as she caught up to him. He noticed she had grabbed her katana from the car. She settled the scabbard across her back as she stepped into the elevator and stood next to him.

"You're not using that to hurt Brynne, Jaz," Dean warned.

"Only a fool goes into a building unarmed with potentially out of control vampires on the loose," Jaz replied. "Besides, it's a precaution only. I'm sure there's nothing wrong. It's probably just a cell tower problem."

Dean wished it were that simple a solution. He looked at the phone in his hand. The bars were full on his screen: not a cell phone problem.

The elevator stopped on the first floor even though Dean had pushed the button and used his keycard to access the Penthouse level. When he tried the button again, nothing happened. He decided they'd have to take the stairs. He stepped off the elevator and was met by one of James' security guards. He was a human but one who knew his boss' true nature.

"I'm sorry, Mr. Flynn but there's a problem on the sixth floor, and I've been instructed to lock down access to the upper floors for the time being."

"The sixth floor?" Dean asked.

The guard nodded.

"What's on the sixth floor?" Jaz asked them both.

"It's the private apartments for the human employees who work for James," Dean replied. "I used to have a place up there for a while." He turned to the guard. "You know who I am, right?"

"Yes, sir. But I have my orders," the guard responded. "If anyone gets hurt because I disobeyed them, I'll lose my job."

"Unless I'm wrong, and I hope I'm not," Dean said. "People are already getting hurt. You have to let us up there. Losing a job will be the least of our worries. Unlock the elevators for us to go up and then call 911 and request an ambulance from Station U. Understand?"

The guard pondered the request for a moment and then turned and went over to his console behind the counter. He tapped a few buttons there and looked back to where Dean and Jaz stood.

"You're cleared in elevator two up to six. I'll call the ambulance, but you better tell Mr. Lee you made me do this."

"Don't worry; I'll back you up." Dean didn't finish the statement with the thought, 'if I survive'.

As they went back over to the bank of elevators, Jaz led the way. She poked the up button and stepped on the elevator that opened. Dean followed her on, staring at the hilt of her sword jutting up over her shoulder.

"You're not going to kill her. I can talk her back from this, Jaz. I know I can," he said as the doors slid shut.

"It's not my first choice of action, Dean, but I'm not letting her kill you either. If it comes down to it, I'll defend us."

Dean opened his mouth to say something then closed it. Nothing he said was going to change anything at this point. Jaz was a hunter. This was more in her wheelhouse than his. He just hoped they weren't right about Brynne. He watched the lighted numbers over the door tick up to six and the elevator car lurched to a stop. Jaz extended an arm to push him back from the door so an attack wouldn't catch him unawares as it opened.

The first body lay outside the door to the elevator, the woman's hand extended as if she were trying to reach for the button on the panel by the elevator doors. Dean didn't think there was any hope, but he checked her for pulses anyway. Her throat had been ripped open. The poor girl must have bled out pretty quickly. She didn't look familiar, but he didn't know all of James' employees even though he had lived here for a few months before.

The scream from down the hall and around the corner jerked him back to awareness at the moment. Jaz had taken up a position between him and the other end of the hallway. The scream cut off as quickly as it began, ending in a sad, gurgling cry. Dean stood and started rushing down the hall. Jaz stopped him with an arm extended outward, barring his path. He pushed against it and was surprised by her strength.

Jaz looked his way with a brief, steely-eyed glance.

"I'll take the lead. You stay behind me."

He started to protest but quickly gave in. With a nod, he stepped back. Jaz gave him a grim smile and started forward. She had one hand inside her jacket, probably on the grip of her pistol in its shoulder holster rig. The other hand was cocked back over her shoulder, fingers just brushing the hilt of her katana. She advanced in a crouch to the corner and peeked around the corner before pulling back.

"It's Brynne," she said in a bare whisper. "She's feeding. Let me take the lead, okay?"

Dean wanted to leap around the corner but stopped himself. It was one of the hardest things he'd ever done, to stop himself from running forward. He knew a rash action here could spell catastrophe, though. His first responder training served him well. Never rush in without the proper training. Wait for back up and the proper resources. Jaz was the one with the experience here. He had to trust her. He nodded.

"Stop her, Jaz. But please, do not kill her."

The hunter didn't answer she reached out and laid a reassuring hand on his forearm before turning back to the corner. She stood up straight and stepped around the corner while she reached back inside her leather jacket for whatever she'd had ahold of before. Dean couldn't see what she pulled out because she walked forward and he lost sight of her for a moment before he followed.

Dean stood from his crouch and bolted around the corner behind Jaz. There were two more bodies here. One was crumpled on the carpet just around the corner. The other was two doors down. Brynne crouched over the second body, a blond-haired woman in yoga pants and a tank top.

His former paramedic partner, now in full vampire mode, looked up at their approach and bared her fangs at them, the fresh blood of her latest victim dripping from them to run down her chin and onto her chest. Her eyes were rimmed with red, and it almost seemed the irises of her eyes glowed even in the bright light of the fluorescent lighting above them.

Their first warning of the attack was a low guttural growl from deep in Brynne's throat. She launched herself at Jaz from twenty feet away, and Dean was taken aback by her ferocity and speed. He saw death moving in the form of a true apex predator. He was sure he and Jaz were both doomed.

His surprise at the outcome was reflected in the look on Brynne's face when she jerked to a stop in mid-air about five feet from him and Jaz as if she ran into a wall. She dropped to the floor and crouched there snarling at them while she turned as if to shield herself from something. Dean took a step to the side and saw what it was.

Jaz stood in the center of the hall in front of him, her arm extended in front of her holding a large silver cross. The boldly presented holy symbol was holding the rampaging vampire at bay, though she seemed to struggle against an invisible barrier, still trying to reach them.

Dean called to Brynne past Jaz, stepping forward a bit so she could see him.

"Brynne, you have to stop this. You aren't in control of yourself. It's Artur. He's controlling you through some sort of magic relic."

She hissed at him and Jaz and renewed her efforts to push past the barrier to get to them.

"I have to feed. I've been holding back for too long. I need to exert my true power and take what I want." Brynne's expression was horrifying to Dean. He knew her to be a compassionate and caring healer. This monster standing in front of him was not that woman. This was something else entirely.

"You know you can feed without killing, Brynne. Stop this and let me pass so I can help those people you've injured." He could see the feebly struggling blonde behind Brynne trying to crawl away down the hallway.

The motion was not lost on Brynne's enhanced senses. As if she could sense her food source moving away, Dean watched her turn away from the barrier she couldn't pass through to reach the meal she could have. He lurched forward to stop her and in that instant realized his mistake. As he stepped in front of the holy symbol held by Jaz, the only thing keeping Brynne at bay, the barrier holding her back came down.

With a howl of feral joy, Brynne hurtled past him, her arm throwing him into the wall with enough force to knock the wind out of him. He saw her bowl over Jaz, sending the silver cross flying to the floor. The two women rolled over and over as he fought to regain his breath and stand.

Dean watched as Brynne rolled on top of Jaz and bared her fangs to sink them into Jaz's exposed neck and shoulder. He thought Jaz was done for, but he should have known better than that. She drove her head up and forward, delivering a brutal head butt to Brynne's face that appeared to stun both of them for a moment. Dean pushed himself to his feet, still having to steady himself against the wall with one arm. This was his only chance to get the stronger vampire off of the hunter before she was killed. He didn't know what he could do, but he had to try. He reached out with one unsteady hand and tried to grab at the back of Brynne's shirt at the neckline.

Something deep inside whispered for him to utter a prayer as he reached for her. His fingers brushed against Brynne's skin as he tried to grab her shirt to pull her backward. In that instant, he felt a surge of strength and his vision gained a strange clarity as if he could see colors he'd never been able to discern before. Instead of grabbing the shirt, his fingers clamped on the back of Brynne's neck, and he pulled upward.

The raging vampire stopped struggling and sat upright staring straight ahead with vacant eyes for a moment. In that instant, Dean could see through her, through the control link to Artur on the other side. He pushed hard against the other's mind he found there and discovered to his surprise a sense of fear resonating back down the link between Brynne and the ancient vampire. Whatever Dean was doing, it scared Artur. The ancient vampire lord shouted something in anger Dean couldn't understand and released his mental hold on Brynne, leaving Dean in his place.

Dean felt his control over Brynne superseding the other vampire's. He sent a command to stand, and Brynne got up off of Jaz, standing and staring off with the vacant stare she'd had since he touched her. He didn't know what to do next. He was afraid to let go of her for fear she'd fall back under Artur's control.

Jaz rolled to her feet. She was bleeding from a deep cut on her forehead where she'd split the thin skin in her attack against Brynne. Wiping the blood from where it trickled down into her eyes, Jaz retrieved the silver cross from the floor and held it ready. Another voice sounded down the hallway.

"Dean, what are you doing?"

The voice was Celeste's. She had stepped unseen from the stairwell door behind him. She startled him, but he didn't let go of Brynne. He was afraid to stop.

"I can't let go. Somehow, don't ask me how, I'm controlling Brynne after Artur let go. I'm afraid to release her. What if she doesn't revert to her normal self?"

"Artur was controlling her?" Celeste asked. She shook her head. "Well, that explains some of what happened tonight." The redheaded vampire stepped around Dean to stand in front of Brynne, examining her face.

"I think she's past the rampage. She might have a problem with all the blood in this hallway when you let go, but I think she'll return to her normal self. I can control her if she doesn't. I'm older and stronger than she is as long as she doesn't sucker punch me first and I'm ready this time."

Dean wasn't sure if he should let go or not, but he knew he had to take the chance. He relaxed his grip on the back of Brynne's neck, pulling his hand away. As soon as his fingers lost contact with Brynne's skin, his vision and mind returned to normal. In addition to that, his weariness from the brief confrontation returned.

Brynne blinked and shook her head as if to clear her mind. She looked around and took in the carnage, the blood soaking her clothes and her friends standing around her. With a guttural cry that wrenched at Dean's heart, he watched his friend and former partner collapse to the floor in a heap as heart-wracking sobs overtook her.

Chapter 13

Dean and Jaz sat in the Penthouse atop the Nightwing Building. It was the early morning hours of the next day after Brynne's attack, and James had just arrived back from his trip. He was in with Brynne in their room, probably trying to comfort her. Dean hoped James was more successful than he had been. She was overcome with grief at the discovery she had killed people and that it was likely not the first time based on what Dean and Jaz learned about the earlier incident with the bodies found in the alley outside the building. Dean discovered that piece of information from Celeste as she was putting together what happened to Brynne with what Dean and Jaz knew from their research.

He had been able to save Brynne's last two victims, though they'd both need extensive surgery and recovery time from the loss of blood alone if not the traumatic injuries they'd received. Jaz had jumped in to help him as he worked alone to stem the flow of blood from both living victims in the hallway at the same time. Celeste called down to the security guard and had him let the police and paramedics from Station U up. Brook and Tammy showed up and brought the supplies with them he needed to help them dress the wounds and prep the two patients for transport.

Tammy called for another transport unit. It would be a regular ambulance team, not a station U team but they'd tell the other crew of paramedics it was an assault victim without the specific details of what they were dealing with. Brook and Dean administered the needed garlic extract to stave off a vampire change just in case one of them died and Brynne had initiated the change. Dean knew James would have to get someone to watch the dead woman he and Jaz had first found by the elevator to make sure she didn't change as well.

The police had extensive questions for all of them. They were a little skeptical about the whole mind-control thing, but they were from the police version of station U and knew Dean and Celeste well enough. They decided only to take a report on the assault and let the higher-ups in the DA's office handle the need for any arrest and charges to be filed later. Dean was surprised they did this given the body they must have passed on the floor by the elevator. He was about to say something, but Celeste changed the subject.

When the officers finally finished with their questions, the small group, including Brynne, headed back around the corner to the bank of elevators. Dean saw the large blood stain on the carpet outside the doors to the elevators, but there was no sign of the body. He looked around and then back at Celeste and Jaz, his eyes full of questions. Jaz laid her hand on his arm and gave her head a little shake. Whatever his questions were, this wasn't the place to answer them.

Now he was seated in the penthouse, still trying to sort it all out.

"So you hid the body by the elevators in the janitor's closet?" Dean asked Jaz.

"I would have hidden the other victims if I'd had the time," Jaz replied. "As it was, I barely had the first body stowed away before the first police officer arrived with Brook and Tammy."

"But, why? Isn't that tampering with evidence?"

Jaz gave a shrug as if it was no big thing to worry about. Celeste jumped in to forestall his asking further questions of her.

"Jaz did the right thing, Dean. I'm glad she had thought of it before I did. We know it wasn't Brynne's fault that the woman died, not any more than she was responsible for the deaths in the alley outside the building. That blame rests squarely on Artur."

"I know that, but we can't go around lying to the police…" Dean started.

"Look," Jaz said. "Do you want Brynne to go through the process of a trial and exposure of who and what she is? She'll never get anything approaching a fair trial. This is how things are done when something like this happens. It's collateral damage in the fight we have against the evil that is Artur."

"But, don't those people have families and loved ones who deserve to know what happened or at least that they died?" Dean asked. "You can't just disappear people, you know." He looked from Jaz to Celeste and back again.

"You'd be surprised," Jaz said with a snorted laugh.

James came into the room at that moment and must have picked up on the gist of the conversation.

"Dean, I assure you, my employees are adequately compensated for their risks living in this building. I offer them full life insurance packages to help support their families in the event of an untimely death." James explained. "They understand this when they come to work here."

"So you just pay them off," Dean said, his anger and frustration bubbling to the surface as his old antagonism with James came forward. "They're only a balance sheet item to be written off as an expense of doing business with a vampire lord."

James stopped where he stood and held Dean's gaze until he looked away.

"You know me better than that now, Dean. If you think I'm not deeply hurt by the way this attack unfolded, you forgot all we've learned about each other over the last year. I'm bothered by this on many levels, I assure you."

Celeste stepped forward to intervene and change things up.

"The question is more a matter of how Artur is controlling Brynne from afar like that. Dean and Jaz have a theory."

James looked at him and Jaz. "What is it? If we must combat this, we need to know what it is and how he's doing it."

Dean and Jaz gave a brief explanation of what they'd discovered in their research earlier the night before.

"The Finger of Azriel?" James asked. "I'd thought that thing was lost to the ages long, long ago. How can you be sure that's what he's using?"

"The way the incidents unfolded match earlier accounts almost word for word," Jaz explained. "Then there are the attacks on Brynne. They all point to this relic."

"That is not good, then," James said. "He could use it to control almost any of us, as long as we're younger and less powerful than he is. Why attack Brynne and not me?"

No one answered at first, then Jaz spoke up.

"Based on your previous encounters with Artur, he has focused on ruining you and discrediting you, so you lose control of Elk City. He wants to destroy you, James, not control you. He wants you to get distracted and not pay attention to what he's doing on the side. From his standpoint, that strategy starts with hurting Brynne."

"She's right, James," Celeste agreed. "These attacks on Brynne have distracted us from other things we should have been doing to track him down and assist the local authorities with the zombie outbreaks. We never connected them together or thought that he could be behind it all."

"I have a question we haven't covered yet." Dean said. "How is he getting to Brynne?"

James gave Dean a puzzled look. "We've covered that. It's got to be the relic."

"No, I know it's the relic that's given him the ability to control her but how did he get to Brynne here?" Dean asked. "Every other time he's used it, he's had to get close. We have the video surveillance footage to prove it. Artur has to be able to see his intended victim to control them. He wasn't in the building when we got here. We would have seen him." He gestured to both he and Jaz.

Jaz thought for a moment and snapped her fingers. "You said the magic words, Dean. It's surveillance cameras. That has to be the way he's doing it." The hunter clan leader looked to Celeste and James. "I assume you have surveillance cameras in the building."

Both James and Celeste nodded.

"Did you have surveillance cameras in the room you were using to test Brynne?"

"Yes, we always video those sessions with new vampires," Celeste answered. "It helps us figure out if we're doing anything wrong for each one when reviewed by the person leading the testing. You think Artur hacked our system somehow?"

Jaz shrugged. "It seems like the most logical conclusion to come to. It would explain how he was able to direct her so easily from outside the building. You're pretty sure he couldn't get inside, right?"

"Every entrance is watched," James said. "And we've started running facial recognition looking for certain individuals, Artur among them, ever since you showed us how easy it was to implement. We'd know if he'd been in the building, even if we didn't catch him in the act of entering."

"That means he was nearby and using some sort of hack to watch our video surveillance systems to control Brynne," Celeste said. "I'll have Rudy run a check on neighboring buildings with his team. Dean, you said you could see him in a room of some sort, not a car?"

Dean nodded, not quite comfortable with the direction the conversation was headed.

James was the one who asked the question he was dreading. "Dean, what exactly did you do? I've never heard of a human doing what you said you did, even one who had powerful magical abilities."

"I don't know how I did what I did, James," Dean said. He looked at Jaz for some support, and she smiled and nodded. "I had to think fast, and the idea sort of popped into my head that if I touched Brynne, I might be able to disrupt the connection. In my previous encounter with Artur, I think I had some sort of protective aura from Ashley." He shrugged. "Maybe it had a residual effect. All I knew was I had to stop her, so I just did it. The next thing I knew, I was looking back through the link Artur was using on her, staring him in the face. He was in an office or apartment of some sort, and he was afraid of me."

James nodded. "I can understand the fear part of it. You shouldn't be able to do what you did, Dean."

"He's full of surprises, James," Jaz said with a snort of laughter. "He has a way of catching you unawares with some new ability of one sort or another."

She pointed to Dean.

"Someday I'm going to figure out what's going on with you, Dean Flynn. You have the ability to command demons, you can touch a heavenly blade with your bare hands with no side effects, and now this. If we didn't know better, I'd think you were an Eldara yourself."

Dean was uncomfortable with the whole line of questioning. He was a completely normal human as far as he knew. He'd been raised by his mom and dad until his dad left them. He had normal memories of childhood like anyone else. Jaz often found a way to work a question about his past into her conversations with him. He knew she was prying for information, trying to get past his descriptions of a normal childhood to something she thought was hidden underneath, but there was nothing there to find. He was sure of it.

"Leave Dean alone, guys," Brynne said from the hallway. Dean wasn't sure how much of the discussion she'd heard since coming out of her room. "He's been through a lot for all of us at one time or another. If he says he doesn't know, he doesn't know."

Everyone looked up as she entered the room. She'd cleaned up and looked a little better, though her eyes were rimmed with red from crying. Dean wanted to tell her to stop trying to protect him, but he knew she would always see him as her probie medic. That sort of mentoring relationship didn't fade even with being turned into a vampire, apparently.

"Thanks, Brynne."

"Thank you, Dean. If it hadn't been for you, I could have done even more harm."

"I'm sorry I couldn't stop it sooner," Dean said thinking of the woman Brynne had killed. He stopped there, not wanting to bring it up again. Brynne knew what she'd done under Artur's control.

"The only person at fault here is Artur," Brynne said, steel determination showing in her tone. "I got set up to think I'd done it. I've been blaming myself, and for that, he's going to pay."

"Careful setting off on that sort of vendetta, Brynne," Jaz said. "It can consume you. My whole clan started because of that sort of thing directed at Artur."

"I'm a patient woman, Jaz. I'll bide my time. I've got centuries to live, right? Might as well have a goal in life. Maybe we can team up and take him down together."

Dean laughed and when they all looked his way he shrugged. "I was just thinking of Artur being chased by you two and the other woman he's eternally pissed off."

"Who's that?"

"Ashley's sister, Ingrid," Dean said. "If he keeps adding female enemies like you all to the list like this, he's definitely in more trouble than he knows." While Ashley was an Eldara Sister, a healing angel, her twin sister Ingrid was a different kind of angel altogether. As a battle angel or Valkyrie, she was a formidable foe to have.

James snorted a laugh. "Careful how you say her name, Dean. She's attuned to you just like her sister was. The last thing we need here right now is the chaos of a Valkyrie in town."

Chapter 14

It had been a week since the incident with Brynne at the Nightwing building. That week had turned into another week of constant ambulance calls at Station U followed by research with Jaz in the off hours. Artur had stepped up his attacks, with new incidents happening every night. The Elk City officials who dealt with the Unusual citizens had tried to distract the human population with stories of gang activity and college pranks gone wrong. Those efforts were starting to unravel as people started asking questions that weren't so easily answered.

This prompted the formation of a new quick response team operating within the police version of Station U. They were staged around the city with Errington hunter teams Jaz had assembled, to respond and take a more aggressive stance against the undead incursions. When Jaz had told Dean of the new strategy, he became livid. They couldn't just kill these people. They were sick, under another's control, and not responsible for their actions. She tried to get him to see it her way more than once, citing the need to be proactive to ensure public safety.

He didn't see her point at all. It seemed to be reactive and not proactive to shoot first and ask questions later. The police should be focusing on tracking Artur down. He was the true enemy. Jaz understood his frustration but for the time being she had advised the city to take this course of action and James was going along with it. Dean thought it was wrong and decided to take action on his end with the other Station U paramedics to try and stop the violence before it started by getting to the scenes ahead of the QRT squads.

It had meant that Dean was taking as much overtime as he could, working nearly every night shift because, if he could get there first, he could sever the connection between Artur and his victims. Dean didn't know where he came by this new power or even how it worked, but he was determined to use it to save as many lives as possible.

The current call had come in reporting a behavioral emergency with the agitated individual attacking bystanders at a convenience store. He was riding with Bill tonight since Lynn had the night off. They were racing to the scene, hoping it was not another attack but worried that it was. The QRT had been dispatched, too, so they had little time to spare. Guns and a police sniper bullet to the head were not the solution to a person with mental illness or suffering from mind control.

The ambulance arrived on the scene, pulling into the parking lot of the Quik-Mart. Dean was pleased to see no other flashing lights evident on the scene, which meant they were the first ones there. He could see people running out of the front doors of the convenience store and knew the problem was still located inside and contained for the time being. The police and the QRT hunter squad couldn't be too far away, so he and Bill needed to act fast. Bill was driving, and Dean jumped out of the ambulance before it had even come to a complete stop. A definite no-no, but he didn't care. A life was at risk here.

Grabbing his trauma and med bags from their compartments on his side of the ambulance, Dean jogged to the front doors of the store and looked through the glass. He was not prepared for what he saw.

Inside the store was a partially decayed human form, wearing a black overcoat and shuffling back and forth in front of the counter.

The creature couldn't move very far because of the cloth wrappings that had unraveled and tangled around its feet and legs. Dean didn't know what to make of it at first.

Bill came jogging over with the cot and the rest of the gear. He stopped next to Dean, looking inside.

"Bill, you've been doing this longer than I have," Dean said. "Have you ever seen anything like this?"

"This is a new one to me." The older paramedic looked around and then pointed across the street. "But if it walks like a mummy and looks like a mummy, maybe it's a — well…"

Dean followed his partner's gaze and pointing finger to see the Elk City Municipal Museum. There was a banner hanging over the front entrance, lit by the building's floodlights. It read "Wonders of Egypt" across the vinyl sign. Dean turned and looked back at the creature in the convenience store. It had fallen over and was struggling to rise to its feet amidst the tangling strips of cloth.

"Come on," Dean said. "The QRT will be here any minute. We need to get our mummy into the back of the ambulance before they arrive and start shooting up the place."

Entering the convenience store, Dean approached the struggling mummy and talked to it in a soothing voice.

"I'm Dean Flynn. I'm a paramedic from the local station. I'm here to help you."

The mummy stopped struggling and stared up at him with open black eye sockets. Dean cleared his throat and tried something else.

"Uh, I don't know if you understand me or speak English."

"Of course I speak English. What else would I speak?" The rasping voice asked. There was a slight British accent and a hint of something else there, but the English was excellent otherwise.

"Oh, good. Well, how about we help you get yourself wrapped up again?" Dean and Bill came forward and lifted the mummy to his feet. Bill rolled the cot over, and they helped the ancient corpse sit on the edge and then lay back in a semi-seated position. Dean scooped the loose wrappings off the floor and laid them on the mummy's lap.

"Is there a reason you can't re-wrap me here. I really need to get back to the exhibit before the guard notices I'm missing."

Dean started pulling the stretcher outside and to the ambulance while he answered. "There've been some issues lately with undead Unusuals attacking humans. We thought that was what you were before we got here."

"I wouldn't attack people. I love getting to see new people in my travels."

"Well, the local human authorities are a bit strained because of the attacks. There's an armed police team set up to neutralize any threats. That includes you."

"Whoa, neutralize? I know what that means. Why would they shoot me? All I wanted to do was to try the cherry slushy. I could see the sign advertising it from the window at the museum, and it intrigued me. I thought I could come over and get a taste and still get back before anyone would notice me missing. I put on a coat I found outside the security guard's break room so I'd be mostly dressed."

Dean shook his head. This wasn't an attack at all, just a case of mistaken identity from the dispatchers. "Let us get you hidden in the back of the ambulance and then we can help you get yourself situated and back over to the museum."

They had just closed the doors on the ambulance when the first police van pulled up, and armed SWAT team members unloaded and swarmed into the convenience store. Dean turned and looked through the back windows of the ambulance to see Bill starting to replace the cloth wrappings around the mummy's legs and torso. His attention was drawn back to the front of the convenience store by a shout from one of the officers there. He saw a person who must have been the store clerk standing next to one of the black-clad officers. The clerk pointed to Dean, gesturing wildly while he talked.

The officers all turned and looked his way. He couldn't think of anything else to do, so he waved and shot them a big, toothy grin. One of the officers waved back until another QRT member smacked him across the back of his head. The leader of the team said something to the clerk, and then the group of heavily armed policemen crossed the parking lot to where Dean was standing.

"Flynn, do you have our suspect in the back of that ambulance?"

Dean recognized the voice as that of Officer Craig Hamm from the police department's own Station U unit. He waited until the officers came closer to answer.

"Hey, Craig. I think we've got a case of mistaken identity here. This wasn't one of our attacks at all, just a hungry mummy with the munchies. He's in the back getting wrapped up again."

Craig came over and looked past Dean into the back of the ambulance. The officer shook his head and glanced back at Dean then turned to his SWAT team.

"Stand down."

The weapons were lowered, and the police officers turned to go back to their van.

Craig Hamm turned back to Dean.

"You guys have to be more careful. You're supposed to stage and wait for us."

"I had a hunch."

"A hunch?" Craig said, his voice rising in volume and pitch. "You can't go rushing into a situation like this because of a hunch."

Dean hooked a thumb over his shoulder at the ambulance. "This guy had nothing to do with any attacks and didn't deserve to be potentially shot by you guys before he had a chance to explain himself. I would have thought you all would be thankful not to have to shoot anyone."

"It doesn't matter what happened here or didn't happen here. This isn't how the response is supposed to go, and I'm going to have to file a report about this. You all are supposed to stage first and let us come in ahead of you. That's protocol."

"I've been in trouble before," Dean replied with a shrug. "I'll be in trouble again. In the end, I can live with myself when I'm doing what is right and saving people's lives."

"We'll see about that." Craig turned back to the few of his team members who were still standing around. They were starting to grumble among themselves. "Come on guys, let's get back to the station. This was a false alarm."

Dean waited until the officers loaded back into their police van and left the convenience store parking lot before he opened the back of the ambulance and checked on Bill's progress with their patient. The other paramedic was just finishing up securing the final strip of cloth. Bill looked at Dean with a big grin.

"Perfect timing, Dean. As you can see, I'm just wrapping up."

Both Dean and their mummified patient groaned at the pun.

Bill laughed and introduced Dean to the patient.

"Dean, meet his royal highness Prince Ahmat of the royal house of Egypt."

"Ahmat is just fine, Paramedic Bill. I thank you, both for your understanding and assistance. Perhaps I can offer some assistance to you at some time in the future."

"All in a day's work, Ahmat," Dean said. "No need to do anything special."

"What was all that commotion with the officers about?" Ahmat asked.

Dean explained about the recent attacks around the city. "When the description came in about you in the store, I think the dispatchers assumed it was another zombie attack."

"I'm no zombie," Ahmat said. He sounded indignant. "I'm a proud example of my nation's heritage. I travel around to talk with museum curators and historians, demonstrating how mummies were made back in the day and how to spot fakes."

"Like I told them out there. I had a hunch you weren't one of the attackers when we got here. I'm glad I was right. Now, if we can just find the location of the person orchestrating all the attacks."

"How are they controlling the zombies?" Ahmet asked. "That kind of thing takes a great deal of power."

"We think it's through the use of a relic called the Finger of Azrial. It belonged to an Eldara once upon a time. Now an ancient vampire with a grudge is using it to try and raise an army of undead in the city, and we can't find him to stop it."

"Hmmm, I used to know a high priest who used a locator incantation based on a pyramid's natural focusing ability, locating powerful magic used in the city of Alexandria."

"Wow, that would be something we could use in a situation like this. Too bad he isn't a mummy, too." Dean responded.

"Oh, he is," Ahmet said. "I'll have to see if I can track him down. He might be able to tell me how to cast the spell in the simulated pyramid they have me living in while at the museum. How can I reach you if I figure this out for you?"

Dean fished a piece of paper out of his pocket and wrote his name and number down on it. He handed it to the mummy. "If you manage to get that spell, we could stop this whole thing and find the vampire behind it all."

"I'll see what I can do," Ahmet said taking the paper and tucking it into a fold in his wrappings. "Well, I think I've caused enough excitement for the night. Can you drive me over to the museum's back lot? I can get back inside that way past the guard station."

"Sure," Dean said. He climbed out while Bill buckled their passenger into the back seat for safety. A few minutes later they were backing up to the museum loading dock and unloading their royal passenger. Dean leaned out his window and waived goodbye as their patient shambled back into the museum. He waited until Bill climbed back into the front seat and then pulled away. They both could check off a Station U bucket list item tonight. Neither of them had ever met a real-life mummy before. They both laughed as they drove back to the station. The other paramedics were going to be so jealous.

Chapter 15

By the end of his shift, Dean was exhausted. He could barely keep his eyes open on the way home from work and was looking forward to doing nothing but grabbing a quick bite to eat and going straight to bed. He was in the process of making a peanut butter sandwich when Jaz called. Dean picked up the phone and opened it in speaker mode so he could keep working on his dinner.

"Hey, Jaz. What's up?"

"Dean, you're off work, right?"

"Uh, yeah," Dean replied. "I'm home and making a snack before bed. I'm totally exhausted."

"Great, but no time for sleep. I need your help. I'm on my way over there now. I'll explain after I pick you up."

Dean started to complain and ask for more information, but she'd already cut the connection. It took him a moment to process what to do next. He was standing there in shorts and a T-shirt, ready for bed. His sandwich was half-made, and he was apparently supposed to head off on some secret mission in a few minutes. Dean shook his head and went into his bedroom to shower and change his clothes into something more appropriate for going out again. He hoped the shower woke him up a little bit.

He was out of the shower and finished making his sandwich fifteen minutes later. Dean was taking his first bite of the snack when he heard a car's horn honking outside, and a text message lit up his phone. Jaz was here. Well, that was fast, he thought. Even though he was tired, he was looking forward to seeing Jaz again and was a little intrigued about what she had going on that needed his immediate attention. Grabbing the rest of his sandwich and his keys, Dean headed out of his apartment over his landlord's garage and headed down to the street.

Jaz was pulled up in front of the driveway in one of the Errington Security unmarked black SUVs. He heard the door locks disengage as he approached and he pulled open the passenger door and climbed into the front seat. Jaz was in her black tactical outfit with a web harness over a black T-shirt. She had a black Errington logo ball cap on with her blonde ponytail pulled through the back. She was in assault mode. Dean felt overdressed in his khakis and a navy blue polo shirt.

"Geeze, Jaz, you look like you're going to war."

"Not sure what we're running into on this one, Dean. Better to be prepared than caught flat-footed."

She gunned the engine and pulled out into the street, heading west into the city. Dean hurried to put on his seat belt while she sped down the street and headed for the highway.

"What's the hurry? Do we need to call in to dispatch for some help?"

Jaz shook her head. "No, this is a private job. I thought I might need your input, though. Besides, you're always saying we need to hang out more together." She shot him a glance and a broad smile.

Dean had to admit she looked good, even in her work clothes. He had said they should spend more time around each other. While he hadn't necessarily meant more time doing work-related things, Dean guessed this was as good as it was going to get for a while given the crisis nature of things right now. He pushed his tiredness down and sat up in the seat and paid attention to where they were going.

Jaz was heading out towards the coastal region on Elk City's outskirts. That could mean the marinas and harbor area, or it could mean some of the more expensive waterfront properties kept by the area's wealthiest citizens. It turned out to be the latter as they passed the exit for the harbor and turned off the expressway and headed out onto Elk Point where all the rich folks lived.

"You said this is a private job. Are we headed to one of your client's homes?"

"One of my former clients, actually," Jaz replied. "Max Herron used to be one of our best local clients. He has business interests all over the country, and we used to provide all of his security. That changed with the current situation. Between the death of my father and the onset of what looks like a zombie apocalypse, Max decided to look elsewhere for his personal security needs."

"So we're headed out to try and win him back?"

"Not exactly," Jaz explained. "He's having some sort of issue with his new security boss and called me to come and fix it. I'm not sure what the issue is exactly. He wouldn't tell me over the phone. I didn't have any of my regular security backup available to come along, so I called you."

"Why me?" Dean asked. "I'm not even armed, and I don't want to be."

"You're better at this than you realize. You think quickly on the fly, and something tells me that there's an Unusual side to this problem. Something in the way Max skirted my questions about who he'd hired."

Jaz pulled the SUV up to the gate blocking access to a long, tree-lined drive. Dean could see a huge mansion in the distance, set right on the water. Jaz pulled up to a speaker box next to the entrance and pressed a button. They waited for a few minutes, and then she pressed it again. Still no answer.

Taking her phone out, Jaz was tapping a message into her phone when the unmistakable sound of two gunshots sounded from the direction of the house. Jaz shoved the phone back into a cradle mounted on her harness and dug in her pocket until she produced a keycard. She reached out and swiped it through the reader in the speaker box and looked to the gate. She sighed in relief as the gate swung inward.

"We installed this system, and we had a backdoor master key installed so we can always gain access," Jaz said, putting the magnetic card back in her pocket. "I guess Max never had his new security head change the locks. Good for us, though. Hang on."

Dean was pressed backward into his seat as she gunned the big eight-cylinder engine in the SUV to full speed and raced up the long, winding driveway towards the mansion. They pulled around to the side of the large home next to a detached garage big enough for six or more cars. More gunshots sounded from the rear of the home on the waterfront side.

"Dean, grab the emergency first aid bag from the back. It has all the normal supplies you might need plus a few extras I threw in when I figured you were coming along."

Jaz jumped out of the car, pausing only long enough to grab her katana and slide the sword scabbard over one shoulder into the loops set in the back of her harness to hold it. Then she drew her pistol and ran for the corner of the house. Dean opened the rear lift gate and found the first aid trauma bag in the back amidst the other assorted cases and supplies she usually kept back there. He jogged over to join Jaz at the side of the house.

She was peeking around the corner to see where the shots had come from. He leaned out to look as well. When he did, he saw a man and woman running across the lawn, pursued by a group of five or six zombies. The man was holding a revolver and was trying to reload on the run, something Dean thought was probably impossible since the man was dropping the bullets as fast as he could pull them from his pocket.

Jaz cursed aloud and started running after the man and woman. Dean followed, figuring it was better to stay close to his armed companion in case there were more rampaging zombies around. The man and woman ran down to the water and into some sort of boathouse there. They slammed the door shut behind them just as the first of the zombies reached the building. The creature bashed at the glass window set in the top half of the door, breaking it inward and started climbing inside. Dean could hear shouts and screams coming from the boathouse's interior.

His partner assumed a shooting position and with a quick succession of double-tap shots, dropped each of the zombies clustered around the entrance to the boathouse. Dean was taken aback by her ferocity. These zombies were likely under Artur's control and not responsible for their actions. They didn't deserve to die like this. Still, as he considered the current situation, it might have been the only option. There was still screaming coming from inside, and Dean knew at least one of the zombies had made it into the building.

He and Jaz ran up to the door and looked inside through the broken window. The man and woman were backed into a corner, and he was fending off the zombie with an oar, pressing the blade end against the creature's chest, holding it at bay. Jaz stopped to take another shot, but Dean placed a hand on her arm.

"There's only one. Let me try something first. Cover me, though, in case it doesn't work."

Jaz started to protest but stopped and stepped back so he could open the door and enter. Dean reached around through the broken window and unlocked the door, swinging it open and walking inside. The man and woman looked his way and shouted for help. Dean cringed as the zombie noticed their shift in attention and turned to see him sneaking up behind it. The zombie was a woman, dressed in a maid's uniform of some sort. Dean held out a hand and tried to talk to her.

"Ma'am, I'm Dean Flynn. I'm a paramedic, and I just want to help stop whatever is controlling you. I'm going to come closer and try to help you, alright?"

The zombie woman seemed confused by something. She snarled at him, not saying anything intelligible he could understand, but she didn't advance on him either. Dean took a step forward extending his hand forward, palm out. He was trying to do something he'd never consciously tried before. He wasn't sure if it would work, but he didn't want this woman to go the way of the other zombies outside if he could help it.

He took a step and then another until he was at arms' length away from the woman. She had still not attacked him, though she seemed to be struggling against some internal control. He reached out and placed his hand on her forehead while he said a quick prayer for help.

The instantaneous effect was evident as she stopped her guttural snarling and stood up a bit straighter. From Dean's side of things, he got the same glimpse into the mind of the person controlling the zombie woman as he did when he touched Brynne in the same way. This time, he didn't see Artur, though. This time he was looking at another woman. He looked up in alarm and pointed at the woman standing next to the man in the corner.

"You. You're the one who turned this poor woman into this form." Dean shouted to Jaz. "She's the one behind all these zombies. She turned them but lost control, and they started attacking her."

Dean wasn't sure how he knew all this exactly, but it was as evident as it could be to him through the connection he had through the zombie maid. He didn't want to let go right away for fear she'd revert to her previous feral state. Looking to Jaz, now walking up to stand next to him, he asked for her advice.

"Jaz, I've got control of this woman, but I'm not sure what to do next. That one might still have a way of controlling her." He pointed to the woman in the corner. She wore a Caribbean print dress and head wrap. She had a necklace of large crystals and had somehow managed to keep her heels on her feet despite the rapid flight down from the main house to the boathouse.

The woman gave Dean a defiant look while the man next to her looked at her in horror. Jaz pointed her semi-automatic pistol at the woman while she talked to the gentleman standing next to her.

"Max, be a dear and take two steps to the right," Jaz said. "I want to make sure I have a clear shot in case your friend tries anything."

Max did as he was told. He still stared at the woman standing next to him with a shocked expression plastered on his face.

"I assume you're the new security consultant he hired when he fired us?" Jaz asked.

The defiant woman lifted her chin in defiance as she answered. "I am Sephrina, and I'm a high priestess of the islands. I'm not afraid of you."

Jaz laughed. "You should be. I don't take kindly to those who try to cheat old family friends, even ones who try and dump us when we need them the most."

Dean saw Max wince at that last remark directed at him. Jaz could lay it on thick when she wanted to.

"Jaz," Max spluttered. "I'm sorry. I didn't think you would get Errington back up and running so quickly and then all this zombie nonsense started. Sephrina approached me and told me she could control zombies if any attacked. Then I started noticing things were going missing from my home. That's why I called you. When I confronted her with my suspicions, we were attacked by my staff; all turned into zombies."

"It was all part of her plan from the start, right Sephrina?" Jaz asked. The voodoo priestess didn't answer. Jaz continued. "She was going to exert her control over the 'attacking' zombies just in time to ensure you'd stay on her side and keep on paying her for services she created the need for."

"Something went wrong, though, and Sephrina couldn't control them on her own. There's something else controlling zombies in Elk City that's more powerful than she is and it took over. That's why you both had to run."

"I would have wrested back control in time," Sephrina challenged. "I just needed to adjust my spell some."

"There'll be no more spells today," Jaz said. "You're going to answer for your crimes here. Then, if and when you resolve your legal troubles in Elk City, you're going to leave this town and stay away from it and my friends." Jaz took out her cell phone and snapped a photo of the woman. "I have your picture on file now, and I'll be forwarding it to all my satellite offices as well as to the local and federal authorities. If you try something like this again, we'll know about it, and the next time, I can't say I'll be as forgiving."

Sephrina started to say something but at the last minute clapped her mouth shut and nodded. Jaz seemed satisfied. She looked back at Dean.

"You can let go of her now. She's out from under anyone's control, for the time being, I think."

Dean looked at the maid and took his hand away, ready to jump back if she lunged at him. The zombie woman blinked once or twice and then looked around in surprise.

"How did I get out here?" She spotted Max in the corner. "Mr. Herron, sir, what happened to me?"

"Maria, you're going to be alright," Max assured the woman. "I'm going to make sure to take good care of you. I promise."

———

THE SITUATION with Max Herron resolved as they wandered back up to the house. There was the problem of the bodies involved. The rest of the household staff was dead. Jaz made a few calls and said her security clean up team would come in and take care of the bodies. It was a service they provided for their wealthiest clients, and Max was definitely an Errington client again. He'd written Jaz a huge retainer check as soon as he got back to the main house.

Jaz had handcuffed Sephrina and put her in the SUV. She would answer for the deaths here at the estate. The Errington teams on loan to Elk City were acting as deputies of local law enforcement during the current emergency situation. They could take the report and turn it in following their arrest of the voodoo priestess.

As they went out and got ready to turn Sephrina over to the security team that had just shown up, she stopped and looked at Dean.

"You are special, Dean Flynn. May I do a reading of you?" Sephrina asked.

Dean looked at Jaz who shrugged. It was up to him.

"Sure, I guess so."

"Please remove the handcuffs."

Jazz stepped up and took off the cuffs. Sephrina rubbed her

wrists for a moment and then reached into a fold in her dress and took out a small deck of tarot cards. She shuffled the deck and then held the cards out in a fan shape to him.

"Take a card."

Dean paused and then reached out, pulling a card from the deck fanned in front of him. Turning it over, Dean saw a round shape. There were symbols written at different positions spaced along the outside edge of the wheel.

"Show me the card."

Dean turned the card and showed it to her. Sephrina sucked in a sharp breath muttering a single word in a quiet voice.

"Nephilim."

"What?" He turned the card over in his hand and looked at the face of it again. He didn't see anything that made any sense to him. "What did you see?"

"Nothing, I'm sorry," Sephrina said, though something clearly shook her. "Sometimes the cards have nothing to say." She held out the deck to him, and he replaced the card in it.

Sephrina hastily shuffled the deck again before putting it back where she'd gotten it. Placing her hands behind her back, she waited for Jaz to put the cuffs on her again. She didn't look at Dean again or say anything else no matter how many times he asked her to explain herself.

Jaz stepped forward and re-cuffed the woman, but her eyes were on Dean. There was a puzzled expression on her face as she led the woman away to turn her over to the security team.

Dean pulled out his phone and tried to look up Tarot card descriptions on his phone. He tried to remember the word Sephrina had said but she had been so quiet he couldn't quite remember it clearly. He did find the card he'd pulled from the deck. It was one known as the wheel of fortune card. It was supposed to signify change, destiny, life cycles or a turning point in life.

Well, given how fast his life shifted of late, he wasn't surprised, though he didn't put much stock in things like fortune tellers and tarot cards. He was a scientist at heart, after all. Dean shrugged and put his phone away while he followed Jaz back to the SUV.

Chapter 16

It was late by the time Jaz dropped him back off at his apartment. Dean was exhausted by the long day at work, followed by the side job with Jaz, and he looked forward to getting in bed and grabbing some much-needed sack time. Dean got in bed and closed his eyes, expecting a long, uneventful night ahead of him. It was not meant to be, though. Just as he was drifting off, the phone on the nightstand rang, startling him out of the early stages of sleep.

Dean reached for the phone and considered shutting it off and ignoring the call. He looked at the screen. The caller's name read "Gibbie." Dean sighed and tapped on the call to answer.

"Dean, thank God you picked up. You've got to help me. She's gone berserk, and I don't know what to do to stop her."

Dean sat up and tried to clear his head as he processed the words from the frantic voice on the other end of the phone. Gibson Proctor, or Gibbie, was a local character in the Unusual community. He was a slightly overweight, middle-aged vampire who always seemed to find his way into trouble of one sort or another.

"Gibbie, you know better than to call me at home when something like this happens. Call nine-one-one. Barry and Lynn are on tonight. They'll be able to help you."

"I did call them. She's got them cornered in a utility closet, and I think she bit Barry."

That woke Dean up right away.

"Wait, tell me what happened. She bit Barry, you said?"

"Just get over to the Metroplex on Route 40. I'll explain when you get here."

Dean looked at his watch. It was close to midnight. The movie theater complex was known for their late-night screenings of current movies popular with the humans of Elk City. Members of the Unusual nocturnal community had taken to attending them as well, adopting the theater as a place to let their hair down and be themselves.

Pulling on his clothes but taking the time to grab his fire department ID badge in case he needed to get past anyone to get inside, Dean rushed out and jumped in his pickup truck. Racing through the late-night deserted streets, he made good time and pulled into the Metroplex parking lot seven minutes later. The presence of numerous police lights amidst other emergency vehicles told Dean that the quick response team had shown up. That wasn't good if Gibbie's girlfriend was still out of control.

He parked at the edge of the cordoned-off area and walked up to a police officer standing near the entrance to the theater's lobby. The officer held up a hand to stop him from entering. Dean decided to try and bluff his way past since he didn't recognize the policeman.

"I'm with Station U and we have two paramedics in there," Dean said showing his photo ID badge with the fire department logo on it. "What's the situation?"

The officer shrugged as he looked scanned the badge with his eyes. "I'm not sure what's going on exactly, I got here and was told to keep people outside. Some sort of disturbance with a violent patron from what I've heard."

Dean nodded and started to walk past, reaching for one of the doors.

"Hey, why aren't you in uniform?"

Dean gave the honest answer to the question. "I was called out of bed, and this was all I had that was clean. I was supposed to be off-duty and asleep until this came up."

The officer snorted. "Yeah, sometimes you can't catch a break. Go on inside."

Dean smiled and pulled open the door, walking inside. He was going to have to think fast. He wouldn't be able to fast-talk someone from the QRT. They would know he wasn't there in any official capacity.

Once inside the lobby, Dean looked around, searching for options on where to go next. There was a crowd of police and what looked like theater managers on the opposite side of the lobby. He'd stay away from them. He just needed to find Gibbie.

A sound drew his attention away from the crowd near the snack bar.

"Psssst. Dean. Over here."

Dean searched for the source of the voice and found Gibbie peering around a door marked "Staff Only." He glanced around to make sure no one was paying attention to him and moved over to the door. Gibbie held it open long enough Dean to enter and pulled it shut behind them.

"Come on." Gibbie led him up a set of stairs to a long hallway. There were metal utility shelves along one side of the hallway holding cardboard boxes of cups and lids and other supplies for the snack bar downstairs. The other side was lined with a series of numbered doors.

"Where are we?" Dean asked.

"This is the projectionist's access hallway. Each of these rooms corresponds to the individual theaters below. The police haven't looked up here yet."

"That just means the police will be up here soon, Gibbie. They're going to lock this place down."

"I know. That's why we have to hurry. Come on."

The portly vampire gestured to Dean to follow as he took off down the long hallway at a jog. Dean had no choice but to follow him if he wanted to avoid getting kicked out of the building by the police before he had a chance to help out.

They came to a stop at the end of the hallway and entered the door marked with the number twelve. Inside Dean saw a projector. It was smaller than he expected but then he realized it was digital and didn't need to be big enough to house a giant film reel like they used to use. Gibbie had opened a small metal door in the wall. The opening was tiny, barely two feet across.

"What's that for?"

"It's a utility access point," Gibbie said. "I used to date the former projectionist. She was big time Emo and loved to bring me up here to fool around during the horror films showing at the time. She told me that through this access door, you could get anywhere in the building. There's a similar opening in the utility room Evie is holed up in with Barry and Lynn. It's the only other way in there besides the door."

"Wait," Dean stopped the vampire by holding up his hands in protest. "You want me to climb in there and find my way to where your girlfriend is holding my friends hostage?"

"Well, I can't fit through that hole. That's for sure." Gibbie grabbed a double handful of his gut for emphasis.

"What am I supposed to do when I get there?"

"I don't know. You'll think of something. She's not a bad person. For some reason, she just started freaking out in the theater and tried to bite a bunch of people. I don't know why. It was like she was under another person's control or something. I called nine-one-one and Barry and Lynn showed up. She grabbed them and pulled them into the closet. That's the last time I've seen them."

Dean's radar was tweaked by something he heard Gibbie say. He said, "she was under another person's control." Dean looked around and realized that a crowded, dark theater would be a perfect place for an attack from Artur's standpoint. It might be he could break the connection to the vampire lord like he did with Brynne if that was what was going on here. It could be something else entirely. Dean shook his head.

"I don't know Gibbie. I might be able to help, but she could be having a normal medical or psychological emergency. There might be nothing I can do."

"Dean, you have to try."

Gibbie's last words sounded desperate. Dean knew this was the only option for a quick fix without waiting for the police to try to negotiate their way inside. They'd run out of patience, though, and eventually, they'd just break in. Who knew who would get hurt in the process of neutralizing the threat in the utility room?

"Alright, I'll do it," Dean said.

Gibbie clapped with delight.

"You said her name is Evie?" Dean asked as he shrugged off his jacket. "What else can you tell me about her?"

"She is a relatively new vampire. She's only been turned about twenty years or so. She is super gentle. She works at an all-night emergency veterinary hospital taking care of sick pets. I know she didn't mean to hurt anyone, Dean. You have to help her."

"I have to help my friends first. I'll try and help Evie along the way if I can."

Dean leaned down and looked through the narrow opening behind the access door. There was not a lot of room in there. He could see pipes and a narrow access ladder that would allow him to descend inside the wall to the ground floor where the utility room was located, he presumed.

"You're sure this leads to the utility room?" Dean asked.

"Yeah. My old girlfriend told me these were the only two places to get into the crawl space."

Dean took the pocket flashlight he always carried on him. Its LED lamp was surprisingly bright for the size. It would provide him plenty of light along the way. Getting down on his hands and knees, Dean placed the penlight in his mouth to hold it until he climbed through the opening. As he was climbing inside, he heard loud voices from the hallway outside the projection room. He hurried to get through the opening and barely pulled his feet through before Gibbie pushed the access door closed. Suddenly, there was no light but what shined from the penlight in his mouth.

Perched on the narrow ladder, Dean looked around to get his bearings before he started down. He could hear a police officer begin to question Gibbie from the opposite side of the utility access door. The voices soon faded, though, as he climbed down to the ground floor level. He stepped off the ladder and looked around. He could see the passage leading off in both directions and he tried to get his bearings. The utility room should be to the left, he decided, so he headed in that direction.

The utility access space was narrow and he had to turn sideways to go past the pipes and conduits running from the floor to the ceiling high above. Soon he reached a section where there was another small panel in the wall near his knees. Dean crouched so he could examine the access door from this side. There was a handle that he presumed would unlatch it. It looked like the door opened into the room on the other side so he'd be hard pressed to sneak through or even open it much to try and look around without being noticed.

Dean leaned forward and pressed an ear to the cool metal of the door panel. He could hear voices on the other side. One was Lynn's.

"You need to let me check my friend out, Evie. You have to let him go so I can make sure you didn't kill him. It's not too late to do that."

"I have to kill, to drink. It's what the voice in my head is telling me to do," said another woman's voice.

"No, you don't. Listen to me," Lynn said. "The voice in your head isn't real. It's someone else trying to control you and get you to do things you don't want to do."

Dean was worried about Barry. He had obviously been injured by Evie, maybe seriously, judging by Lynn's words. It was also apparent that Evie had exerted some sort of control over the voice she heard, unlike Brynne. It might have to do with being a vampire longer. Brynne might not have had the sort of self-control yet to manage it. That was good news for this situation.

Dean took his phone out of his pocket and sent a brief text message to Lynn.

I'M *close by and want to come in. Make a distraction. Say "yes" if you understand.*

. . .

IT WAS a long shot but he had to try something. He just had to get close enough to touch Evie and break the hold Artur had on her. Dean still didn't know how he could do what he did but it worked and that was all that mattered right now. He had to try and save Barry.

His ear was still pressed against the metal and he heard Lynn's voice loud and clear.

"Yes."

"Yes, what?" Evie asked.

"Yes, I want to help you. That's all."

"You got some sort of message on your phone. What did it say? Show it to me."

"Sure, here you go."

Dean then heard some sort of scuffle begin on the other side. He decided to take advantage of the noise and pushed the access door open. He pushed his head through and saw Lynn and another woman struggling on the floor over control of the cell phone. Barry was slumped to the floor. His head was tilted to one side and Dean could see the bloody wound on the side of his neck. He seemed to be breathing but was unconscious.

Pulling himself the rest of the way through the opening, Dean scrambled across the floor as fast as he could and reached out to grab Evie's arm. She had raised it to strike at Lynn. With her superior strength, it could have been a deathblow. However, as soon as he touched her, she stopped struggling and looked around in confusion.

Dean stood up and pulled the vampire off of Lynn. The paramedic rolled to her feet and raced across the room to tend to Barry. Dean wanted to help her but he needed to attend to Evie and make sure she was back in control of herself. The woman was tall and was what he would term big-boned if he were told to describe her. She had brown hair and striking hazel eyes. They were currently gazing at him in wonder.

"How did you do that?" Evie asked him. "One minute I had

another voice in my head trying to get me to do horrible things and then next, it's gone."

"It's just a little trick I learned," Dean said, avoiding the question. "How do you feel? Are you back in control of yourself?"

"I think so." She turned to look at where Lynn was crouched over Barry. "Oh my God. Did I do that?" Her hand flew to her mouth and Dean saw tears in her eyes.

"You did, but it wasn't your fault. There's a person running around with a powerful artifact which is taking control of people like you to try and hurt humans."

"Did I hurt anyone else? The last thing I remember was sitting at the movie with my boyfriend. The movie was just about to start."

"I don't think you hurt anyone other than Barry here. Gibbie said he held you back while the people ran out of the theater."

"Gibbie?" Evie looked around. "Where is he?"

"He couldn't fit through the access panel," Dean pointed to his entry point. "He's somewhere close by, though. First, we need to work on our friend. You stand here and wait while I help Lynn out."

"Alright."

Dean crossed over to where Lynn was working on the unconscious paramedic.

"How is he?"

"He's lost a lot of blood. I've got an IV started and fluids running but he's going to need a transfusion and a dose of garlic extract to remove the vampire virus from his system. We need to get him to the hospital."

"Agreed," Dean said. "I need to get Evie out of here and around the police cordon. If we can get her out of this room, then I can go back up the way I came and meet you from the other side."

"Sounds like a plan," Lynn said nodding. "Don't take too long."

"I won't."

Dean turned his attention back to Evie. She was pacing back and forth in the small space scrubbing her hands together.

"Evie, if I can get you out of here, can you change form into something smaller and get away? I know you have to be a certain age as a vampire to do that."

"I can change into a bat if that's what you mean. I hate it, though. I'm afraid of flying."

Dean sighed. Of course, she was afraid of flying. Why would Gibbie have a girlfriend who was a normal vampire?

"Look, you don't have to fly far, just far enough to hide up in the rafters of the building. If you can stay put for a while, the police will leave and then you can just walk out."

"I guess I can do that," Evie agreed.

"Good. You go through here." He pointed to the access hole. "Hide up high and in the shadows in case the police search in there."

She nodded and started to climb through. Dean turned back to Lynn.

"The police are going to come soon. Tell them you and Barry hid in here after the attack and you didn't see the attacker. I'll help Evie get away. This wasn't her fault and I know Artur was behind it. Are you alright with that?"

"Yeah, just hurry up with getting the police here. I'll cover for you."

"Alright, I'll be outside and can drive the ambulance once we get Barry loaded up."

He turned to crawl back through the opening and pulled the door shut while Lynn continued to tend to her partner. There was no sign of Evie on the other side, so he returned to the ladder and climbed back to the projection room upstairs. Gibbie was gone and there was no sign of the police either. It was time to get back downstairs and help Lynn out once the police found them.

No one saw him as he returned to the lobby. The police had obviously cleared the upstairs access hall and didn't expect anyone to come from there. This time he clipped his paramedic ID on his shirt and crossed to the command group.

"I'm Dean Flynn. I came to help the paramedics on scene," Dean announced himself.

One of the police officers turned and looked at him, glancing at his ID.

"Good," the officer said. "Your team was holed up in a utility closet. One of them is injured. We just found them. You can go help. They're going to need a stretcher."

"Got it," Dean said.

He left to get the stretcher from the ambulance; happy his plan had come together. All that was left was to get Barry to the hospital and tell Gibbie where Evie was hiding. Dean let himself show a brief smile. All things considered, this had worked out about as well as he could have hoped.

ACROSS THE PARKING LOT, inside a car with tinted windows, Artur watched Dean exit the building and walk to the ambulance. The vampire lord growled a curse under his breath then started the car and pulled from the parking lot, driving off into the night.

Artur Torrence finished feeding on the woman in his arms and stepped away, letting her near-lifeless body slump to the bedroom floor. He muttered a curse as his mind turned to thinking about the meddling of the paramedic, Dean Flynn.

"God dammit, that bastard has crossed me one too many times."

"I don't know why you let him get to you," Felicity said as she walked away from the man's body in the corner. She stopped next to the groaning woman on the floor. "Are you gonna finish this?"

Artur waved his hand in dismissal and Felicity pounced down, sinking her fangs into the woman's shoulder with a giggle of delight. Artur looked down at his protégé's feeding and marveled again at how easy it was to change a human from their civilized ways back to their base nature as animals and predators. Felicity had been a nurse and healer before she was turned into the creature wantonly feeding on his leftovers. Look at her now. He snorted a short laugh and then looked away as an idea inserted itself into his mind.

He needed to rid himself of this Flynn character. Somehow the man was breaking into the connection between he and the undead he was controlling. It must be some artifact that was doing it. There was no way he had some innate power to interfere in this way. If Artur could get his hands on that artifact and separate Flynn from the tool he was using to defeat him, then the paramedic would not be a problem for him anymore. All he needed was some leverage against him, some way to convince Dean Flynn to give up the method of his interference.

Artur walked over to the bedroom window and looked out over the small townhouse community he had taken as the location of his lair. He was careful to keep from feeding too close to home, in case there was some way for the local authorities or James Lee's security goons to track him down. As far as the neighbors were concerned, he and Felicity were a couple who both worked night shifts.

He was watching a young couple who lived a few doors down return from a late outing. The man doted on her and opened the door for her as they walked into their home. Watching the two of them, an idea began to form in his mind.

"Felicity, dear, when you're done with that one, dispose of the bodies in the usual way and then come straight back here. I might want to have some fun when you return."

The female vampire looked up from her meal with a bloody smile on her face. "You're in a good mood all of a sudden. What changed in the last two minutes?"

"I think I finally have a way to convince our meddlesome paramedic to turn over his methods for breaking my controls over the undead. If it works, he'll have to tell me how he's doing it."

"Are you going to tell me or keep me in suspense?" Felicity asked.

"The best way to get to a man like Dean Flynn is to threaten someone he holds close. For me, it's a doubly attractive option because it also offers the opportunity to rid myself of the Erringtons once and for all."

"Oh, good. I want a chance to try my new strength on that hunter bitch. She can't be as good as she thinks she is."

"You'd never last more than a few minutes against her, my dear. You've never faced a trained hunter before, and this one is among the best," Artur warned Felicity. "No, we'll have to be careful and come up with a way to trap her and keep her alive but contained long enough to convince Mr. Flynn to come to her rescue and exchange whatever magical tool he's using to win her back."

"You mean you're going to let her go once you capture her? That doesn't make any sense, Artur."

"No, of course not. I will not let the Errington woman go, no matter what Mr. Flynn does. We'll only keep her alive long enough to force him to do what we want. Then we'll finish off them both."

Chapter 18

Dean slept in on the morning of his first real day off in two weeks. He rolled over in bed and looked at the clock. It read eleven AM. Dean sighed. He was exhausted from the continual running and overtime from the department plus the additional time spent running down leads with James, Jaz and the rest of them. They were still no closer to narrowing their search for Artur and catching him with the relic. James said if they could prove Artur was using the relic actively against James, it would be enough to convince the Unusual powers at the federal level to take action against the rogue vampire lord.

That was a great idea in the abstract, but it had proven difficult to do in reality. Artur was hiding well in plain sight, despite several sightings on surveillance cameras after the fact, they still had no clue where he was hiding out. James had Rudy and his pack out nightly searching the industrial parks and abandoned warehouses in and around the city as they were likely hiding places. They had turned up nothing.

Because Dean was their only sure-fire way of combatting the undead onslaught, he had been called time and again to scenes where an Unusual wasn't acting normal. Most of the time, it wasn't Artur at all and Dean could do nothing to help. Then he'd return to the station, or home if he was off duty, and try and go back to some sort of normal routine. Jaz had noticed how stressed he had become and made the executive decision that he needed some rest. She was taking him out to dinner that evening and had given both James and the local authorities strict instructions to leave him alone and let him rest for a few days. He was annoyed at having to be rescued from the workload but also glad to have the opportunity to stand down.

Jaz called it an operational decision. She said no one could stay on the front lines with no break for weeks on end without losing their edge. It was important for him to have a real break from the action in a way that kept him from focusing on work. Her idea was for the two of them to have a night out without any work-related discussion. They'd have to talk about other things. She said it would be good for them both to talk about things that didn't involve hunters and undead running amok.

He had to admit; it would be nice to go out with Jaz and not worry about such things. The two of them needed to get to know each other outside of their work. It seemed like every time they would get close to a personal breakthrough, something would come up and pull them apart or force them to work together in their official capacities. He wanted to get to know the woman with whom he was destined to have a child and start a family. Up until now, Dean felt like they were taking one step forward in that direction then taking two steps backward. It was time to push things in the right direction despite the events that surrounded them.

Dean got up and went out to the kitchen in his apartment over the landlord's garage. He poured himself a bowl of cereal and milk then sat down on one of the barstools at the counter to eat. He had some chores to do around the house today since he had fallen behind in helping the elderly couple from whom he'd rented the apartment. The Baxter's were very nice and gave him a break on his rent in exchange for him helping them out around the property. He had a list of things he needed to attend to before he could go out with Jaz that night.

It was a good thing, he figured. The physical workout around the yard would keep his mind off of work problems and be a positive break for him. He finished his late breakfast, got dressed in a pair of old jeans and a T-shirt and headed downstairs to grab the tools he needed from the detached garage's tool shed. He had a hedge to start pruning.

DEAN HAD BEEN RIGHT about the therapeutic nature of some work outdoors. He felt better as soon as he started and the mood altering work carried him through the rest of the afternoon. He finished up and went back to his apartment after putting his tools away to clean up. When he re-emerged, Dean felt refreshed and better than he'd felt in weeks.

Mrs. Baxter was out front, working in her flower garden when he walked to his pickup. He was wearing a pair of freshly pressed khaki pants and a blue button-down shirt under his jacket. She noticed his outfit right away and commented on it.

"You look nice, Dean. Off to a date with that pretty blonde girl I've seen you with lately?"

"Yes, Mrs. Baxter. Her name is Jaz."

"That's pretty. Is it short for Jasmine?"

"No, Jaswinder. I think it's a family name of some sort."

"Well, that's a lovely name, too. I hope you both have a good time. You've been working so hard lately. I was telling my husband just the other day that we've hardly seen you at all."

"I know, and I also know I've been slacking off on the chores. I'll finish the rest of them soon, I promise."

Mrs. Baxter waved him off. "Don't you worry about all that. You'll get to it in time. I know there's a lot going on in the city lately that has you and your paramedic friends really busy. We'll hold down the fort here."

She pointed to his truck. "You should get going. You don't want to explain that another pretty woman made you late for your date."

Dean laughed at her joke and waved goodbye as he got in his

truck and headed across town to pick up Jaz at her apartment. They planned on having dinner at the new Sabatani's and then maybe catching a late movie. It would be fun to get away and, who knows, he thought, the two of them might be able to take their budding relationship further than just a friendship tonight. As far as he was concerned, it might be time for that next step.

He parked his truck out in front of Jaz's apartment building and went upstairs to pick her up. She came to the door wearing a dress, which surprised Dean. His first thought was she looked fabulous. His second had him wondering where she was keeping her customary sidearm. He'd expected her to wear something a little more utilitarian. He was sure she was armed in some way.

Jaz noticed him looking her over and guessed at what he was thinking.

"Yes, I'm armed. You don't have to search me, though. Maybe, if you're lucky, I'll show you where I keep my pistol." She gave him a wink and walked past him to the elevator.

Dean followed her, his imagination racing even faster as he wondered both where her pistol was and, moreover, what she meant by her comment as she passed. He caught up with Jaz just as the door opened. He waited for her to enter and followed her on board.

"You look nice," he said in an attempt at small talk.

"So do you," she replied. "I figured we both needed something of a normal night out together. We've got to make up for lost ground, Dean. I feel like we don't have a lot of time left to get together as a couple, so I went out today and bought this little black dress for our date tonight."

"So, this is a date?"

"What would you call it?" She replied in kind.

"Oh, it's a date," Dean chuckled. "I mean, we both got dressed up and all. We're catching dinner and a movie. It has all the hall-marks of a date."

"Agreed. So, where are you taking me for dinner? I hope it's somewhere where this outfit won't be out of place."

"I thought we'd hit Sabatani's. Kristof has rebuilt the restaurant, and I hear it's fabulous."

"Perfect. I hope you'll not stand on chauvinistic conventions and let me pick up the check. I know I make like four or five times what you pull in as a city employee."

Dean smiled at her as they walked outside to his waiting pickup truck.

"I'm a fully liberated man of the new millennium. I'd be happy to let you spend your riches on me."

Dean watched as she was about to give what he was sure was a snappy reply when a white panel van pulled up and parked behind his truck. The side door slid open, and a group of six men jumped out, rushing the two of them. Jaz gave a yell of surprise as two of them reached for her arms and started pulling her towards the van. She punched one of them in the throat and then reached under the hem of her skirt, pulling out a small semi-automatic pistol. She was about to bring it to bear on one of her attackers when another of the men jumped at her and opened his mouth to sink his fangs into her forearm. Great, Dean thought. They're vampires.

Jaz yelped in pain and dropped the gun, yanking her bloody arm from the vampire's mouth. She tried to swing a punch at his face, but two more attackers piled on grabbing at her arms. Dean tried to come to her rescue, but one of the first attackers turned and plowed into him, knocking him to the pavement hard. It was all happening so fast. He gave an awkward roundhouse punch to the side of his attacker's head, and there was a flash of light that momentarily blinded him. The vampire's dead weight fell on top of him, and for a moment he was unable to free himself. He twisted his head to look back and watched as the other five attackers pulled the struggling Jaz into the van. The door slid shut and they pulled away, driving away into the night.

Dean finally managed to free himself from beneath the dead weight of the vampire collapsed on top of him. He wasn't sure if the guy was dead or alive, unsure what exactly had happened when he hit the vampire's temple with his fist. It didn't matter in the end. What mattered was they had Jaz. He didn't wonder who "they" were. Dean had little doubt they'd been sent by Artur. He was sure

Jaz had been on the vampire lord's hit list ever since he failed to kill her along with the rest of her family.

Pulling out his phone, Dean dialed James first. He could have called the police as well, but he knew they'd be of little help with this particular situation. The line picked up after only a few rings.

"Dean, what are you doing calling me," James said. "You're supposed to be taking a night off. Jaz was very specific with me about that."

"They took her. Right off the street. We were supposed to go out, and then they swooped in and took her away from me. I couldn't do anything."

"Wait. Slow down, Dean. Tell me where you are. Rudy's here, and I'm sending him to you right away."

"I'm outside of Jaz's apartment building," Dean exclaimed, his voice rising in pitch. He knew he was beginning to panic a little but he couldn't stop. "They took her right here in front of her building. I got one of them, but the rest took her and got away."

"Alright, try and calm down," James said, his voice even and steady over the phone. "Rudy just left, and he'll be there soon. You said you got one of them? Are they dead or what?"

"They were vamps, James. You and I both know who sent them. It has to be Artur. The guy they left is here, but I can't tell if he's alive or dead. It's not like I can check for a pulse or breathing. I hit him pretty hard, though, and then something weird happened. Something flashed bright white, and he collapsed on top of me."

"Vampires," James answered. "He can't have too many of those he'd trust out from under his direct control. Rudy and a few of his pack mates are on their way there. He'll be able to help you with the one you have. If he's not dead, we'll get him back here and try and get some answers out of him."

"What do I do if this one wakes up before Rudy gets here?"

"I don't know, Dean. Hit him again until he stays down. He's our only connection to Jaz right now."

Dean disconnected the call and stood looking down at the vampire lying on the ground in front of him. If this was the only way he was going to find and rescue Jaz, it didn't seem like much. It was all he had, though. He had to hold on to that. With nothing better to do but wait, Dean stood over the body on the sidewalk, waiting for Rudy to arrive.

Chapter 19

Dean stopped pacing the white, tiled floor and looked at Brynne. "When are we going to go in there and start questioning this guy?" Dean asked. He was feeling more frantic by the minute because every minute was another chance for something to happen to Jaz. He paced across the room to look out over the night-time cityscape of Elk City below. He didn't know why. It wasn't like he could make out anything meaningful on the streets far below them.

"Dean," Brynne soothed. "James and Rudy know what they're doing here. You need to trust them."

"But what's taking them so long to come back from City Hall?" Dean asked.

He was alone in the apartment with Brynne and Celeste while they awaited the return of the Elk City vampire lord and his head of security. They had left soon after Dean was picked up with his hostage, saying only that there was an urgent matter to attend to at City Hall. Dean saw two of Rudy's werewolf pack mates haul off the captured vampire. He was just starting to regain consciousness.

"There is a great deal of wheeling and dealing going on behind the scenes right now, Dean," Celeste replied. "The mayor has never been comfortable with the Unusual population living in Elk City being so prominent. With the current state of affairs, he wants assurances from James that the human populace is receiving the proper protection from their Unusual neighbors."

"But this guy could lead us to Artur," Dean explained pleading his case. "We could wrap up the whole problem if we can find Artur and deal with him once and for all. I, for one, am interested in that. Why isn't anyone else?"

"Dean," Brynne said trying to reassure him. "James and Rudy know that. They've got a lot on their plate right now but believe me when I tell you, Artur is priority one. We'll get him. We'll get Jaz back, too."

The conversation stopped when they heard the elevator chime from the entry foyer, and Dean heard James and Rudy talking as they came into the penthouse. The two of them were in the midst of an animated discussion as they walked into the room.

"James, this is serious. The mayor can make things very difficult for you if he stops working with you to keep the peace. You have to be careful how you approach him over this current problem."

"I don't care, Rudy," James replied. "That man is in office partly because of the support of my community. If he wants to stay in office after the next election, he'd better remember who helped put him there."

James noticed Dean and the two women and stopped the conversation. Brynne asked him about the meeting with the mayor.

"That man said he expects me to pay for the overtime needed to manage the attacks in the city since they were perpetrated by what he called 'one of my kind,' as if I had some control over what was happening."

Dean had never seen James angry before. He was always the pinnacle of self-control. The mayor of Elk City must have been pretty disrespectful for him to react this way.

"We need to find Artur, and we need to do it now," James said.

"That's just what I was saying to these two." Dean pointed to Brynne and Celeste. "Let's get started questioning the guy we captured, James. He's got to know something about where they took Jaz."

"We've got to have a plan, Dean," Rudy said. "We can't just walk in there and start slinging questions at him. He's got to have a reason to cooperate or fear something we can do to him. If he doesn't, we won't get anywhere."

The werewolf pack leader and head of security could be imposing. Dean didn't understand why he couldn't just go in and get the answers they needed, one way or another.

"Vampires can be intransigent, Dean," James added. "There isn't much we fear, especially when we're young in our transformation. My guess is that Artur has turned this individual recently. That way he'd still be under control of the master who turned him. That control fades with time and would be of little use after five or ten years have passed."

"So what do we do?" Dean asked. He was tired of waiting. "Jaz is in the hands of an insane vampire lord who has no problem inflicting pain and death on anyone who gets in his way. We have to find her, and soon."

"No one's disagreeing with you, Dean," Brynne said coming over and laying a supportive hand on his shoulder.

Dean looked at his former partner. He wondered if she understood how he felt. Every time he started to get close to Jaz, something got in the way. He felt a close bond to the hunter now, and he now knew she felt the same way. It wasn't fair that people like Artur kept getting in between them.

"Come on, Dean. Let's you, me, and Rudy head down and take a look at our captive," James offered. "We'll see if we can't find a way to convince him to see things our way."

Dean nodded and followed James and Rudy from the penthouse and back to the elevators. Taking the elevator down to the fifth floor, they got off, and Dean realized he'd never been on this level before. The panel on the wall opposite the bank of elevators read "Nightwing Security." This must be where Rudy ran operations for James' personal and business security.

They walked down the hallway, past a guard station with a man in a navy blue sports coat watching a series of monitors. He nodded at them as they passed. Turning a corner, they reached a pair of doors with two men standing outside. They were huge, bursting at the seams of their khaki pants and navy blazers. Dean assumed they were pack members, but they could have been bulky vampires, too, he supposed.

Rudy led them to the left-hand door, and they went inside a darkened room. One wall had a large window set in it, and Dean soon realized this was an observation room for the interrogation room next door. He looked through the window that, he realized, must be a two-way mirror. On the other side was the man he'd captured. He was pacing the room like a caged animal, trying the doorknob from time to time to check if it was locked and looking around for some means of escape.

A blonde woman in a navy blue pants suit entered the room as Dean scrutinized the captured vampire in the adjacent room. She handed a file folder to Rudy and nodded to James.

"We don't know much about our visitor here," the woman said. "He says his name is Grant. I have no way of verifying that. He had no identification on him when he was picked up. Other than his name and his repeated threats that we'd better let him go or his master will come and kill us all; I don't have a lot to tell you."

James gestured to the woman. "This is Victoria. She works with Rudy and usually handles things when our, uh, guest is a vampire. She's been with me almost as long as Celeste has." He pointed to Dean. "Victoria, this is Dean Flynn, Brynne's former paramedic partner."

The woman extended her hand and shook Dean's hand in a firm handshake. The cool skin confirmed for him that she was a vampire.

"It's a pleasure to meet you, Dean. I've been following your exploits for some time now."

"Really? I guess I'm flattered," Dean said. He felt a little awkward.

"No big deal, really," she replied. "We look into the backgrounds of all the Station U paramedics. It helps us identify when one might become a problem down the road like your predecessor Zachary."

Dean remembered how the paramedic who'd been Brynne's

partner before him had ultimately turned on his Unusual patients and started carrying out hate crimes against them.

"I'm glad I passed the test, then." Dean pointed through the glass. "Is there any way we can get him to tell us where Artur is or where they took Jaz?"

"We haven't figured out the trigger to make him talk yet. It's hard when a vampire is so new. They feel invincible. They know that we only have the option to either kill them or let them live. Anything else we do will regenerate with no lasting effects. It makes interrogation — challenging, shall we say."

Dean looked through the glass at the vampire. He felt anger rising inside. Anger at this vampire, anger at Artur, and anger at how helpless he felt.

"I want to talk to him."

"Dean," Rudy said. "I'm not sure that's a good idea."

"Come with me if you want," Dean offered. "You can keep him for hurting me or the other way around."

Rudy looked at James. After a moment, the vampire lord nodded.

"All right, Dean," Rudy relented. "But follow my lead. Let me start the conversation. This can be delicate, and we have to proceed carefully."

"I'll be careful." Dean hoped they didn't notice he didn't agree with Rudy in that statement. He didn't want to lie to his friends. He had an idea of how to get the vampire to talk, but he wasn't sure how the others would react.

James and Victoria settled in front of the two-way mirror to watch as Dean and Rudy left the room to go next door. Dean knew he was going to only get one chance to try his idea out on the prisoner. It was either going to work, or he was going to get hurt, or worse, in the process of trying. It didn't matter, though. He had to try something. Rudy and Victoria had gotten nowhere so far.

Rudy opened the door and led the way into the room, flanked by the two enormous guards from outside. Dean followed, his hand reaching into his pocket. He pulled out his pocket knife and opened the small blade, making sure no one could see what he was doing, using the burly guards and Rudy to block the view from the mirror in the left wall. Grant backed against the far wall, holding himself in a defensive crouch ready to fight.

"I won't tell you anything, but if you want to fight, I'm willing. Maybe I'll find out what werewolf tastes like before the night is over." The vampire said.

"Grant," Rudy said. "I'm Rudolf Finney. I'm in charge of security here. We have a few questions for you."

Grant started to answer but stopped suddenly as he sniffed the air. Dean had slid the blade of the knife through his palm, gritting his teeth at the sudden stinging pain. Just as Dean expected, the new vampire smelled the fresh blood instantly. Grant growled and launched himself across the room, catching Rudy and the two security team members completely off guard.

Dean held his bloody palm up in front of the charging vampire, luring him in. He knew he had to time this perfectly, or the more powerful Unusual was going to have more than enough time to injure or kill him before Rudy and the others could separate them. Just as the vampire closed on him, Dean brought the flat of his uninjured hand around and struck the side of vampire's face. There was the familiar flash of light Dean was hoping for, but this time, he tried to hold onto the light. It was something he'd never done before: try to use his hidden powers consciously. He was hoping to use his ability, wherever it came from, to exert some control over the vampire in front of him.

Grant stopped as if he hit a wall as soon as Dean's palm impacted his face. Dean brought his other, bloody hand up and grabbed the vampire's head between both his hands before he fell and broke the connection. He concentrated on holding onto the flash, or whatever it was he was doing. It seemed to be working. The vampire stood still, staring at him wide-eyed, his lips quivering as if he was trying to talk.

Rudy was advancing on Dean to pull the vampire away but Dean shot him a steely-eyed glance and shook his head. Something in his eyes must have convinced the werewolf because Rudy held up a hand and held his guards back.

Dean decided to try and command the vampire to say something.

"Grant, do you know who I am?"

"Y-y-you're the paramedic, the one who knocked me out."

"Yes, that's right," Dean said. He was making this up as he went along. He decided to try something else.

"Did you know I could knock you out like that before you and your friends attacked us on the street?"

"N-n-no. Master just told us to grab the woman and bring her back to him. If we could grab you, too, we were to do so, but she was the primary target."

"And so your friends left you, left you with me after taking my friend. You know that makes me angry, right?"

Grant nodded his head a little between Dean's hands gripping the sides of his face.

"I've been told that vampires don't fear much. You know that you might die but there isn't much else out there that can truly harm you in the long-term. The problem with that assumption is that it doesn't take me into account."

"W-w-what do you mean?"

Dean could sense the fear in the vampire. Good. That was exactly what he wanted.

"I can command you, Grant. I can tell you to do something and you will have to obey as long as you live. No matter how painful it will be, you will follow that command to the last letter."

"W-w-what do you want from me?"

"It's simple, Grant. I want my friend back. If you help us find her, and she's alive, I'll take back my command, and you can go back to normal."

"I-I don't have to tell you anything. Master said the other vampire lord would not kill me."

"I'm not going to kill you, Grant. I'm going to do much worse than kill you." Dean paused. This next part was coming from pure instinct. He didn't know if it would work or not but this latent power of his was working so far.

"Are you hungry, Grant? Can you smell my blood?"

The vampire gave another small nod.

"Grant, I command you. You are now to feel the depths of your greatest hunger at all times, but you are never allowed to drink another drop of blood, not ever."

Dean watched the change come over the vampire in his grasp. He could see the horror of what he'd done dawn on the man. He was a vampire, he would never truly die, but he would also never be able to truly live since he'd never be able to feed again. It was cruel. It was a punishment worse than death. Dean didn't care. He only wanted one thing and this vampire was the one who could help him get it.

He let go of Grant's head. There was no danger here anymore, not from this vampire. Grant collapsed into a heap on the floor, sobbing. Dean nudged him with a toe and the whimpering increased.

"Grant, you don't have to feel this way forever. Tell us where your master is hiding."

"I-I don't know the address, b-b-but I can take you there."

Dean looked up and saw Rudy staring at him, a grim expression on his face. Dean knew he'd crossed a line here. He was a healer and he also knew there were rules to what Rudy would allow to happen to a prisoner in his custody. Dean had violated both his own standards and those of his friend. He didn't care. He wanted Jaz back safe and sound. Without saying a word, Dean turned around and left the room.

Chapter 20

Artur got out of the car and walked to the front door of the abandoned mansion on the outskirts of town. Felicity drove the car around back to hide it from sight behind the home. He'd known it was time to move from the townhouse they'd been using as their base of operations when one of his followers failed to return from their errand to pick up the hunter. Felicity had told him of an old mansion on the outskirts of town a few days before. She thought it would be perfect for them to use once the townhouse became too small to hide their growing numbers.

Looking around the grounds as he walked to the front door, Artur was happy with the decision to relocate. The house was set well back from the road so any noise from the home's Unusual residents and their victims would be masked. There were numerous rooms in the house to provide a place for the growing army of followers to stay. He would have to reward Felicity for her initiative. Perhaps he would let her turn a vampire on her own the next time they went hunting. The former public health nurse was surprisingly vicious in the way she preyed upon human victims. She showed promise of being one of his best children in a long time. That type of promise must be rewarded.

Artur stepped inside the entry hall and looked around. A vampire in a business suit came around the corner at the far end of the hall and noticed him standing there.

"My lord, we didn't know you were arriving quite so soon."

"Never mind that, where is she?" Artur asked looking around the grand entry hallway with a large chandelier overhead and a broad staircase leading up to the second floor.

"I'm sorry, sir. Who did you mean?"

"The hunter girl. I got word she was captured and brought here."

"Ah, the captive is being held in the basement, your lordship," the man said with a bow. "May I show you the way?"

"Just point me to the stairs and then go out back and help Felicity bring in my belongings," Artur ordered.

"Yes, sir. As you wish, sir."

Artur followed the servant. The man led him to a door that opened to reveal stairs down into the basement. Artur started downstairs while the other vampire left to bring in his belongings from the car. Felicity would ensure the bedroom was arranged the way he liked it and that his clothes were unpacked and put away.

The basement of the home was finished into a recreational area with one large room and several smaller rooms off of it. In the main room, there was a wet bar made of wood off to one side. Someone, probably one of his followers, had screwed eye bolts into the front of the wooden counter top. They were currently being used as positions to secure the bindings of one Jaswinder Errington, her arms tied, so they were spread wide across the front of the bar while she was seated on the floor, still wearing the tight little black dress in which she'd been captured. She looked up at him as he came down the stairs.

He expected her to be somewhat cowed by her captivity, but she was not. On the contrary, she stared him down as he approached, raw defiance lending a fiery glint to her eyes.

"Ms. Errington," Artur said. "This moment has been a long time coming. I will finally realize my aim to rid the world of your meddlesome family once and for all."

"I don't think you realize what kind of trouble you're bringing down on yourself, Artur," Jaz replied. "You've bitten off more than you can chew this time."

"Ah, my dear, that is delightful. Such defiance in the face of impossible odds. There is nothing you can do, no one you can count on for help, no possible escape. I hold all the cards here."

"So, what? You toy with me until you tire of the sport, and then you kill me? I promise you; I won't give in that easily."

"You prefer 'Jaz' don't you?" Artur asked. "Well, Jaz, I would certainly not want to miss out on the chance to torture you endlessly in the interest of getting back at your family for hounding me all of these long centuries. I'm not going to do that, though. I think I'm just going to rip your throat out and have a long drink as the last of the Errington clan leaves this earth."

"That would be a mistake, Artur, one that you'll live to regret, if only for a short time," Jaz replied.

"Oh, how do you mean?"

"I mean that you should be aware of things I've discovered about Dean Flynn's true nature that you might want to know. He's the real opposition to your attempt to take over Elk City from James Lee."

"That human paramedic is no threat to me," Artur lied. He wondered what this hunter girl knew about the paramedic that he didn't. It was true they were companions, that much he knew, but what else was there?

"Tell me what you know, and perhaps I'll make your death a little less painful."

"I think not," Jaz said. "I just know I don't want you using me to lure him here. I don't want any part of the carnage that would follow such a vain attempt at killing him. He probably won't come unless there's proof I'm alive anyway."

"Tell me what you know, girl. I know he has fallen under the protection of the Eldara in the past, but I rid the world of that particular bitch for a while. What else has he managed to find to protect himself?"

"His power is getting stronger all the time, Artur. That's all I know. Every time he's stepped in to counter you, you've failed to stop him. Isn't that evidence enough of his capabilities?"

"Whatever method or tool he's discovered to protect himself if he comes here, he'll never walk out alive. Still, you will be useful as bait to lure him into the little trap I have planned." Artur liked the idea of killing them both together. The girl was right. The paramedic had been a thorn in his side since he started working at that station.

"I'll leave you alive for a short time longer. Perhaps you and the paramedic can die together down in this basement." Artur laughed. All this gloating had made him hungry, but he resisted the urge to have a sip from the prisoner. That was a meal he wished to savor in its entirety. He smiled down at the girl one more time and turned to go back upstairs. He wanted to see who his followers had procured as feeders for himself and Felicity. He was suddenly famished.

JAZ WATCHED him go and counted her blessings again. Her hasty plan had worked for now. She was sure for a moment the vampire lord was going to go ahead and kill her no matter what it meant to his other plans. It was only her quick thinking about how Dean and the others might impact his ultimate goals that saved her.

Once Artur reached the top of the stairs and closed the door, the lights shut off again and she was plunged into near total darkness. Luckily, the vampires who kidnapped her didn't take her hunter charm from her. It still dangled on the gold chain at her throat. Closing her eyes, she said "Lumos," and when she opened them again, she could see much better in the darkened room. Not as well as with the lights on but sort of a muted green haze over the contents of the room.

Looking around, she tried again to find a possible way to escape from the ropes that bound her arms. Her shoulders were already cramped from being extended in this position for so long. She tried to tense and relax the muscles in alternate cycles in order help alleviate her cramping pain. There was nothing else she could do until she managed to find a way out of her bonds.

She had one trick she could try, but it would take a long time, time she might not have. These ropes were thick. Jaz was glad she had taken to wearing finger blades in the past year. They were small, narrow razor-edged blades glued under the fingernails of her index fingers. They were invisible unless you looked closely at her hands. The blades weren't much, and it would take a long time to saw through the stout ropes they'd used to bind her, but it was all she had right now.

Twisting her hands to a painful angle, she was able to press her finger against the edge of the rope knots binding her wrists. She had to make sure she attacked the underside of the knot so it wouldn't be visible to any casual inspection. It was awkward to do, but she managed to slowly move her fingertip back and forth and start fraying rope in one part of the knots on either side. It was hard work, but it wasn't like she had anything else to do.

While she worked at her bonds, Jaz let her mind drift to thinking about Dean again. The two of them were getting along well, and she had planned to invite him back up to her apartment after dinner that night. She figured it was time for them to move forward in their relationship. Now it was all falling apart, and that pissed her off. She hoped Dean was smart enough to enlist some help at least when Artur tried to trap him into coming to rescue her. He wouldn't be that pig-headed, would he?

Chapter 21

Dean returned to work the next morning feeling like the walking dead himself. He'd been up all night after going on the raid Rudy and James assembled on a townhouse in the suburbs. The vampire they had captured assured them it was the hideout for Artur and his crew. Dean doubted it. He couldn't see the haughty vampire lord living in a small home like that.

It turned out Dean was both right and wrong. There was definite evidence of Artur's presence, but the vampire lord had clearly moved on. There were at least twenty bodies stacked in the basement in various stages of decomposition. Rudy said he detected the smell from outside the home, though Dean couldn't smell anything. Once they made entry to the home, the smell was obvious. It was probably the reason they moved on to another location. The neighbors were so close in these townhouse communities that it was only a matter of time before someone passing by detected the odors.

They checked on all the neighbors to make sure everyone was all right. The houses on either side of the target home were both empty. Someone lived there but no one was home. Dean suspected they would find that some of the bodies in the basement belonged to them. After they checked in with the police and turned the crime scene over to the ECPD and the coroner's office, Dean and the rest of the small group loaded back into their black SUVs and rode back downtown to the Nightwing Building. Dean returned home with only enough time to check his mail and get a quick shower before going to work.

He didn't want to be at work. He wanted to be out searching the city for Jaz. She was still out there, and he knew, somehow, she was still alive. He couldn't say how, but he knew deep inside that there was still time to get to her. Instead of looking for her, he was stuck here at the Station because the crews were stretched so thin.

As soon as he walked in the door at Station U, Dean could tell his co-workers detected his fatigue and distraction. He was usually talkative and upbeat. Today, he was sullen and withdrawn. He saw Brook and Tammy make eye contact and shrug at each other while they packed up to leave work. Barry must have detected his desire to be alone because he went into the ambulance bay and started the beginning shift checks on their gear and meds, leaving Dean alone in the squad room.

Dean stared at the computer screen in front of him, trying to make sense of what had happened overnight. His emotions had been riding a roller coaster for the last twelve hours, and he wasn't sure he could take much more of this. The kidnapping knocked him to his knees emotionally, and then the capture of the vampire and the hope they could question him for information brought him back up. He was excited when they finally got an address only to have his hopes dashed again when they found nothing to lead them to Jaz. He was emotionally spent.

He needed rest and sleep to right the ship, but that wasn't going to happen anytime soon. He had to work the rest of the day, and while he might get lucky and catch a short catnap here and there, it wasn't the same as a real night's sleep. Dean knew he was running at less than peak effectiveness. His training told him to be very careful at times like this and make sure to avoid making errors in judgment and patient care. He couldn't think about anything but Jaz, though. His thoughts centered on her.

Looking at the computer screen in front of him, Dean decided to get to work, to go through the motions until he found a way to get himself back on track. He logged in and started going through the morning email from headquarters. There were the usual medication shortage updates and notifications of upcoming training sessions available for the crews. He sorted through them, tagging some to forward to Barry's account until he came to one that caught his eye. There was a report of several individuals going missing on the outskirts of town with descriptions of the missing people. All stations were to keep their eyes open and report if anyone matching the descriptions and photographs in the email was spotted.

It struck Dean as strange that all of the reported missing people were males in their mid to late twenties. It didn't strike him as the normal type of missing person. Usually, such missing people were teen girls or women from at-risk situations. To have all four of the missing people listed be men in their prime was strange. He read the whole email twice thinking it must be important to have caught his eye like that but no other information leaped out at him. He shrugged and went back to sorting emails and filing the morning reports until the first ambulance call came in.

As Dean and Barry rode to the address provided, Dean listened to the dispatcher's description of the patient. They were responding to a female with a severe laceration with uncontrolled bleeding. Trauma calls were always interesting, and Dean perked up a bit to get back into a routine in which he had some control.

They pulled up in front of a small single-family rancher on the western edge of town, and Dean got out to help Barry back into the driveway. He didn't see any sign of a patient. They must be inside the house. He and Barry unloaded their gear and walked to the front door. Dean was just about to knock when the door creaked open, revealing an empty hallway into the home.

Dean looked at Barry who shrugged his shoulders.

"After you, Dean. You're the lead medic today, and this is why you get the big bucks."

Dean snorted at the comment. No one in EMS made anything resembling big bucks. He looked into the darkened interior of the home from the front stoop and called out.

"Hello. City paramedics. Did anyone call for help?"

A woman's voice called from inside the home. "I'm in here. In the back bedroom."

Dean took a step inside and tried a light switch inside the door-way, but nothing happened. There was enough sunlight streaming in to reveal a short hallway that opened on the left into a living room and continued to the rear of the home, turning to the right at the end. The daylight didn't penetrate beyond the first ten feet, though. It was dark at the back of the house. Dean pulled the mini-Maglite from his belt and shined the bright LED beam into the rear of the hallway as he advanced in that direction.

Turning the corner, he saw another light switch and tried it. Nothing happened. The electricity must be out for some reason. Dean looked behind him to reassure himself that Barry was right there then continued towards an open door at the end of the short rear hallway.

"I'm in here," the woman's voice called. "I can see your lights."

"Why aren't the lights working?" Dean asked.

"I think the electricity is shut off. The owner must not have paid his electric bills for a while," the woman answered.

Dean walked forward up to the doorway and looked inside. To the right was a pile of dark clothes on the floor and to the left, there was a bed with someone in it, but their back was to him. He relaxed a bit and took a step inside towards the bed. That was when the pile of clothes shifted, and a pasty white hand reached out to grab his ankle. With a shout and a jump backward, Dean shifted his light to shine on what he thought was a pile of clothing. His heart was racing, and he had very nearly pissed himself.

"I'm sorry," the voice from the pile of clothes on the floor said. Dean realized as the pile moved that it wasn't a pile of clothes after all. It was a woman collapsed in a heap on the floor wearing black robes. She had flipped the robes back to reveal herself. The woman had one hand gripping her thigh where he could see the wet fabric that was probably blood from a deep gash. The other hand had reached out to him.

"You startled me," Dean said. He looked at the figure on the bed and then back at the woman. The person on the bed hadn't moved despite his shout. "Barry, check the person in bed while I look over our patient here."

Dean wasn't sure if they'd stumbled on a burglar who'd injured themselves or what, but he needed to be careful.

"Don't worry about him," the woman said pointing to the bed. "He's dead. That's why I'm here."

"You killed him?" Dean blurted out the question before he realized he'd said it.

"No, silly," the woman laughed. "I'm here to collect him. I'm a reaper."

Dean looked at the woman, took in her black robes and the pale complexion. Barry said it before Dean could gather his thoughts.

"You mean like the Grim Reaper? You're kidding me, right?"

"Do I look like I'm kidding, dude?" She paused only a moment before continuing. "I was here collecting this guy's soul. None of the lights worked, so I was using my night vision to see, which isn't perfect in zero light conditions like this. The next thing I know, I tripped and was on the floor with my scythe blade sticking out of my leg. I pulled it out and tried to stop the bleeding but I can't, and now I feel weak and too dizzy to stand."

That last statement hit Dean, and his training moved him to action. He unzipped the trauma bag and grabbed an absorbent trauma pad impregnated with a quick-clotting product and slapped it over the wound in the woman's leg. Barry was checking on the man in the bed. Dean saw him shake his head and move back towards Dean and the woman.

"Hold this in place and press down hard while I get some things together," he told the woman. While he gathered the IV supplies and handed them to Barry, he introduced himself, trying to get back into control over the situation.

"I'm Dean, and this is my partner Barry. What's your name?"

"I'm Katya." She hissed in pain when he pressed harder over her hand on top of the dressing on her leg. "Man, I'm gonna get in trouble over this."

"Why's that?" Dean asked. "It's an accident and accidents happen all the time. I would suspect as a reaper you'd know that."

"It's my first job," Katya said. "It was supposed to be a cake walk. My superiors don't like to throw us to the wolves right away, and so I came here to collect Mr. Anderson's soul. He had died in his sleep after a long battle with cancer. It was his time, and I was to escort him along his journey to the afterlife."

"So there's an afterlife," Barry said as he tied a rubber tourniquet around her arm to get the IV started. She needed fluids. "I guess that makes you a sort of angel of death."

"I'm not the angel of death; I just work for her," Katya said.

Dean was cutting away the denim of her black jeans from around the wound so he could see what he was doing.

"So you're a sort of Eldara like the Valkyries are?" Dean asked.

"We're not Eldara; like I said, we just work for them. We can sense the lingering souls of the dead who don't want to leave this world. We use our scythes to cut the ties that bind them to their mortal bodies and help them on their way."

Dean looked around for a long pole with a curved blade like in the pictures he'd seen of grim reapers. "Where's your blade? I don't want to trip over it and lose a toe."

Katya shifted her robes to show a small hand-tool-sized scythe that could be held in one hand. It lay on the floor next to her leg.

"I was all excited and anxious about my first reaping. The rules say you don't deploy your blade until you need it, but I couldn't wait, and I was a little freaked out by the darkened house. Man, I'm in so much trouble," she said again shaking her head.

She shifted her position, and the dressing moved a little where she held it in place, renewing the flow of blood from her leg. Dean reassured her while he slapped another pile of gauze on top of the first and renewed pressure on it, holding it himself this time and pressing down hard.

"Don't worry about that. We'll help you explain to your bosses if you want. Right now, though, we need to make sure you don't lose any more blood so hold still, alright?"

Barry had the IV flowing and was getting a set of vital signs while Dean continued to try and stem the flow of blood. He decided he needed to stop fooling around and pulled his tactical tourniquet from his pocket and started wrapping it around Katya's leg above the wound. He cinched the strap tight before securing the end and looked at his patient.

"Katya, I'm going to twist this windlass and tighten this tourniquet. That's going to hurt. A lot. I need you to try and hold still so I can get the bleeding stopped, though."

She nodded and gritted her teeth as he started winding the windlass, tightening the tourniquet down until the blood flowing from the wound stopped. Katya was gasping in pain by the time he was finished securing and labeling the tourniquet with the time of application using a permanent marker. That would be important when they got her to the ER, and the doc's started working on her leg.

"I know it hurts. You're doing great, and I've been able to stop the bleeding. We'll get you to the ambulance and keep giving you fluids. I can also give you something for the pain when you're all loaded up."

Katya nodded and pointed to the bed.

"You have to help me collect Mr. Anderson's soul. He has to be freed from this world."

"What do you need us to do?" Dean asked. "If you tell me, maybe I can sever the connection."

"I have to do it. It's my job, and I can't leave until it's done," Katya insisted.

Dean looked at Barry, and his partner shrugged. They lifted the woman up with ease. She had grabbed her scythe, and she reached out over the body with it and grabbed at something with her free hand, swiping her blade in the air just below her closed fist. Dean thought he could see a wisp of smoke or something extending from her fist upward for an instant then it was gone.

"It is done," Katya said, relaxing in their arms. "I can go with you now."

Dean and Barry set her down on the edge of the bed and Barry left to bring in the stair chair to wheel her out to the ambulance. There was no way they'd get the stretcher in these narrow hallways.

While they waited for Barry to return with the wheeled stair chair, Dean and Katya talked about her work as a reaper. They continued chatting in the back of the ambulance while Barry pulled out of the driveway and headed to the hospital.

"You know, it's been strange lately around Elk City. I've heard my superiors talking about it. So many dead we've been called to serve here, only to arrive and find no body and no lost soul."

"There's been a problem with a power struggle in Elk City of late. Someone is raising the dead and creating new undead to serve his own purposes," Dean explained.

"Well, I hope they find the person who's doing it soon," Katya said. "There's an imbalance happening, and it's strongest on this side of town right now. I can feel it."

"I hope we find them, too," Dean said. Somewhere out there that person held the woman he had grown to care very much for. He thought about Jaz and watched out the back windows of the ambulance as Barry drove them down the street past a large, run-down mansion with an overgrown yard.

Chapter 22

After dropping Katya off at the hospital to get her leg attended to, Dean and Barry ran a series of non-stop calls taking them from one end of the city to the other. As a result, Dean never got the catnaps he had hoped to take during the day, and he was even more exhausted at the end of the shift. They finally returned to the station, but then he was tied up for another hour wrapping up his patient reports and making sure they were filed before he was finished for the day.

By the time Bill and Lynn arrived to take over, Dean was done. He wasn't just finished with his work; he was finished with everything. He was closer to total exhaustion than he'd ever been before and it showed in his every movement. Lynn commented on it when she walked into the squad room and saw him for the first time.

"Damn, Dean, you look like crap."

"Gee, thanks," Dean replied managing a half-smile.

"Don't worry about him, Lynn," Barry said. "He's running on a solid thirty-six hours with no sleep right now. He just needs a good night's sleep."

"Well then, get the hell out of here, Dean. We've got this," Lynn offered.

"I still have to go and run the final shift checks on the gear I used today," Dean said. "We've run a lot of calls since this morning."

"Nonsense," Lynn said. "Barry and I will finish up. Bill's running late, so one of you has to stay late anyway. Barry will do it, won't you?"

"Sure thing, partner. Go home, Dean. Get some sleep. I'll see you in the morning."

Dean sat for a moment longer, his exhaustion-slowed brain processing what his friends and coworkers told him. Then he nodded and stood up.

"Thanks, guys. I owe you one."

"Nonsense," Lynn said. "You'd do the same for us. Get some rest. We'll see you in twelve hours."

Dean picked up his coat and phone and walked from the squad room to the parking lot. The sun was setting over the buildings to his right as he walked to his truck. His phone buzzed in his pocket with a text message. After he climbed into his pickup and started the engine, Dean checked the message on his phone. His heart skipped a beat when he saw it was from Jaz; then he read the message itself.

"I HAVE YOUR HUNTER FRIEND. *If you want to see her again alive, come to 1367 Mockingbird Lane. Come alone, or she dies.*"

DEAN DOUBLE CHECKED the address and entered it into his GPS. He thought only once about calling James and Rudy and asking for help. The message had been clear. "Come alone, or she dies" was the kind of thing you expected from a kidnapper but in this case, Dean knew it was meant in all seriousness. Dean pulled out of the parking lot and gunned the engine, heading out into the darkening city streets.

As Dean pulled away, a dark SUV pulled from the lot across the street and followed him down the road.

⬜

"HE'S ON THE MOVE," Rudy said, hanging up his phone.

Brynne looked up from the magazine she was reading. "Where's he headed? Is he going home?"

Rudy shook his head. "He's headed across town. My guy watching him said he got a message on his phone and then drove away in a hurry. He's following Dean now."

"That has to be a message from Artur to lure Dean in," Brynne said. "Let me get James and Celeste from the other room. They're on a conference call with one of the Nightwing Corporate factors overseas."

Brynne walked back to the large office Celeste used to help run James' international business empire. She was helping James on the call, handing him documents while the caller on the other end of the video conference talked about numbers and figures that meant nothing to Brynne.

She wrote a hasty message on a piece of scrap paper and handed it to Celeste. The redheaded assistant glanced at the paper and passed it along to James.

"I just got an urgent message, Bernard," James said after reading the scrap of paper. "I have to attend to something. Do you have all you need to move forward right now?"

"I do," the man on the other end of the connection said.

"Very well, then," James reached out and disconnected the call. He looked at Brynne. "Dean's not going home or coming here?"

She shook her head. "He's not going home, and if he's coming here, he's not taking the most direct route. He got that message and took off at a high rate of speed. It has to be a message from Artur."

"Alright," James said. "Rudy and I will head out and catch up with the vehicle tailing Dean. We'll get back in touch with you when we know where he's headed."

Brynne shook her head. "No way. I'm going with you."

"Are you crazy, Brynne," James protested. "You can't do that. You're not able to control yourself well enough to go on a mission like this."

"Artur has a lot to answer for, not the least of which is how he made me kill people. I'm a healer, James. I won't be compromised that way, ever again. I was working towards getting back on the street, doing the things I cared the most about. I was doing fine until Artur started messing with my mind. Ask Celeste. She said I was progressing in my tests. On top of that, I owe Dean too much not to be there when he needs me. If you leave me behind, I'll just come on my own and follow you."

James started to protest again, but Celeste raised a hand to stop him.

"I'll come along and be responsible for her, James. She's right on both counts. I think she's ready to go out on her own and she needs to be there for herself and Dean."

James opened his mouth to say something but stopped and nodded. "Come on then. We've got to catch up with him before it's too late. I can't believe that Artur is going to let Dean live for long, especially once he finds out about Dean's newfound power over vampires who seek to harm him."

"Do you think Jaz is still alive?" Brynne asked as they walked back into the main apartment. "I don't know what Dean will do if she's harmed in any way."

"I don't know, Brynne. Maybe. Artur would surely like to cause them both a great deal of pain before he kills them. I can imagine inflicting that pain on one of them while the other watches would be something he would seek to do."

Rudy looked up as the three of them entered the main room of the penthouse. "I just got off the phone with my security teams. They're all spread out around the city. Aside from the one guy tailing Dean, it's going to take me a while to pull a tactical team together for a raid."

"I don't think we have time for that, Rudy," James said. "Dean's on the move, and I've got a feeling he's not going to wait for us to catch up if he calls us at all. I'm sure Artur told him to come alone in that message."

"And Dean's just pig-headed enough to do it," Brynne added.

Rudy nodded. "He is if history is any judge. So it's just you, me, and Celeste?"

"And Brynne," James added. "She's convinced me she should join us." He shot her a glance. "But, she's assured me she's going to stay back and let us handle things, right?"

"I'll let you take the lead," Brynne said. She hoped he didn't notice that she didn't promise to stay out of the action. She was gratified to see James turn back to Rudy as the two of them started talking about plans and how soon they could expect any backup.

"Should we notify the human authorities?" Rudy asked.

James shook his head. "We may be going on a wild goose chase. We need to know more about where we're going and what we're facing first. I suspect, though, that this is going to be a problem we're better off solving for ourselves. The human police authorities, even those from their Station U will only get in our way."

"Agreed," Rudy said. "I just wanted to hear it from you. I'll start my teams moving west after they gather and arm up. Hopefully, we have time to wait for them."

"I hope so, too," James agreed. "Let's get to it."

Brynne smiled, and she had a spring in her step she hadn't felt for some time. She was going to get out of this penthouse apartment and do it under her own power and control. Dean needed her help, and she wasn't going to sit on the sidelines and watch while everyone else went to his rescue without her. This was her fight, too.

<hr>

Chapter 23

<hr>

Dean stood on the street outside the address the text message had given him. He recognized it as the dilapidated mansion he had seen from the back of the ambulance earlier in the day. He couldn't believe he'd been so close and hadn't realized it. What if Jaz was already dead but had been alive when he went by on an ambulance call earlier in the day? He couldn't bring himself to think about it. She had to be alive; she had to be.

He had parked by the gate, but it was shut, and there was no call box or anyone in attendance to let him inside. Getting out, he walked along the street, looking for a way in past the tall, wrought-iron fence. There were pillars along the fence built with cut stone blocks. They were spaced periodically securing the fencing and acting as posts. Examining one of the pillars, he saw some gaps in the masonry he thought he could use to climb over but he'd rather not if there was another, easier way inside. He needed a quick way out if he managed to rescue Jaz and they had to get out on the run.

He checked a section of fence overgrown with bushes and found what he was looking for. There was a gap in the fence where the bushes had pushed through the fence and caused it to rust away over the years. He was able to detach and move a couple of the bars aside, creating an opening large enough to climb through.

Satisfied with his work, he returned to his truck and retrieved Jaz's Katana from behind the seat. He'd been carrying it with him since she'd been taken, knowing if he found her, she'd want it back to take her revenge on Artur. He looped the sword's belt over his head and settled it across his back the way he'd seen Jaz carry it so many times.

He returned to the open section of fence and squeezed through, crouching in the bushes on the other side as he scanned the grounds in the moonlight for any signs of movement. He was thankful for the full moon tonight. It would provide him some light to see. He'd never be able to see as well as an Unusual could at night, but beggars couldn't be choosers. He watched in silence for a solid ten minutes before he left his position of cover and started across the overgrown lawn towards the main house. He decided against going to the front door. They'd expect him to do that and might be watching it. Instead, he moved to the side of the house and worked his way around to the back. He was about to turn the corner and walk into the backyard when he saw a figure walk out from the door closest to him and onto the patio. He thought it might be Artur himself, but when the person stepped from the shadows and into a pool of moonlight, he saw it was a man or probably a vampire in a three-piece suit. He soon saw it was a vampire. Dean could see the elongated canines when the man yawned as he looked around the yard. He could also see the white earbuds in the vampire's ears and, judging the nodding of his head, he was listening to music.

Dean reached up and grabbed the hilt of the katana for a moment, thinking about using it to kill the vampire. He wanted to kill one of the bastards but decided against it at the last minute. He wasn't a killer, and he wouldn't start now. He would try and use his other ability, new as it was, to try and control or overcome the vampire in front of him. He waited until the man turned around to go back inside to make his move.

He rushed from his hiding place, vaulting over the low patio wall and opened his left hand to strike at the side of the vampire's head with the flat of his palm. He felt rather than saw a flash of whiteness coming from the point of contact and the vampire crumpled to the ground at his feet. Looking around to see if anyone had spotted him, Dean reached under the unconscious man's arms and dragged him back to the low patio wall. With a grunt of effort, he dumped the limp form over the edge and jumped down after it. He pulled the body into the bushes at the side of the house and crouched down there to plan what he was going to do next.

He still didn't know if Jaz was even here. It could all be a trap to capture him. Dean snorted a chuckle at that thought. Of course, it was a trap. He decided he needed information most of all. He crouched next to the vampire lying on the ground at his feet. He unwrapped the bandage covering the cut on his hand so he could grip the vampire's head with skin-to-skin contact. Just like with the vampire they'd interrogated back at the Nightwing building, he was doing this by instinct alone since he had no idea what or how much he could do. Grabbing the vampire's head in his hands, he whispered a single word.

"Wake."

The vampire's eyes sprang open, and though his body was immobile, his eyes darted around as if trying to get his bearings.

"Look at me," Dean ordered.

The eyes moved to lock on his own. Dean could feel some more of the power behind what he was doing this time as if with each use, he became more attuned to the ability. He could also sense for the first time that the power was finite. If he weren't careful, his source of this strange energy would run out. He might only have one shot at this, so he needed to work quickly.

"Whisper when you answer me. Where is the hunter woman?"

The vampire tried to twist his head in Dean's grasp but his struggles were weak, and Dean maintained his grip. Despite the resistance, an answer was forced from the vampire's lips.

"Sh-she's in the basement."

"Is anyone down there with her right now?"

Again, Dean could sense resistance. This vampire was older than the other vampire was, more established in his control. He realized this would never work against James or Artur. They were far to powerful for him to use this power against.

"Th-the master was down there, but he retired an hour ago to his chambers to share a meal with Mistress Felicity."

Dean wondered if that was the same Felicity as the health department nurse who had gone missing weeks before. He thought for a moment before continuing. He needed an easy way in and out of the house that avoided any other vampires or servants inside.

"Is there an outside entrance to the basement?"

"Y-y-yes."

Dean was taking a chance that his commands would hold long enough for him to get to Jaz and bring her back out the way he came in. He could already feel his resources weakening, his control over the vampire slipping. He drew up all his will and directed it at the vampire for one last push.

"Good, you're going to lead me there. If anyone approaches us, you'll tell them you're on an errand for the Master. Once we are at that entrance, you will stop anyone from following me. Do you understand."

The vampire resisted longer this time, but after a moment of struggling, Dean heard a murmured "Yes."

This was the moment of truth. Once he let go, the direct control would be gone. Dean let go and stood up in one motion, reaching up for the katana's hilt, ready to defend himself if he needed to. The vampire stood up and, without hesitation, began walking towards the back of the house.

Dean had to jog a little to catch up to the vampire who had taken off at a purposeful marching step. Dean could see a shadowed alcove in the wall at the back of the home. That must be the basement entrance. The vampire was making a beeline for it.

He was only twenty yards away from the entrance when the two figures across the back yard called a greeting to his guide.

"Gary, where are you going and who is that guy behind you?"

Gary didn't answer or even turn to acknowledge their query. Damn, Dean thought, the vampire was following his commands to the letter, but the problem was he couldn't deviate from them, and

Dean couldn't tell him to answer them either without reconnecting with him. He doubted he had the power reserves left to make that work anyway.

"Gary, you alright? You're acting strange," the second voice called out.

Dean tried to use his will remotely to get the vampire to move faster. It didn't work. He maintained his purposeful stride towards the alcove. Ten yards now and Dean could make out the door set in the masonry of the foundation. He decided it was now or never. He hoped that door was unlocked.

As the pair of voices shouted for Dean and his guide to stop, he darted past the vampire ahead of him and ran for the basement door. He reached it as he saw the pair at the back of the yard start running in his direction. Grabbing the doorknob, Dean felt the latch open as he turned it and he pushed the door open, rushing inside. He slammed the door shut behind him and searched for a way to secure if from the inside. He was rewarded when he saw the outline of a sliding deadbolt lock set into the door. He reached up and slid the bolt home into a slot cut in the foundation from the inside. The door was a steel exterior door. It should hold them for a short time if his guide failed to stop them from following him as ordered. Dean turned and pulled out his flashlight in the darkened basement. It was time to look for Jaz.

Chapter 24

Brynne silently urged Rudy to drive the SUV faster as they sped through the night. She knew Dean well enough to know he'd try and bull his way into rescue Jaz without a real plan. He was running on little sleep and wasn't making good decisions. It was a recipe for disaster.

Rudy was in contact with the pack member following Dean via a radio and wireless earpiece in his ear. With her enhanced senses, she could sense the buzz of occasional updates coming into the pack leader while he drove. She couldn't make out what was said, but that didn't matter. Rudy was passing the updates along to the rest of the passengers in the SUV as he got them.

"He's stopped at the Old Heritage mansion on the edge of town, and he's poking around to try and find a way inside. My guy is watching him from a distance and says he's pacing along the front of the main fence."

"How far out are we?" Brynne asked. She looked around to get her bearings but had trouble figuring how long it would take them to get there.

Rudy turned off the next exit from the interstate as he answered her.

"I'd say ten minutes, maybe a little less."

"Brynne, don't worry," James consoled her. "He'll realize he needs help and call us or call the authorities."

"No, James, he won't. I know him. He's going to try and be the hero and go in to rescue her on his own because, like you said, Artur probably told him to come alone." She thought for a moment before continuing.

"What about that trick he tried on the prisoner? Could that be used again against Artur or his minions?" Brynne hoped the answer was yes. She had not realized her former probie had any special powers at all. They were going to have a long discussion when all of this was done.

James shook his head in answer to her questions. "I don't know, Brynne. It's not something I've ever seen a human, even a witch or other magic user use before. I don't know where he discovered how to do that."

"Most powers like that are finite. He's used it once already in the last twenty-four hours," Celeste chimed in. "He needs to rest. He can't be at full strength after being up all night and working all day today."

"My thoughts exactly, Celeste," Brynne agreed. "He needs us to get there before he brings things to a head with Artur."

Rudy held up a hand and pressed his hand to his ear for a moment.

"Damn, he's found a way inside, and he's approaching the main house," the werewolf reported. "He has no idea who or what is waiting inside. What is he thinking?"

"He's not thinking. As Celeste said, he's tired and running on instinct alone," Brynne replied.

Rudy relayed another message to them.

"My guy has lost sight of Dean. He's gone around the back of the house. I told him to wait until we got there. It's not too much further."

Brynne looked ahead as Rudy sped through the dark, residential streets. She hoped they were in time.

DEAN HEARD a commotion start up behind him outside the entrance as he started searching his way through the basement's many rooms. He was in some sort of storage area filled with broken furniture and various tools for use around the grounds. Using his flashlight, he found the door out and entered a long, carpeted hallway with many doors branching off of it. The far end of the hall opened up into a larger area, but he couldn't see too far there using just the beam of his flashlight. He started trying the doors to either side as he worked his way down the hall. The rooms were small bedrooms or offices, and most were filled with assorted junk discarded and stored down here from the rest of the house.

He was halfway down the hall when he heard banging on the door to the main storeroom behind him from the outside. Attackers must have overcome his vampire guarding the door, or the effects of Dean's control had worn off. Either way, he wasn't going back out that way. He needed to pick up the pace of his search, or he'd never make it out of this basement alive.

He decided to take a chance and called out once to see if Jaz answered him.

"Jaz, where are you?"

Dean heard her voice faintly from the open area at the far end of the hall. He rushed down the hallway into a large open room. He shined his light around the room looking for Jaz. He found her; hands tied wide to the front of a built-in wet bar in the corner. She shied away from the blinding light of his flashlight. He shifted the beam to one side as he ran over to her.

"Dean, you are a sight for sore eyes. I thought I was going to have to rescue myself."

"Not hardly," Dean said. "I came for you as soon as I found out you were here."

Jaz looked past him, searching the hallway behind him for a moment.

"Where's the rest of the team?"

"Uh, well…"

"Oh, my God. You idiot. Dean, you didn't come here by yourself did you?" Jaz asked in shock while Dean struggled to loosen the knots.

"I couldn't wait for help. Artur contacted me and warned me to come alone without any police or other assistance. He threatened to kill you otherwise."

"Of course he told you to come alone. Now he's going to try and kill both of us." Jaz tried to pull at her bonds, hoping the cuts she'd been able to make in the ropes had weakened them enough to break.

"Stop struggling. You're making the knots tighter, Jaz."

"Dean, you've got my sword. Use the blade to cut the knots. We have to get out of here. Artur has to know you're coming. He'll be down here to check on me soon."

"Oh, yeah," Dean said. He couldn't believe he didn't think of that, but he'd forgotten about the blade across his back. He was so tired he wasn't thinking clearly. He reached up to draw the blade just as the lights in the basement room switched on. Dean spun around and saw Artur standing on the stairs.

"Well, well, well," the vampire lord said as he lifted a scabbarded sword he carried as if to invite Dean to keep drawing the katana blade. "I see you got my invitation to come and pay me a visit. How very rude of you to sneak in the back way, though."

<hr>

BRYNNE JUMPED out of the back of the SUV as soon as Rudy screeched to a stop outside the main gate. A dark-haired man stood by another black SUV nearby. He must be Rudy's pack mate who'd been following Dean. She joined James, Celeste, and Rudy in front of the SUV to get the latest report. The security agent pointed to the big house on the other side of the fence.

"I heard shouting coming from the back of the house but that has stopped now, and it's been pretty silent for the last few minutes."

"Good work, Ricky," Rudy said. "Stay here and direct the teams that are coming soon to surround the house and be ready to come in if we call them. Stop anyone trying to leave and detain them."

"Got it, boss."

Rudy turned to James. "I think we should head inside. We can leave Brynne and Celeste here with Ricky."

"No way," Brynne answered. "You need our help, too. You can't go in there alone, just the two of you. Celeste and I are coming with you."

James started to protest, but he must have seen the dangerous glint in Brynne's eyes. He sighed and nodded.

"You can come with us, but you're going to stay close to Celeste and listen to what she says, alright?"

"Agreed," Brynne said. She understood the need for a chain of command here. She also knew they had to hurry and get inside. Arguing out here wasn't going to solve anything and would only delay the help that Dean was going to need. She hoped they weren't already too late.

James and Rudy led the way, easily leaping over the fence. Brynne followed Celeste, marveling at the powerful strength in her vampire muscles propelling her up and over the fence with a single bound. She landed on the balls of her feet and took off at a jog after the other three Unusuals. They covered the ground between the street and the main house in a few seconds and stood outside the front door. James looked to Rudy. Brynne was shocked to see a partially shifted wolf form standing where Rudy had been standing. His fingers had sprouted talons, and his face was slightly elongated as his upper and lower jaws now featured long sharp canines.

Rudy gave a grunting growl and hurled his shoulder against the double doors in the front of the mansion. The wooden doors burst inward in a shower of splinters. She heard a howl of rage and sounds of fighting on the other side. Brynne followed James and Celeste inside after the werewolf to find a semi-circular array of people squared off facing them. Two were already pinned to the floor beneath Rudy's massive taloned hands. There were about ten others scattered about the entry hallway and on the broad staircase leading upward. James stepped forward.

"I'm James Lee. I'm the Lord of this region. I promise each of you fair treatment and safe passage if you let us pass now."

Brynne could feel the power of James' ancient vampire power washing over all the other vamps in the room. The offer hung in the air between the two groups for a few tense moments frozen in time. Then a brunette woman standing on the stairs behind the others spoke. Brynne recognized her as Felicity Richards, the missing public health nurse. It was obvious she had been turned into a vampire.

"The master said he was not to be disturbed. We outnumber them, you fools. Kill them. Now."

Rudy growled once and slashed at the two vampires he had pinned to the floor as Artur's other minions rushed the small group of rescuers. Then all sense of time disappeared for Brynne as the entry hall devolved into a massive melee for life or death. She stepped up next to Celeste and began fighting for her life as the other vampires closed on her. She wondered where Dean and Jaz were and if they were too late to save them as she dodged the first of her attackers and kicked out at another with a wicked round-house that knocked the vampire back into a wall with backbreaking force. Then she had no time to think as the rest of their attackers closed in.

Chapter 25

Dean backed away from Jaz and extended the blade of her Japanese style sword out, pointing it at Artur. The vampire lord stepped down the last step into the room and slid his own blade from the scabbard. The sword was different, looking more like a sword he might see in a movie about the Three Musketeers than Jaz's Japanese katana. He had no doubts about Artur's ability to use it compared to his non-existent skill, though.

"I won't let you kill her, Artur. Not now, not ever," Dean said through gritted teeth. He knew it was mostly bluster, but he felt like he had to say something.

"Dean, don't," Jaz warned. "He's a master swordsman. Finish cutting me free before it's too late."

"Oh, it's already too late Miss Errington. I don't think your friend here can finish cutting your bonds before I run him through. He's been a thorn in my side for too long as it is and I want him stopped as much as I want you dead. It's time I put you both in your place."

Dean knew Jaz was right. He didn't stand a chance against this guy. He wasn't sure he had an alternative, though. He'd managed to free one of her hands and was working on the other one when Artur arrived. She was tugging at the knots with her free hand but wouldn't get free anytime soon. Dean knew his only chance was to slow the vampire down enough that she could free herself. Then she might have a half a chance.

A wolf's howl from somewhere in the house above them stopped all for a moment. There were sounds of a struggle coming from upstairs. Dean knew what he had to do.

"You may be a master swordsman, Artur, but I'm going to do my best to stand in your way. That howl means my friends are here. It's only a matter of time before James comes down here and finishes you off himself. I only have to slow you down."

"Boy, you are less than a flea to me. An inconsequential fool who won't slow me for even an instant. Now, out of my way." Artur advanced on him with a flurry of sword jabs and slashes.

Somehow Dean knocked them away from him as he backpedaled across the room to get some space between himself and the deadly blade. He stopped backing up at one point and slid to the side. He had to keep himself between the vampire lord and Jaz. That limited how far he could back up. As soon as Dean stopped backing up, Artur had him where he wanted. With two well-placed thrusts, the vampire slashed open deep wounds in both Dean's thighs causing him to fall to his knees.

Dean almost dropped the katana because of the pain. He could see the blood pumping from one of the wounds. Artur's blade had at least nicked the femoral artery there. If he didn't do something in the next few minutes, he was going to bleed out. He knew he only had a moment before he'd start to lose consciousness. In a last, desperate action, Dean leaned backward and pushed himself off with his injured legs to try and reach Jaz. He smiled as she reached out and grabbed the katana from his outstretched hand. Dean's last conscious thought was how glad he was to have given her a fighting chance.

BRYNNE SPARED a glance at her companions as she threw the woman she was fighting over her shoulder and into the stairs. She heard a satisfying snap as her opponent landed. James and Rudy were a whirlwind of teeth and talons as they waded through the opponents who faced them on the main floor below. She and Celeste had taken on the group coming down the stairs. Celeste led the way. She had produced two wicked-looking knives from somewhere, and she had been putting them to good use as the two of them fought their way upward. Brynne followed and tried to watch her friend's back with her more limited skills. She'd been practicing kickboxing in the gym for a long time, but it was entirely different in a practical application.

It helped that their opponents weren't very competent fighters either. Most were just launching themselves in a sort of whole-body assault on the intruders. If they had charged en-masse, it might have worked, but they came in piecemeal in groups of two or three at a time. Soon she and Celeste had reached the top of the stairs and were fighting their way towards a rapidly retreating Felicity. She was backing away now, looking from side-to-side for some avenue of escape.

Celeste finished off the final vampire between her and Felicity and pointed a bloody knife blade in her direction.

"I'll let you live if you tell us where Dean and Jaz are right now."

"I don't know where the paramedic is. He was supposed to show up tonight. Artur had sent him the address and told him to come."

"Fine," Celeste replied. "Tell us where you're holding Jaz Errington."

Felicity paused for a moment then shrugged. "She's being held downstairs in the basement. I don't think she's still alive, though. Artur took his blade down to finish her off himself before the paramedic arrived."

Celeste turned and looked at Brynne. "Go, find her and you'll probably find Dean, too."

Brynne started to leave but stopped when Felicity took advantage of Celeste's turning to talk to Brynne and ran down the hallway. She disappeared into a room at the end of the passage.

"Don't mind her, Brynne. I'll track her down. You go and find Dean. He's going to need you to stop him before he does something heroic and stupid."

Brynne nodded and turned, racing down the stairs. She reached the bottom and stopped, trying to get her bearings and to figure out where the basement door might be located. She decided to find the kitchen. There was probably a basement door somewhere near there. She skirted the melee where Rudy and James were battling the bulk of Artur's remaining minions and went in search of the kitchen.

She found the kitchen without any further encounters. The sound of the brawl in the main entry hall had drawn all potential attackers there. She tried all the doors off the kitchen and found the pantry and a door to the back yard but no stairs down to the basement. Moving down a side hallway, Brynne let her enhanced senses expand outward to try and hear or smell something that might indicate which way to go. That was when she caught the first whiff of human blood. It was fresh. She could tell. She sniffed the air again. It was coming from - that way.

Brynne moved down another hallway until she found a half-open door. She heard the sounds of clashing steel below her and again detected the unmistakable odor of fresh human blood. She fought down the predatory urge to charge down and drink from its source. Instead, she took the stairs down in slow, measured steps. This was all about self-control. If she tried to hurry, she'd be unable to control herself.

Reaching the bottom of the stairs, Brynne saw a furious battle of steel on steel as Jaz fended off a flurry of attacks from Artur. Jaz must have seen Brynne enter because she called out to her.

"Brynne, you have to help him. Dean. He's over at the bar. He's dying."

That set Brynne's mind into motion, and she scanned the room for a moment before she saw Dean's crumpled form on the floor next to the built-in bar. That was where the blood smell was coming from, and she had to clamp down on her urges again to keep from rushing over and feeding. Forcing herself to walk, she crossed to where Dean lay on the floor. He was unconscious and had lost a lot of blood due to two vicious sword wounds in his legs. She battled again with her inner vampire nature for a moment before she was able to kneel down and set to examining his wounds in detail. One was worse than the other, but both were serious.

Thinking quickly, Brynne spotted the thick hemp ropes that had been used to secure someone, probably Jaz, to the bar. She grabbed a length of the rope and wrapped it around Dean's upper thigh, fighting against the urge to drink from the fountain of blood that surged from his wound when she moved his leg. She tied a single loop in the rope and used her increased vampire strength to pull the ends of the rope tighter and tighter until the blood slowed to an oozing flow and then stopped entirely. She tied off the rope ends and repeated the same action with the other, less seriously wounded leg.

She checked to make sure the bleeding was indeed stopped before she continued checking Dean for other wounds. Not finding anything, she grabbed his wrist and checked for a pulse. She realized after she started feeling his thready, weak pulse that she could hear his heart beating, too. It was starting to slow down, a sign that the shock was taking over. He needed fluids, preferably blood, and a trauma center's operating suite as soon as possible. Brynne took out her phone and started to dial nine-one-one to get help when she stopped and felt a tugging at her mind.

Before she could stop herself, Brynne put her phone on the floor next to Dean and stood up. She was looking at the ferocious display of sword fighting happening mere feet away from her. Something was tugging at her mind, compelling her to stop Jaz, to leap at her and take her sword away. Brynne shook her head and tried to clear her mind. She knew she should not interfere. She knew that attacking Jaz would almost ensure her death at the hands of Artur, but she couldn't stop herself. Taking a few hesitant steps forward as she tried to resist, Brynne reached out for Jaz from behind.

Jaz must have noticed what she was doing and shouted at her, out of breath from the battle.

"Brynne, what are you doing?"

"I—can't—stop—myself," Brynne forced herself to speak. "He's —in—control."

Brynne felt another sudden urge, and she took a swing at Jaz's head. The hunter ducked under the blow which allowed Artur to get past her guard and score a deep slash across her shoulder. Jaz let out a gasp at the pain. It didn't slow her, though. The hunter appeared to redouble her attacks to push Artur away, so she was farther from Brynne's advance. It didn't matter. Brynne felt the command tugging at her mind, and she continued to move forward.

She saw something in the way Artur was holding himself as he fought. There was something in his off hand. She realized what it was. He was holding the relic, the Eldara finger there. As long as he did, he'd be able to command her to do his bidding. She was able to resist, sort of, probably because his attention was divided between her and the formidable sword skills of the hunter he was fighting.

"He's—got—the—relic—in—his—hand," Brynne managed to stammer as she continued to close in on Jaz. She knew once she was close enough, there's be nothing Jaz could do, and then the hunter would die, either at her hands or Artur's.

Jaz must have seen what she was talking about. In a move Brynne was surprised by as much as Artur, Jaz tucked and rolled in toward the vampire lord's feet, springing upward and delivering a slashing blow to his free hand with her katana blade. With a spray of dark, almost black blood, Artur's hand was cut free and spiraled across the room, the fingers releasing a long cylindrical object to fall free.

As soon as Jaz's blade detached Artur's hand, Brynne felt the compulsion leave her, and she fell to the floor as if puppet strings holding her aloft had been cut. Artur howled in pain and rage as he used the pommel of his sword to bring a crashing blow down on Jaz's exposed head. The hunter crumpled to the floor at his feet. Artur was about to deliver a killing blow when James and Rudy leaped down the stairs. The rebel vampire lord snarled with rage and threw his sword at the two interlopers before he turned and raced down the hallway into the depths of the basement.

Rudy dodged the flying blade and then took off after Artur. James came over to check on Brynne and then Jaz. Brynne was getting her strength back, and she moved over to attend to Jaz as well. The hunter was bleeding from the blow to her head. James raised his arm to bar Brynne's approach, but she pushed him aside.

"I'm fine. I can control myself," Brynne assured James. "Let me look at her wounds." She knelt down and started assessing the bleeding. It looked worse than it was. Heads always bled a lot. She was more concerned about an internal, closed head injury. Jaz needed a trauma center as much as Dean did.

"James, are things cleared out upstairs? We need to call them an ambulance right now."

James nodded. "Rudy's backup arrived, and we captured the remainder of Artur's followers. Celeste is trying to track down the woman you two were following. She's afraid she got away out a window."

Brynne turned and went to grab her phone off the floor from where she dropped it next to Dean. Placing the nine-one-one call and waiting for the dispatcher to pick up, Brynne looked around. She felt a grim smile come across her face. For the first time in months, she felt like a paramedic again.

HIGH ABOVE THE MANSION, Ingrid watched the scene below as her wings beat silently behind her, hovering in place. She tensed when she saw two figures leave the building within moments of each other. The first was a female vampire. She leaped from a second-story window to the ground below, crouched for a moment among the bushes and then started for the edge of the fenced-in grounds. A few seconds later, a male vampire left from the basement entrance and sprinted after the female.

Ingrid didn't know who the female was, but the male was one she recognized the instant she saw him. She tensed and started to draw her sword. Her companion laid a hand on her wrist, stopping Ingrid with her sword half drawn.

"Why did you stop me, Gabriel? That's Artur Torrence down there." Ingrid pointed at the figure sprinting across the grounds towards freedom. "I've been hunting him for centuries. He's responsible for banishing Ashley and the loss of countless lives. He might have even killed your son down there, for all you know."

"My son is injured but will survive. I can sense his life-force, and it is strong. Besides, look, Artur is being pursued already." The other Eldara pointed to a wolf-like figure bounding from the basement exit. The creature sniffed at the air for a moment then howled and took off after the fleeing vampire.

"Artur will elude the werewolf if given enough time. You must let me intervene."

"No," Gabriel ordered. "You must go and prepare the hall of heroes. This is the moment we've anticipated. The final battle is coming soon unless we can do something to stop it. I think I now know why I was sent here all those years ago to father a human child. He may be the key to preventing the impending Armageddon."

"You think it is that close, just because of an isolated attack by a deranged vampire lord?" Ingrid asked. She was concerned. Ragnarok, or Armageddon, or whatever you called the end of the world, had always seemed so far away. To be told it was close by Gabriel, the trumpet bearer himself, was frightening.

"I think it is time for me to return to Dean Flynn's life and tell him more about his father. There are things he needs to know, important things, that may help him stop Armageddon from coming."

Ingrid watched as Gabriel flew off, gliding on his mighty wings. She spared one last glance in the direction in which Artur fled and turned in the air to follow. Soon the darkness swallowed both Eldara as they returned to their ethereal plane.

Epilogue

Dean got dressed and winced as he went to stand up. His legs were sore from all the physical therapy he'd been receiving since the surgery the previous month. He was pushing himself faster than the PT guys wanted him to but he wanted to get back to work and back on the ambulance. Despite the objections of his caregivers, the hard work had paid off. He was due to start back to work in two days. He was happy, as were all his friends. There was a celebration planned for tonight at the Nightwing Building penthouse to congratulate him on his recovery and also to welcome the new permanent night shift supervisor for Station U, Brynne Garvey.

"Jaz, honey, are you almost ready to head out?" Dean asked

Jaz came out of the bathroom, her head turned to one side, putting in a pair of diamond stud earrings. Dean watched, enjoying seeing her back on her feet, too. She'd been laid up with a concussion for two weeks until the after-effects started to fade. In the time of their combined convalescence, the two of them had gotten the downtime they needed to see each other on a more social basis, and it had paid off.

"Here, Dean, help me zip up." She turned so he could pull up the zipper for her dress, a little black and red number that showed off her curves and athletic build. He pulled the zipper to the top, and she turned and delivered a quick kiss in thanks before going off to put on her shoes. Dean watched her as he grabbed his truck keys and wallet.

Dean checked his watch. "I know you don't like to be late. We should be going."

"I'm coming," Jaz said as she grabbed her purse and her familiar leather jacket. Dean knew it contained numerous weapons. She never left the house unarmed, especially since Artur had evaded Rudy's pursuit that night last month. He was out there, somewhere, planning some other way to bring them all down, Dean was sure.

As the two of them left Dean's apartment over the Baxter's garage, Jaz pointed to his white pickup truck.

"I know you want to keep your independence but there's really no reason you need to drive that thing. I have a fleet of SUVs for use by the Errington security teams."

"I don't need a new truck," Dean protested. He secretly wanted to drive one of the Errington SUVs, but his pride prevented him from taking her up on the offer.

"I'm going to keep offering," Jaz said. "Eventually I'll wear you down."

"Maybe I just keep saying no so you'll keep coming back to ask me," Dean said with a broad grin as he held the truck's door open for her.

"Careful what you wish for," she smiled as she chided him and climbed into the passenger side of the truck.

Dean walked around to the driver's side and thought about his life as it stood right now. Things were going pretty well, and he was excited about the direction things were headed in the future, too. He and Jaz were together, Brynne was coming back to work. Everything felt right again. It wasn't the same, that was for sure, but it was back to normal and had even gotten better in many ways. He smiled at Jaz as he started the truck and drove off into the night to celebrate with the friends who'd become his family.

GO AHEAD and read the next three book box set in the series.

Also by Jamie Davis

Get a free book and updates for new books.
visit JamieDavisBooks.com/send-free-book/

Extreme Medical Services Series

Book 1 - Extreme Medical Services

Book 2 - The Paramedic's Angel

Book 3 - The Paramedic's Choice

Book 4 - The Paramedic's Hunter

Book 5 - The Paramedic's Witch

Book 6 - The Paramedic's Nemesis

Book 7 - The Paramedic's Doom

Book 8 - The Paramedic's Amazon

Book 9 - *The Paramedic's Sorceress (coming soon)*

—

Eldara Sister Series

The Nightingale's Angel

Blue and Gray Angel

—

The Huntress Clan Saga

(A 6-book Urban Fantasy series starting with)

Huntress Initiate

—

The Broken Throne Series

(A 5-Book Dystopian Urban Fantasy

starting with)

The Charm Runner

—

The Accidental Traveler LitRPG Series

(with C.J. Davis)

(A 6-book Epic Fantasy Series starting with)

The Accidental Thief

—

Lone Wolf Squadron Scifi Series

(A multi-book space opera series starting with)

Marshal the Stars

—

Follow on Facebook for updates, news, and upcoming book excerpts

Jamie's Fun Fantasy Readers Facebook Group

Help - Leave a Review!

I Need Your Help ...

Without reviews indie books like this one are almost impossible to market.

Leaving a review will only take a minute — it doesn't have to be long or involved, just a sentence or two that tells people what you liked about the book, to help other readers know why they might like it, too. It also helps me write more of what you love.

The truth is, VERY few readers leave reviews. Please help me out by being the exception.

Thank you in advance!

Jamie Davis

About the Author

Jamie Davis, RN, NRP, B.A., A.S., host of the <u>Nursing Show</u> (<u>NursingShow.com</u>) is a nationally recognized medical educator who began educating new emergency responders as a training officer for his local EMS program. As a media producer, he has been recognized for the <u>MedicCast Podcast</u> (<u>MedicCast.com/blog</u>), a weekly program for emergency medical providers like EMTs and paramedics, and the Nursing Show, a similar program for nurses and nursing students. His programs and resources have been downloaded over 6 million times by listeners and viewers.

Jamie lives and writes at his home in Maryland. He lives in the woods with his wife, three children, and a dog.

Follow Jamie Online
www.jamiedavisbooks.com